This book must be returned by the date specified at the time of issue as
the DATE DUE FOR RETURN.
The loan may be extended (personally, by post, telephone or online) for
a further period if the book is not required by another reader, by quoting
the above number / author / title.

## Enquiries: 01709 336774

## www.rotherham.gov.uk/libraries

Cover Designer: Angie Fields, i love it design studio
Editor and Interior Designer: Jovana Shirley, Unforeseen Editing

This book is a work of fiction. Names, characters, places, and
incidents either are products of the author's imagination or are used
fictitiously. Any resemblance to actual persons, living or dead,
events, or locales is entirely coincidental.

Visit my website at http://www.authorkellyelliott.blogspot.com

ISBN-13: 978-0-9887074-7-4

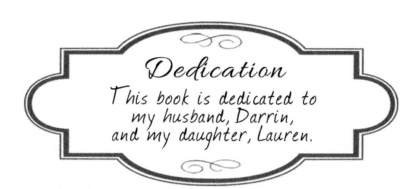

*Dedication*

This book is dedicated to
my husband, Darrin,
and my daughter, Lauren.

# Contents

# Prologue

## Heather

### *High School*

"Heather?"

I heard Ari say my name, but I was so numb that I couldn't even turn around.

*They left me.*

I felt a hand on my shoulder as I closed my eyes. *Why did I ever tell Ari about my secret place?* It was the only spot I could escape to when I needed time to think.

"Heather, Ells and I are really worried, sweets. Please come back to my house with me. You can't be all alone tonight."

I felt a chill run through my whole body. *How am I going to sleep in that house, knowing they'll never come back?*

I tried to talk, but nothing would come out. I looked up toward Ari as tears ran down my face.

Ari dropped to her knees and grabbed my hands. She put her head on my lap as she started to cry. "I'm so sorry, sweets. God, you know I would do anything to bring back your parents. Anything. Just please tell me what to do, Heather. What can I do to help you?"

I smiled as I looked down at her beautiful dark brown hair. Ari was filled with so much spit and fire but also with so much love. I knew there wasn't a damn thing she wouldn't do for any one of us.

"Will y'all stay with me tonight? I can't leave the house, but…I can't stay there alone either," I said as I began to stroke Ari's hair.

She sat up and smiled at me. "A slumber party?"

I let out a small giggle. "Yeah, a slumber party. You, me, Amanda, and Ells."

Ari stood up and reached out her hand for mine.

"Will you give me just two more minutes?" I asked as I glanced back to the water.

"Sure, sweets. I'll be waiting in my Jeep. I'll go ahead and call Amanda and Ells, too," Ari said as she rubbed my back before leaving me to my thoughts.

I closed my eyes, took in a deep breath, and held it for a few seconds. I would never forget the first time Daddy brought me to this gazebo. I'd felt like such a princess. He'd told me that this was our special place—a place where we could always come and feel each other's presence, a place to feel safe when we were scared, lost, or lonely.

"Daddy…it isn't working. I feel so lost…so completely and utterly lonely without you and Mom. I can't do this. I can't do this by myself."

A warm feeling captured my whole body as I thought of my father's last words to me.

*"Princess, you'll never find anyone who will love you like your mother and I do. Remember to guard your heart, and don't let just anyone in. To love strongly is a great thing. To be loved just as strongly in return…well, that is a miracle in itself."*

I would never love anyone again like I loved my parents. *No, I'll guard my heart and never let anyone in, so I'll never be hurt again.*

I stood up and took one last look at the river. Closing my eyes, I decided right then that I wouldn't cry anymore. It did no good. They were gone, and they were never coming back.

"I'm sorry, Daddy. I'm sorry I couldn't get there in time to be with you and Mommy one last time. I love you both. Good-bye."

I slowly turned and started to walk toward Ari's Jeep.

*All because I wanted to go on a stupid date.* If I'd just gone with my parents to Marble Falls instead of insisting on meeting them there the next day, I would've been driving, and they would be alive today.

*This is all my fault.*

# *Josh*

## **Sophomore Year of College**

"Dude, how many times do I have to tell you? You're gonna get in trouble," Jeff said as we walked onto the football field for practice.

I let out a laugh. "Jeff, I'm careful. I'm not going to get a girl pregnant. Besides, I'm too damn young to settle down with just one girl. I wanna have fun."

Jeff rolled his eyes as he looked over at Gunner, who was talking to Smitty.

"Gunner agrees. You have to take it easy, Josh. You're a fucking manwhore."

When my eyes darted toward the bleachers, I saw Victoria sitting there. *Shit.* I let out a sigh as I threw my stuff down on the ground.

Jeff glanced over to where I was looking.

"Your latest? She's cute. What's her name?" Jeff asked as he turned back to me, raising his eyebrows.

"Fuck off, dude. I actually liked this one, but she's so damn clingy. Gonna have to break it off."

"Yeah, they tend to get that way after you sleep with them. You'll have to forgive them, Josh. Most girls don't put out for just a one-night stand."

I smiled at Jeff, shaking my head. "Most of the girls I meet have no problem with a one-night stand."

"You ain't all there." Jeff pushed my shoulder back and started running off toward Gunner.

When I glanced over at Victoria again, I decided to just get it over with. As I walked toward her, I noticed her beautiful, long dark brown hair. She had it down today, and the thoughts running through my head were making my dick rock-hard. I'd hooked up with her more than any other girl, and she knew it. Something was missing though. I just wasn't feeling it with her.

*Fuck. I want to meet a girl I feel something for. I want someone to love me for more than just my looks.*

As I got closer, the smile spread wider on her face. *Yeah, she's definitely beautiful, great in bed, and smart as hell, but she's too fucking needy.*

"Hey there, handsome."

"What's up, Tori?" I asked, giving her my signature smile.

"I was hoping you were," she purred back.

*Oh god, I think I just threw up in my mouth.*

"I thought I'd come and watch y'all practice. Afterward, maybe you and I could go...you know, play around a little back at my place."

*Tempting, but...* "Listen, Tori, I don't think this is working out for me," I said as I noticed her friend Michelle sitting near her.

"What?" Victoria said, almost shouting.

*Ah hell, here we go.* "Listen, it was fun. It was, um...it was a lot of fun, Victoria, but it's just not working out. I'm not really ready to settle down yet, and to be honest, you were giving me that vibe."

She leaned over and said something to Michelle. Her friend quickly looked over at me and smiled before she turned and walked away.

"Baby, let's go back to my car and talk about this. I'm sure I can...change your mind," she said, glancing down toward my junk.

I let out a sigh.

*Damn, a blow job would feel really good right about now.* I shook my head and cleared my thoughts. I needed to find a girl who would not put out just because I smiled at her. *Fuck me. Does someone like that even exist?*

"While you're thinking pretty hard about it, Josh, I'm feeling a little wet with excitement," she said with a wink.

*Yeah, fuck this shit.* "Sorry, Victoria. It was fun, but I'm done. Good luck with nursing school. You're gonna make a damn good nurse."

With that, I walked away, and she called out my name twice.

*Just keep walking, Josh. Just keep walking.*

Her hand grabbed my arm, pulling me to a stop. "Wait, Josh! Just one more time? Please. Just as a good-bye, that's all. I promise."

I looked back at the field where Gunner, Jeff, and Brad were all talking. I reached in my back pocket and pulled out my phone to see how much time I had before practice started. *Fifteen minutes. I could do that.*

I glanced back at her with a smile on my face. "Lead the way to your car, baby," I said as she smiled back.

*Yeah, she's beautiful, and we have great fucking sex, but she's definitely not the one.*

# Chapter One
## Heather

I glanced over at Ari. She was staring out the window, and I could see tears running down her face. I looked up to the front seat where Jeff was on the phone with Gunner. I assumed Jeff was giving Gunner the details about the accident.

*Oh my god. I didn't even tell him that I loved him before I walked out the door. I just left.*

Ari squeezed my hand. I was guessing it had been about twenty minutes since I'd stopped crying hysterically.

"It's gonna be okay, sweets," Ari said with a weak smile.

I tried to smile back at her. My heart was pounding in my chest as images of Josh flashed through my mind. Leaning my head against the seat, I thought back to when he'd made such passionate love to me in the rain.

### Two Nights Ago

I was sitting on the sofa, watching his every move. He started his iPod and then walked toward me. With that panty-melting smile on his face, he held out his hand.

My heart was racing. *How does he make me feel this way?*

I smiled as I reached up, and his warm hand took mine.

"Will you dance with me, princess?" he asked with a look that just melted my heart.

"Yes."

He pulled me into his arms and captured my lips with his. As he led me outside, I could hear Ed Sheeran's "Kiss Me" playing on the outdoor speakers. *Damn, he knows how much I love this song.*

The rain was coming down at a steady pace as he guided me down the steps and out to the patio. Looking up, the rain hit my face, instantly cooling me off. *God, that feels so good.* After days of having a fever, the drizzle felt like heaven on my skin.

He drew me closer to him and put his lips against my ear. "I love you, Heather."

"I love you, Josh, more than anything."

Heartbeat to heartbeat, we danced in the rain.

"Are you feeling better, princess?" Josh asked against my ear.

"Yes…especially here in your arms," I said, slightly leaning back to gaze into his beautiful green eyes.

While the music played, he slowly moved us over to one of the patio chairs.

"I'm going to make love to you in the rain, Heather," he said with so much seduction it felt like my knees were about to go out from under me.

"Oh god," I said as he started to pull my T-shirt up and over my head.

Leaning down, he kissed me so softly that I just wanted to pull him in for more. I needed to feel him against me, getting as close as I possibly could to him. I needed him inside me.

Slowly turning me around, he placed gentle kisses on one shoulder before moving to the other while his hands slid down to undo my bra.

*Oh god. He's trying to kill me.* I glanced over my shoulder. "Josh, please…it's been so long."

He let out a small chuckle as he pushed my bra off my body. Wrapping his arms around me, he said, "I know, baby, but you had bronchitis, a sinus infection, the flu, and God knows what else. There was no way I was getting near you, let alone having sex with you!"

I spun around and smacked him on the shoulder, making him laugh. "Nice. You just ruined one of the most romantic moments of my life, you ass!"

Then, he smiled that smile—the one that always made me think of our lunch in Marble Falls. With his crooked smile and the dimple in his cheek, I felt the throbbing between my legs. His expression turned into a smoldering look that just about had me on my knees, ready to beg him to make love to me.

He took my hands in his. "I love you, Heather."

"I love you more, Josh."

"I love you more times infinity," he said with a wink.

"Make love to me, Josh."

His hands released mine, and he gently caressed them up my wet arms, over my chest, and down my shorts. By the time he had them off, I was ready to explode. *Oh god.* The way he made me feel was like nothing I'd ever experienced before. Every time with him was like the first time.

When he stood back and stared at me, I so desperately wanted to cover myself, but I knew how that would upset him. He always told me how perfect and beautiful I was. I didn't think I'd ever get used to how he made me feel so special, so wanted.

I watched as he took off his T-shirt and dropped out of his shorts. I raised my eyebrows at him and smiled. "Commando today, huh?"

"Easier access for you, baby," he said with a wicked smile.

Throwing my head back, I laughed, again reveling in the feeling of the rain on my face. *Is this really happening?*

I snapped my head back up and looked at him. "We can't do this!" I practically yelled.

"What? Why the hell not?"

"This is your parents' house, Josh! What if they come home? I mean, what if your mom…oh god, I don't even want to think about it!" I turned to get my shirt.

Josh grabbed my hand and pulled me to his wet, warm body. "Princess, my parents are at their lake house. They're not coming home until tomorrow. It's just you and me."

He pressed his lips to mine and kissed me with so much passion that I knew I would have an orgasm the moment he touched me. He slowly lowered himself to the lounge chair and moved back, allowing me to straddle him. When I sat down and pressed against him, I let out a moan. Between his warmth and the cool drizzle on my body, I was in heaven.

"Oh god, I've missed you so much," I said with desperation in my voice.

"Jesus, Heather, you feel so damn good. I love you, princess," Josh said as he lifted me up and down onto him.

Wrapping his arms around me, he covered me in soft kisses as we made the sweetest, most romantic love of my life…in the rain, heartbeat to heartbeat.

Ari's voice suddenly awoke me from my memory.

"Heather, sweets, we're at the hospital," Ari said with sadness in her eyes.

As soon as Jeff parked the car, I jumped out.

"Heather, please slow down!" Ari called out from behind me.

I had to get to him. I kept running. *What if he doesn't make it? I never even told him I loved him before I left. Oh. My. God. We were fighting.*

On the way toward the hospital, I sent Josh's mom a text message, letting her know I was there and asking where she was.

*Elizabeth: Second floor. Surgery waiting room.*

I crossed through the ER and headed straight to the elevator. I heard Jeff tell Ari that Gunner and Ellie were praying for Josh. *Don't cry, Heather. Do. Not. Cry.*

As we stepped into the elevator, I looked at Ari. *That was a mistake.* I immediately felt tears building in my eyes. I turned away and looked down at the floor.

"Heather..." Ari started to say.

"Please don't." I glanced back up at her as the doors opened.

Ari grabbed my hand, and we rushed to the waiting room. I saw Elizabeth and Josh's father, Greg, standing there, talking to a doctor dressed like he had just come out of surgery.

I stopped just short of them, unable to take another step. *What if he's telling them that Josh didn't make it?*

Elizabeth glanced in my direction and immediately walked over and took me in her arms. "He's going to be okay, baby girl. Breathe. Just breathe, Heather."

*Oh god.* That was what Josh told me all the time when he knew I was upset or nervous.

I pulled back and looked at her. She took her thumbs and wiped the tears away from my face.

"He's going to be okay? But I thought he was in critical..." I couldn't finish.

When I started to sob, Ari rubbed her hand on my back, trying to soothe me.

"Come on, Dr. Michaels was Josh's surgeon. He just came out to talk to us."

As we walked over to the surgeon, Jeff's phone started to ring. All I heard him say was, "Hi, Gunner." *Poor Ellie. She just had her baby, and she doesn't need this added stress.*

"Dr. Michaels, this is Heather Lambert, Josh's girlfriend," Elizabeth said as she gave me the sweetest smile.

After Dr. Michaels and I greeted one another, he began to tell us about Josh. "It looks like we were able to stop the internal bleeding from the blunt force trauma to his abdomen. His spleen was lacerated, probably by one of his two broken ribs. With a procedure called exploratory laparotomy, we were able to stop the bleeding by using a heat probe to seal the blood vessels. He lost a lot of blood, so we also had to give him a transfusion. His brain scans show that he suffered a slight trauma to the head, resulting in minor swelling. We're treating that with IV steroids and mannitol, and we'll observe him. We won't really know any more until he wakes up. He is stable now, and he's breathing very well on his own. His blood pressure is good, and all his vitals are normal."

Greg cleared his throat. "What about his head trauma? Do we know if he had any significant injury to his brain?"

"We'll have to wait until he wakes up to see how significant it was. All the brain scans appear to be normal, and the swelling is steadily going down, so I didn't see the need to induce a coma."

Looking over at me, Dr. Michaels gave me a weak but genuine smile. I smiled back the best I could, but my heart was racing.

*He's going to be okay.*

"We're going to keep him in the ICU overnight, and then we'll move him to another room tomorrow. Although he's not awake, y'all are more than welcome to go in. We just ask for only two people to visit at a time."

"Of course, of course," Elizabeth said.

My heart started racing even more. *Oh god.*

"We'll be right back." Greg leaned over and kissed me on the cheek.

I watched as Josh's parents followed the doctor through the double doors. Jeff must have sensed what was about to happen because he rushed to my side and grabbed on to me when my knees gave out. With Ari on one side of me and Jeff on the other, we walked over to the small sofa.

After Ari and I sat down, I just let go. I had never cried so hard in my life. Even after my parents passed, I'd tried not to cry. This time though, I couldn't hold it in. Thinking back to the last forty-eight hours, every emotion I'd felt came crashing down on me,the beautiful moment in the rain when Josh had made love to me, my anger over him and Lynda and the fight we'd had before I left, the excitement about Alex, Josh's car accident, and how scared to death I was when I'd thought I lost him.

As Ari gently held me in her arms, I let it all slip away.

*He's okay.*

*We'll be okay.*

Chapter Two

Josh

## *Twenty-Four Hours Before the Accident*

I looked down at my cell phone in my hand. *Fuck, why is Lynda calling me again?*

Heather was staring at two dresses on my bed, trying to decide which one to wear to my mother's office Christmas party tonight.

"I'll be right back, babe," I said as I turned and walked out into the hall.

"Lynda, what do you need?" I asked in a hushed voice as I quickly made my way down the stairs.

I headed through the kitchen and out onto the back patio. The last thing I wanted was for Heather to hear me talking to Lynda.

"I'm so sorry to bother you, Josh. I'm just having a really hard day. Christmas is so close, and I feel so alone. Can't we just meet for lunch, please?"

I took a deep breath and looked out toward the pool. As my eyes locked on to the lounge chair where Heather and I had made love the day before, I smiled. I slowly let out the breath I'd been holding in.

"No, Lynda, we can't meet for lunch. You have your family. You'll be fine. You need to get out and meet someone."

"I don't want to meet anyone else. What we had was such a good thing. You know it was."

"No, what we had was nothing, Lynda. You knew from the beginning that I loved Heather. I'm tired of having this conversation with you. Listen, I need to go. You're gonna be okay, trust me. Please just get out there and look for someone. You're a beautiful girl, and I promise that you'll have no problem finding someone."

When I turned around, I found Heather leaning up against the door. She had obviously been listening to me.

*Fuck me.* "Listen, I have to go and get ready for a Christmas party. Later." As I hung up the phone, I started to walk toward Heather.

She put up her hand to stop me from coming closer. "You felt the need to come outside to talk to her? How often do you sneak away to talk to her on the phone, Josh?"

"Heather, I know it upsets you, so—"

"So, you snuck outside? Why can't you see that this girl is playing you? This whole feel-sorry-for-me shit is getting old." Heather turned and began heading back into the house.

"Heather, wait. I'm trying the best I can here," I said.

She stopped immediately and spun around to look at me. The expression on her face told me that I had just said something very wrong.

"You're trying your best? No, you're not trying your best. When she calls, you drop everything to comfort her, and she knows it. You need to ignore her. I'm tired of this, Josh. I'm ready to move on and leave all of that behind, but we can't. Every other week, she calls you with some sort of breakdown. She's lying to you. Why can't you see that?"

I pushed my hands through my hair as I let out a long breath. I glanced over at the clock. My parents would be home any second, and the last thing I wanted was to be fighting with Heather when they walked in.

"Okay, Heather. You're right. I need to learn to just ignore her. I care about her though, and I worry, so—"

Her mouth dropped open as she shot me the dirtiest look.

*Oh fuck.*

"What? You care about her?"

*Jesus H. Christ! I can't believe I just said that.* "Okay, this is getting fucking ridiculous, Heather. I love you. I'll only ever love you. I want to be with only you. Why are you so fucking jealous over someone who's only a friend?" I shouted.

I watched as tears began pooling in her eyes before she lowered her head. *Oh, holy shit. Why did I just yell at her?* I was nervous about proposing to her tonight, and I was taking it out on her.

She started to shake her head as she looked back up at me. "She'll never go away, will she, Josh? How would you feel if I talked to Jerry on the phone all the time? If I told him how handsome he was? If I snuck outside to talk to him? If I told you I still cared about him?" Heather asked as she tried to hold in her sobs.

"Baby, I meant to say, I cared...as in past tense. I feel nothing for Lynda. I just worry that she'll do something stupid," I said as I moved closer to Heather.

"She. Is. Not. Your. Problem. The problem you have right now, Josh, is the fact that you can't open your eyes and see she's coming between us. She's doing the very thing she set out to do the day we walked into that hospital room together."

"Heather, Lynda is not trying to keep us apart. That's just stupid. Why do you keep saying that?" I asked as a tear rolled down her cheek.

*Jesus.* My whole world just stopped at the sight of that tear.

"Whether you want to see it or not, that's exactly what she's doing." Heather turned and walked inside and then made her way upstairs.

Just then, I heard my parents, so I went inside to meet them. I watched as my mother and father came into the kitchen, laughing. I put on a smile, trying to act like nothing was wrong.

"Josh, darling! Is Heather here also?" my mother asked, looking toward the family room.

"Uh, yeah. She's upstairs, trying to figure out what to wear for the party." I glanced at my father, who was giving me a knowing look. *How the hell does he know when I'm putting up a show?*

Turning to head up the stairs, my mother said, "Wonderful! I can't wait to see what she has planned for tonight. I'm going to go say hello and see if I can help her pick out a dress."

Once she was gone, my dad looked at me. "What happened?"

"Lynda called, and I took the call outside. Heather overheard me talking to her, and that led to a fight."

"Josh, you need to cut these ties with Lynda...now," Dad said as he took a water bottle out of the refrigerator.

"Oh fuck. You, too, Dad? What exactly am I doing wrong? The girl has problems, and I'm just trying to be her friend." I sat on the bar stool and put my head in my hands.

My dad let out a laugh that caused me to look up at him.

"What the hell is so funny?"

He stopped laughing and gave me a look. "Are you kidding me, Josh? The only problem that girl has is the fact that you love Heather and not her. The other night, your uncle told me he saw Lynda out with his neighbor, and she was hanging all over the kid. Wake up, Josh. Stop acting like a fucking idiot, and give a hundred percent of yourself to the girl you love. She deserves at least that. I think she's been patient enough with your ass." He reached for an apple and took a bite.

"Well, shit. Don't hold anything back, Dad," I said, standing up.

My mother walked into the kitchen. She stopped and placed her hands on her hips, shooting me the look she always gave when she was pissed. "What in the hell did you do to Heather?"

"Oh. My. God. You, too?" I said as I started to walk past her.

My mother grabbed my arm, stopping me. "She just left, Josh. She said she's not going to the office party tonight. She wanted me to tell you that she's heading to Mason. So, I'll ask you again, Josh. What the hell did you do or say that caused her to walk out of my house with tears in her eyes?"

When my father cleared his throat, my mother and I looked at him.

"Lynda," he said, raising his eyebrows.

*Traitorous bastard.*

"Josh, oh no. Josh, you didn't..." My mother started shaking her head.

"I didn't, what?"

"Will you just kick that girl to the curb already? Can't you see that she's trying to pull you two apart?"

*Holy hell. Not her, too?* "This is bullshit. I'm going upstairs to take a shower and get ready for your Christmas party, Mom."

"Josh, what about Heather? She left!" My mother pointed toward the front door.

Reaching down, I held on to the ring box in my pocket. "I'm not going to force her to go to the party. If she doesn't want to go with me, then I'll have to go without her," I said as I walked out of the kitchen.

Before I hit the stairs, I heard my father say, "Stupid bastard is going to lose the only girl he's ever loved just because some twisted nutcase won't let go of him."

With each step I took, my heart starting beating faster. I couldn't lose Heather. I'd rather die than live without her.

*What the hell am I supposed to do?*

## Chapter Three
## Heather

Sitting in the waiting room, I thought about everything that had happened between Josh and me. The love I felt for him was beyond anything I'd ever felt before. My hands started shaking as I recalled what had happened yesterday. I had walked out of his parents' house without even telling him that I was leaving. I'd just left, like I had done with my parents. I'd just left without a single word to him—no, *I love you*…no, *we'll talk later about things.*

*Nothing.*

"Heather, I see the wheels spinning in your head. You heard the doctor. Josh is going to be fine."

I looked over toward Ari. She was curled up next to Jeff on the small sofa.

"I just left him. I didn't even say good-bye to him. I just walked out. What if—"

"Don't do that to yourself, Heather," Jeff said as he got up and walked over to me. Sitting down, he pulled me closer to him.

I wanted so badly to be in Josh's arms right now. I wanted him to tell me how much he loved me and how he wanted no one but me. *Why was I so upset with him?* I'd heard him tell Lynda he was in love with me.

"I was so mad at him when I left. He went outside to talk to Lynda, and at the time, I thought he was just trying to be sneaky about it. Now that I look back…oh god, Jeff. He was just trying not to hurt me. I'm such fool."

Ari stood up and came toward us. Getting down on her knees in front of me, she grabbed my hands. "The moment he wakes up, just tell him. Tell him how much you love him and that you're sorry for walking away like that. Tell him you'll never walk away again," Ari said, giving me that smile of hers.

Greg cleared his throat. "Um, Heather, honey, would you like to go in and see him?" he asked. "Liz is still in the room."

Getting up slowly, I nodded. Greg reached out and took my hand. As he led me to Josh's room in the ICU, my heart started racing, and my head was spinning.

When we stopped right outside the door, Greg turned me to face him. "I want you to know something before you walk into that room."

Tears began building again, and I did everything I could to not cry. "Okay," I whispered.

"Josh was on his way to Mason when he had the car accident."

I felt all the air leave my body at one time. *What?* "What do you mean, 'Josh was on his way to Mason'?"

"When we were at the Christmas party, I could tell he was so miserable. He told his mother and me that he'd made the mistake of not going after you the moment he knew you'd left. He wanted to make things right with you. He said he was going to Jeff and Ari's because he figured that would be the first place you'd go."

*Oh. My. God. It's my fault he had the car accident. He was coming after me!* "Oh no. Oh god, no. This happened because of me," I said, barely able to get the words out.

Placing both of his hands on my face, Greg brought my eyes to his. "No! This is not your fault, Heather. This is no one's fault. It was an accident, and he's going to be okay. He is going to be okay, Heather. I want you to repeat this to me right now, 'This is not my fault.'"

Tears were rolling down my face as I looked at Greg. He was the closest thing I had to a father, and I felt like I had just let him and Elizabeth down.

"Heather, repeat it to me right now. You have to say it."

I slowly started to open my mouth to speak, but instead, I broke down and began crying.

Greg pulled me into his arms. "Everything is going to be okay. He's going to be okay."

"I'm so sorry, Greg. I'm so sorry I left. If I had just stayed and talked to him—"

Just then, I felt another hand on my back. I looked over my shoulder to see Elizabeth smiling at me.

"Heather, you will never utter those words out of your mouth again. None of this was your fault. Josh could have just as easily run after you to stop you from leaving. Things happen. This is life, sweetheart. He's going to be okay. You're both going to move on from this. You'll get married and give me grandkids, damn it!" Elizabeth said, taking me into her arms.

I let out a giggle as I buried my face in her sweater. I loved how she smelled. It wasn't like my mother at all, but it was just the same. Just from being in her arms, I calmed down almost immediately.

Elizabeth held me out at arm's length as she looked me up and down. "Shall we go in, so you can see our boy?" With a smile, she wiped the tears off my face.

"Yes, let's go." I glanced back at Greg before Elizabeth and I headed into Josh's room.

The moment I saw him in the hospital bed, I sucked in a breath of air. His face was cut and bruised. He was just lying there…broken. Then, it hit me. I hadn't even asked how the accident happened.

I stopped and turned to face Elizabeth. "Wait. How did the accident happen?" I whispered.

Elizabeth shook her head and glanced down at the floor and then back up at Josh. "A drunk driver ran a red light. Bastard doesn't have a scratch on him. He'll be sorry though when my law firm gets done with him," she said with a wink.

*A drunk driver?* I looked back over toward Josh. *I love him so much. I'll never, ever leave him again. I'll never give up on him.*

"I love him so much, Elizabeth. I can't live without him," I said, turning back to her.

Elizabeth reached down and took my hand as we made our way toward Josh.

"I know, baby girl. He feels the same way about you. I know how much that boy loves you."

For a few minutes, we stood there, talking.

"Honey, I'm going to give you some time alone with Josh," Elizabeth said.

The moment the door shut, I sat down in the chair next to his bed. I picked up his hand and stared at the IV.

"I'm so sorry I left you, Josh. I promise you, right here and right now, I will never leave you again. I don't care if you tell me to leave you…I never will. With every ounce of strength I have, I will fight for our love. I will forever be true and faithful to only you. I love you so much, and I'd be lost without you in my life. I could never go on without you. You are my every breath, every smile, every tear, and every single laugh. You are my everything. You are my life, Josh Hayes."

Just then, I felt him squeeze my hand. As my heart started pounding, I jumped up, and the chair flew back, landing on the floor with a loud crash.

"Can you hear me, baby? Please squeeze my hand again if you can hear me!"

"Heather! What's going on?" Elizabeth ran in with a nurse following right after her.

"He squeezed my hand! When I was talking to him, he squeezed my hand." I smiled at her.

The nurse walked over and picked up the chair.

"I'm so sorry. I just got excited when I felt him squeeze my hand!"

"No worries, sweetheart. Let me get some vitals on Mr. Hayes," she said as she started to take his blood pressure.

I turned and ran into Elizabeth's arms. "He's going to be okay," I whispered in her ear.

She hugged me for a long time. "Yes, of course he is."

I was so glad Greg and Elizabeth had talked Ari and Jeff into heading home. I knew Ari wanted to get back to Luke. This was the longest she'd ever been away from him, and I was sure that she was worrying herself sick from not being with her baby.

"How did you manage to get Ari to leave last night?" I asked Elizabeth as she poured me a glass of orange juice.

"The same way I got you to come home with us for a few hours of sleep…I threatened her," she said as she winked at me.

I looked at the clock. It was getting close to one in the afternoon. Josh would be moved into a regular room today, but the last update we'd heard from Greg was that Josh was not awake yet.

I stood up and took my plate over to the garbage can. Glancing at my half-eaten bacon and eggs, I sighed.

"Baby girl, just throw it away. I'm not going to make you sit until you clear your plate. I'm just happy you got some food in your stomach. Now, why don't you go change out of Josh's clothes, honey, and then we'll head over to the hospital, okay?" Elizabeth said, leaning back against the kitchen sink.

I looked down at what I was wearing. When we got back to the house early this morning, I had gone straight to Josh's bedroom and put on one of his old T-shirts with a pair of his sweatpants. His smell was everywhere in his room. I'd curled up with his pillow and cried myself to sleep before waking up around nine this morning.

"Just give me five minutes, and I'll be ready to go." I washed off the plate and then made my way upstairs.

Five minutes later, I met Elizabeth at the front door, and we headed out to her Mercedes. I loved Josh's parents. They were super rich, but they never acted like it at all. I remembered going with Greg and Elizabeth when they'd bought this car. She'd hated the idea of owning a Mercedes. She'd wanted a Jeep, like the one Ari had. I giggled as I thought about it.

"Was that a laugh I just heard?"

When I glanced over to Elizabeth, I laughed again. "I was thinking about how you wanted a Jeep like Ari's, and Greg fought with you about it all the way to the Mercedes dealership."

Elizabeth let out a giggle. "That's right. I still want a Jeep, damn it."

During the drive to the hospital, we talked and laughed about that day. Josh and Greg had argued about some piece of equipment that Josh wanted to buy for the business. Greg had said that Josh didn't need a stupid new age machine. When Greg had told Josh that he needed to do it all by hand, Josh's face fell.

Those two would fight all the time, but they loved each other so much. Josh's eyes would light up when his dad would call and ask if Josh wanted to go fishing. I'd never seen so much love between three people…at least not since my parents had passed away.

The last five miles to the hospital, we drove in silence. I was scared to death, and I had the worst feeling in my stomach. Something wasn't right. I could feel it.

My phone went off just as we were walking into the hospital. I looked down to see I had a new text message.

> *Amanda: Hey, I just got to the hospital, sweets. Text me when you get here.*

I sent her a text back, and right when I hit Send, I heard her voice. "Oh, sweets!"

When I glanced up, I saw Amanda walking toward me. I picked up my pace and practically ran into her arms.

"Oh, Manda!"

Somehow, I was able to hold in my tears. I knew Josh was going to be okay, so I needed to get my big girl panties back on and stop with the stupid crying.

Amanda pushed me away from her and looked me up and down. When she smiled, I smiled in return. *I'm so blessed to have three of the most amazing women as my best friends.*

"Hey, Elizabeth, how are you?" Amanda said.

"Hello honey." Elizabeth said.

Then, Amanda reached for me and hooked her arm around mine as we followed Elizabeth into the hospital and over to the elevators.

"I talked to Ari this morning, and then I called Ellie. Ellie's so upset that she can't be here with you. They're going home today with the baby, and she told me to tell you that she'll be at your side in a few days," Amanda said, giving me a wink.

"Are you going to go see Alex?" I asked as we stepped onto the elevator.

"Brad and I plan to head out to Mason tomorrow. I bought the cutest outfit for Alex a few weeks ago. I can't wait to see it on her!"

Elizabeth and I started laughing.

"How did you know it was going to be a girl?" Elizabeth asked.

"I didn't! I bought two. I picked out my favorite outfits for a little boy or a little girl. I'll just hold on to the boy's outfit for the next person in the group to push out a pup," Amanda said as she bumped her shoulder against mine.

Elizabeth spun around and grabbed me. "Oh. My. God! Are you?" she yelled at me as the elevator doors opened and two nurses got on.

"Am I what?" I asked, confused.

"Oh, baby girl, don't play stupid. Are you pregnant and not telling me?"

My eyes darted between Amanda and Elizabeth. "What? Elizabeth, I'm not pregnant!"

The two nurses smiled as they looked back and forth from Elizabeth to me.

*Jesus H. Christ. Why the hell does she think I'm pregnant?*

"Damn it all. You just got my hopes up," Elizabeth said as the doors opened to the fifth floor.

Amanda laughed. "I don't think you have to worry about Josh's mom liking you. Hell, she wants grandkids already!" she whispered in my ear.

I glanced at Amanda as we both started giggling.

*A baby with Josh.* I smiled at the idea.

"Oh shit!" Elizabeth said, pulling me out of my thoughts.

I looked over to see Greg standing at the nurses' station. He was talking to a nurse, and he seemed to know her. She appeared to be my age, maybe a few years older, and she was wearing her dark brown hair up in a ponytail.

"Oh, holy hell, not Victoria," Elizabeth said as she reached down and grabbed my hand.

*What the hell? Who is Victoria?* I peeked at Amanda, and she just shrugged her shoulders. When I turned back to Elizabeth, she winked at me as she leaned down toward my ear.

"Don't freak out. Josh dated Victoria during his sophomore year of college. Don't worry. She was a bitch, and he couldn't stand her, but she was the only other girl he's dated besides you and Lynda. Put your game face on, girl," she whispered.

*Oh. My. God. She did not just dump that on me!*

As Elizabeth started to pull me close to this Victoria chick, I turned around to Amanda. "Oh my god. Did she just—"

Amanda nodded. "Yes. Yes, she did."

"Mrs. Hayes! Oh my gosh! I was so shocked to see Josh's name on the board when I came in this afternoon. Thank God he seems like he'll make a full recovery. I was just letting Mr. Hayes know that Josh hasn't woken up yet."

Elizabeth put on the fakest smile I had ever seen her wear. She squared her shoulders and looked at Greg. He smiled at her and then gave me a wink.

*I love them both so much.* I would never be able to get through this without them.

"Well, hello there, Victoria. It's been a long time. I see you followed your dream and became a nurse. How wonderful." Elizabeth glanced at Greg as he rolled his eyes at her. "I'm glad Josh hasn't woken up yet. I'm sure he's waiting for Heather."

Victoria frowned as she glanced over at Amanda and peeked down at her wedding ring. As she looked in my direction, I noticed when her eyes landed on my bare left hand.

"Heather?" she asked Elizabeth.

"Oh, where are my manners? Victoria Chapman, this is Heather Lambert, Josh's girlfriend," Elizabeth said with a wicked smile.

If I didn't know any better, I would swear she was getting a kick out of this.

I reached out my hand toward Victoria. At first, I was sure she wasn't going to shake my hand, but then she put on a fake smile as she extended her hand.

I smiled as I shook her hand and introduced her to Amanda. "Very nice to meet you. This is Amanda, one of my best friends."

Victoria gave Amanda another fake smile.

"Could we please go see Josh?" I asked.

"Oh, of course. Follow me, y'all," Victoria said.

After she led the way into the room, Elizabeth and Greg started talking to Josh. I walked up next to him, and Amanda came and stood by my side. When I looked across the bed, Victoria was staring down at Josh.

*Could you eye-fuck him any more? Bitch. I hate her already.*

Reaching down, I took Josh's hand and brought it up to my lips. Then, I leaned toward his ear. "Baby, please wake up for me," I whispered.

As I stood up, I noticed Victoria glaring at me. I tried my best to give her a smile, but then I felt Josh squeezing my hand.

"Oh my god. He's waking up!" I could barely get the words out before he opened his eyes.

He looked straight at Victoria.

"Josh, you're in the hospital. You had an accident. Do you remember the accident, Josh?" Victoria asked as she went to grab the blood pressure monitor.

When he smiled at her, my heart started to race. *He must recognize her!*

*More importantly though, I realized he was going to be okay. Thank God.*

"Tori, what the hell are you doing, working at a hospital?" Josh asked.

I peeked over at Elizabeth and Greg, and they were smiling from ear to ear.

Victoria laughed. "I'm a nurse here, Josh."

I must have squeezed his hand because he looked down at my hand holding his. When he glanced up at me, his beautiful green eyes captured mine, and I smiled.

"Hey, there. You really scared us," I said as I glanced over at Elizabeth and Greg.

"Did I now? And who is us?" Josh asked with that damn crooked-ass smile of his.

"Well, for starters, your parents and me," I said with a chuckle.

Josh's smile faded, and he looked at me funny. "I'm sorry. How do you know my parents?"

*Oh god. Oh god…please…no.*

I let go of his hand and brought my hand up to my stomach. I felt sick. When I glanced up at Victoria, she gave me a faint smile. I looked back down at Josh, and he was still staring at me.

"Josh, don't you know who I am?" I asked with panic in my voice.

"Um…no. Should I?"

With that, my legs slowly started to give out.

Greg was next to me in two seconds flat. "Josh, buddy, you don't remember Heather?"

"Hey, Dad. I thought y'all were in Paris," Josh said with a perplexed expression on his face.

*Paris? What the fuck is he talking about? He's confused. That's all. He is just confused.*

"Mr. Hayes, it would probably be best if Heather and…Amanda, was it?" Victoria looked between Amanda and me.

"Yes, it's Amanda," Amanda said with sarcasm dripping from her voice.

"It might be best if they stepped outside for a bit. I'm going to call for the doctor."

Greg gave me a weak smile. "Josh, buddy, I'll be right back. Liz…" He waved for Elizabeth to come over and talk to Josh.

As soon as we got out into the hallway, I wanted to collapse to the floor. Greg and Amanda helped me over to one of the waiting room chairs.

"Oh my god. He doesn't remember me. He doesn't remember me, Manda! Greg, why doesn't he remember me? Why did he think y'all were in Paris?"

"Um…well, considering his confusion with Victoria working at the hospital and then his comment about us being in Paris, he must think it's his sophomore year of college."

"What?" Amanda and I both yelled at the same time.

Greg took a deep breath in before he slowly let it out. His eyes filled with tears, and he looked at me with such sadness that I felt like my whole world was about to be ripped apart.

"The only time Liz and I ever went to Paris was for our anniversary when Josh was a sophomore at UT. He was dating Victoria at the time."

I just started shaking my head. *No, this is not happening. This can't be happening.*

"So, you think Josh doesn't know who we are because…because he thinks he's back in college?" Amanda asked.

"And dating Victoria…he thinks he's dating Victoria," I said as tears started to roll down my cheeks.

## Chapter Four

### Josh

My mother was just staring at me as I watched Victoria walk around the room.

*What the fuck is going on? How in the hell is she a nurse?*

"Mom, what the hell happened? Tori, when the hell did you get a job as a nurse?"

Victoria laughed just as the door opened, and a doctor walked in.

"Good morning, Mrs. Hayes, Mr. Hayes. I'm glad to see that you've woken up," he said as he gave my mother a smile and a wink.

"Good morning, Dr. Michaels. Um, it seems Josh has woken up…in a different time zone!" my mother said with a small smile.

"Can someone please tell me what the fuck is going on?"

My mother spun around and gave me *the look*. "Joshua Michael Hayes, do not use that language!"

Dr. Michaels laughed and walked up next to me. He picked up the medical chart and glanced over it before looking back at me. "Josh, let me start off by telling you that you were in a serious car accident yesterday. You had surgery to repair some internal bleeding, and you got a pretty bad concussion with a small amount of brain swelling. Your brain scans all came back normal. Your vitals are all good. It just appears that you have a slight case of amnesia."

"Slight? A slight case?" my father said from behind the doctor.

Dr. Michaels turned around and shook my father's hand. "Good morning, Mr. Hayes."

"He thinks he's still in college," my father said as he went to stand next to my mother.

*Wait. What? Still in college? Does that mean I'm out of college? What about football? Someone needs to tell me what the fuck is going on! And who the hell was that beautiful girl holding my hand?*

"Okay, stop. First of all, my head is pounding. Second, Dad, what do you mean by I *think* I'm 'still in college'? Someone tell me what the hell is going on! And where did that girl go?" I glanced at Victoria, who was giving me a funny look, and then over to my mother, who was smiling from ear to ear.

"You mean Heather?" my mom asked.

Victoria walked right in front of my mother and grabbed my hand. "Don't worry, sweetheart. It'll all come back to you when it should. Heather is a friend of yours. As soon as your brain has healed, you'll remember everyone when you're ready." She turned around and looked at my parents. "Isn't that right, Dr. Michaels? We don't want to force Josh into remembering things. His memory needs to come back on its own."

My mother was glaring at Victoria. *Damn, Mom has never liked Victoria.*

Dr. Michaels said, "Well, um…thank you, Ms. Chapman, for that explanation of sorts. Josh, I wish I could tell you exactly why you don't remember the last four and a half years, but—"

"Four years? I've lost four years of my life? Did I finish college? What am I doing now?"

My head was spinning. Then, I remembered the beautiful blonde who was holding my hand. The moment I looked into her eyes, my stomach had dropped.

*That has never happened to me before…ever. Victoria said she's a friend, but the girl didn't look at me like we were just friends.*

"Mr. Hayes, just calm down." The doctor glanced over at my parents as he took in a deep breath. "With amnesia, we can't say that you'll regain a hundred percent of your memory. In most cases, we've seen patients get all of it back, but then in others, people seem to only get some of it. It could happen in a day or maybe a year. We just don't know. Don't force yourself to remember, and don't feel pressured by others who want you to remember. The key is to let your memory come back on its own."

I shook my head. *I don't remember four and a half years of my life.* I looked at my parents and then back to the doctor. "Well, can I ask questions about my life?"

"Of course you can. Just try not to take in too much right now. First, Victoria needs to change your IV." The doctor turned to Victoria. "Ms. Chapman, please give him some of the pain meds I prescribed. I'm sure he needs it right about now." Looking back to me, Dr. Michaels gave me a wink.

*Oh, I'm feeling it.* Not only was I in pain, but I was also completely confused.

Victoria walked over and leaned down. After she kissed my cheek, she moved her lips to my ear, so no one else could hear her. "Maybe after everyone is gone, I can help ease some of your pain," she whispered before she pulled away.

I tried to give her a smile, but my stomach turned at her words. *Okay...I'm pretty damn sure we're no longer together. Didn't I break up with her? Oh yeah...right after the blow job. Best fucking blow job of my life...at least from what I can remember.*

Then, my mind flashed an image of the beautiful mystery girl. *Who is the blonde?*

I glanced at my mother, who was watching Victoria leave the room. *If looks could kill, Tori would be flat on the floor.*

For a few minutes, the doctor talked to us about the rest of my stay in the hospital. He mentioned that I'd need another brain scan before I could leave, and then I'd need follow-up appointments with the internal medicine doctor.

Once he was out the door, my mother walked up to me and leaned down to give me a kiss. "Baby, you scared the shit out of me."

I let out a laugh and then winced in pain. "What happened?"

My dad pulled up a chair next to me and sat down. "You were heading out to Mason when a drunk driver hit you." He began shaking his head with anger.

"Mason? Was I going out to the ranch to meet Gunner and Jeff?"

My mother smiled. "No, you were—"

"Liz...too much information, maybe?"

"Oh please, I know exactly what that little witch was doing with the whole don't-force-him-to-remember shit!" Mom said with a disgusted look on her face.

"Yes, but the doctor said the same thing, and..."

I tried to suck in a deep breath, but everything hurt. *Fuck, just tell me already.* "I want to know everything. Don't hold anything back. Fuck what they said. Mom, where was I going?"

Smiling, my mother said, "You were going to see Heather."

"Heather? The girl that was in here earlier? That's Heather, right?"

My dad cleared his throat and nodded. "Yes, Josh. You and Heather are, um—"

"More than friends," I said.

My mother sat straight up and gave my dad a huge smile. "What? He's figuring it out on his own!" she said with a wicked grin on her face.

I let out a laugh. "Okay, I was just taking a guess. My stomach dropped at the sight of this girl, so I knew we had to be more than friends."

My father and mother looked at each other and then at me.

My mother smiled. "Oh yeah...more than just friends."

I smiled at the idea of being with this girl. There was something about her that made me feel...different, and I sure as shit couldn't wait to figure out what it was.

## Chapter Five
## Heather

I watched as Victoria came out of Josh's room. She glanced over at me, and the smile on her face gutted me. I didn't trust her as far as I could throw her.

A few minutes later, the doctor came out.

When I looked over at Amanda, she was holding her stomach.

"What's wrong? Are you feeling sick?" I asked as I got up and walked over to her.

She stood up and put her hand on her mouth.

"Oh god, are you going to throw up? Shit!"

I grabbed her free hand and pulled her to the restrooms. We barely made it in time before Amanda started throwing up in the toilet.

"Jesus, Manda. Do you have the flu? That hit you out of nowhere."

As I stood outside the stall, waiting until she was done, I turned on the warm water and wet a paper towel for her. When she opened the door, I saw tears streaming down her face.

"Amanda! What's wrong?" I asked as I watched her walk to the sink.

She started to splash water onto her face. Looking in the mirror, she began laughing as she wiped off her smeared makeup. Turning around, she leaned against the sink and smiled at me. "You know what's so funny, Heather?"

"Um, no. What's so funny?"

"I should be happy, but I'm not. He doesn't want kids—not now, not ever."

I stood there, staring at her. She was making no sense whatsoever.

"Who doesn't want kids?"

"Brad. He told me last night. He doesn't ever want kids."

I sucked in a breath of air. *Oh no.* "Amanda, are you pregnant?"

When she placed her hands on her stomach, I saw the bump. *Holy shit. How far along is she?*

"I'm almost four months," she said with a weak smile.

"Holy hell! Why didn't you tell us?" I took a step toward her and hugged her.

"He said he didn't want kids right away. We've been married for almost two years now, so when this happened, I thought he'd be okay with it. You'd think he would be happy, right?"

"Of course he's happy, sweets. Why would you think he wasn't?"

She started laughing. "Last night, he told me he doesn't want kids. Ever. When I told him he should have mentioned that minor detail before we got married, he said…he said…" Amanda broke down, crying.

*I'm going to kill Brad.* Placing my hands on her face, I forced her to look at me. "He said what?"

She tried to control her sobs, but she couldn't. Finally, after three good minutes of uncontrollable crying, she blurted out, "He said he'd lied to me because he knew I wouldn't marry him if he never wanted kids. He knew how much I wanted kids, Heather. He knew, and he lied to me. He just hasn't been himself for the last six months."

"Oh, honey. Well, you know what? That dickwad asshole will just have to get used to the idea of kids because he's going to be a dad in five months," I said with a smile.

"No, Heather. I haven't told you everything."

*Oh god, can I take any more bad news?*

"He told me I either have to give up the baby, or he's leaving." She started sobbing again.

"Are you kidding me? What does he mean, you have to 'give up the baby'? Amanda, he doesn't mean…" I trailed off as I moved my hand up to my mouth. I felt sick.

"I told him I would never have an abortion, and he yelled at me for thinking that he could be such a monster. Then, he said he meant adoption. He's already talking about hiding me from his parents for fuck's sake. He doesn't want anyone to know. He wants me to give up the baby, Heather. Give her away. I don't know what to do! It's like he's not even himself. I don't know him anymore." Amanda slid down to the floor, crying.

*Shit a brick…this sucks.* I knelt down next to her, pulled out my phone, and sent Ellie and Ari a text message. We needed a code blue, but I couldn't leave, and Ellie was still in the hospital. *Shit.*

Just then, the restroom door opened, and Victoria walked in. Amanda flew up so fast that she knocked me back on my ass. I jumped up as fast as I could.

"I thought I saw y'all come in here. Mr. and Mrs. Hayes are looking for you," Victoria said to me, looking me up and down as if I were a bug she wanted to step on.

Turning to Amanda, I asked, "Are you okay?"

She smiled and nodded.

As we made our way to the door, Victoria grabbed my arm. "Heather, can I talk to you for a second...alone?" She directed a fake-ass smile toward Amanda.

Amanda threw her hands on her hips. "No. Whatever you have to say, you can say it in front of me. Right, Heather?"

I couldn't even think to talk. *Why does she want to talk to me? What could she possibly have to say to me?* "Um...yeah, right Manda. I mean, is something wrong with Josh?"

Victoria gave Amanda a dirty look before she turned back to me with a smile.

*God, her smile is pure evil. I think Lynda has a twin sister who she doesn't know about.*

"Listen, I get that you and Josh *were* together," she said, throwing her hand back in the air like she couldn't care less. "However, I'm telling you this now. Don't push him into remembering you and your relationship. If you force it and he never gets his memory back, he could very well just be with you because everyone tells him he should. He needs to have the memories return to him...on their own. Right now, he only remembers...well, a relationship with me," she said with a smile.

"You know what...Tori? I have this gift," Amanda said, taking a step closer to Victoria.

Laughing, Victoria put her hands on her hips as she tilted her head to the side. "Oh yeah? And what's your gift...Manda?"

*Oh my god! What a bitch!*

"Well, you see, I can spot a bitch a mile away. And, honey, I spotted you from two miles away. Mess with my friend, and you'll have three very angry girls waiting for you in a dark alley one night." Amanda cracked her knuckles.

I wanted so badly to start laughing, but a thought crossed my mind. *When did Amanda start cracking her knuckles? She hates it when Ari does that.* I shook my head to clear my thoughts.

Victoria stood up a little taller. "Are you threatening me? And who are these other girls?"

Throwing her head back, Amanda laughed. "Oh, honey, you should wish it was only a threat. I forgot to mention my two other friends. We have each other's backs—always have and always will. You hurt Heather in any way, and I'd be more than happy to introduce you to Ari and Ellie."

Victoria gave Amanda a dirty look before turning at me. She leaned in toward me and smiled slightly as she got right in my face. "I'm sure you've never satisfied him like I did. You'll never be able to give him a blow job like I did. BJs from me were his favorite thing, but I'm sure you know all about how much Josh likes his BJs…now, don't you, Heather?" She tapped my nose with her finger before walking out of the restroom.

*I'm going to be sick.*

"Holy fucking hell. What a bitch! Ari is so going to kick her ass. God, I can't wait to tell her about this one. She makes Lynda look like a—" Amanda turned around to see me with my hands on my knees.

*I can't breathe. Oh. My. God.*

"Holy hell, Heather. What's wrong?" Amanda asked.

I looked up at her. I didn't even know what to say. It was Lynda all over again. So many times, she had called or sent emails, detailing her sex life or relationship with Josh. Now, it was happening all over again. I'd only talked to Ari and Ellie about it. I'd told Josh that Lynda was contacting me, but I never told him what she'd said. I couldn't handle it anymore, so I'd finally changed my number and my email address.

"Oh my god. Ari told me about how Lynda would call and write you. Oh god, Heather."

I glanced up at Amanda with a shocked look on my face. I shouldn't be surprised though. None of us could ever hold anything back from the others.

"Fuck her, Heather. Josh loves you, and his relationship with her was years ago. Trust me. The love you share with Josh is strong and true. He's not going to forget that."

I felt tears building in my eyes. "Amanda…I've never given Josh a blow job…ever."

Amanda stepped back and covered her ears. "Oh. My. God! Heather…TMI! I don't want to know if you've ever given Josh a blow job or not!"

Just then, Elizabeth walked in, looking between Amanda and me.

My face instantly grew hot. *Fuck me. Just shoot me! Shoot me now 'cause this can't get any worse.*

"Okay…I'm going to pretend that I never heard those words come out of your mouth, Amanda," Elizabeth said as she walked over to me. "Baby girl, Josh wants to talk to you," she said with a smile.

My heart started pounding. "Me? He wants to talk to me? But he doesn't even know who I am," I said, confused.

She laughed and pulled me in for a hug. "Oh, it was the most romantic thing ever, Heather. He knows."

I leaned away from her. "He remembers me?"

Her smile faded some before it returned. "Well, no…but he knows that y'all are more than friends."

"Oh no. Did you tell him that, Elizabeth?" I asked, thinking back to what Victoria had said about forcing him to remember.

"No, not really. He asked Greg and me about you. He said when he saw you, his heart dropped to his stomach, and he has never felt like that before. He also mentioned that the whole time the doctor was talking, he just kept wondering who you were!" Elizabeth clapped her hands and then grabbed Amanda in for a group hug.

Amanda started laughing as she and Elizabeth began jumping up and down like little kids.

"See! A love like y'all's can never be forgotten," Amanda said with excitement.

"Listen, Josh, I know your parents told you we were dating, but I don't want to force—"

"Dating, huh?"

I watched her as she gave me a confused look.

"Oh, um…well, your mom said you figured out we were more than friends, so I just assumed you thought we were dating." Then, her eyes filled with anger. "Wait, did you think we were fuck buddies or something?" She stood up and stared at me.

*Oh shit, this is turning south fast.*

Considering my mother had told me they'd found an engagement ring in the pocket of my pants, I safely assumed that Heather and I were much more than fuck buddies. Just the way she made me feel in her presence told me that.

"What? God no, Heather. I didn't think that at all!"

Her eyes instantly softened.

*Damn, she's cute as hell when she's mad. I wonder if I used to purposely get her mad just to see that spit and fire come out of her.*

"Oh. Well, okay…because…well…"

"Heather, please tell me about us. I know everyone keeps saying to let my memory come back on its own, but please tell me about you and me. I feel something between us that I've never felt before," I said as I reached out for her hand.

The smile that spread across her face caused me to suck in a breath of air. *Fuck.* I wanted to know everything about this girl, and I wanted to know it yesterday.

She moved closer to me, and then she put her hand in mine. The moment she touched me, an electric shock ran through my whole body.

*This is what I've been waiting for—for a girl who makes me feel like this.* I couldn't help but let out a laugh.

She tilted her head. "What's so funny?"

I shook my head. "It's nothing. I've just waited so long to feel this way, and I can't imagine how or why I would forget it."

"To feel what way?" Heather began to sit back down, not letting go of my hand.

*I can't move too fast. I need to do this right.* "Do you think we could maybe start out by being friends?"

I noticed when her whole body sank. *Shit, that didn't come out right.*

She tried to pull her hand away, but I held on to it.

"Wait, that didn't come out right."

As she stood up, she took her hand away from mine. "No, it's fine. You're right. I don't expect you to just jump into this like nothing happened. I mean, you don't even know me." She gave me a weak smile.

*Ah shit. Why do I feel like I just ripped out her heart?*

"Heather, please…" I reached out my hand for hers, willing her to take it.

Just as she placed her hand in mine, the door opened with no warning, and Victoria walked in. She glanced down at our hands before her eyes snapped back up to focus on me and then Heather.

"Well, looks like you two are getting to know each other again," she said with a fake-ass smile.

When she turned and leaned over, I couldn't help but notice her ass. *Damn…girl has been working out these last few years.*

I quickly looked away and glanced at Heather. She was watching Victoria's every move.

*Thank God she didn't see me checking out Victoria's ass. God, I'm such a dick.* I closed my eyes, wishing I could punch myself.

"Well, sorry to break up the reunion between you two, but I have to take Josh for his scan now." Victoria winked at me.

*Fuck. Why is she flirting with me in front of Heather?*

When I glanced over at Heather, she was staring at me. I smiled at her, but she looked back over to Victoria.

"Not sure how long this will take, so feel free to stay in the room or go to the waiting room." Victoria moved past Heather and lifted up the side rail of my bed.

"That's fine. I'm going to meet Greg and Elizabeth down in the cafeteria for lunch." Heather turned back to me and smiled.

I liked how she'd called my parents by their first names. Considering that along with how much my parents adored her and the engagement ring…*yeah, we must have been really serious.* It was bothering me that this was probably killing her. *Shit. This girl has me in knots, and I can't even remember a goddamn thing about her.*

Heather stepped closer and leaned down slightly, like she was going to kiss me good-bye, but then she stopped herself. "Okay…well, I guess we'll see you in a bit. Good luck with the scan." She took a step away from the bed.

"I don't even get a good-bye kiss?" I asked, knowing how that would make her smile.

*Bingo! Right on cue.*

I stared as that beautiful smile spread across her face. Just as Heather was about to walk back toward me, Victoria stepped in front of her and started to push the bed away from the wall.

"Say good-bye for now, Josh," Victoria said to me before looking over her shoulder at Heather. "Don't worry, honey. I'll be sure to take real good care of him."

I rolled my eyes. I went to look back at Heather, but my whole body screamed out in pain when I did. Closing my eyes, I tried to memorize her. Her blonde hair was beautiful, and it looked so soft. She had the most amazing blue eyes I'd ever seen. Her laugh was…incredibly sexy as hell. She was wearing jeans that fit her body like a glove and a Longhorn T-shirt that was a bit too big on her small frame. Deep down inside, I was hoping like hell that it was my T-shirt on her body.

I heard the elevator doors close, and then I felt lips on my lips. *Those beautiful, soft-looking lips…*

I opened my eyes to see it was Victoria kissing me. When her tongue pushed into my mouth, I started exploring it with mine. I let out a moan as I remembered all the times we'd been together. She responded with her own moan that ran through my body, causing my dick to jump.

Then, her face flashed in my mind. *Heather. This is wrong. This just feels so damn wrong.*

I pulled my lips away from Victoria's and shook my head. "No, please don't do that. This is wrong, Tori."

Smiling, she moved her hand under the covers and grabbed my dick. "Doesn't feel like it's wrong, babe. God, I've missed you, Josh. I can make a small detour if you need a little…attention down here."

*Oh god, this girl gives the best blow jobs.* "I, um…I don't think that's such a good idea." I cleared my throat as I tried to ignore her hand stroking up and down my dick.

"Why? Because your parents tell you that you're with some girl who they clearly want you to be with? How do you know they weren't trying to push you two together before the accident? Do you really know if you were with this girl, babe?"

As much as I would have loved to have her suck my dick right now, something inside me was telling me it was a bad idea. "Thanks, Tori, but no thanks. Let's just get this damn scan done and over with. My head is killing me." I pushed her hand off my dick. As good as it had felt, I needed her to stop.

"Fine, but you know where to find me when you come to your senses."

Victoria leaned down and kissed me on the lips before I quickly turned my head away.

When I closed my eyes again, I pictured a beautiful blonde lying on a blanket next to a river. She was reading, and as I walked toward her, she lifted her head to me…but her face was blurred. *Is that Heather? Is this a memory?*

I needed to find out more about Heather, but damn…I was aching for Victoria's touch again.

*Chapter Seven*

*Gunner*

In the backseat of my truck, Ellie was sitting on one side of Alex while I was on the other. Looking to the front, I saw my parents holding each other's hands as my father pulled up to our house. I smiled and glanced over to Ellie. She was smiling back at me.

"Are you happy?" she asked as she reached over the car seat and grabbed my hand.

I brought her hand up to my lips and kissed the back of it as I grinned. "Never been so happy in my life!"

After Dad parked the truck, he jumped out and ran around to open Mom's door. He helped her out and then opened my door.

"Mom, where's Gus?" I took the car seat out of the truck and held on to it with all my might as I looked around for the little bastard.

Then, I heard Ellie laughing before she started talking to Gus.

*Figures he would run to her first. Bastard. If he thinks he's sleeping in the middle tonight, he has another thing coming.*

As I started toward the house, I heard my dad laughing behind me.

"Jesus, Drew. Think you could walk any faster? You're gonna have to let him meet her, or he won't stop trying to figure out what the new thing is," my dad said, catching up to me.

*Asshole.* I was still pissed that he had joined up with Gramps, and they had been spreading their little story about me fainting to anyone who would listen. I needed to think of a way to get back at them.

When I turned around, Ellie was bending over, giving Gus some lovin'. *Damn, she loves that dog.*

She had read up on how to introduce the baby to Gus, and apparently, we were just going right for it with introductions off the bat.

*Well, not if I can help it. I'm taking little bear in the house and locking the rest of them out.*

As I opened the front door, Ellie called out from behind me, "If you even think about locking us out, Drew Mathews, I'll make you sleep on the sofa for a week!"

I stopped dead in my tracks. I moved out of the way to let Gus run in, and as he passed by, he must have caught Alex's scent. I had to let out a laugh as he slid around the tile floor, trying to stop and turn around all at the same time.

"What's wrong, dipshit? Haven't figured out yet how to stop on the floors?"

When I felt a hand smack the back of my head, I turned to see my father walking by. *What the hell?*

"Don't call that dog names, Drew," my father said as he winked at me.

"Are you kidding me, Dad? You call him every name in the book!" I looked at Ellie and then back at my dad.

"Gunner, take Alex out of her car seat and bring her over to the sofa, so Gus can meet her," Ellie said, practically skipping into the living room.

*She's way too excited about this.*

"Dad, can you go get my twelve gauge?"

My dad gave me a confused look. "Shit, Drew. You gonna introduce her to your gun?" my dad asked.

"What the hell do you need your gun for?" Ellie asked me as she sat down.

As she held out her hands for little bear, I glanced down at Gus lying on the floor near Ellie's feet.

*Damn dog puts on a good show.*

"I need it in case he hurts Alex. If he tries anything, I'm gonna shoot his ass," I said, holding my baby girl in my arms as I looked down at her. I smiled at the sight of her sleeping so peacefully. *God, I love her.*

"Oh. My. God. You did not just say that about my dog!" Ellie stood up and put her hands on her hips.

Gus just stayed in his spot, his eyes moving from Ellie to me and back again.

"Look at him. He's acting so calm now, but I know what he'll do. He's gonna think she's a toy!" I turned to my mother with a pleading look. *She'll be on my side.*

"Oh, for the love of all things good, Drew. Give Ellie the baby, so Gus can meet her already," my mom said as she moved to sit down on the floor next to the dog.

My mouth was hanging open as I just stood there, staring at her, while she rubbed Gus's ears. *My own mother.*

"Fine, but someone better be ready for when he makes his move," I said, glancing down at Gus as I handed little bear to Ellie. *Did that dog just smile at me?* "He just smiled at me! Did y'all see that?"

Ellie let out a laugh as she kissed Alex on the cheek. When Gus slowly sat up, Ellie held Alex down near him. I sucked in a breath of air and just watched. Gus smelled, wagging his tail a little. After he smelled again, he looked up at Ellie.

"Hey, bubs, this is Alex, your baby sister," Ellie said as she smiled at Gus.

*Baby sister? What the hell?*

"I need you to always watch over her and protect her, baby boy. She needs you."

I watched as Gus sat down, still wagging his tail. I was waiting for him to pick up his paw and slap it down on the baby, but he didn't. He just sat there, staring at Alex. Then, he put his head on Ellie's leg.

I looked over at my dad as he slowly let out the breath he'd been holding in. He glanced over at me and shrugged his shoulders. *Son of a bitch was just as worried as I was.*

Ellie looked up at me with that smile of hers. I smiled back before leaning down to kiss her.

"I told you he would be a good boy. He loves her already," Ellie said, glancing down at Gus.

I walked over to the table by the front door and grabbed the PetSmart bag. As soon as I took out the rawhide bone, Gus got up and ran over to me. After I opened it and gave it to him, he ran through the dog door in the kitchen and headed outside.

"Easy-peasy!" my mother said as she began heading toward the kitchen. "Who wants lasagna?"

My dad walked up and kissed her on the cheek. "I'll make the salad."

As they both went into the kitchen, I could hear them laughing and talking about how scared I'd been about Gus attacking Alex. *Some parents they are.*

I turned to look at Ellie as she started to softly sing to Alex. My heart burst from chest with so much love that I had to sit down slowly. I watched the both of them until my mother called us for dinner.

I sat down on the bed and stared at the bassinet holding the love of my life. As I felt Ellie crawling into bed, I saw something that shocked the shit out of me.

"Holy shit, I can't believe it!" I said.

Ellie sat up. "What? What's wrong?"

"Ells, look at your dog." I pointed over to the bassinet.

Gus had walked up and peeked in at Alex before lying down near her.

"Aww…see, he loves her. I told him to protect her, and he's taking his job seriously," Ellie said, lying back down on the bed.

I looked over at her, and my mouth dropped open. *Motherfucker.* She had on a white silk nightgown, and I could see her nipples through the lace.

"Jesus, Ells, are you trying to kill me? You heard the doctor. No sex for six weeks," I said, trying really hard not to jump on her.

She slid under the covers and smiled at me. *God, how I love this girl.*

"I'm sorry! It's just…well, when I tried it on to see if it fit, it did, and I got excited. I want to feel sexy again, Gunner, and this makes me feel sexy," she said as she rubbed her legs together.

"Good god, Ellie. You're going to kill me. Do you know that? I'm not going to be able to wait six weeks, baby. I want you now." I got under the covers and rolled over next to her.

"Touch me, Drew," she whispered in my ear.

*Fuck me. Where the hell do I touch her?*

"Ellie…sweetheart." I slipped my hand under her silk nightgown. I felt her body shiver as I moved my hand up and down the inside of her leg.

"Oh god, Gunner," she said in between breaths.

She was breathing so hard I could barely stand it.

"Ells…I love you so much."

I moved my hand up, taking her nightgown with it. She sat up a little as I slipped the gown over her head. I pulled the covers away from her, so I could see her entire body. She was perfect. No one would ever know that she had just had a baby. She was beautiful, and the stretch marks from being pregnant with Alex just turned me on even more. I needed to make her feel loved and wanted…at this very moment.

"Shit, Ellie...your body is so damn beautiful." I traced one of the stretch marks with my finger.

She let out a moan that traveled through my whole body. If she were to touch me right now, I swore that I would come.

"I need to feel you up against me, Drew. Please…let me feel you."

I flew out of bed quickly, and I almost tripped as I tried to take off my shorts. After I pulled my T-shirt over my head, I got back into bed. Pulling her toward me, I took her nipple in my mouth as I moved my hand down her stomach to between her legs and then into her panties. I knew she was still sore and bleeding, so I only touched her clit.

She jerked her hips and grabbed my dick. The moment she started moving her hand up and down, I knew I wouldn't last.

"Gunner, I'm so close. Oh god, I'm so close."

I leaned up and captured her lips with mine. As our tongues started moving together, she let out a long, soft moan. When I moved my thumb faster on her clit, she held me tighter in her hand.

I pulled away slightly from her lips. "Jesus, Ells. I'm gonna come, baby."

And just like that, we both called out each other's names at the same time.

There was nothing I enjoyed more than making my wife have an orgasm.

Her orgasm seemed to last forever. By the time she came back to me, her breathing was moving her chest up and down. I placed my hand there to feel her heartbeat.

*She's mine. This incredible woman who just gave me the greatest gift in the world...is mine.* "I love you so damn much, Ellie."

She smiled at me, and my world stopped. *I'd do anything for that smile.*

"Drew, I love you more than life itself. I'd be lost without you," she whispered as she put her hand on my face.

Just then, Alex started moving around, barely letting out a cry.

"That's my girl. She waits until Daddy gets his lovin' before she wakes up!" I leaned down and kissed Ellie on the nose.

"And so it begins...the late-night feedings." Ellie giggled.

I reached down and picked up her gown from the floor. After I helped her put it on, I slipped on my shorts and T-shirt, washed my hands, and then walked over to my little bear. Gus sat up and watched as I leaned down and picked up Alex. I moved to the changing table to change her while Ellie went to heat up a bottle.

I figured Gus would have followed Ellie because he never left her side, but he didn't. He sat next me, watching my every move.

I lifted up Alex and walked into the kitchen with her in a full-blown screaming cry.

"Shit, I think she's pissed 'cause I changed her first!" I smiled at Ellie.

She was testing the milk on her arm with a frown I knew she was upset that Alex hadn't taken to breastfeeding. Ellie had been looking forward to that. She had talked about it the whole time she was pregnant. When we had ended up having to bottle-feed, I thought Ellie was going to break down and cry. She was a trooper though, and she'd made a joke out of it, saying I had no excuses now to not get up in the middle of the night.

Alex was still crying, so I pulled out the little binky blue thing the hospital had given us. I put it in her mouth, and she sucked on it five times before she spit that bitch out. I swore that it flew halfway across the kitchen. I looked up at Ellie as she started laughing.

"Beautiful and smart!" Ellie said as she handed me the bottle.

When I put it up to little bear's mouth, she went to town.

"Holy hell, this girl likes her milk!" I said as I followed Ellie into the living room.

I sat down on the sofa, and Ellie curled up next to me. Gus practically sat on my feet with his head on my legs, just watching my every move.

The next thing I knew, he slid down my legs and began snoring. My beautiful bride was sleeping next to me, and the most amazing little girl in the world was looking into my eyes while she ate.

"Life doesn't get any better than this, baby girl."

Then, I thought about Josh and Heather. We'd gotten a text from Amanda earlier, saying that Josh didn't remember Heather…and something about him thinking he was still in college.

When Alex stopped drinking, I looked down at her, and she was just staring back at me. I smiled at her and said a prayer for Josh, hoping that someday, he would be looking down at his little girl while Heather slept peacefully next to him.

"I love you, baby girl. I love you so much."

# Chapter Eight
## Ellie

As I opened my eyes, I saw the light shining through the window. I rolled over and looked toward Alex's bassinet. Gus was gone, so I was guessing that Gunner had gotten up to feed Alex. I had to smile as I thought about how Gus was now following Alex all over the place. *Damn, I love that dog.* It was driving Gunner nuts, which made it all the more fun.

I sat up and stretched as I remembered the two times Gunner had satisfied me last night. *God, I'm so horny but also so damn sore. Six weeks…shit.*

After I brushed my teeth, I made my way toward the kitchen. I stopped when I heard Gunner singing. I slowly walked up to the kitchen entryway and peeked around the corner. I smiled when I saw Gus following behind Gunner as he walked around the kitchen. Gunner was singing "(Everything I Do) I Do It for You" by Bryan Adams as he held Alex in his arms. My heart started beating so fast. He'd sung that song to me when we danced on the beach during our honeymoon.

*Oh. My. God. This man is beyond perfect. How can one person give so much love?* I felt a tear slide down my face. Gunner loved her unconditionally. Alex would always feel loved and wanted.

"I'd die for you and your mama, baby girl. I'll protect you from all those disgusting, evil little boys who will break your heart. Their parents might be upset when I break their faces, but that'll be their problem."

I tried so hard not to giggle as I imagined how he would scare away every boy who would come to our house. Gus must have heard me because he looked right at me and wagged his tail.

When I stepped into the kitchen, Gunner's back was facing me. When he started to sing "Twinkle, Twinkle Little Star," I had to stop and grab on to the kitchen island. My heart was pounding as the ache between my legs grew. His voice was amazing.

Alex let out a little sound, and Gunner laughed.

"You like that song, baby girl?"

"She likes you singing to her, just like I do," I said as I finally got my legs to move.

Gunner turned around and smiled that drop-dead gorgeous smile of his. *How is this man mine? I am one lucky-ass girl.*

"Good morning, sweetheart. Did you sleep good?" he asked as he winked at me.

I walked over to him and reached up to give him a kiss. "I did, thanks to you and your magical fingers."

Gunner threw his head back and laughed.

"How did you sleep?"

He yawned and then handed Alex to me. "I tossed and turned all night, thinking about Josh."

"Shit. I need to call Heather. The last time I talked to her, they had brought Josh back from some scans, and she said he had been sleeping for four hours. I can't believe he doesn't remember her, Gunner. How could he forget her?" I put Alex in her bouncy chair and then started to make coffee.

Gunner let out a sigh as he sat down. He ran his hands through his hair and then down his face. "I don't know. I can't even imagine how Heather's feeling. I wasn't going to say anything, but…" He stopped talking and shook his head.

"What? Don't stop mid-sentence and leave me hanging like that!"

"Well, Josh was planning on asking Heather to marry him after the Christmas party. Jeff and I had gone with him to pick out the ring." Gunner looked up at me with such sad eyes.

*No…*

"Oh, Gunner. Oh no. Why is this happening? Oh god…poor Heather. Like she hasn't been through hell and back enough times. Does she know he was going to ask her?"

"No. I'm not even sure his parents knew." Gunner stood up and grabbed a coffee mug out of the cabinet. "Listen, Jeff is heading back into Austin today to go see Josh. I'm going to follow him in Heather's car since Jeff drove her to the hospital. I know Brad and Amanda are coming out to visit, and—"

I spun around and looked at Gunner. "Oh. My. God! You need to kick Brad's ass!"

Gunner gave me a confused look. "What? Why?"

I shook my head, remembering Heather's text to Ari and me.

> *Heather: Amanda's pregnant, like four months along, and Brad told her if she didn't give the baby up for adoption, he was leaving. And he told her she had to hide it from his parents. It's like someone snatched the real Brad and replaced him with this asshole. This dickwad also told*

*Amanda he had lied to her about wanting kids because he
was afraid she wouldn't marry him if he said he didn't.*

"He lied! Never wanted kids…she's pregnant, and he's talking
crazy…hide the pregnancy! Adoption? Psht!"

Gunner stood there, just staring at me. "Wow…somehow, I think I
understood everything you just rattled off." He sat back down. "Okay, so
let me get this straight. Amanda told Brad she was pregnant, but Brad
doesn't want kids. So, he told her she had to give the baby up for adoption?
Ellie, that doesn't even sound like Brad. He's never once told us he didn't
want kids. As a matter of fact, when Ari was pregnant, he told Jeff he
couldn't wait to have kids!" Gunner said, running his hand through his
hair.

"I don't know. That's what Amanda told Heather yesterday. Brad
freaked and told Amanda he didn't want kids. Ever."

Gunner got up and took out his phone.

*Oh shit. He's calling Brad. Good thing Gunner won't be here when
they come visit.*

Just then, my cell phone went off. I grabbed it out of my purse and saw
a message from Amanda.

*Amanda: We're on our way! Can't wait to see the baby!*

Clearly, she didn't know Heather had told us. When Heather called the
code blue, Ari had called me right away, and we'd decided to wait to talk
to Amanda in person.

*This is insane. No way is she giving up her baby because some asshole
said she had to. Ugh, I can't believe he lied to her about wanting kids.*

"Okay, I'll see you in a few minutes." Gunner slipped his cell phone
into his back pocket. "Jeff and Ari are on their way. Jeff is driving
Heather's car, and my dad can give Ari a ride back home when she's ready
to leave."

"Did you mention Brad to Jeff?"

"I didn't have to. Ari told him last night. He's ready to kick his ass,
and to be honest, I'm ready to put him in the hospital," Gunner said as he
made a fist.

"Good Lord, can't we just have a few months of no drama in this
group of ours? First, it's Josh and Heather, and now, there's this whole
thing with Brad and Amanda. I'm not sure if I'll be able to look him in the
eye and not say something, Gunner." I looked over at Alex as she started to
wake up.

Gunner let out a sigh. "Jeff thinks he knows what the problem is with
Brad."

I was just about to pick up Alex when I stopped and looked at Gunner. "Okay…what's the problem?"

"All he said was that Smitty had called him a few weeks ago and said he saw Brad at lunch with a girl."

I felt sick. *Brad's cheating on Amanda?* "Oh no, Gunner…you don't think…"

"I don't know, baby. Jeff asked Brad about it, and Brad said Smitty must have been wrong because he was out of town that week."

I picked up Alex and held her close to me as I felt tears building in my eyes. *Did Brad cheat on Amanda? Please, God, no. Please don't let that be true.*

# Chapter Nine
## Heather

As we walked into the hospital, I thought about everything that had happened yesterday. Josh had been so cold and distant when he came back from his brain scan, and Victoria had been flying high as a kite.

*Did she say something to Josh? What could she have said to make him so withdrawn?*

Elizabeth grabbed my hand. "Heather, honey, are you okay? You seem so far away."

I had talked to her about how Josh wanted to start off by being friends. I'd seen how disappointed she was, and I knew exactly how she felt. I didn't want to push Josh into anything, but at the same time, I felt like he was slowly slipping away from me.

"I guess I'm just trying to figure out how you go from being head over heels in love with someone and spending every moment you can together to…just being friends."

Elizabeth stopped and gave me a weak smile. I tried so hard not to cry, but it was getting harder and harder to hold it back.

"Don't give up on him. Don't give up on the two of you. What you shared is too strong to be forgotten," she said as she wiped away the single tear rolling down my face.

"That's just it…he did forget, Elizabeth. He forgot about me, about us. He doesn't remember any of it."

"I'm telling you right now he knows that you both shared something. He even told Greg and me that you took his breath away when he first saw you. Please have faith that he'll come back to you, baby girl. Please don't give up on him, not when he needs you," Elizabeth said as tears started to pool in her eyes.

"Elizabeth, I love Josh with every ounce of my being. My life would be nothing without him. If I didn't have him…I…I just couldn't live without him. He's every breath I breathe. I'll never leave him. Ever."

She pulled me into her arms, and we stood there, crying for a few minutes.

Then, Greg walked up. "Girls, are you ready to go in and see Josh?"

I pulled back and smiled as I wiped the tears from my face. "I promise you, I'll stay faithful to him forever."

She tried to return the smile, but it didn't reach her eyes. I knew exactly what she was thinking because I was thinking the same thing.

*I would remain faithful to our love…but would Josh?*

As we got closer to Josh's room, I could hear Victoria laughing. *Holy hell…does this girl never go home?*

Greg opened the door and held it for Elizabeth and me to walk in. Unfortunately, I went in first and saw Victoria leaning over the bed, like she was about to kiss Josh. They didn't see us right away, and the way he was looking at her caused my whole body to start shaking. Following me in, Elizabeth saw them and grabbed my hand.

"Jesus H. Christ, Victoria. Do you ever go home and sleep?" Elizabeth asked.

I almost laughed since I'd just thought nearly the same thing.

Victoria stood up straight, and her smile dropped from her face when she saw me.

*Bitch. I will never leave him.*

I glanced over to see Josh staring at me. When our eyes met, the smile that spread across his face made me weak in the knees. He was looking at me like he…loved me. But the way he had looked at Victoria was like he lusted after her.

When I smiled back at him, he held out his hand for me. I watched as Victoria noticed Josh's hand stretched out toward me. Her head snapped back up, and she just glared at me.

Elizabeth gave me a little push from behind, and I made my way over to Josh's side. Victoria gave me a fake-ass smile as she stepped closer to the bed, blocking me.

"Well, I have to go check on my other patients. Josh, I'll see you in a few, honey," she said as she leaned down and kissed him on the cheek.

I sucked in a breath of air. *Oh. My. God. She did not just do that!*

"See ya later, Tori," Josh said with a smile.

She turned and gave me a look that I just wanted to slap off her face. *Okay, bitch, it's on now.*

"You don't have to rush back anytime soon. I plan on hanging out all day." I gave her my own bitchy smile. I glanced over and saw Elizabeth holding back a smile.

Victoria let out a gruff laugh. "Well, just remember that he needs rest. Too much company isn't good for his recovery."

"Maybe you should remember that yourself." I raised my eyebrows at her.

Her smile faded as she excused herself. "Greg, Elizabeth, good morning," Victoria said as she made her way out the door.

Once the door closed, I looked at Elizabeth, and she winked at me. Slowly letting out the breath I had been holding in, I tried to calm myself since my hands were still shaking from being so upset.

Then, Josh reached for my hand, and the electric shock that ran through my body surprised me. It was as if he were touching me for the first time. I turned, and holding his hand in mine, I smiled at him.

"I missed seeing your face this morning when I woke up," he said with that damn panty-melting smile of his.

My heart was beating so hard that I swore everyone in the room could hear it. "Really?"

"Really, really!" He let out a small laugh and then made a face like he was in pain.

"Oh, sweetheart. Do your ribs hurt?" Elizabeth asked as she moved to the other side of the bed.

"Yeah, they were in here earlier, making me take deep breaths. Fucking hurt."

"Language, Josh." Elizabeth leaned down and kissed him on the forehead.

*Oh god.* I wanted to kiss him so badly. As I looked at his lips, I started licking my own. *I miss those lips.*

When I felt him squeeze my hand, I pulled my eyes away from his lips to see him staring at me. I shook my head to clear my wayward thoughts.

"Have you had anything to eat yet? I could go and get you some banana nut bread from Starbucks," I said, feeling heat warm my cheeks.

He smiled the biggest smile I'd seen yet. "I love their banana nut bread!"

I laughed as I sat down in the chair Greg had just pushed up for me. I wasn't even thinking about my actions when I pulled his hand up to my lips and kissed the back of it. "I know you do!"

Elizabeth let out a giggle and looked over at Greg. "Come on, babe. I could go for a nice hot chocolate from Starbucks."

"Sounds good to me. Heather, honey, would you like something?" Greg asked before he kissed me on the top of my head.

I glanced up at him and smiled. "I might take a slice of banana nut bread also if you don't mind."

I turned back to Josh and winked. He tried not to laugh, but he did. The moment I saw the pain on his face, I felt sick to my stomach.

"Oh shit! I didn't mean to make you laugh," I said as I held his hand tightly.

"No worries." Josh looked over at Greg. "Take your time, okay, Dad?"

Greg winked at Josh and grabbed Elizabeth's hand as they turned to leave.

I watched as the door shut. *We're alone…and I'm nervous as hell.*

"Heather?"

I turned back to look at Josh. "Yeah?"

"Um, you're squeezing the hell out of my hand," he said with a small smile.

"Oh my god! I'm so sorry, Josh." I let go of his hand. *Shit! Shit! Shit!*

"Ah, damn, don't make me laugh. Shit, you're the cutest thing I've ever seen."

*Cute? What the hell am I? A puppy?* I tried to smile at him. "Oh, um…well, I, um…" *Damn, I can't even talk.*

"I've never seen anyone as beautiful as you," he said, looking at my lips.

I couldn't help myself. I licked them again before biting down on my lower lip. *Why do I feel like I'm falling in love with him all over again?*

"You look like you want to kiss me, Heather," he said with seduction in his voice.

"Josh…" *Please give me strength.*

"How long have we known each other?" he asked, pulling me out of my moment of weakness.

*Thank God because I almost leaned over to kiss him.* "Um…two and a half years. We met at Ellie's graduation party. Ellie and I went to high school together."

"So, you're still in college?"

"No, I graduated last August," I said with a smile.

"What? How the hell did you manage that?" he said as he tried to sit up some more.

"Do you need help?" I asked as I stood up.

"I just wanted to try to sit up a little bit more." He put his hands on each side of the bed to push himself up.

When I reached over to help him, he stopped moving.

"Don't touch me, Heather!" he said with panic in his voice.

"Oh shit! Did I hurt you?" I asked, stepping back.

"No! Shit, no, you didn't hurt me at all."

He moved himself up a little, and the pain on his face gutted me.

*I wish I could take the pain away.*

"That's sweet of you, but I wouldn't want you in this kind of pain," Josh said with a smile.

"What?" I asked, confused.

"You said you wished you could take the pain away, but I wouldn't want to ever see you in this kind of pain."

"Wait, I said that out loud?" I asked, confused as hell.

Josh let out a laugh and then quickly stopped and swore.

"Can I ask you something, Josh?" I said as I sat back down in the chair.

"Of course. Ask away. Not going to promise I'll remember if you ask me anything about us, but I can try!"

I let out a giggle, shaking my head. "No, it's just…why did you just tell me not to touch you?"

His smile faded. "Heather, I have to be honest with you. I haven't been able to stop thinking about you all night and all morning. I kept wondering when you'd come back. Actually, I was hoping to God that you'd come back early this morning," he said, his smile reappearing. "I've never felt like this before. Well, shit, I guess I have, but I don't remember a damn thing. I'm guessing I felt this way the first time we met. It scares the shit out of me. In my mind, I'm still in college, still fucking around with other…" He stopped talking as he looked away.

I closed my eyes, trying so hard to not start crying. I wanted so badly to tell him that he was my everything, to tell him how much we loved each other.

When Josh turned back to look at me, his eyes were filled with so much confusion. I instantly felt guilty for feeling the way I did.

"I want so badly to…"

*Please don't stop talking.*

"You want so badly to what?" I asked as I took his hand in mine. I had to touch him in some way, or I was going to lose it.

When he looked down at my mouth, I realized I was biting my lower lip. I instantly stopped and snapped my eyes to his lips. His lower lip was swollen just a bit, and I wanted nothing more than to kiss it.

Josh started to talk, but his voice cracked. "I just want to kiss you so fucking bad." He cleared his throat and gave me that damn crooked smile of his. "I want to know if you make noises when you kiss. I want to feel your body against mine. I want to know what you smell like. Is your skin as soft as it looks? I want to know everything about you."

I felt a tear rolling down my face. Butterflies were taking off in my stomach like I'd never experienced before, not even when we'd first made love. "Josh—"

He shook his head as if he didn't want me to talk. "Please don't say anything for a minute…please."

I sat there in complete silence while his eyes held mine captive.

When he smiled at me, I swore my stomach just about dropped to the ground. *Is it possible to fall in love with someone I was already in love with?*

"I want to get to know you again. Will you let me, Heather?" he asked, squeezing my hand with his.

I pulled his hand up to my mouth and kissed it. As he closed his eyes, my heart started pounding.

"Of course, Josh. I lov—" *Shit! I almost told him that I love him.*

"I want to hear you say it. Please tell me how you feel about me." Josh tried to adjust himself to a more comfortable position.

I closed my eyes as I felt tears coming. This time, I didn't care, and I just let them fall as I opened my eyes. "I love you. I've loved you since the first moment I saw you, since the first time you asked me if you could help me out of my clothes, and since you told me your tongue wanted to show my tongue how to dance," I said with a giggle.

I watched as a smile spread across his face.

He chuckled. "Sounds like something I would say."

"You're the only one I've ever loved. You're the only one I will ever love. You're my every breath, Josh," I said as I looked away from him. *I'm telling him too much.*

"You asked me why I didn't want you to touch me," Josh said.

I slowly glanced back toward him.

"It's because I feel something. I feel something so incredibly strong toward you, and the moment you touch me, I feel like I'm gonna want more, much more. I have this need to just be with you, and it blows my mind because I don't ever remember feeling like this toward anyone. I don't want to blow this, and I usually fuck things up by moving too fast." He gave me a small smile.

*I didn't know what to say. Does he really have these feelings? Or did I just tell him too much? Maybe he thinks he should be feeling like this. Oh fuck.*

"I, um…I'm not sure if I should have told you all that. Maybe I just confused you. I don't know. I'm so sorry, Josh. The last thing I want to do is confuse you." I wiped the tears away from my face.

He shook his head and held on to my hand tightly. "No, I'm glad you told me. I just…I just want to take things slow. I want to get to know you, and when I said that I wanted to start off as friends, I just meant…fuck, Heather. If it weren't for a few broken ribs or me lying in this hospital bed, I would want to make love to you. But I don't want it to be like all the other girls. I want to get to know you again. I want to know everything about you."

*What? Oh. My. God. Breathe. Breathe, Heather. Daddy, help me to breathe.*

"Heather, breathe, honey. You're holding your breath," Josh said.

I snapped my head up. "What did you just say?"

"Um, I told you to breathe. You looked like you were holding your breath."

When Josh glanced down at my lips, I looked to his, and without thinking, I got up, leaned down, and kissed him. I needed to feel some kind of contact with him.

Placing his hand on my neck, he held me closer to him and kissed me back.

I let a small moan escape my mouth. *Oh god, I miss him.*

We kissed until we needed to stop for air. After I slowly pulled my lips away, I rested my forehead on his.

*I love him so much. I'd wait an eternity for him.*

"I'm sorry, Josh. I shouldn't have done that," I whispered, keeping my eyes closed. I was so afraid to open them.

"Heather, please don't ever apologize for kissing me. As a matter of fact, feel free to do it anytime you want!" Josh said.

I opened my eyes, and when I saw him smiling, my heart dropped to my stomach. It had almost felt like it was our first kiss. I let out a giggle that made him smile.

"Um...should we come back?"

I spun around to see Gunner, Jeff, and one very pissed-off Victoria standing there, staring at us. Gunner was smiling from ear to ear.

"Y'all look like you were having a...moment," Jeff said as he walked up to the side of the bed. Leaning down, he kissed me on top of the head before he moved toward my ear. He whispered, "What the fuck? Victoria is his nurse?"

I let out a laugh. "Yep. We need to talk later."

I stepped back, so Jeff could talk to Josh.

"Jesus H. Christ, dude. You look like shit," Jeff said, gently shaking Josh's hand.

"Thanks, dude. Holy shit. Do you have a wedding ring on?"

When Josh glanced over toward Gunner, Gunner held up his wedding band for Josh to see.

"Motherfucker. Both of y'all are married?"

"Yep. I just had a baby girl two nights ago...the night of your accident." Gunner's smile faded a bit.

"No shit. You're a dad, Gunner? Well, goddamn!" Josh looked back at Jeff.

"I've got a six-month-old little boy. His name's Luke," Jeff said with such pride in his voice.

I was bursting with joy. I was so happy for my friends. *I really need to go see Ellie and Alex.*

"Excuse me, but I need to get in there and take some vitals. Josh also needs to take his pain meds," Victoria said as she smiled at Jeff. Then, she gave me a look that should have dropped me on the spot.

"Sure, Victoria. By the way, it's good seeing you again," Jeff said as he gave her a wink.

"Yep, y'all, too. Been a long time. We'll have to get together for old times' sake," Victoria said to Jeff before she glanced at me with an evil grin.

I smiled back at her, shaking my head.

*I'm going to put this girl in her place. Time to pull out my inner bitch.*

## Chapter Ten

## Josh

I sat there and listened to Gunner and Jeff talk about their lives. *Married and with kids? Fuck me.*

Then, I remembered the engagement ring. My parents had already come back from Starbucks, but they'd left with Heather for a bit to let Gunner and Jeff visit with me. Victoria had kept coming in every fifteen minutes. She was back again, and this time, she was leaning up against the bed, talking to Gunner.

"Hey, Tori, do you think I could have a few minutes alone with Jeff and Gunner? I need to talk to them about some things in private," I said as I winked at her.

I watched as a blush slowly crept up her face. I wanted to roll my eyes at her reaction, but instead, I gave her my smile.

"Sure, babe. I'll be back in a bit."

Leaning down, she went to give me a kiss on the cheek. When I turned my head away, she stood back up.

"Oh shit, sorry. Old habits are hard to break," she said as she smiled at me.

Once she shut the door, Jeff let out a laugh. "Motherfucker, some things never change!"

"Fuck, Josh, what did you ever see in that girl?" Gunner asked as he ran his hand through his hair.

I let out a laugh, but I stopped as soon as the pain in my side shot through my whole body.

"Fuck, don't answer that. I already know what you're gonna say…especially since your ass thinks you're the old you!" Jeff smiled at me.

"The old me? What's the new me like?" I asked as Jeff and Gunner looked at each other.

"Well, from what we saw when we walked in, I take it you know that you and Heather are dating?" Gunner asked with a grin.

I nodded. "There's something about that girl. She's exactly what I've been looking for. I've never felt like this before."

Jeff smiled at me and shook his head. "Josh, you're fucking madly in love with her. You were even gonna ask—"

Gunner hit Jeff in the arm.

I let out a laugh. *Shit, the pain.* "I already know I was going to ask her to marry me the night I had the accident. My parents told me they found the ring on me when they brought me into the hospital."

Gunner smiled. "Yeah, dude, we went with you to pick it out. You were fucking nervous as hell, too."

Jeff started laughing. "You were shaking from head to toe, but man...you picked out a beautiful ring."

"Can I ask y'all something?"

"Of course, Josh. We're like brothers. You know you can always ask us anything," Jeff said.

"Have I been...well, you know...with Heather...have I been, um...well..."

"Jesus, spit it the hell out." Gunner started to laugh.

"Have I been good to her? I mean...I haven't fucked around on her, have I?"

Jeff looked at me and smiled. "Dude, the moment you realized you loved her, you went for, like, months without sex. I actually started to worry about you." He threw his head back and laughed.

"Let's just say, the road y'all have traveled on was not so straight, but when you finally got together...dude, you loved her with all your heart. There's a reason you're feeling the way you are, Josh. A love like what you and Heather share...it never goes away. Just take it slow. It'll come back. For now, just enjoy it. Get to know each other again. In a way, you're a lucky bastard." Gunner smiled, shaking his head.

I looked at Gunner, confused. "How the hell do you figure that? I've lost all these years, Gun. I can't even remember the girl I'm in love with. For fuck's sake, I was planning on asking her to marry me!"

Gunner smiled at me. "Josh, you get to fall in love with her all over again. You can experience all those first moments with her. Dude, you get to sweep her off her feet again and make her fall in love with you even more."

Jeff stared at Gunner and shook his head. "Jesus H. Christ, who the fuck taught you this sappy-ass shit?"

I started to laugh as I grabbed my side. "Oh shit. What about my truck?" *If anything happened to my Dodge, I swear I'm going to kill that motherfucking drunk driver.*

Gunner and Jeff both looked at each other.

"Dude, it's totaled," Gunner said.

"But don't worry. You were actually getting ready to buy a new truck," Jeff said as he glanced back at Gunner.

"My truck is totaled? Fuck! I was gonna buy a new Dodge? What was wrong with mine?"

Jeff smiled. "You weren't gonna get a Dodge, dude. You were tired of that truck. Bitch had no balls. You were looking at an F-250 diesel. You needed power for pulling the trailer with your furniture."

Gunner snapped his head over to Jeff.

*I was getting a fucking Ford? Jesus, I really have changed.* "Wait, what do you mean, 'with your furniture'? I'm working for my dad?"

"You bought out your dad. It's your business, dude, and you're doing great," Gunner said with a smile.

*No fucking way. I own my dad's business.*

Just then, Victoria came back in. "Time to get you to do some deep breathing, babe," she said as she winked at me.

Jeff looked Tori up and down as if she were a bug that should be stepped on. Gunner looked everywhere but at Tori.

Victoria noticed Gunner avoiding her. She walked up to him and ran her hand through his hair, and he immediately pulled away from her. "You still a deep breather during sex, Gun?"

Gunner turned and glared at Victoria.

*What the fuck? Gunner slept with Victoria?*

"Oh fuck no, Gunner!" Jeff said.

Victoria threw her head back and laughed. "Oh fuck yeah. I dare say Josh gave Gunner a run for his money though." She looked back at me and smiled.

I couldn't even think. *Gunner slept with Tori. When? Before or after me? Fucking bastard never said a word to me.* "When the fuck did this happen?" I said as I tried to sit up some.

Gunner gave Victoria a dirty look. "Shut the fuck up, Victoria." He stood up and walked over toward me.

"Gunner, when the fuck did you sleep with my girlfriend?"

"First off, Josh, Victoria is not your girlfriend. Heather is. It was months before you started dating her, dude. It was one time, and it meant nothing," Gunner said.

"Why didn't you tell me that you'd slept with her, dude? You knew I liked her."

When I looked over at Victoria, she was standing behind Gunner with a shit-eating grin on her face.

"Um, Josh—" Jeff said, walking up next to Gunner.

"Not now, Jeff! Gunner, why didn't you tell me that you slept with the girl I'm dating?"

"You're not fucking dating her, Josh. It was over four years ago, dude. You're with Heather now." Gunner threw his hands in his hair and let out a sigh.

"Josh—" Jeff said again.

Something snapped in me. "I'm not fucking dating anyone, and I don't want to date anyone or be tied down to anyone!" I yelled.

With that, I heard someone suck in a breath of air.

"Ah fuck," Jeff said.

When I looked over toward the door, I saw Heather and my mother standing there.

"Excuse me," Heather said before she turned and left.

When I glanced at Victoria, she was smiling from ear to ear.

*Why do I get the feeling she set that whole thing up?*

"Heather, wait!" I called out. Pain shot through my body, and I threw my head back against the pillow, letting out a sigh.

"Jesus, Josh. Next time I try to tell you to shut the fuck up, you should listen." Jeff turned and followed my mother out the door.

I glanced back at Gunner. "Fuck, Gunner. I'm sorry, dude. I don't know what the hell came over me just now. It just feels like it's all happening now and not four years ago." I looked over toward Tori.

Gunner shook his head. "Don't worry about it. I'm sorry I never told you about sleeping with Victoria." He turned to Victoria. "You mind giving us a few minutes?"

"I'm so sorry, Josh. I wasn't even thinking," Victoria said.

"Can you just please give us a few minutes?" Gunner said, a little angrier this time.

"Oh yeah, sure. I'll be back in a few minutes for that breathing exercise, Josh." She winked at Gunner before she walked out the door.

Gunner closed his eyes and shook his head. "I really don't like that girl," he said as he looked at me.

I let out a small laugh. "Victoria is just being Victoria, that's all."

"Well, she better not ever pull that shit around Ellie," he said, sitting back down.

"What did you want to talk about, Gunner?"

"Josh, you need to know something about Heather. I should probably let her tell you, but…" He trailed off, looking down at the floor.

"What is it? Is she sick or something?"

Gunner snapped his head up. "No! Oh god, no. It's nothing like that. During Heather's senior year of high school, her, um…her parents both died in a car accident."

*Holy fuck. That poor girl.* "I'm all she has, aren't I?" I asked, feeling tears build up in my eyes. This was the first time in my life I'd even cared about a girl, and I'd just hurt her.

Gunner nodded.

"And my big fucking mouth basically just told her that I didn't want her as a girlfriend." I closed my eyes and saw the look on her face when I'd said it.

When I opened my eyes, I turned to Gunner. "I always fuck things up, Gun…always."

## Chapter Eleven
### Jeff

"Elizabeth, let me talk to Heather."

She nodded and gave me a weak smile. "I think I'll go have a few words with Victoria."

*Fuck, I hate Victoria.*

I caught up to Heather just as she was getting on the elevator. We rode down to the first floor in silence. I followed her as we walked outside. She sat down on a bench and leaned her head back.

"Why did this happen, Jeff? Am I just not meant to find happiness?"

When she looked at me with tears in her eyes, my heart dropped to my stomach.

*Shit, this girl can't catch a break.* "Sweetheart, he didn't mean it. I promise you, he feels something for you, something very strong. He's just scared of how he's feeling, Heather. In his mind, he's this young kid in college, just having a good time. He's confused, and Victoria threw some shit out there on purpose to confuse him even more."

"That's just it, Jeff. What if that's the life he wants again?" Heather started shaking her head. "Damn it! I'm so damn confused. Do I back off? Do I keep telling him about us? I mean, I want him to remember us on his own, not because I'm feeding him with my memories. At the same time, I need him so much that I…" Heather's voice broke off as tears began rolling down her face.

"You know what to do. You don't give up on him. You love him, Heather. You need to be there for him as his girlfriend." I grabbed her hand and held on to it.

"He told me he wants to start off as friends. I don't know if I can just be his friend, Jeff. I mean, of course, I will, but…even earlier…shit, I couldn't help myself. I kissed him!" she said as she covered her face with her free hand.

"Heather, just try your best to do what he asks. If he needs time to adjust to all of this, give him time. Deep down inside of him, he knows he loves you. We just need him to remember it."

"Yeah…I know. Thanks so much, Jeff," Heather said with a small smile. "Thank you for bringing me to the hospital to see him. I love you and Ari so much."

"I know, sweetheart. Let's head on back, okay? I'm sure Josh is worried that he upset you." I stood up, still holding her hand in mine.

Gunner and I were quiet almost the whole way back to Mason.

I was still trying to process that he'd slept with Victoria. *Fuck me.*

Then, I thought back to a party when I'd come close to hooking up with her. *Damn. How fucked-up would that have been?*

"Dude, I still can't believe you slept with Victoria. Why didn't you say something to Josh when he started going out with her?" I asked as I looked over at Gunner.

"Because it was Josh, and I figured he was going to sleep with her and move on. How the hell was I supposed to know he'd end up dating her? Besides, I only hooked up with her once, and I was drunk when it happened."

I shook my head and smiled. *Glad those fucking days are over.*

For some reason, I couldn't wait to get home to Ari and Luke. I glanced over to see how fast Gunner was going.

"I know, dude. I want to get home to Ellie and Alex, too." Gunner smiled.

"Jesus H. Christ. It must be in your blood. How the hell did you know what I was thinking?" I asked.

We both started to laugh, and Gunner shrugged his shoulders.

"Dude, I gotta know. Where the fuck do you come up with all that sappy shit you throw out there?"

"What the hell are you talking about? I just say what's in my heart, that's all," Gunner said with a wink.

"Okay, dude, like that shit. You just say what's in your heart? Who says that?"

"I do, and my sappy shit makes your sister happy." He quickly glanced over toward me with a smile and a wink.

*Bastard.*

"Did Ellie tell you about the visit with Brad and Amanda?"

Gunner shook his head. "She just sent me a text and said one word—*awkward.*"

"Yeah, Ari sent me a text, too. She said she pretty much dug holes in her hands with her nails to keep from saying anything to him."

"What the fuck do you think is going on, Jeff? I mean, come on. Do you really see Brad saying that shit to Amanda?"

"No, but he's been acting weird lately. All this traveling out of town, and Smitty swears that Brad was with another girl. I mean, he loves Amanda so much. None of it makes any sense, Gunner. None of it." I looked out the window.

"Dude, I think we need to have a chat with our buddy Brad."

I glanced back to look at Gunner. His jaw was set, and I knew how he felt. My heart was breaking for Amanda. She was four months pregnant, and her husband had told her she had to hide it and then give up the baby for adoption. *Yeah, none of it makes a lick of sense.*

Just then, my cell phone rang.

*Holy fuck, speak of the devil.* I looked at Gunner. "It's Brad."

"Hello?" I answered.

"Jeff, I need to talk to you and Gunner right away!" Brad said in a panicked voice.

"Okay…well, dude, we're almost back to Mason."

"I just dropped Amanda off at home. I'm coming back out there. Can I meet y'all in a few hours?"

I glanced over at Gunner, and he must have been able to hear Brad because he nodded.

"Sure, dude, just, um…come to Gunner's house or mine—"

"No. I could tell Ari and Ellie were pissed at me today. I'll meet you at the main barn. Just give me a couple hours to get there," Brad said before he hung up.

I looked over toward Gunner. "What the fuck is going on?"

"He must really need to talk if he's going to drive all the way back out here again," Gunner said as he shook his head.

"Yeah, he must."

When I walked into the house, I could smell lasagna. *Damn, Ari makes the best lasagna ever.*

It was dead quiet in the house. I walked into the kitchen to see my beautiful bride sitting at the kitchen island with her head resting on her arms. The baby monitor was next to her, so Luke had to be sleeping. As I stepped closer, I could tell she was fast asleep.

I smiled as I leaned down and scooped her up into my arms. Snuggling her head into my chest, she let out a small moan.

"Don't forget the monitor," she whispered.

I smiled as I went to grab it before heading to our bedroom.

Once in our room, I gently laid her down on the bed. She still had her eyes closed, but a small smile was playing across her face.

"How is Josh? Heather sent me a text saying you were her knight in shining armor today. How long is he going to be in the hospital?"

She just kept asking question after question. Instead of answering her, I leaned down and took her lips with mine.

The next thing I knew, I was taking off my clothes as I watched her strip out of hers.

"I missed you so damn much today. I love you so much, baby," I said as I crawled on top of her.

"Hmm...I love you, too. Oh god," she said as I slowly entered her body.

*Fuck, she feels like pure heaven.*

"Jeff...you feel so good. Please go slow. I need you so bad," Ari said as she pulled my body closer to hers.

I started covering her with kisses. I stopped moving as I paid attention to only her nipples. When she kept bucking her hips into mine, I smiled.

"Move, Jeff. For Christ's sake, move!"

"Baby, you told me to go slow...so I'm going slow," I said as I looked at her and smiled.

The next thing I knew, she was on top of me, and my world was completely and utterly rocked by her. We called out each other's names at the same time as we both came together.

*Life is so perfect when I'm with Ari. Fuck, I love this girl so damn much.*

We were lying there, holding each other, for what seemed like forever.

"How long has Luke been asleep?" I asked.

Ari let out a sigh. "I put him down right before you came home. He was being a stinker. He loves Alex, and I think he was wondering why she wasn't on the floor, playing with him. Amanda played with him so much that I think she wore his little ass out. Brad even played with him...a lot. That surprised me since the fucker doesn't want kids."

"Yeah, about Brad...I'm gonna have to go meet him here in a little bit. He called and said he dropped off Amanda and was heading back out to talk to Gunner and me," I said as I stroked Ari's hair.

She pushed up and looked at me. "What? They just left a few hours ago. Now, he's coming back out? What the hell for?"

I shrugged my shoulders. "Said he needed to talk to Gunner and me, and he sounded desperate."

Ari sat up straight and pulled the sheet around her. "You know, they were both acting so weird. They weren't even talking to each other. At one point...well...oh shit, never mind."

"What? Tell me, Ari," I said.

"Okay, but you're gonna think I'm crazy. At one point, I swear Brad was high. He went outside to take a call. When he came back in...I don't know...he was different. I swear, Jeff, he was high on something."

Running my hand through my hair, I shook my head. "Impossible, Ari. Brad would never do drugs. No way."

Ari frowned and just looked at me. "I don't know, Jeff. I would stake a million dollars on it. Even Ells thought he was acting strange."

Just then, we heard Luke over the baby monitor. Ari got up and started getting dressed. Lying there, I thought about everything Ari had just said.

*Brad's doing drugs? No fucking way.*

# Chapter Twelve
## Gunner

Sitting on the porch with Ellie, I was holding Alex in my arms while she was asleep. Jeff had called a few minutes ago to tell me he was on his way to pick me up to meet Brad. I had the worst feeling in my stomach.

"Ells, how did Brad act when he was here with Amanda?"

Ellie looked at me with concern in her eyes. "Well, um…honestly, Ari and I both thought something was wrong. Ari swears he went outside and got high, but Amanda told her that she was crazy. He was acting differently though after he came back in from taking a phone call."

"How did Amanda and Brad act toward each other?"

"Like strangers. She told me she was going to call me later. She'd talked to Brad this morning, and she said things were not good. Maybe that's why he wants to talk to y'all?"

Jeff was pulling up, so I handed little bear to Ellie before I leaned down and kissed her good-bye.

"I'll see you in a bit, sweetheart." I gave her a sad smile. I hated leaving her again.

When I looked up, I saw my mother standing in the doorway. She smiled and nodded as if she knew it was killing me to leave my girls. I was so grateful my parents also lived on the ranch.

"I love you, Gunner. Just don't beat the shit out of him, okay?" Ellie said with a wink.

I laughed as I turned to walk to the truck. The feeling in my stomach was telling me something was very wrong with this whole picture.

Jeff parked in front of Grams and Gramps's place. I jumped out and glanced over at Brad's BMW. I waved to Grams and Gramps as I walked up to the porch.

"Brad inside or down at the barn?" I leaned down and kissed Grams on the cheek.

"He's down at the barn, but he did come up and say hello. He looks tired. That boy needs to slow down," Grams said with a smile.

I glanced over at Gramps. The look he was giving me told me he thought it was something different.

As Jeff and I walked to the barn, I could see Brad pacing back and forth in front of it. He was wringing his hands together, and—

*What the fuck? Is he talking to himself?*

"Hey, dude!" Jeff called out.

Brad jumped. "What the fucking hell, asshole? You scared the shit out of me!" he yelled as he threw his hands in his hair.

He looked like shit, and Grams had been right. He did look tired.

"You want to tell us what the fuck is going on? You told Amanda you didn't want kids? What kind of game are you playing?" Jeff asked, not even giving Brad a moment to think.

"Oh, fucking son of a bitch. She told the girls?"

"Of course she told them, you douche bag. Why the fuck would you tell your wife that? Let alone, tell her to hide it," I said.

Bending down, Brad put his hands on his knees.

"Dude, are you going to get sick?" Jeff asked right before Brad started throwing up.

I ran to Dewey's office where he kept a small cooler of waters and grabbed one. By the time I got back over to them, Brad was crying.

*Brad's crying?*

"Oh god, oh god. I fucked up so bad in so many ways. I don't even know what to do!" Brad called out as he fell to the ground.

Jeff and I looked at each other. We walked over, picked up Brad, and helped him into the barn. Jeff grabbed three chairs, and Brad practically slumped onto one of them.

"Brad, what the hell is going on?" I asked.

As soon as he lifted his face, our eyes met…and I knew. I'd seen that look before when we were in college.

"You didn't, Brad. You didn't cheat on Amanda, did you?" I asked.

Jeff snapped his head from me to Brad.

"What? Wait. Why would you even think that, Gunner?" Jeff asked, confused.

"Because I've seen this look before. Remember when he was dating Stacy Malloney? He cheated on her, and this was the exact same look he had when he told me," I said, glaring at Brad.

Sitting down, Jeff stared at him. "Brad?"

Brad sat back and took in a deep breath. "I was at a business meeting in Dallas, and we all went out to this nightclub. I never go out with the guys, but Amanda and I had gotten into a huge fight right before I left. She was bitching yet again because my mother had kept pushing her to work full-time at the office. Then, she started complaining about how my mother keeps giving her a hard time about having kids. The fight wasn't even about having kids. It was about my fucking mother constantly pushing Amanda. She told me she was sick of my mother. When she said how she'd given up her dreams for me, I just lost it. I told her to stop acting like a bitch, and then one thing led to another, and words were said that shouldn't have been said. It was the worst fight we'd ever had. When I left for Dallas, I was mad as hell at her."

"Okay, so you went out because you were pissed at Amanda. Keep talking," Jeff said.

"So, I ran into a girl I knew from college—Michele Walker."

"Ah shit, Brad. Your fuck buddy from college?" Jeff shook his head.

"Yeah, Jeff, my fuck buddy from college," Brad said, glaring at him.

"Go on," I said. The terrible feeling in my stomach was growing bigger.

"Long story short, she flirted, I flirted, and then she asked if I wanted to go back to her hotel room to get high. I was shocked that she'd even asked, and I told her no. Then, Amanda sent me a text message. Said my bitch mother wanted me to call her. It pissed me off, so I went back to Michele's hotel room."

When Brad looked down at the ground, I saw a tear rolling down his face.

*Motherfucker. This does not sound good at all.*

"You know I've never touched drugs before in my life. Y'all know that. But, fuck, we got back to her room, and she started taking off her clothes. She was just walking around in her bra and panties. I wanted so badly to just forget about everything—Amanda, the fight, my controlling parents...my fucking job I hate. So, I took a hit of coke, and it felt fucking great. I was happy, I had a ton of energy, and I didn't give a fuck about anything."

"Or anyone," Jeff said.

Brad looked at Jeff with a weak smile. "Yeah...or anyone. Michele started feeling on me, and for one brief moment, I gave in and kissed her. That was it though. I had the sense to stop myself."

Jeff glanced over toward me before we both turned to look at Brad.

"By the time I got back to Austin, I felt like such a piece of fucking trash for doing that to Amanda. I needed to forget. I needed to feel happy...like I did that night with Michele. She had told me she lived in Austin, so I gave her a call. Told her I needed more coke, and she hooked me up. I've been doing it for the last seven months now."

"Jesus H. Christ, Brad. What the fuck were you thinking? You need to get help, dude. You need to get off of it," I said.

I glanced over at Jeff. He was just sitting there in shock. None of us had ever done drugs. We'd even made a pact our freshman year of college, promising that we wouldn't try any of that shit…ever.

"That's not the worst of it," Brad said, tears rolling down his face. "That day Smitty said he saw me with a girl…it was Michele. She's been harassing me for months, threatening to tell Amanda about the drugs. I've bought the bitch so much shit just to keep her ass quiet. Then, I started to realize that something was different with Amanda. I've been such a fucking dick to her the last four months, and I didn't even think that she could be pregnant. To be honest, I'm surprised she's stuck around. I've just been pushing her away because I've been so afraid she'd find out about the drugs or that I kissed another woman."

"Were y'all trying to get pregnant?" Jeff asked.

"Not really. When I came back from Dallas, I told her if she wanted to try, we could, but I never had sex with her. I felt so fucking guilty that I just couldn't stand to touch her. Then, one night she started asking questions. She just kept hounding me. I had just taken a hit of coke before I came into the house, so I was high as a damn kite. I got so damn angry that I…I…"

"God, please no, Brad. Tell me you didn't," I said, feeling sick to my stomach.

Brad instantly started crying again. "I practically raped my own wife. At first, it was hot as hell for the both of us…but then…I think she knew something was wrong with me. She started asking me to stop…but I didn't. Afterward, the only thing I remember was her lying there, crying. I packed up a bag and stayed at a hotel for a few days."

Jeff stood up and grabbed Brad by his shirt. "You dirty, rotten motherfucker. How could you do that to your wife?" Jeff pulled his arm back like he was going to punch Brad.

I jumped up and grabbed him. "Jeff! That's not going to help anything, dude! Calm the fuck down!" I yelled as I pulled him away from Brad.

"You don't know how many times I wanted to tell one of y'all, so you would beat the shit out of me," Brad said as he stood there and cried.

After I talked Jeff out of beating Brad's ass, I looked at Brad. He was now sitting in the chair, shaking.

"Why did you tell Amanda she couldn't keep the baby, Brad?" I asked.

He snapped his head up at me. The next thing I knew, he was outside, throwing up.

"I hope the motherfucker throws his goddamn guts up," Jeff said as he sat down.

Brad walked back in and sat back down on the chair. After taking a deep breath, he said, "Amanda hasn't let me touch her since that night. I don't blame her. I hate myself for what I did to her. I just need to find a way to get off the coke and then tell her about Michele. I just need more time."

Brad looked at Jeff and then me. "I got off the coke for a couple of days, but the other night, I caved and bought some. When I got home, I was feeling pretty damn good. I was even going to apologize to her because I missed being with her so damn much. I just fucking miss her so much. But my world stopped when she told me about the baby. Everything hit me all at once, and I panicked. My wife is pregnant, and the only reason she's pregnant is because I forced her to have sex with me. I flipped out and lost it. It was like it wasn't even me talking. I was listening to myself tell her that she had to keep it a secret, and she needed to give up the baby. I was so scared and high. I didn't even know what the fuck I was saying." Brad leaned over and cried hysterically.

"Jesus. Why the hell would you tell your wife that? Why, Brad? Why would you tell Amanda that?" I asked, trying to make sense of all of this.

"I don't fucking know, Gunner! Michele's been threatening to tell my parents and Amanda about the drugs. She said she would even show them the video. I just fucking panicked. The moment I said it, I wanted to take it all back, but Amanda was so devastated."

"Whoa…holy hell. What fucking video?" Jeff said as he stood up.

"I guess Michele thought it would be fun to tape our little escapade, so she set up a camera and videotaped the whole thing—me taking the drugs and then making out with her." Brad started shaking his head.

I pulled out my phone. "Okay, Brad, the first thing you need to do is get off the coke, and then you need to tell Amanda the truth." I was ready to start looking up rehab places. Just by the way he was shaking, I could tell that he needed more drugs.

"After spending time with Luke and Alex and seeing how happy Ari and Ellie are, I tried to tell Amanda today. I mean, I want this baby with Amanda, y'all. I love her. I've dreamed of having kids with her since the day I met her. This is not me. When I started to tell her, she…she…"

"She what?" Jeff asked.

"She told me she wanted a divorce, and she would raise the baby on her own. She's going next week for the sonogram, and she said…" Brad lost it again and started sobbing uncontrollably.

Jeff and I gave Brad a few minutes to get himself back together again.

He looked up at us and took a deep breath. "She told me she didn't want me there. She saw no reason for me to be there since I didn't want to have kids with her. But that's not true! I tried to explain, but she wouldn't let me. She walked out of our bedroom with her suitcase, and she said she was going to stay with her parents. What the fuck do I do, y'all? I can't lose her. I love her so much."

Jeff had been walking back and forth for a while, and he finally stopped to look at Brad. "You love her so fucking much that you told her to give up her child? You fucking deserve everything you're getting. You love her? Listen to what you're saying. Listen to the things you told her. You're a fucking druggie asshole!" Jeff turned to walk away.

"Jeff! Stop." I got up and reached for his arm.

He pulled it away and turned to look at Brad, who had tears rolling down his face.

"Jeff, I need help. I'm asking you as my friend...please help me get through this. Please," Brad said in between sobs.

I dropped my grip on Jeff's arm. He walked over to Brad, and Brad stood up.

Jeff grabbed him and pulled him into a hug. "Don't worry, dude. We're gonna get you and Amanda through this. I'm sorry, Brad. I'm so fucking sorry," Jeff said while Brad kept repeating back how sorry he was.

Just then, I felt a hand on my shoulder. I turned around to see Gramps.

"Gramps," I said, stunned.

"My good friend, William Schmidt...do you remember him? Well, he has a son, Bryan, who runs a recovery center in Austin. I already called Bryan, and I sent you a text with the address. He's waiting on y'all," Gramps said, looking over toward Brad.

"How did you...I mean...how did you know, Gramps?"

"Son, I've had a friend or two in my lifetime who found themselves in trouble. Nobody in this world is free from making mistakes. Some mistakes are just grander than others." Gramps slapped me on the back. "Y'all best get a move on before it gets too late," he said before he turned and headed back to the house.

I turned around and looked at Brad and Jeff. They were just watching Gramps walk off.

"Holy fucking shit. I want that gift when I get older," Jeff said.

Brad laughed for the first time tonight.

"Come on, let's head out. I need to call Ellie to let her know what's going on. Brad, do you want to call Amanda? Or do you want one of the girls to talk to her?"

Brad shook his head. "What the fuck do I tell her? Do I tell her everything? Over the fucking phone? I mean, she won't even look at me, so—"

Jeff looked at Brad. "Dude, you tell her the truth 'cause that's all you can do."

Jeff called Ari while I was talking to Ellie about what was going on. Afterward, we headed out. I was driving Brad's BMW while Jeff followed in his truck. Brad called Amanda as we got closer to Austin. I knew he didn't want to tell her about the drugs or about Michele over the phone, but it was like he was opening a floodgate that had been closed for so long. Once he started, he couldn't stop himself from spilling it all out. Listening to him pour his heart out killed me. I was gutted. My stomach dropped, and I thanked God for Ellie and Alex.

"Amanda, I was so scared, and I didn't know what to do. I didn't know how to tell you. I want nothing more than to have kids with you. I always have, baby. Please…oh god, please don't say that to me. I'm so sorry, baby…please don't leave me, Amanda, please. I don't care about her, and it was just a stupid kiss. I love you, and I'll get off the drugs. I swear to God, I'll be there for you and our baby," Brad begged.

When he hung up, he placed his head on the back of the seat.

"What did she say, Brad?"

"She told me she'll see me tomorrow at the rehab center, but she needed time to let everything sink in. She said she hates me, Gunner. She hates me," Brad said as he looked out the window. "Gunner?"

"Yeah?"

"Do you think she'll ever be able to forgive me? I mean, I can see her forgiving me for the drugs, but the kiss, and then that night she got pregnant…"

"Would you forgive her?" I asked as I quickly glanced toward him.

Brad stared out the window for the longest time before turning back to me. "I would. I would forgive her because I love her so much. I…I can't lose her, Gun. I don't want to live without her. I can't live without her," he said as his tears came again.

*Chapter Thirteen*

*Heather*

I took a deep breath as I pulled in and parked in Josh's driveway. So much had happened in the last three weeks.

Brad had entered rehab for his drug addiction. Amanda had moved out of their house and moved in with me while she tried to sort everything out in her head. Josh had been released from the hospital, and he was staying with his parents. Josh's dad had taken over the business while Josh was still recovering.

And Victoria…*ugh, that bitch.* Every time I turned around, she was calling Josh, texting Josh, coming to "check up on Josh."

*I hate her more than anything. She makes Lynda look like an angel.*

As I stared at her car sitting in the driveway, my hands gripped the steering wheel just a little harder.

*Great. Just what I needed. I already feel like I'm getting the flu. Now, I have to look at her fucking face.*

One of the reasons I came over was because Josh's birthday was coming up, and his mother wanted to plan a party for him. It was still awkward for both Josh and me. I was trying to give him the room and space he'd asked for, and he was trying his best to take things slow even though I could tell he wanted to be with me as much as I was dying to be with him.

I started walking up the steps when I heard the door open and close. I saw Elizabeth with a pissed-off look on her face. She came down the steps like she was mad as hell.

"Follow me, baby girl," she said, storming past me.

I heard the door open again, and I looked back to see Josh standing there.

"Hey! I'm so glad you stopped by," he said as he flashed that damn smile at me.

*Ugh...that dimple.* I just wanted to run into his arms. I smiled, but then it quickly faded when I saw Victoria walking up behind him.

"Hey, Smeather," she said with a laugh.

She'd taken to the habit of calling me Smeather even though I'd asked her fifty times to please call me Heather. I had no idea why in the hell she called me that.

Just then, I felt Elizabeth grab my arm and pull me along with her.

"Mom, wait! Please, Mom, let's talk about this," Josh called out.

I looked behind me to see Victoria waving at me before she turned and went back into the house.

*Yep, I hate her.*

"Elizabeth, what the hell is going on? You seem so pissed?"

"Oh my god, I'm gonna punch that girl square in the face." She came to a stop and spun around.

"What happened?"

"She just shows up when she pleases. Day or night, she just comes to the house whenever she feels like it," Elizabeth said, her hands flying all over the place.

*Oh god. I feel sick to my stomach.* I had gone back to Fredericksburg since Christmas break was over, and school started back up again, so I wasn't around as much as I wanted to be. During the break, I had stayed at the cottage on Ari's parents' property, so I could be at the hospital as much as possible.

"Oh," was all I could get out.

"I'm ready to run over her with my car," Elizabeth said with the most serious face I'd ever seen.

I couldn't help it, but I let out a laugh. "Is that why you're so mad?" I asked.

"No. I knew you were on your way over, and I told Josh. I said it would probably be best if the bitch, um…Victoria left before you got here."

I waited for her to continue. "Okay," I said, trying to prompt her into going on.

She took a deep breath. "Josh, stupid ass son of mine, doesn't see what this girl is up to, but I do. She's after my son, and she doesn't seem to care who she pushes out of the way to get to him. I've never in my life met a girl like this. I'm ready to slap a restraining order on her ass."

I took another deep breath as I started to feel sick again. I put my hand to my head. *I wonder if I'm getting a fever 'cause I feel like shit!*

"Are you not feeling well, baby girl?" Elizabeth pushed my hand out of the way and started feeling all over my face and forehead with the back of her hand.

"I think I'm getting the flu. I just feel so bad." I leaned against the fence.

"Huh," Elizabeth said, looking me up and down.

"So, what happened that made you storm out of the house like that?"

Elizabeth was staring at me, but then she shook her head as if she were clearing her thoughts. "Josh told me he wasn't going to be rude because Victoria had taken such good care of him while he was in the hospital. He thinks she's just being nice by coming over to check up on him. He said she was just a friend, and everything would be fine. Well, I told him he was a stupid ass. Then, she came walking into the kitchen, and I asked her to leave."

"Wait. What? You just busted out and asked her to leave?"

*I want to be like Elizabeth when I grow up!*

"I did. I told her I had invited you over to talk about plans for Josh's birthday party and that I thought her visit should be coming to an end. That little bitch got all excited and begged Josh to let her stay and help with the party plans. He said...he said..." Elizabeth turned and threw her hands in the air.

"He said what?" I practically shouted.

"He said she could stay and help...that you wouldn't mind. I just stared and told my own son that he was an idiot, and then I stormed out. That was when I saw you."

I rolled my eyes because I could so see Victoria doing just that. For some reason, she had gotten her hooks into Josh, and it scared the shit out of me, especially with me not being around as much as I wanted to.

I started pacing as my mind started spinning. I had to do something. With me being gone all the time, she was getting closer and closer to Josh. I'd brought it up the other night on the phone, and he'd sworn to me that he didn't have feelings for her like he did for me. Even though I believed him, that whole conversation with Victoria in the restroom kept coming up in my mind. I could still hear her bragging about giving Josh blow jobs and how much he liked it.

*Oh god. I'm gonna be sick.*

I snapped my head up at Elizabeth. She grabbed my arm and began leading me toward the back of the barn. I barely made it before I started throwing up.

Elizabeth pulled back my hair and held it up for me while I just threw up over and over again.

*Damn it! The stomach flu again!*

When she started rubbing my back, I almost cried because my mother would do the same thing when I got sick.

After my stomach finally settled down, I stood back up.

"Come on, baby girl. Let's go in the house and get you some water. You need to sit down." Elizabeth began heading back toward the house.

"I'm going to take a leave of absence," I blurted out.

"What?"

"I'm going to take a leave of absence from my job," I said, standing up taller.

*What the fuck am I saying? I love my job…but I love Josh more.*

"Heather, why? You love your job!"

"I love Josh more. I need to be here more since this bitch is moving in on my man. I won't let her take him from me, Elizabeth. I will not let her take him from me. I'll just tell the school I'm having personal issues that I need to take care of. With Amanda staying at my house for a while, I won't have to worry about things in Fredericksburg. I can talk to Ari's parents about staying at the cottage." I started to walk toward the house.

"No," Elizabeth said.

I stopped and turned to look at her. She had a smile as wide as the Grand Canyon on her face. "I think you should stay here…with us. We have three extra bedrooms and all."

"Um…I guess I could stay here," I said as she skipped up and hooked her arm in mine.

She threw her head back and laughed. "Oh my god! Please let me be the one to break the news to Victoria!"

I giggled at the thought of seeing Victoria's face when she found out I would be moving into the same house as Josh. I peeked over at Elizabeth. She was now humming a song as we made our way back to the house.

She looked over at me as her smile grew. "Oh, this day has turned out to be one of the best days of my life!" she said with a wink.

I laughed, shaking my head. "Why?"

When she glanced back at the house, Josh was talking with Victoria at her car. It looked like she was leaving.

"Oh, you'll find out soon enough, baby girl. Soon enough."

As we got closer to the car, I heard Josh telling Victoria about us all going to Luckenbach dance hall next weekend.

*No! Shit! No, no, no, don't tell her!*

"Oh, I love that dance hall! Who's all going?" she asked as she glanced over at Elizabeth and me moving toward the stairs.

"Normal gang, I guess!" Josh said, laughing. "I've only met Ari and Ellie twice now, but they'll be there with Jeff and Gunner. I think Brad's wife will be there, too." Josh turned and looked at me. "Right, Heather? The whole gang?" He smiled.

"Yep," I said with a weak smile.

*Please say no. Please say no.*

"Oh, I'd love to see Jeff and Gunner again. Yeah, count me in. I'd love to meet their wives," she said with a shit-eating grin on her face.

I changed my mind. *Ari will kick your ass so fast you won't know what the hell hit you.*

Just then, Elizabeth leaned in closer. "You must be making evil plans 'cause that smile on your face is speaking volumes!"

I glanced at her and giggled. "This could actually be fun."

"Josh, you might have to take a drive out to Fredericksburg with Heather to help her bring some stuff to the house." Elizabeth dropped her arm from mine and started to head up the stairs to the house.

Josh looked at me and then glanced over at his mother. "Okay…for the party?" he asked, confused.

Elizabeth turned around and gave a smile like I'd never seen before. "Oh no…Heather is taking a leave of absence from work. She'll be staying with us for a bit until you're fully recovered. You know how I hate leaving you home alone while I'm at work," she said with a wink. She turned and walked into the house.

I slowly peeked over toward Josh and Victoria. Victoria's mouth was hanging open, and she was just staring at the door Elizabeth had just walked through. Then, she shot a look at me. I reached down inside and pulled out my inner Ari and Ellie. I gave her the biggest go-to-hell-bitch smile I could muster. Then, I glanced over at Josh. He was completely focused on me.

"Hell yeah!" Josh walked up to me and hugged me.

As he held me in his arms, I picked up my hand and gave Victoria a wave of my own.

"I need to leave, Josh." She pulled open her car door and got in. She didn't even give him time to turn and say good-bye before she was speeding off down the driveway.

"I think my mom pissed her off earlier when she asked her to leave," Josh said with a shrug of his shoulder.

I just looked at him. *Yep. Stupid ass, he was indeed.*

*Chapter Fourteen*

*Josh*

I smiled as I pulled up to Ari's parents' house. The past week had been so fucking great. Heather had moved into the house the same day my mother announced it, and everything had been perfect. Since Victoria hadn't called, texted, or stopped by the house, I could focus all my attention on Heather.

I parked my truck and thought about last night. Heather had packed up some sandwiches and fruit, and we had taken a walk down to the main pasture. *God, it felt so good to be alone with her.* We'd talked, we'd laughed, and we'd even played I Spy. I'd never felt so alive in my life.

When I asked her why in the world she would take a leave of absence from her job, she had pulled away from me and tried to change the subject. I knew she was trying so hard not to push her feelings on to me, but I'd kept asking her to tell me why. When she told me it was because she missed being near me and because she loved me, it had taken every ounce of energy I had to not pull her into my arms and make love to her.

*God, I just want to be with her…but I can't. Not yet. I need to make sure I do this right.*

Just then, someone started knocking on my truck window. I turned to see Gunner holding up a little guy, who I assumed was Matthew, Ari's little brother. After Jeff and Gunner had told me all about Matt, I was dying to meet him, so we were going to take him fishing today. Jeff had said that Matt and I were pretty close, and I used to come over all the time to play video games or just hang out with Matt.

I took a deep breath as I tried to remember everything Jeff had told me. I opened the door and got out as Gunner placed Matt on the ground.

"Josh! I'm going to hug you!" Matt yelled as he grabbed me by the legs and hugged me. "I've missed you, Josh, you assmole!"

*Did he just call me an assmole?*

I glanced back up at Gunner and Jeff as I started laughing. They were both shaking their heads and mouthing, *No.*

*No?*

"Holy shit! Did he just try to call me an asshole?" I laughed harder. I bent down and got face-to-face with Matt.

"Dude!" Gunner said.

When I glanced back at him, he mouthed, *Don't laugh when he swears.*

*Oh shit, that's right! Jeff warned me about that.* "Oh, right! Sorry, but that was some funny shit. Oh shit! Ah, motherfucker!" I stood up and covered my mouth.

"I wanna be a mudderfuckin' cowboy, Josh! Just like you and Gunner and Jeff!" Matt started running around. "Oh shit! Ah, mudderfucker!"

"Nice, dude. Ari's going to be so pissed off at you," Jeff said.

Gunner let out a laugh and shook my hand. "How are the ribs feeling?"

I smiled as I thought about Heather asking me the same thing while I'd watched her make pancakes this morning. She'd been wearing a pair of my boxer shorts—at least I hoped like hell they were mine—and one of my old UT football shirts.

"Almost feel normal again. Doesn't hurt either that I have the most beautiful girl in the world living with me at my parents' house!" I said as I watched Matt running around. "Shit…sorry, I forgot about the whole swearing thing. Funny as hell little guy though. I see why we got along so well."

Jeff walked up and gently hit me on the back. "You remember anything at all from spending more time with Heather?"

I shook my head. I was starting to get frustrated. "No, nothing. I feel something for her though. I feel like I just need her so much, and it scares the fuck out of me. I just want to be around her all the damn time. I wake up, thinking about her, and go to sleep, thinking about her. What the fuck is that?"

Gunner threw his head back and laughed. "That, my friend, is called love!"

*Love?* I knew that I loved her before the accident. *Do I love her now? Is that what this is?*

Jeff started laughing, too, as he shook his head. "Don't push it, Josh. It'll come back, dude, and you'll remember exactly how head over heels in love you were with Heather."

I sure hoped they were both right. I could see the pain in her eyes every day. She would try to hide it, but I knew she wanted so much more from me. I also knew the only reason she took a leave from her job was to keep Tori away as much as possible. I shook my head and let out a small laugh.

"What's so funny?" Gunner asked as he walked over to his truck and started taking out his fishing gear.

"It just blows my mind she would leave her job to stay with me. I mean, I'm fine now. My mother is treating me like I can't do a damn thing. Do you think she asked Heather to stay with me? Or do you think it was Heather's idea?" I asked as I helped Gunner put the poles in the back of my new truck.

Gunner stopped, looked at me, and smiled. He took a deep breath and chuckled. "Well, according to Ellie, Heather did it to keep Victoria at bay."

*No fucking way. I was right.*

"Well, fuck me, I knew it," I said, laughing.

Gunner put his hand on my shoulder. "Josh, you and Heather went through hell and high water before you finally got together. That girl loves you with every ounce of her being. She's not going to give up on you. She's going to fight for the both of y'all. I'm gonna be honest. Your whole let's-be-friends-first thing has her world turned upside down. Just don't string her along, Josh, and please don't hurt her. She's been through enough as it is." Gunner looked away.

"Some girl named Lynda called me the other day. I asked my mother about her, and she pretty much gave me the lowdown of what she knew. She basically told me to keep the fuck away from this chick. She mentioned Lynda was your cousin."

Gunner headed back over toward his truck. He called over his shoulder, "Your mom gave you good advice, dude. If Lynda calls again, don't ever answer the phone." He stopped dead in his tracks and turned to face me. "And don't fucking tell Heather you talked to Lynda. Shit, poor girl already has one to tend with. She doesn't need to worry about two."

After getting everything loaded in my truck, we all got in and headed out. Matt was a hoot. That kid had me in stitches, and I could feel my side every time I laughed. I loved that he knew all the words to Blake Shelton's "Boy's 'Round Here." We had to play it over and over for him. I loved him already.

*Shit!* There was that love word again. *Fuck. I must have really changed.*

I could hear Jeff and Matthew laughing in the backseat as we got closer to the lake. I smiled, thinking about Jeff and Gunner being fathers and how good they both were with Matt. Just then, I had the strangest feeling come over me.

*I want to have kids with Heather.*

"Holy fucking shit! What the hell?" I said without thinking.

"What the hell!" Matthew called out from the backseat.

"Josh!" Jeff and Gunner said at the same time.

I needed air. When I saw a store, I pulled in. I jumped out of the truck and started taking deep breaths.

Gunner came running over. "Jesus, Josh. Are you okay? What's wrong? Are you hurting anywhere? Can you not breathe, dude?"

"Matt, stay in the truck buddy, Jeff said.

"Jesus H. Christ, Josh, stop swearing in front of Matt. Ari's gonna chew my ass out!" He ran his hand through his hair, obviously frustrated.

"Really, motherfucker? I'm having a moment of sheer panic right now, and that's what you're worried about?" I asked.

Jeff shrugged his shoulder. "Hey, I can't help it if you don't remember how Ari is about this kind of shit," he said with a shit-eating grin.

Gunner punched Jeff in the arm and turned back toward me. "Josh, what's wrong?"

I shook my head to clear my thoughts. I looked back and forth between Jeff and Gunner. "I, um…I just, um…I just had a thought, and, um…"

"Good god, son, spit that shit out. I want to get in some fishing at some point today," Jeff said as he leaned up against the truck.

"It's just…I heard you laughing with Matt, and then I thought about the two of y'all being dads, and how much I love that kid in the backseat, and I don't even know him, and then I thought…I thought…"

Gunner was smiling from ear to ear.

"Why the fuck are you smiling at me like that?" I asked.

"You thought what, Josh?" Gunner asked.

I took a deep breath. "I thought it would be nice to have kids with Heather." Bending over, I put my hands on my knees, taking more deep breaths. *Oh. My. God. I said it out loud!*

Jeff pushed off the truck and smiled as Gunner did a fucking fist pump in the air.

"Yes!" Gunner came over and put his arm around my neck, pulling me closer to him.

"You, my friend, are on your way back. Come on, let's go catch some fish." He turned and walked back to the truck, giving Jeff a high five on the way.

*What in the hell just happened?*

I looked down at Matt. He seemed like he was in pure heaven. Jeff had said the feel of the boat on the water made Matt feel calm. It had been a great afternoon so far. We talked about everything from fishing to the girls to trucks to my stupid-ass birthday party tomorrow.

"Why do you like girls?" Matt busted out.

We all just looked at each other.

"Jeff?" Gunner and I both said at the same time.

Jeff snapped his head over to both of us as his mouth fell open. "Why the fuck do I have to be the one to handle this one?"

Gunner let out a laugh. "Dude, you're his big brother." He winked at Matt.

I glanced down at Matthew, and it almost seemed like the little guy knew exactly what he was doing.

"What the fuck? Josh, you handle this one. Matt, you want your best buddy Josh to answer that one, don't you?" Jeff said.

Matthew shrugged his shoulders and looked at me. "What the fuck, Josh? Why do you like girls?"

I tried. I tried really hard, but I couldn't hold it in. I started laughing. I laughed my ass off. Then, Gunner started laughing, and before I knew it, the three of us were laughing so hard we each had tears rolling down our faces.

It didn't help that Matt was now saying, "Holy shit," and "Ah, mudderfucker," over and over again.

Just then, Matt's line started moving.

"Shit!" I yelled out.

Of course, Matt followed suit and yelled out, "Shit," as well.

Jeff told Matthew to start reeling it in. Then, the bastard tried talking Matt into letting him bring in the fish.

"What the fuck, Jeff? Why are you trying to take this away from my little buddy?" I said as I pushed Jeff away from Matt.

"I am not, you asshole. He needs help," Jeff said, pushing me back.

"Josh, you're an assmole like Jeff!" Matt said with a huge smile.

"He's the bigger assmole, Matt," I said with a laugh, pushing Jeff harder.

He stumbled backward, and the next thing I knew, we were both in the water.

"You motherfucker. You just cost me a fish, you asswipe!" Jeff yelled as he kept trying to dunk me under the water.

"Oh shit! My ribs! I can't move!" I yelled out.

Gunner jumped into the water, and it was all I could do to not start laughing. He swam over and pulled Jeff off of me.

"You fuckin' idiot! Are you trying to kill him?" Gunner yelled at Jeff.

Jeff gave me the finger when Gunner pushed him away from me.

I looked around Gunner and smiled at Jeff.

"He's faking! Gunner, that motherfucker is faking! His ribs don't hurt. Lying asswipe!" Jeff yelled out.

I glanced back up toward the boat and saw Matt.

"Oh no! Oh no, little buddy, don't do that!"

Jeff and Gunner turned.

Jeff called out, "No, Matt! Don't jump!"

*Too late.*

For some reason, a feeling came over me, and I shuddered, thinking about how pissed Ari would be about this.

Chapter Fifteen
Heather

When Ellie called and said they were at Ari's parents' house, I rushed over. I couldn't wait to see them. When I pulled up and got out of my car, they both came out of the house, each carrying a baby in their arms. I smiled as I looked at them, and then the strangest feeling came over me.

*I want a baby.*

I stopped dead in my tracks.

"Hey! What's wrong? You look like you just saw a ghost! Ah shit, are you still feeling sick?" Ari asked as she turned Luke away from me.

I felt almost a hundred percent better since I had been staying at Josh's parents' house.

I let out a laugh. "No, I feel fine. I think it was just a stomach bug." I ran up the steps and took Luke from Ari. "Hey there, my little man! Oh my gosh, you get bigger every time I see you!"

Luke giggled, and then he was trying like hell to get out of my arms.

"Yeah, he just wants to crawl everywhere now," Ari said as we walked into the house.

I smiled as I looked at Ellie. She was holding Alex, and I'd never seen her look so happy in my life.

"Hey, Ells. How's motherhood treating you, sweets?"

Ellie smiled even bigger. "It's amazing…beyond amazing. I'm just ready to have sex though."

"Oh. My. God. TMI, Ells," I said as I shook my head.

I put Luke down and watched him take off. I smiled as soon as I heard Susan calling out for me to get in the kitchen and give her a hug. I walked into the kitchen, and when I stepped in, I found myself wrapped up in Sue's embrace. She pushed me back and gave me a once-over. I smiled as she tilted her head.

"What? What's wrong?" I asked.

"Nothing. You just seem…different," she said with a wink.

"Well, Jesus H. Christ, Mom. The love of her life doesn't remember her, she left her job to keep a crazy bitch from getting her claws into said love, and she hasn't been feeling good. Way to bust her self-esteem," Ari said as she grabbed a jar of baby food out of her bag.

"You're not feeling good? What's wrong?" Sue asked as she picked up Luke and put him in his high chair.

I stood there and watched the whole scene play out. The way Ari moved around the kitchen and took care of Luke was wonderful. She seemed so happy, and her skin was glowing. I noticed she kept putting her hand on her stomach.

*Oh. My. God.*

"Ari!" I yelled, standing up quickly.

Ari and Sue both jumped at my sudden outburst, and Luke started laughing.

"Holy hell, Heather!" Ari said. "You just scared the piss out of me!"

"I need to talk to you. Now."

Walking in with a bottle, Ellie stopped and looked between Ari and me.

"Um, okay…right this second, Heather?"

"Yes. Yes. Right this second. Sue, will you excuse us?"

I turned toward Ellie. "Come on Ells."

As soon as we got on the back porch, I spun around to face Ari.

"Are you pregnant?" I busted out.

"Wait! What?" Ellie said as she turned to look at Ari.

The smile that spread across Ari's face caused me to let out a gasp.

"Oh my god! Oh my god, Ari!" Ellie said.

"How the fuck did you know, Heather? I just found out this morning!" Ari said.

I walked over and gave her a hug. "You're glowing like all get out, Ari, and you keep touching your stomach."

I reached for Alex and sat down with her while Ellie took Ari in her arms.

"Does Jeff know?" Ellie asked, jumping up and down with excitement.

Ari threw her head back and laughed. "Nope. I've been feeling like shit, so I bought a test yesterday. I used it when we got here this morning, but then everyone started showing up. I haven't had a chance to tell him."

"How late are you?" I asked.

While looking down at Alex cooing as she drank her bottle, my heart filled with so much love that I wanted to yell it out to the world.

"I was supposed to have my period two weeks ago. And I realized how I was feeling and all, so I figured that I must be!"

Just then, it dawned on me. I was late. I was three weeks late.

*Oh no. Oh my god. I can't be. I'm on the pill!*

"Um…Ellie…can you take Alex real quick?" I asked. I stood up and handed the baby back to Ellie.

"Honey, what's wrong? You look like you're about to be sick," Ellie said, taking Alex from my arms.

I covered my mouth and ran into the house.

"I knew it! I knew she was still sick! If you get these kids sick, Heather Lynn Lambert, I'm gonna kick your ass!" Ari called out.

I ran past Sue and into the bathroom. After five minutes of puking and then dealing with the dry heaves, I heard a knock on the door.

"Come in," I said in a weak voice. I looked up to see Sue standing there. "Sue…" I couldn't manage to get another word out.

Sue fell to her knees and took me in her arms.

I started crying. "I can't be pregnant. I just can't. I'm on the pill."

She stroked my hair. "Shh…it's okay, sweetheart. First, let's find out if you are before you start wondering about anything else."

I glanced up to see Ari standing in the doorway. Her face was white as a ghost.

"I have another test! Let me go get it!" She spun around and ran upstairs.

"What?" Sue pulled back from me and turned to watch Ari leaving. "Why does she have a pregnancy test?" she asked, looking back at me.

I just smiled.

Sue wiped the tears from my eyes and shook her head. "Oh holy hell, this house is going to be filled with kids soon."

After Ari came barreling back down the stairs, she skidded to a stop. "Mom! Who's watching Luke?"

Sue just looked at Ari. "I've raised two kids. I'm not that stupid. Your father is feeding him, or I should say your father is eating all the poor kid's Hawaiian Delight."

I let out a giggle. Josh, Gunner, and Jeff also loved that stupid baby food, and they ate it all the time.

*Josh. Pregnant. There is absolutely no way I could be pregnant.*

I let out a laugh again. "Sue, this is just silly. I'm on the pill, so there is no way—"

Ari let out a gasp and covered her mouth. "Oh my god! Oh my god!"

Sue turned and took the stick out of Ari's hand. "What the hell is wrong with you? And when were you going to tell me you had taken a pregnancy test, young lady?"

Ari peeked down at her mother and shook her head. "Never mind that, Mom. Heather, remember when you were so sick right before the accident? Remember you had, like, all this shit wrong with you? Do you remember?"

"Of course I remember. I was sick for, like, two weeks. Why?"

Now, Sue let out a gasp before she started smiling. "Sweetheart, were you on any kind of antibiotics?"

"Yes…two different ones. Why? What does that have to do with me getting the flu again?"

Ari started jumping up and down as she grabbed on to her mother's shoulders.

"What's going on?" Ellie asked as she walked up behind Ari. "Alex is passed out in her swing, and you're fixin' to wake her up, Ari."

"Oh, sorry, Ells! I'm just excited because Heather's pregnant!"

"What?" Ellie and I both yelled out at the same time.

"Oh my god, Ari! I am not pregnant," I said as I turned to Sue. "Sue, this is just insane. I'm not pregnant."

"Humor me then," Sue said as she put the pregnancy test in my hand.

"Fine!" I looked at all three of them standing there, staring at me. "Um, do think I could piss on the stick in private?"

Ari threw her head back and laughed. When she started jumping up and down, Ellie joined in.

"Yep! She is sooo pregnant. She keeps swearing!" Ari said as she hugged Ellie, who was laughing.

Smiling, Sue backed out of the bathroom and shut the door.

I just stood there and looked at the stick in my hand. I thought back to the last night Josh and I had been together. I closed my eyes as I remembered the sweet passionate love he'd made to me outside in the rain. It was one of the most romantic moments of my life.

*He doesn't even remember that night. He doesn't remember our love. He doesn't remember whispering in my ear how much he wanted to be with me forever.*

I jumped when I heard knocking on the door.

"Piss on the damn thing already, you bitch!"

I smiled. *God, I love Ari.* Only she could make me smile when I was dying a slow death on the inside.

I did what they had said, and then I took a piece of toilet paper and put it on the counter. I set the test down without looking at it, and I washed my hands and opened the door.

"Well?" all three of them asked.

"I don't know. I haven't looked at it."

"Jesus, Mary, and Joseph! Look at it," Ari said with her hands on her hips.

"I can't," I said, a tear rolling down my face. "If I am…then…I'm in this all alone."

"What are you talking about, Heather? Josh will be a wonderful father!" Ellie said.

I shook my head as the tears started falling faster. "He doesn't even remember being in love with me. He doesn't even remember the night this child was possibly conceived. Why would he…why would he want…"

Sue walked up and took me in her arms as I lost it.

"Do you want me to look at it, sweets?" Ari asked.

"Yes."

Ari walked by me and into the bathroom. I buried my face into Sue's chest.

*I can't breathe.*

*Breathe, baby girl.*

I looked up at Sue. "What did you just say?"

Sue looked at me, confused. "I didn't say anything, sweetheart."

I closed my eyes.

*Just breathe…*

My eyes flew open. "Daddy…"

"What?" Sue asked me.

I shook my head to clear my thoughts. "Nothing, um…never mind," I said as I turned to look at Ari.

She was just staring at me.

"Well? I was right, right? I'm not pregnant, am I?"

Ari quickly glanced over to Ellie and then at her mother before her eyes met mine again. She didn't have to tell me. A part of me already knew.

*I'm going to have Josh's baby.*

*Chapter Sixteen*

*Josh*

The moment I saw Heather's car parked behind Gunner's truck, my heart started pounding.

"So, you never did tell me how you like your new truck," Jeff said with a smile.

Gunner shook his head and punched Jeff in the arm.

I still couldn't believe I'd been looking at Fords. I'd always loved my Dodge truck. "I love it. Bitch has a ton of power. Too bad all you fuckers got my new leather seats wet," I said as I helped Matt out of the backseat.

Then, he took off running up the stairs, yelling, "We're home, fuckers!"

Jeff turned and gave me a drop-dead look. I couldn't help it. I started laughing.

A minute later, Ari came storming out of the house. "Josh!"

Jeff walked up and leaned in toward my ear. "You've gone and done it now. She's pissed. You better be glad you don't remember shit right now 'cause you have no idea what the fuck is in store for your ass!"

"Fuck off!" I pushed his wet ass away from me.

The next thing I knew, Ari was standing in front of me. I could so see why Jeff was head over heels in love with her. She was spit and fire all in a beautiful package.

"Hey, Ari, how's it going? You sure look beautiful today."

"Don't you even try that Southern charm on me, you twatwaffling, douche-bag idiot!"

*Ouch. Girl doesn't hold back the punches.*

"Wait. Did you just call me a twatwaffling douche bag?"

"Idiot. Don't forget, I called you an idiot as well," Ari said with a slight smile on her face.

"Did we get along before? Because I'm sensing there might have been some conflict between us." I gave her my sweetest smile possible.

"Don't give me that dimple. Did Jeff and Gunner not talk to you about swearing in front of Matt? He adores you, Josh. He thinks you walk on water, and he does everything you do. He's in the house right now, running around while repeating 'Oh shit,' 'Ah, mudderfucker,' and 'What the fuck?' Let's not even mention how he said, 'What's up, fucker?' to my father. After only one day with you, Josh. You were with him for one day. One. Day," Ari said as she held up one finger in my face.

I glanced over to Gunner and Jeff. They were just standing there, letting me take all the heat.

"And…to top it off, he's soaking wet! Why is he soaking wet?"

"That was not my fault! Jeff pushed me into the water, and then he tried to drown me. Gunner jumped in, and—"

Ari put her hand up to get me to stop talking. She looked at all three of us, just now noticing our wet clothes. Her mouth fell open as she glared at Jeff. "You let Matt swim in the freezing cold lake? Have you gone insane, Jefferson Johnson?"

"No! I didn't let him swim. He just kind of…well, he just…he kind of saw the three of us in the water, and…well, I guess he wanted to join the boys."

The look on Ari's face caused me to start laughing. Then, Gunner and Jeff started laughing. By now, Ellie and Heather had come out. Ellie was laughing, and Heather was just standing there, smiling. The moment her eyes caught mine, her smile faded. It was quickly replaced by a panicked look. She almost seemed like she was about to get sick. She threw her hand up to her mouth, turned, and ran back inside.

I took off running up the stairs to the house and went in after her. I watched as she bolted into a bathroom and slammed the door shut.

I knocked lightly on the door. "Heather, are you okay?"

"I'm okay, Josh. Thanks. I just feel sick. I'll be out in a few minutes," she said in such a sweet, soft voice.

Leaning my head on the door, I just stood there for a few minutes. I swore I could hear her crying. *I'm hurting her. By not remembering…I'm hurting her.*

I felt a hand on my shoulder. I turned to see Jeff with Luke in his arms. When Luke reached out for me, I looked at Jeff, confused.

"Dude, he wants you to hold him," Jeff said with a smile.

I held out my hands, and Luke came right to me. He wrapped his little arms around my neck and put his head down on my shoulder.

*Oh. My. God.* My knees felt like they were about to give out. When I put my hand on his little back, I could feel him breathing. He smelled so damn good. I took a deep breath and closed my eyes.

*God, please…please just give me my life back. I just want to remember all of this. I want to remember Heather.*

I wasn't sure how long I'd been standing there, just taking in this sweet little man, but neither one of us moved.

"You feeling better, Heather?" Jeff asked.

I slowly turned around and saw Heather leaning against the doorjamb. She had the sweetest smile on her face.

"He always did love you so much," she said.

I smiled back at her. I didn't even know what to say. Her beauty left me speechless. As I looked her up and down, my heartbeat started racing. I handed Luke back to Jeff. When I turned back around, she was looking at Luke in Jeff's arms.

I walked up to her and reached my hand behind her neck, pulling her to me. I leaned down and captured her lips with mine. She wrapped her arms around my neck and kissed me back with so much passion that I thought I would explode. I'd never in my life experienced this type of kiss, this type of emotion.

Barely pulling away from her lips, I whispered, "I want that to be my last first kiss."

She smiled, and then she let out a giggle. "That wasn't our first kiss though."

"It was for me. I've never before experienced so much emotion in just one kiss. Everything I experience with you is new, beautiful, and breathtaking."

She pulled back from me and looked into my eyes. I saw the tears forming in her eyes, and the last thing I wanted to do was hurt her more. I reached down and gently kissed her on the lips again. The low moan that came from her mouth moved through my whole body.

*I love this girl. I love her. I need to tell her right now.* "Heather, I—"

"Sorry, y'all, but Luke's getting fussy, and we need to head home," Ari said from behind me.

Heather looked at me with pleading eyes.

I smiled and kissed the tip of her nose. "Tonight?"

She gave me a sweet smile and nodded.

I turned and saw Luke trying with all his might to get out of Ari's arms. I laughed as I reached for him, and then I started to fly him around like an airplane. My fucking side was killing me but I'd never felt so damn happy in my life.

By the time I made it back to my parents' house, my ribs were killing me. I showered and took some pain medicine since my little romp in the lake and then playing with Luke were doing me in now.

When I walked down the stairs, I heard my mother talking to someone. I looked at my watch and wondered where Heather was. She'd said she had to stop at Party City to pick up supplies for my birthday party tomorrow.

Right as I was turning into the kitchen, I heard Heather's voice. My heart stopped and fell into my stomach. *Shit. Did it feel like this the first time I fell in love with her?* My fucking hands started sweating, and I almost turned to go back upstairs. *What the hell is wrong with me? Why am I so nervous? Just tell her how you feel, Josh. That's what Gunner said. Be honest.* I took a deep breath and walked into the kitchen. They were both laughing, and then my mother looked up at me and smiled.

"Hey, handsome. I heard you had an exciting day," she said as she winked at Heather.

I laughed. "I'd say. I taught Matthew a few new words, I think. I swam in the freezing cold water at Lake Travis while Jeff tried to drown me, got chewed out by Ari, and discovered that I…" I stopped myself.

Heather tilted her head. "Discovered what?"

"Um…I discovered…that I'm still a damn good fisherman," I said, trying to cover up my almost confession of love.

My mother opened the refrigerator and started looking around. "Huh. You must not be that good 'cause I don't see any fish in here," she said, turning to me with a smile.

"Thanks, Mom."

For two hours, we talked about everything from the party to when I would move back into my apartment.

"Mom, I think I'm more than ready to move back into my apartment. Are you going to be moving in with me, Heather?" The blush that covered her cheeks turned me on so fucking bad that I found myself daydreaming about what it would be like to make love to her.

An image of me making love to Heather in the rain popped into my head. I closed my eyes as I tried to make it come into focus. *Where are we? Is this real or just my imagination?*

"So, we can set up a small table by the spa side of the pool. We can move the lounge chairs, so people can walk around a little bit more…" my mother said.

*The lounge chairs! We're in the lounge chairs.* I stood up so fast that my chair fell backward, scaring Heather and my mother. I hustled outside, heading to the pool.

"Holy hell, Josh. Where's the fire?" Mom called after me.

I walked up to the lounge chairs and stared at them. *Goddamn it! Remember!*

"Josh?"

Just the sound of her voice had me wanting her so fucking bad. I couldn't look at her. If I were to look at her, I would take her right here in this damn chair, and I wouldn't even care if my mother were watching or not. *Okay, that's a lie. That'd be fucked-up.*

"Josh, are you okay? Is something wrong?"

*Oh god, that voice.* I turned around and looked at her. *That was a mistake.*

Those beautiful blue eyes were looking right back into mine. It was like she could see into my soul, but I couldn't see into hers.

"I, um…I think I overdid it today. I took some pain medicine, and I'm really tired right now," I said, glancing down at her lips. *Oh god, I want her so much. Control, Josh. Fuck, get control of yourself.*

I looked back up into her eyes. She was smiling as her eyes glanced at the lounge chair for a quick second before she looked back at me.

Another image flooded my brain. Heather was on top, making love to me in the lounge chair. Her head was thrown back, and she was moving slowly while I was holding her in my arms. I closed my eyes and shook my head. *Am I remembering this? Or is this just a dream?*

I swore I could feel an electric bolt moving through my body. My eyes flew open, and she was standing right in front of me with her hand on my arm. Her touch felt like a million tiny zaps of electricity.

"Josh, are you okay?"

I pulled her to me and started to kiss her. I kissed her like I would never see her again. When my hand started to move up her shirt, I felt her whole body shudder.

*I need you.*

She ran her hand through my hair and gave it a tug.

*Oh god. I want her so much.* "Heather…"

"Josh, I've missed you."

"I want you so much, baby," I whispered to her.

"Yes," she whispered. "I want you, too, Josh. I need you so much."

"Josh? Heather?"

"You've got to be fucking kidding me! That's twice today." I leaned my forehead against hers.

When she giggled, my heart melted.

"Meet me downstairs at midnight, okay?" I said as I looked into her eyes.

She gave me the biggest smile ever and I felt my legs wobble.

"Are we sneaking out tonight, Mr. Hayes?" she asked.

"Fuck yeah, we are, Ms. Lambert!"

She threw her head back and started laughing. When I glanced up, I saw my mother walking toward us, and she looked pissed.

"Hey, Mom. What's with the sour look?" I grabbed Heather's hand and started toward my mom.

Just then, I saw Victoria walking toward us with a big grin. *Fuck me.* Her smile faltered just a little when she looked down at my hand holding Heather's. I didn't mean to, but I tightened my hold on Heather.

"Look who dropped by for a visit," Mom said with sarcasm in her voice.

Victoria walked right up to me and kissed me on the cheek. "Oh, hey, Heather. How are you?"

"I'm just fine, Victoria," Heather said.

I glanced over at my mother as she winked at Heather.

"What brings you by?" I asked.

I could feel Heather trying to pull her hand out of mine. *No way, girl. This is the most contact I've had with you since I woke up in this nightmare.* I glanced at her as I brought her hand up to mouth. When I kissed it, a flush spread across her cheeks, and it nearly sent me down to my knees. Knowing that I could make her feel this way did crazy things to me.

I let my eyes travel down her body. *Fuck, she has a nice body. I need to make her mine again.* When my gaze moved back up, I stopped to stare at her eyes. Those beautiful blue eyes just made me want to get lost in them for hours.

"Josh? Josh! Hello? Earth to Josh!" Victoria said as she snapped her fingers in my face.

Slowly, I pulled my eyes away from Heather to look at Tori. "What did you say?"

Victoria glared at Heather like she wanted to stomp on her. "I thought we could maybe go out to dinner, but I see you have a friend over."

Now, it was Heather's turn to squeeze the shit out of my hand.

"Yeah, I don't think so, not tonight. Heather and I have plans with my parents for dinner. Next time, it might be a better idea if you called ahead before you drove all the way over here."

As Victoria looked my body up and down, I remembered the kiss. When I'd kissed her in the elevator in the hospital, she'd felt me up with her hand. I instantly dropped Heather's hand before I started to walk into the house.

*Oh my god. I cheated on Heather.* I felt sick. I needed to get away from both of them. *I knew it. I knew I would fuck this up.*

"Josh?" Heather called out to me.

Then, I felt someone grab my arm, and I turned to see Victoria. "What?" I snapped at her.

She took a step back. "Your face went white as a ghost. Are you feeling okay, Josh?" she asked, looking concerned.

I ran my hand through my hair and then down my face. "Yeah, I'm fine. I just want to fucking remember my life. Hey, are you still coming to see the Matt Kimbrow Band at the Luckenbach dance hall on Saturday night?"

Tori smiled and put her hands on her hips. "Oh, I wouldn't miss it for the world. What time should I meet you there?"

I glanced at Heather, and she looked hurt as hell. She was holding her stomach, like she was going to be sick again.

"Heather, what time will we be meeting everyone there?" I was hoping to show Victoria that I would be going with Heather while I was wishing to God that Heather knew I wanted to go with her and not Tori.

"Um…they go on at nine, but I think everyone is planning to get there around seven or seven thirty."

Victoria turned around and then looked between Heather and me. "Should we drive together or—"

"No. You should probably just meet us there," I said, looking back at Heather.

As Heather started to walk past us, heading back into the house, I reached out and grabbed her hand. She came to a stop right away, but she never once looked at Victoria or me.

"So, um…listen, I hate to send ya off when you just got here, but we're fixin' to leave. Right, Mom?" I glanced over to my mother.

"Yep, we are. Let me show you out, Victoria," Mom said.

"Okay…well, I guess I'll see you at your party tomorrow." Victoria went to kiss me good-bye.

As I took a step back and away from her, I noticed that Heather was watching my every move.

"Right. Well, see y'all tomorrow. Have a good evening. It was nice seeing you again, Smeather Heather!"

Heather rolled her eyes and jerked her arm away from me. "Yep. You, too," she said as she started to go into the house.

*Fuck! Fuck! Fuck! Why the fuck did I remind Victoria about Saturday night?*

I thought back to my conversation with Gunner about Lynda. I started pacing back and forth. I was so ready to sleep with Heather, and I'd forgotten all about what happened between Victoria and me.

Just then, I felt a hand on my shoulder, and I turned around to see my father. I wasn't sure what made me do it, but I walked up and crashed myself into him. When he put his arms around me, I lost it.

"Jesus, Josh. What's wrong, son?"

"Oh god, Dad. Oh god. I fucked it up with Heather." I felt tears running down my face.

My dad pushed me away from him and stared at me. "Josh, I've never in my life seen you cry, not even when you broke your leg or arm when you were a kid. What the hell happened?"

I sat down on one of the chairs, and put my head in my hands. "I cheated, Dad. I cheated on the only girl I've ever loved in my life." I looked up at him.

"Wait a minute, Josh. Slow the hell down. When? Before the accident? Did you remember something?"

I shook my head. "No…no, Dad. It was the first day I woke up in the hospital. It was after you and Mom told me about Heather. Victoria came to take me for a brain scan, and she kissed me in the elevator, but I told her to stop."

My dad laughed. "Son, that's not cheating."

"I also let her feel me up for a minute before I pushed her hand away," I said as I looked away.

"Oh…well…listen to me, Josh. In your mind, you weren't with Heather."

"But from the moment I saw her, I felt something for Heather, Dad. The whole time Victoria was doing it, I was picturing Heather lying on a blanket next to a river. I was thinking about her, Dad. What kind of fucked-up person does that?"

"Josh, stop being so hard on yourself. You were just in a major car accident, and you have memory loss."

"That's no excuse. I have to tell her, Dad," I said, standing up.

"What?" my dad grabbed my arm. "Josh, why would you hurt her like that?"

When I glanced up, I saw Heather watching us from one of the kitchen windows.

I looked back to my dad and smiled. "Because I love her, Dad, and I owe it to her to be one hundred percent honest with her."

My dad shook his head. "I get that, Josh. I do. Believe me, I would never, ever under normal circumstances tell you to hide something like this from her…but, son, this girl has been through so much pain and hurt in her life. Why would you even want to plant that seed of doubt in her mind when nothing really happened?"

My dad started to pace and then stopped. "Did you just say you love her?"

"Yeah, I did," I said with a smile.

"You just came up with this feeling all on your own? Your mother hasn't been pushing you, has she?"

I laughed. He knew better than to ever think that Heather could have pushed me, but he didn't hesitate to put it past my mom.

"No, Dad, she hasn't pushed me. It hit me like a ton of bricks today. I've been trying like hell to tell her, but something keeps happening, and I haven't had the chance." My smile faded.

"Okay, listen to me. You do what's in your heart, Josh. What's your heart telling you to do?"

I looked back up at the window. She was gone, and my heart dropped to my stomach.

I turned to my dad. "It's telling me I need to always be one hundred percent honest with her."

"Then, you know what you have to do, son." Dad brought me in for a hug. "I love that girl like she's my own daughter, Josh. Your mother feels the same way. The moment she walked into this house, she captured all of our hearts. You fuck this up, and I'll kick your ass!" My dad pulled away from me and winked.

"Jesus H. Christ, Dad." I shook my head and made my way into the house.

I walked into the kitchen, and my mother was on the phone.

"She said she would be upstairs, waiting for you in your room," Mom said with a sad look on her face.

I quickly left the kitchen and went up the stairs two at a time. When I opened the door to my room, I found her standing at the window, looking out at the pasture. The horses were all out, and from the few days she'd stayed with us, I already knew how much the horses could calm her down.

*She knows.*

"Heather—"

"What happened between you two? And when did it happen?"

Her voice was so cold and distant that it gave me chills.

*How the fuck does she know?* "Um…it was the first day I woke up."

Heather spun around and looked at me.

I waited for her to say something or ask me something. When she didn't, I just went on with my confession. "She was taking me down for the brain scan, and when we got into the elevator, she started to kiss me and touch me with her hand. I asked her to stop kissing me, but I didn't…I didn't stop her right away from…" I couldn't even finish. I wanted to throw up.

I watched as Heather closed her eyes. When she slowly started to sink to the floor, I ran over to her and grabbed her. I sat down on the floor and pulled her onto my lap. I held her as she began crying. *Ah hell. I should have listened to my dad. All I ever do is hurt her.*

I could tell she was having a hard time breathing, so I stroked her hair. "I pushed her hand away. I didn't come. I swear to you." I was trying to reassure her, to let her know that I didn't want Victoria.

"Breathe, baby, just breathe," I whispered in her ear.

She grabbed on to my neck with both arms and clutched on to me tightly.

"Is that all that's happened between you two?"

"Yes! The whole time, all I could do was picture you, and I was so fucking confused." I held her as close to me as I could.

"She didn't...she didn't use her mouth, did she?"

*Oh Christ. Why the hell is she asking me that?* "God no, Heather. Why the hell would you even ask that?"

She pulled away, and her eyes met mine. The tears on her face made me want to punch myself in the stomach. *I never want to be the reason she cries...ever again.*

"That day at the hospital, she told me in the restroom how much you loved blow jobs and how good she was, and I've never done that with you, and—"

"Stop. Please don't say anything else. Heather, I never want to hurt you or be unfaithful to you. No matter what happened in my past, it doesn't matter anymore because I only love you. You're the only one I want to hold in my arms. You're the only one I want to wake up to every morning and kiss like it's my first kiss all over again. You're the only one I want to be with."

She stared at me, stunned. "What did you just say?"

"Uh...do you want me to repeat all of that? I thought it sounded pretty damn good the first time. I'm not like Gunner. I don't think I could repeat it exactly even if I tried."

She shook her head and laughed. "No, did you say you love me?"

I smiled as I placed both my hands on her face. "Yes, I love only you. I think I knew it the moment you looked at me with those breathtakingly beautiful blue eyes of yours."

I lowered my lips to hers. I slowly started to get up, and her body moved right along with me. When I backed her up to my bed, she started to lie back. Never once did we break our kiss.

The passion and love I felt in her kiss was making my heart beat a mile a minute.

Then, right on cue, there was a knock on my door.

I stopped kissing her when she started laughing.

I smiled as I looked down at her. "I don't think the gods are on our side today, princess."

I jumped up and pulled open my door. My mother was standing there with a shit-eating grin on her face. Then, she looked around me at Heather, and her smile disappeared. She snapped her head back to me and pushed me out of the way.

I turned around to see Heather crying. *What the hell? She was just smiling and laughing a second ago!*

"Oh, my baby girl. What did he do to you?"

"Wait a minute! Mom, everything was fine until you knocked on the door. Heather, baby, why are you crying now?"

She looked at my mom and smiled.

*Oh Jesus, I'm so confused. Is she crying 'cause she's happy? Because my mom stopped us from doing something? What the fuck is going on?*

"Elizabeth, Josh is perfect! He...he just said..."

After quickly getting up, Heather ran and jumped into my arms. I held on to her as she cried.

*Thank God I took two pain pills earlier.*

"What did you say to her?" my mom asked.

I shrugged my shoulders. *Hell if I knew!*

"I love you, Josh Hayes. I love you so much!"

She kissed me, and I kissed her back, even with my mom sitting on my bed.

Heather pulled away and looked at my mom. "He called me princess!"

My mother jumped up and screamed. "Shut up!"

"I know!"

*Okay... now, I'm really fucking confused.*

My mother walked up to me and hugged me.

Heather looked behind me and ran past me. I turned around to see Heather jumping into my dad's arms. "He called me princess!" Heather squealed.

"Mom..." I said, still confused.

My mother moved her mouth to my ear. "Her father called her princess, and that's what you called her, too. You called her that the first time you ever kissed her, Josh," Mom whispered. "I think she's slowly bringing you back to us again."

I pulled away from my mom, and I watched my dad spinning Heather around in the hallway. I smiled, knowing I made her that happy. I wanted to make her that happy every single day of my life.

Dad put Heather down and winked at me. "Come on, let's go to dinner. My treat!"

# Chapter Seventeen

## Ari

As soon as we started to drive out of my parents' driveway, Luke fell fast asleep. I was so nervous. *How am I going to tell Jeff I'm pregnant?* Then, I remembered that Heather had said Jack would be DJing at Josh's party tomorrow. I couldn't help but grin.

"What are you smiling about over there?" Jeff asked, glancing over at me.

"Um…nothing." *Oh shit, I can't slip up.*

Jeff laughed. "Come on, Ari. I know when you're thinking hard about something. Spill it, baby."

Before I even knew what I was saying, it was out of my mouth. "Heather's pregnant!"

Jeff slammed on the brakes and then let off of them when he realized what he had done.

"Jesus, Mary, and Joseph, Jeff! Give me damn whiplash, why don't ya?"

"Well, what the hell did you expect? You just threw that out at me, Ari! Does Josh know?"

I rolled my eyes. "Pesh…no! She just found out this afternoon."

"How?"

"Well, you see…when you make love and the man comes, he spreads his seed in the girl, and then all those little sperms move on up in there and look for the egg."

"Funny! I meant, when did this happen? No, don't answer that. I know it was before the accident. Oh fuck. How far along does she think she is? I thought they were on birth control?"

"You remember when she was so sick, right before the accident, around when Alex was born?"

"Yeah."

"Well, she was taking antibiotics, and some antibiotics can negate the pill. Her doctor obviously didn't bother to mention that to her. She knows the exact date it happened! She's probably a month or so along." I smiled, thinking about our own little baby growing in my stomach.

"Holy shit. I can't even imagine what the poor girl is thinking right now. I mean, with Josh not remembering their relationship and all," Jeff said.

"I know. She freaked the fuck out. I mean, Ellie and I got a little scared for a few minutes, but Heather just kept saying that she couldn't do it alone. Then, she started talking about Amanda and how they would both be living in her house, raising kids alone. It was a little weird to see her freak out like that." I shook my head as I thought back to it.

"Well, let's just hope that Josh gets his memory back, and he gets it back quickly," Jeff said.

"Speaking of Amanda, how is Brad doing? I know Amanda has only seen him twice. She won't take calls from Ellie or me. Since Heather has been staying with Josh, Heather said Amanda hasn't been taking her calls either. I'm so worried, Jeff. She's pregnant and all alone. Brad's mom called me yesterday, begging me to tell her where Amanda was."

"They don't know she's staying at Heather's place?"

"No! She made us swear we would not say a word about where she is," I said.

"But wait…Brad knows she's there. He mentioned it to me," Jeff said, looking confused.

"From what Amanda told us, his parents flipped when they found out he was in rehab. Of course, Amanda had to tell them because Brad's too chicken shit to stand up to them, and they are part of his problem. Then, when she told them she was pregnant, they were all ready to forgive and forget. Did you know that Brad's dad is thinking about firing Brad? His own son!"

Jeff chuckled and looked at me. "That would probably be the best fucking thing that could happen to both Brad and Amanda. His parents are so damn controlling, and his dad has been working him into the ground. I know the major reasons he turned to drugs was because of all the stress from his job along with his mother always being on Amanda's ass. Now, the fact that he kissed the bitch…that was his own stupid-ass fault."

We drove for a few miles, not saying a word.

"Jeff, I'm not so sure Amanda will be able to forgive him."

Jeff glanced at me and frowned. "I know, baby. Did she happen to mention to y'all about the night she got pregnant?"

My eyes filled with tears. "Yes." I looked out the window and didn't say another word until we got home.

I collapsed on the bed next to Jeff. When I looked over at him, he was typing something on his laptop.

"Scott's bringing another stud by tomorrow. Asshole," Jeff said under his breath.

I let out a laugh. "Are you still jealous of him? My god, Jeff. He's engaged to be married! I'd say he is well past his little flirty days with me."

Jeff closed his laptop and set it on the floor. He reached for me and pulled me to him. He kissed me so passionately that I was ready to do anything he asked of me.

"Wow! What was that for?"

"I just wanted to show you how much I love you," he said with lust in his eyes.

*Oh my.* I was getting that familiar buildup between my legs that only he could satisfy.

"If you want to convince me, I think you're gonna have to show me a little better than that," I said with a purr.

He smiled that smile that always melted my heart. "It would be my pleasure, Mrs. Johnson." Before I knew it we were both undressed.

The moment his hand touched my stomach, I jumped.

"You that excited, baby?"

I smiled against his lips. I wanted to tell him so bad, but I had a plan that I had to stick to. "I always want you, babe."

He leaned down and took one of my nipples into his mouth.

*Oh motherfucker!* My breasts felt sore. *Shit, I don't remember feeling like this with Luke.*

I started to let out a moan because it was so uncomfortable.

"Does that feel good, baby?" Jeff asked before he started to kiss down my stomach.

When he stopped, I held my breath.

"I want another baby," he said as he moved his lips across my body.

*Oh. My. God. Could he be any more perfect?*

"God, Jeff...please touch me," I begged.

"All in good time, baby. I want to kiss every inch of your body."

And that he did. By the time he got back to my lips, I was dripping wet and so ready to come that it wasn't even funny.

He got on top of me and started to tease me. He slowly entered me just a little and then pulled it out.

"Jesus H. Christ, I can't take it!" I thrashed my head back and forth.

When I felt him near me, I pushed my hips up to him, and then he was inside me, moving so fast and hard that I was coming within seconds.

"Oh god, don't stop, Jeff...please go faster..." There it was again—that familiar buildup. *Jesus...how is it always like this with him?*

Right as I was coming down from my orgasm, Jeff whispered in my ear, "I'm going to come, baby."

Then, he was lying on top of me, panting, with sweat dripping off of him and onto me.

*Oh shit.* It was turning me on. *Already? Fuck, I love being pregnant!*

"Do you think we could maybe try that again?" I asked.

Jeff pushed himself up and looked at me. "What? Like, right now, Ari?"

I smiled as I pushed my hips up against him.

He smiled and rolled us over until I was on top.

"This time, I get to tell you faster and harder," he said.

I raised my eyebrows as I felt his dick growing harder.

I started off slowly. "Oh..." I moved myself up and down. "Feels. So. Good."

I looked down at Jeff, and he was staring at me. Leaning down, I bit on his lower lip.

"Fuck, Ari."

"I am, Jeff," I said with a wink.

We both started laughing, and then Luke started crying.

*No! Oh no! No, no!* I kept moving.

"Baby, Luke is crying, and I'm not even all the way up," Jeff said as he tried to move me off of him.

*Oh hell no.* I'd worked for this orgasm, and I'd be damned if I wasn't getting it. I pushed his hands away and threw my head back as I moved faster.

"Ari," Jeff said before he started moaning.

Luke was still crying.

*Tune it out, Ari. Just five more minutes.*

I moved faster and slammed myself down on him harder each time. I could feel him getting harder as he moaned more.

"Jesus...Ari, baby, hurry 'cause I'm about to come. Shit, I'm gonna come again, baby."

*No, the fuck he is not, not before I get mine.* I adjusted myself...and there it was.

"Oh yes! Oh god, yes! That's it, Jeff." I called his name over and over again as I had the most intense orgasm ever.

I collapsed onto his chest, our sweaty bodies sliding against each other, as I tried to catch my breath. "Shit. That felt so damn good!"

Jeff laughed as he held on to me.

I noticed it was quiet. "He stopped crying," I whispered.

Then, through the baby monitor, I heard him jabbering on and on.

"Dada."

Jeff and I looked at each other. The next thing I knew, Jeff was pushing me off of him.

He jumped up and threw on his shorts. "Holy fuck! He just said dada!"

He was out of the room before I could even get my wits about me.

I heard Jeff running up the stairs, and then I heard him open the door to Luke's room.

"Hey, little bit, what's going on?"

I smiled to myself because I could imagine Luke's smile as he saw his dad walk in.

"Dada."

"That's right, buddy. Dada is the boss and ruler of the house. Always remember that," Jeff said.

"Dada!" Luke said with a laugh.

*Funny 'cause I thought that was a joke, too!*

I looked over at the monitor and watched as Jeff picked up Luke and brought him over to the camera. *That bastard!*

He looked up at the camera and waved. "Tell mama who's the boss," Jeff said as he smiled at the camera.

"Mama!" Luke screamed into the monitor.

*Wait! What?* "Oh my god!" I yelled. I got up and threw on a T-shirt and panties. I was quickly up those stairs and in his room.

Jeff was standing there, looking at Luke. "Dude…ah, man, I can't believe you did me like that!" He kissed Luke on the cheek.

Luke was smiling at him. I leaned up against the doorway and just watched them. I loved my simple life with my sexier-than-fuck husband, beautiful baby boy, and precious gift in my stomach.

I frowned slightly as I thought of Amanda and then Heather.

*Dear Lord, I know I don't converse with ya much, but you know you're in my heart. Please…please take care of my two girls.*

I watched as Jeff changed Luke's diaper, and then he walked around, singing to him.

It didn't take long for my little man to drift back to sleep.

By the time Jeff and I crawled back into bed, I was ready for round three. I rolled over to whisper sweet nothings into Jeff's ear, but I was greeted with a loud-ass snore. I flopped back down and let out a sigh.

Just then, he started mumbling in his sleep. I moved closer to him to see if I could hear what he was saying.

"Ari…another baby…baby girl…"

I sucked in a breath of air and held it. I slowly let it out as I touched my stomach.

*Yep…this one's a girl. I just know it.*

## Chapter Eighteen
### Jeff

I watched as Scott jumped out of his truck, wearing a stupid-ass smile. *Bastard.* I took a good look at him and his stupid perfect blond hair and blue eyes that Ari would go on and on about.

He smiled as he walked up to me with his hand held out for me to shake. "Hey, Jeff! What's been going on? How is your friend Josh?"

*Wait, how the hell does he know about Josh?* "He's doing good. How did you know? Did you see Gunner?"

With the way he was smiling at me, I already knew the answer.

"Nah. I ran into Ari at the store the other day, and she filled me in on everything. I need to stop by Gunner's place and see the baby. Speaking of…where are Ari and Luke today?"

*Fucking dickwad. I'm just glad his ass is getting married.*

Just then, I heard Luke calling out, "Dada."

My heart swelled at least ten times its normal size. I looked over to see Ari walking down to the barn with Luke in her arms. She was wearing a light jacket and jeans.

*Thank fuck it's chilly outside.*

"Hey, Scott! How's it going?" Ari asked. She glanced at me and smiled.

"Hey there, Ari. How is that adorable little man of yours?" Scott asked with a grin on his face.

"He's good. He said 'mama' last night! And not the jabber mamamama…but the real mama."

"And dada! He said 'dada,' too." I walked up and took Luke out of Ari's arms.

"So, how are the wedding plans coming along?" Ari asked.

Scott's smile faded as he looked down toward the ground. "Uh…Chelsea called it off. She, um…broke up with me two weeks ago, so…yeah, there isn't gonna be a wedding."

I almost felt sorry for the fucker—almost.

"Oh no, Scott! I'm so sorry. Is there anything we can do?"

*What? What the fuck would we be able to do?*

Scott let out a little laugh and looked at me.

*Yeah, you better think before you talk.*

"I'm just trying to stay busy. I haven't been out in forever, so I might head into Austin this weekend."

"You know what? You should come to Luckenbach dance hall with us all on Saturday night. Everyone is going. Dewey and Aaron and Jenny will be there, too!"

I just looked at Ari. "I'm sure he would rather go to Austin, babe. Isn't that right, Scott?"

That fucking bastard winked at me and shook his head as he turned back toward Ari.

"You know, I haven't see Dewey and Aaron in so long. It would be fun to go out with my old high school buddies. Count me in!"

*Fuck me.*

"Awesome!" Ari took Luke back and turned to head to the barn. She looked over her shoulder and called out, "Feel free to bring a date!"

I smiled because I knew my girl did that one just for me.

"Holy hell!" Ari said as we pulled up and parked in Josh's parents' driveway. "When Elizabeth said she wanted to have a party for Josh, she wasn't kidding." Ari looked over at me.

I let out a laugh. "I guess with the accident and all, she kind of felt like she had a little more to celebrate." I got out of the truck and jogged around to open Ari's door.

She hopped out and smiled at me. "I'm so glad my mom and dad said they could watch Luke. I can't wait to just let my hair down!"

"I hear ya, babe. Feel free to get tipsy. We can stop at a hotel for a quickie before we get to your parents' house." I reached down and kissed her quickly.

"Oh, I, um...yeah, I don't really want to drink anything." She was looking everywhere but at me.

"Why? Are you not feeling well?"

"Oh no, I feel fine. Perfect in fact. I just don't want to be out of it when we pick up Luke, that's all."

We started to walk up the steps when Heather and Josh came out the door. I hadn't seen Josh smile like that since before the accident, and Heather...well, she looked like she was on cloud nine. I knew she hadn't told Josh about the baby yet, or Ari would have told me. I looked over at Ari. She must have noticed the difference in them, too. She winked at me and grabbed my hand.

"What the fuck are you two smiling so big about? Did you get lucky last night?" Ari asked.

"Oh nice, Ari. Really nice," Heather said.

"I wish! My damn parents talked to us until two in the morning. My ass fell asleep on the sofa last night, and I woke up with a stiff neck," Josh said, rubbing his neck.

Ari walked up to Josh and gave him a kiss on the cheek. "Happy birthday, sweets!" she said with a smile and a wink.

"Thanks, Ari," Josh said.

I reached out and took his hand, pulling him into a bear hug. "Happy birthday, dude. I take it you and Heather are getting closer?" I whispered in his ear.

He pulled back and smiled. "Not close enough."

Just then, Ari let out a small scream as she turned to look at Josh. "Yep...that true love shit is good stuff!" she yelled out.

Heather laughed and hooked her arm around Ari's as they walked into the house.

"What was that all about?" I asked, slapping Josh on the back.

Josh let out a laugh as he shrugged. "I guess I used to call Heather *princess*, and I called her that last night. Shit, everyone thinks it's a big deal, but I don't get it. I mean, I know her dad called her that and all, but it just seemed natural for me to say it."

I stopped and grabbed his arm. "Dude, that's fucking huge. I mean, you don't remember, of course, but you calling her the same thing as her dad meant the world to Heather. It just shows how much you love her. It's down in there, Josh. Something just needs to trigger your memory," I said as I watched him look down to the ground.

"I love her, Jeff. I told her yesterday. I mean, I'm sure what I'm feeling is love. I've never felt this way before. Well, at least, I don't remember feeling like this. I want to be with her every second of the day. I think about her anytime she's not right there by my side. I dream of making love to her. I want to give her that damn ring so bad, so I can ask her to stay with me forever."

I smiled as I looked at him. He was like a brother to me, and I was so happy to see him feeling this way. "Josh, I'm really glad you feel this way, but do me a favor. Don't rush anything. Just take your time. Keep the ring in a safe place, and you'll know the right time to ask. Make it special for her, a time she'll never forget, because you won't get a do-over." I winked at him.

Just then, I saw Ellie running up.

She stopped and kissed Josh on the cheek. "Happy birthday, Josh!" She turned and took the steps two at a time to head into the house.

Gunner walked up and slapped Josh on the back. "Happy birthday, dude. Sounds like you made Heather one happy girl yesterday," he said with a smile.

Josh laughed and looked at me. "Yeah, well, she's made me pretty damn happy as well."

I watched as Ari and the girls stood off to the side, talking and laughing with each other.

*Damn that girl.* Everything about her turned me on.

She glanced over at me and smiled. She was having a blast. Josh's dad had set up a huge dance floor, and the girls were taking advantage of it. They were all having a good time without any babies around.

I watched as Ari walked over to Jack.

*Ah shit.* It was never a good sign when she would request a song.

She practically skipped over to me and reached out her hand for mine. When I took her hand, I instantly felt that familiar shock run through my body.

"Twirl my ass around on the dance floor!" she said with an evil smile.

I grabbed her, picked her up, and carried her out onto the dance floor. Just as I was letting her body slide oh-so-slowly down mine, "Two of a Kind, Workin' on a Full House" by Garth Brooks started playing.

I laughed. "Did you request this song?"

She smiled, and we took off two-stepping. As the song played, she was only singing the same damn line, not the other lines in the song.

"Workin' on a full house," she sang softly.

I pulled away and looked at her. The moment her eyes met mine, I knew. *Holy shit.* "Baby…you're pregnant?" I silently hoped I wasn't reading this wrong.

When she gave me a big smile, I saw that glow on her cheeks. Then, I thought about last night and how she couldn't get enough of me.

She slowly nodded.

"We're having a baby?"

"Yep. I took a home test yesterday at my parents' house. I made an appointment for us next week!" she said as she placed her hand on the side of my face.

I put my hand over hers, and then I pulled her to me and kissed her. The small moans coming from her were driving me mad. I leaned away and looked around. I grabbed her hand and started walking toward Josh. He was sitting at the bar by the pool, talking to a few people. *Ah shit.* Victoria was one of them.

"Josh, something's come up, and Ari and I need to leave, dude. I'm sorry, but we'll see you tomorrow night."

Josh got up. He kissed Ari on the cheek and then held out his hand for me. "Sure, I hope everything is okay?" he asked as he glanced at Ari.

She looked confused as hell.

I gave his hand a quick slap. "Yep, all is good, dude. When you see Gunner, tell him I said I'll talk to him later."

Pulling Ari along, I started walking toward the gate to get to my truck.

Over her shoulder, Ari yelled, "Good-bye," to Ellie and Heather.

I practically dragged her back to my truck. I opened the door for her and helped her in.

"Jesus H. Christ, Jeff. Where the hell are we going?" Ari asked.

When I got inside my truck, I looked over at my sexier-than-hell pregnant wife and smiled. "Baby, we are going to celebrate…at The Driskill Hotel."

Ari threw her head back and laughed. "You horny bastard. You just left one of your best friend's birthday parties to have sex with me?"

I looked over at her like she had just said the stupidest thing ever. "Hell yeah, I did. Baby, I haven't forgotten how fun sex is with you when you're pregnant." I gave her a wink.

She smiled that beautiful smile of hers. "Neither have I, Mr. Johnson. Neither have I!"

Josh was having a great time at his birthday party. He was talking and laughing with his friends. Elizabeth was moving around, being the perfect host. I smiled as I watched Josh talking to Gunner and a few friends from college. Victoria had been hanging around him for the last hour. He would talk to her every now and then, but every time he did, he would look at me and smile.

"Jesus...you know you should have been dead like forty minutes ago," Ellie said.

"Huh?"

"You know, with the drop-dead looks Vict-bitch-ia is giving you."

I let out a laugh and looked at Ellie. "Fuck her," I said.

Ellis snapped her head at me and gasped. "Holy hell! Did you just say that?"

I winked at Ellie. "There's no way in hell this girl is going to get anywhere near him. I'll fight tooth and nail if I have to."

When I looked back toward Josh, Victoria was whispering something in his ear. He shook his head before he started walking toward me.

Just then, Jason Aldean's "Staring at the Sun" started playing. The smile that spread across his face caused my stomach to take a dive.

"Good Lord, do you see the way that boy is looking at you?" Ellie pushed my shoulder back.

My heart started racing. When he walked up to me, he held out his hand. I reached for it, and the moment I touched him, I sucked in a breath of air as he pulled me into him. He backed us up onto the dance floor, and we started to dance.

"Breathe, princess," he whispered.

I grabbed on to his shirt and just held him as tightly as I could. *Oh god, I miss his touch so much.*

He leaned into me and put his mouth right next to my ear. "You're the most beautiful thing I've ever laid eyes on."

I slowly felt my legs going out from under me.

He held on to me tighter, and then he laughed. "I can't take credit for that one. Gunner told me to tell you that!"

I pulled back and smiled as his eyes captured mine.

*I love him so much it hurts.*

He took the back of his hand and ran it down my face. "So beautiful."

When he leaned down and kissed me, I poured as much love into that kiss as I could. I needed to show him that he was mine, and I'd wait an eternity for him.

He bit my lower lip before leaning back slightly. "I love you, Heather."

"I love you more," I barely whispered.

He laughed. "I love you more times infinity!"

I pulled back and looked at him. "What?"

"I love you more times infinity," he said again as he looked at me with that smile.

When I grabbed his shirt, his smile faded.

"What's wrong?"

"You said that to me the last night we made love. We made love in the lounge chair right over there, and you said that to me, Josh. We laughed about it, and then we said we were going to get infinity tattoos on our wrists."

His face went white as a ghost. "Heather, I thought that was just a dream!"

"You remember that?"

He shook his head, and when he looked at me, he had tears in his eyes.

*Oh. My. God. Is he starting to remember things?*

"Yesterday, when I came out here…I saw you and me in one of these chairs, but I thought I was just daydreaming about you. So, you're telling me that was a memory?"

I wanted to scream out, *Yes, it's a memory!* Instead, I just smiled at him. "That was a memory indeed, baby."

The smile that spread across his face made me giggle.

"By a river…you were reading a book, lying on a blanket—"

"That was the first time we ever made love. It was on Jeff and Ari's property, next to the Llano River. It was the best day of my life."

Grabbing the sides of my face, he kissed me. He kissed me as if he were never going to kiss me again.

"Can I leave my own party?" he said against my lips.

I let out a giggle. "I don't think so."

"I want it all back, Heather. I want back every single moment with you—every kiss, every laugh, every fight, and every time we ever made love. I want it back so fucking badly," he said as a single tear rolled down his face.

At the sight of that one tear, my legs just about buckled underneath my body. "Josh…"

When I reached up and wiped his tear away, he took my hand and kissed my wrist.

As I glanced to the side, I could see Victoria walking up to us.

"Josh, your mom wants you to cut the cake now," she said, putting her hand on his shoulder.

I glared at her, and she removed it as quickly as she could.

He never took his eyes off of me. "Thanks, Tori. I'll be there in a minute." He took my hand, leading us over to the table where his parents were standing. "Tonight, we're going for that drive," he said with a wink.

Elizabeth and Greg talked about the accident for a few minutes before announcing that Josh was turning twenty-four. All the while, he kept squeezing my hand and looking at me.

*Is this really happening? It feels like I'm falling in love with him all over again! It's almost like a do-over.*

After blowing out the candles, Josh leaned down and whispered in my ear, "I'll be right back, baby." He walked over to talk with Jack for a bit.

"So, Jeff and Ari took off, huh?" Gunner asked with a smirk on his face.

"Yep! As soon as Jeff heard Ari was pregnant, that was all she wrote," Ellie said with a laugh.

I looked up only to see Victoria heading our way. *Fuck. Can she please just go away?*

She looked like she was making a beeline right toward Gunner.

*Oh hell.*

Smitty stopped her and started talking to her.

*God, I love that guy.*

Jack asked for everyone's attention, so we all turned to face him. When I looked, I saw Josh walking straight to me with a big smile on his face.

"The birthday boy would like to have this dance with his girl," Jack said.

*Oh. My. God. Could he be any more perfect?*

Lifehouse's "You and Me" began playing as Josh took my hands and brought me out to the dance floor. I glanced over at Elizabeth and Greg, and they were both smiling.

Josh pulled me in close to him just as the lyrics started. My heart was beating so hard that I was sure he could hear it. When he started singing the chorus to me, I melted on the spot. I buried my face in his chest as I tried to catch my breath.

*God, please don't let this be a dream.*

"I love you, Heather. I'll never stop loving you. My love for you is infinite."

I looked up at him and smiled. Tears were running down my face, and he used his thumbs to wipe them away.

"I love you so much, Josh. There's something I have to tell you—"

Just then, I felt a tap on my shoulder, and I turned to see Victoria standing there.

"Mind if I cut in?"

*Oh no, she didn't!*

I glanced over to Ellie. She had her hands on her hips, mouthing, *No*, to me. When I turned back to Victoria, she wasn't even looking at me. She was staring at Josh. I quickly looked at Josh, and he had his eyes on me.

"Yes, actually, I do mind, so if you don't mind, I'd like to finish dancing with my boyfriend."

She snapped her head to me before looking to Josh. "Josh, I'm leaving soon. I thought we could have just one dance together for old times' sake," she said, putting her hand on his arm.

Josh pulled his eyes away from me and looked down at her.

She smiled. "Listen, Heather, I just want—"

Taking a step closer to her, I got in her face. "No, you listen. I've been patient with your ass, but now, I'm just gonna come out and tell you what I've wanted to tell you from the first day I met you."

She smirked. "What's that?"

Just as Miranda Lambert's "Only Prettier" started to play, I smiled. Looking right into her eyes, I said, "Fuck off, Tori!"

Victoria's face dropped.

"Now, if you'll excuse us, my man is gonna twirl me around the dance floor."

Josh started laughing and grabbed me as we took off two-stepping. My whole face felt like it was on fire, and my heart was pounding so hard.

"Jesus H. Christ, Heather. Why do I get the feeling, baby, that you don't say the word *fuck* too often?"

My hands were shaking, so I grabbed on to him tighter. I looked at him and started laughing. "I reached deep inside and pulled out my inner Ari!"

He threw his head back and laughed as he pulled me in closer. The closer he pulled me into him, the more I felt his hard-on.

I looked up at him and raised my eyebrows.

He smiled that damn smile at me and winked. "I fucking love two-steppin', but I think we need to find a way to leave!"

"I agree," I said.

I glanced over at Gunner and Ellie cutting it up on the dance floor. I smiled at how happy they looked. Then, I couldn't help but notice Victoria's eyes following them.

*I have a really bad feeling we haven't seen or heard the last from Victoria.*

Chapter Twenty

Josh

Every time I tried to sneak away with Heather, we'd get stopped by someone. I was beginning to think it wouldn't happen again tonight.

She was standing near the door, talking to my mother and Ellie, and I couldn't pull my eyes away from her. She must have felt me staring because she looked over at me. The blush that crept up on her cheeks turned me on so fucking much. I smiled, knowing she wanted me as much as I wanted her.

"She's a very beautiful girl," my father said from behind me. "Inside and out."

I let out a small laugh. "I wish I knew more about her, Dad. I want to know everything about her," I said as I turned to him.

"Take your time, son. It'll come back. You seem to be getting bits and pieces, so just let it come back on its own."

"I know, Dad. I'm trying not to push it, but…"

Just then, Heather glanced back over at me, and my heart started pounding.

I looked at my dad. "Dad, did I love her this much? I mean…am I just feeling what I felt before? Or is this all new? I feel like I can't breathe without her near me. Can you really fall in love with someone so damn fast?"

My dad cleared his throat and smiled at me. "Josh, when you came to your mother and me and told us you were planning on asking Heather to marry you, we were beyond happy. Not only do we love that girl like she's our own, but you also love her with your whole heart. When I asked you if you were one hundred percent sure about asking her, you looked me dead in the eyes and smiled. Then, you said to us, 'I know that I don't want to live a single day in this life without her in it. I want to wake up every morning to her beautiful smile and go to sleep to that same smile. I want to have kids with her and grow old with her. I want everything with her and only her.' Son, a love like that is too strong to be broken…by anything! A love like that will remain faithful until the very end."

"I said all that, huh?" I asked with a shit-eating grin on my face.

He let out laugh and grabbed me by my shoulder. "Yep, you must have gotten that from Gunner 'cause you sure as hell didn't learn it from me!"

When we both laughed, Heather glanced over again.

"Don't rush it. I know how much you want to be with her, and it's not like y'all haven't been together before. I just don't want you rushing into this."

"Oh god. Really, Dad? You're gonna go there?" I rolled my eyes. "I believe you gave me the sex talk when I was twelve years old."

My dad laughed and shook his head. "No, I'm not gonna give you the sex talk, you little bastard. I'm just telling you…take your time. Make it special for both of you. Make it a night she'll always remember. That's all I'm saying. Now, I'm going to find your Uncle Pete. He owes me an arm-wrestling rematch."

*Make it special. How the fuck am I going to make it special?*

I looked around for Gunner and found him making his way over toward where Heather was talking. I walked as fast as I could and grabbed him by the arm.

"I need to talk to you right now!" I said as I pulled him past Ellie, my mom, and Heather.

"Um…okay."

I dragged him upstairs and into my room, and then I shut the door. I felt like I was about to hyperventilate.

"Shit, what the fuck is wrong with you?" Gunner asked.

I shook my head. I couldn't talk. *I'm gonna fuck it up! Did I fuck up our first time?* "I'm gonna fuck it up, dude. I know I am." I gasped for air.

"Fuck what up?"

"The first time with Heather…I just know I'm gonna fuck it up."

Gunner threw his head back and laughed. "First off, you stupid bastard, you've already had sex with her. From what Ellie has shared, even though I begged her not to, it was the most romantic moment of Heather's life."

"Oh fucking great! I don't remember that, Gunner. So, I'm really gonna fuck it up now 'cause I have nothing to compare it to. Ah shit!" I started pacing back and forth as I ran my hands through my hair.

"Jesus, Josh, calm the hell down. Is it going to be tonight?"

I stopped and looked at Gunner. "I thought I wanted it to be, but now, I'm not so sure. I think I need to wait, but…I don't think I can wait. I just want to rip off her clothes and devour her. I want to see and touch every inch of her body."

"Okay, first off, just stop. I love Heather, and I think of her as a sister. You're totally grossing me the fuck out with the picture you're putting in my head, you asshole. Second, don't worry. It's going to be perfect no matter what you're doing or when it is or even where it is. Just let it happen when it feels right."

"What did you do for Ellie?" I stopped pacing and stared at Gunner. He started looking everywhere but at me.

"Gunner? What did you do for your first time with Ellie?"

Gunner looked at me and shook his head. "Dude, I don't think you really want me to tell you what I did."

I just stared at him. "Yeah, I do. What did you do?"

"I, um…well, I had Jenny…she's Aaron's wife. You know Aaron, Drake's son? Anyway, Jenny decorated the old deer cabin that I had remodeled. She filled it with daisies and other flowers and champagne and chocolate-covered strawberries and all of that good shit. But I, um...I...well, first I…"

"Jesus, spit it out."

"I asked her to marry me first," Gunner said with a shrug of his shoulders.

"Wait…what? How long did you date her before you asked her to marry you?"

"About six months," he said with a smile.

"You dated her for six months and never had sex with her?" I asked, stunned.

"Yep. I didn't want to rush it. I wanted it to be perfect. Believe me, there were a few times we almost went too far, but I always stopped it before we got carried away."

"You're my fucking hero!"

Gunner let out a laugh and sat down on my bed. "Just don't rush it, dude. I know you want to remember everything about those years you lost, especially your memories about Heather, but it'll come back. And if it doesn't…well, you'll make new ones."

Just then, there was a knock on my door. I walked over and opened it to see Ellie and Heather standing there. Heather's face instantly blushed. *Shit, why does she get so flushed around me?* I smiled as she walked in, and the smile she gave back almost brought me to my knees. *There isn't a damn thing I wouldn't do for this girl.*

"Hate to interrupt guy time, but we better head back before it gets too late. I don't want to leave Alex with your parents for too long," Ellie said as she walked by me and gave me a wink.

*She's the sweetest thing ever.*

Gunner got up, took her in his arms, and kissed the shit out of her.

When I looked away, I caught Heather staring at me. My heart started pounding, and my hands started sweating. *Jesus H. Christ. Am I in high school?* I winked at her, and there went the blushing again. I let out a little laugh, and she tilted her head at me. Then, she bit down on her lower lip. I was pretty sure a small moan escaped from me. She giggled and looked away.

The next thing I knew, Gunner slapped the shit out of my back.

With a wink, he said, "Remember what I said, dude." He turned, leaned down, and kissed Heather on the cheek. "Take good care of the birthday boy, sweetheart."

When Ellie hugged Heather good-bye, she whispered something in Heather's ear that made her smile and blush again.

I felt my dick getting harder by the second. *Calm the fuck down, Josh. Think about something else.*

Before Gunner walked out, I called out to him. "Gunner! What did you think about?"

He turned and smiled.

*Bastard knows exactly what I'm asking.*

"Dogs."

"Dogs?" I asked, confused as hell.

He let out a laugh and nodded. "Yep…fucking dogs."

Ellie looked at Gunner, and then she glanced over at Heather. Heather just shrugged her shoulders. I watched as Gunner and Ellie started walking out.

Ellie turned, and before she shut the bedroom door, she gave me a wink. "Happy birthday!"

Once the door was shut, I pulled Heather into my arms. I pressed my body against hers, so she could feel how much I wanted her. I looked down at her mouth and ran my finger along her lower lip, pulling it out from between her teeth.

"Let me." Leaning down, I took her lip in my mouth and sucked on it. *God, she tastes like honey.* Then, I kissed her with as much passion as I could.

"Oh god," she whispered.

"You want to go for that drive?" I looked into her beautiful blue eyes.

"What?" she asked, confused. She almost seemed like she was in a daze.

"Our drive that we've been trying to go on for the last few nights," I said with a smile.

She giggled and nodded. "Okay. Can I go change into some jeans though? It's getting kinda chilly outside."

"Okay. Hurry and meet me at my truck. I'm gonna try and sneak out without anyone seeing me," I said with a wicked grin.

She raised her eyebrows at me before she reached up and gave me a quick kiss. "It's a date!" she called out as she opened my door and skipped down to her room.

I shut my door and quickly changed into some jeans and a long-sleeve shirt.

When I got downstairs, I heard my parents talking to their best friends in the kitchen. I tiptoed around the corner and hustled down the back hallway to the garage. I went out the garage and jogged over to my truck. Thankfully, I'd parked down by the barn, so no one was blocking me in.

The next thing I knew, I heard Heather laughing as she was running to the truck. When I turned, she jumped into my arms.

*Oh my god, my ribs.* I couldn't help it. I let out a grunt.

"Oh my god! Oh shit, shit, shit! I forgot about your ribs. Oh, Josh, I'm so sorry!"

I laughed and pulled her back to me. With one look into those eyes, I forgot all about the pain. I kissed her quickly before I picked her up and carried her over to the passenger side of my truck. Once she was in, I jogged around to the other side and got in.

As I pulled out of the driveway, I saw my parents standing outside the garage door, smiling. I gave them a quick wave and headed off to the back pasture.

I parked the truck in my favorite spot and turned it off. I looked over at Heather and smiled. She was grinning from ear to ear.

"I thought we were going for a ride?"

"We did. This is my favorite place to come to when I just want to relax and think. Wait until you see the stars." I rolled down the truck windows and turned up my iPod. "Come on, the sun is going down. They're gonna start popping out!"

I jumped out of the truck and went over to help her out. I took her hand and led her to the front of the truck. "Climb up," I said.

"Up where?"

"Onto the hood of the truck."

"You want me to climb up on the hood of your brand new truck? And do what?"

I let out a laugh. *God, she's so damn adorable.* "Just lie back and look at the sky, princess. I promise it'll be worth it." Then, I stopped and stared at her. "Have I ever brought you out here?"

She smiled and shook her head. "Nope, this would be a first!"

*Perfect.*

I wasn't sure how long we were on the hood of my truck, just talking. We talked about everything from the grades we made in high school to our first fight. I couldn't get enough of her. She cried once when she started to tell me about her parents. I hated that she had to live through it all over again, just to tell me once more, but I wanted to know.

Everything about her was…amazing. She was beyond perfect in every way.

"I still can't believe Jeff talked you into buying a Ford. You loved your Dodge so much."

I sat up on my elbows and looked at her, stunned. "Wait, Jeff said I wanted to get a Ford because my Dodge was having a hard time pulling my trailer with the furniture on it." I started to get a sick feeling in my stomach.

Heather let out a laugh. "Your Dodge pulled your trailer just fine! Jeff always teased you about your truck, and…" She stopped when she realized what was going on. "Oh no, Josh!" She giggled.

"That dirty, rotten, motherfuckin' asshole. I'm gonna kill him! I'm. Going. To. Kill. Him."

Heather couldn't stop laughing.

I just sat there in shock. *I let that bastard talk me into a Ford truck.* "I trusted that motherfucker. And Gunner! Why didn't he say anything?"

"Probably because they both love Fords," Heather said with a shrug.

I leaned back and looked up at the sky. I was tired of talking. I just wanted to enjoy this time with her.

Then, I heard Jason Aldean's "Talk" playing through my speakers. *So perfect.* I grabbed her hand and slid us down the hood. "Dance with me."

She smiled and walked into my arms. I pulled her in closer to me and just held her as we danced under the stars.

"I want to make love to you so damn bad, princess," I said in her ear.

"Yes," she whispered back.

"But I won't do it in my truck or in my parents' house. I want it to be perfect for you."

She grabbed on to my shirt and took a deep breath. "Amanda's in Austin this weekend, staying at her parents' house. She has to go see Brad and meet with his counselor. We could, um…well, we could go and stay the night at my house after Luckenbach. Then, you could head to your apartment in the morning, like you planned," she said with a twinkle in her eyes.

When I smiled at her, her face lit up like Christmas morning.

*I love this girl so much.* "It's a date, princess," I said before I leaned down and kissed her.

# Chapter Twenty-One
## Gunner

I watched as Ellie bent down and kissed Alex for the fourth time.

"Ellie, sweetheart, let's go!" I called out.

Grams and Gramps started laughing.

"Ellie, I raised two boys, darling. I've got this," Grams said before she kissed Ellie on the cheek.

Ellie skipped over to my truck. I opened the door, and she jumped in.

"Let's go cut a rug, Mr. Mathews!" she said with a smile.

After we parked and got out of the truck, I heard Ari call out, "Ellie!"

Ellie's face brightened as she waved at Ari.

"Hey, bitch! Dropping the baby off two days in a row! Aren't you brave?" Ari said as she winked at me.

"Shut up, Ari. You're gonna make me turn around and go back and get her," Ellie said as she pouted her lips.

I grabbed her and pulled her chin up to me. "I've arranged to have Grams keep Alex all night," I said as I winked at her.

"Really?" Ellie gave me a wicked look.

"Six weeks, baby." I captured her lips with mine.

"Oh, for Christ's sake, I don't need to hear that shit!" Jeff grabbed Ari's hand and headed into the Luckenbach dance hall.

Ellie and I both started laughing.

Once we got in, I spotted Josh and Heather on the dance floor. I smiled as I watched the two of them. When Ellie had told me that Heather was pregnant, my heart just broke. Heather had gone to the doctor yesterday morning and confirmed it all.

"Ells, do you think it's a good idea for Heather to not tell Josh about the baby?" I asked.

Ellie turned and looked at me with such sadness in her eyes. "Ari and I talked about it with her. She wants to wait just a little longer. With Josh getting little bits and pieces of his memory back, she's holding out hope that he'll get it all back." She turned and looked at them both dancing.

Kenny Chesney's "Don't Happen Twice" was playing, and Josh had the biggest smile on his face.

I smiled and let out a laugh. "That boy is head over heels in love with her."

Ellie reached up and took my face in her hands. "He is…just like I'm head over heels in love with you. I love you, Gunner."

I leaned down and kissed her so softly. *God, she tastes like heaven.*

"How sweet are you two?"

I pulled my lips away and looked behind me to see Victoria standing there. *Oh fucking great.*

I turned back and winked at Ellie. "Let's dance, sweetheart." I grabbed her hands and led her away from Victoria. *That girl is nothing but trouble.* I couldn't even believe she had shown up after Heather told her to *fuck off* yesterday.

After dancing for at least four songs, Ellie looked exhausted. "Gunner, can we grab a drink and sit for a bit?" Ellie asked as she made her way over to Heather and Ari.

I noticed Victoria trying to talk to Josh. I glanced over to where the girls were sitting. Heather, Ari, and Ellie were all shooting daggers at Victoria. As I laughed, I felt someone slap my back.

"I feel really sorry for Tori if she messes with these girls tonight. Ari's in a mood!"

I smiled as I looked at my best friend. "Congratulations, Jeff." I held out my hand.

He smiled so big that it made me smile harder.

"Fucking great, isn't it? I can't believe she's pregnant again." Jeff glanced back toward Ari. Then, he looked at the dance floor. "What the fuck?"

I turned and saw Josh dancing with Victoria. *What the fuck is he thinking?* "That stupid fucker. What the hell is he doing?"

"At least it's a fast song, and he's staying a good distance away from her," Jeff said.

I looked over at the girls. Heather was smiling as she stared at Josh and Victoria dancing together.

*Why is she smiling?*

She turned and said something to Ari. Ari jumped up and did a fist pump before she started walking over to the DJ.

*Ah hell.*

I smiled when I saw Jeff was watching Ari.

Turning to me, he said, "Shit, they are up to something."

We walked back over to our tables, and Ellie jumped up.

"Okay, listen. There was a song we made a dance to in high school. Well, really, Heather made up the dance 'cause she had taken dance lessons for years," Ellie rattled off.

"Wait, I thought Ari took dance lessons," I said.

"She did, but so did Heather. Focus, Gunner!" she said.

I let out a laugh. "Okay. Sorry, baby."

"So, anyway…just don't really pay attention to how we dance here in a second, okay?"

"Oh motherfucker. Ells, what are y'all gonna dance to?"

Just then, Josh walked up, shaking his head. "Don't bitch at me. I see the look you're giving me, Jeff. She wouldn't leave me alone, so I asked Heather if I could dance with her once." He rolled his eyes as he sat down.

I handed him a beer, and then I glanced behind Ellie to see Ari walking up with a smile.

She grabbed Ellie. "It's up next!" She walked over to Jeff, straddled him, gave him a kiss, and told him she loved him.

"That can't be a good sign," Jeff said with a laugh.

The three girls walked onto the dance floor and started dancing to the song playing.

Josh looked at us, confused. "What's going on?" he asked, looking between Jeff and me.

"I think Heather is about to make a statement," I said as "Give It Up to Me" by Shakira started.

"Oh fuck," Jeff and I said at the same time.

Ari started first, then Ellie, and then Heather. In all the times I'd ever seen these girls dance, I'd never seen them move their hips like they were moving them now.

"Dude, did you know they could move like that?" I asked Jeff as I turned toward him.

He had his beer frozen to his lips. I glanced over at Josh, and I'd be damned if his mouth wasn't hanging open. He looked shocked as shit.

I turned back to the girls. I couldn't help but notice that Heather really knew how to dance. She was dancing just like Shakira. Her hips were moving all over the place.

Then, I looked at Ellie. *Holy motherfucking shit.*

"Holy shit," Jeff said.

"Um," was all Josh could get out.

I couldn't pull my eyes away from Ellie. I was thanking God that we'd hit our six-week mark. I moved around to adjust myself.

Once the song ended, the girls walked back over to us.

Ellie came and sat on my lap. She raised her eyebrows at me as she smiled.

"Motherfucker. Ari…are you trying to kill me?" Jeff asked.

Ari laughed. "God, I haven't danced like that in years. I didn't know my hips could still move like that!"

"If I knew your hips moved like that, we could have—"

"Eww! Stop, Jefferson! Just stop!" Ellie scrunched up her nose.

I couldn't help but laugh. "Baby, I think we can skip Matt Kimbrow and just go home!" I said with a shit-eating grin.

Ellie threw her head back and laughed. "Oh no, Gunner. I'm gonna have me a good time tonight!"

Just then, Selena Gomez's "Come and Get It" started playing. Heather was standing in front of a still stunned Josh. When she reached her hand out, he took it, and they made their way to the dance floor.

"Get it, girl!" Ari called out.

I looked at Ari. "Did you ask for that song, too?"

Ari smiled and winked at me. "Fuck yeah, I did!"

I looked back out, and those two were really dancing. With the way Heather was moving up against Josh, I felt sorry for the poor bastard.

"Damn…I'm even getting turned on by watching them dance!" Ari busted out.

Ellie started laughing. "You're pregnant. Everything makes you horny when you're pregnant!"

"True dat!" Ari said as she stood up. "Dance with me," she said to Jeff.

"You wanna dance?" I asked Ellie.

She shook her head and moved a little on my lap. I smiled as I pulled her closer to me.

*I fucking love this girl.*

I'd never seen Ellie have so much fun. She loved the Matt Kimbrow Band. They were playing "If It All Goes Right," and Ellie, Heather, and Ari were dancing.

Every now and then, she would look over and smile at me.

Jeff had been pouting ever since Scott showed up. Scott had danced once with Ari, and Josh had practically held Jeff down the whole time.

I had to laugh at how Scott loved to get Jeff worked up. Scott had absolutely no interest in Ari, but he loved to torment the fuck out of Jeff.

"So, Josh, I hear you're gonna be spending the night with Heather!" Jeff yelled over to Josh as I was sitting in between them.

The smile that spread across Josh's face said it all.

"This the night?" I bumped him with my shoulder.

He turned to me, took a drink of his beer, and winked.

I leaned in closer, so he could hear me. "You remember anything else?"

"I don't think so. I mean, I keep having dreams and shit. Stuff will pop up in my head, especially when I'm with her. I don't know if they're memories or not. I sure as fuck hope they're memories," Josh said with a laugh.

Just then, I felt someone put a hand on my shoulder. I looked around to see Victoria standing there.

*Oh great. Just what we need is for her to start some shit.*

It wasn't lost on me how she had been watching Ellie and me all night.

"You need something, Victoria?" Josh asked.

"Well, since I can't have you, Josh, I was thinking maybe Gunner here would want to pick up where we left off all those years ago. You remember, don't you, Gunner? If my memory is any good, I'm pretty sure you said it was the best fucking blow job you ever got. That statement still hold true?"

"You fucking bitch!" Ari said.

When I turned my head back toward the dance floor, I saw Ellie standing there with Ari. Ellie had tears in her eyes, and Ari looked like she was about to go apeshit.

*Fuck. Me.*

Victoria started laughing. "Oh, now, now, Ari. Don't worry. You're the lucky one. You see, Jeff here...he would never let me get any further with him than a quick grab of his dick." Victoria looked at Jeff and winked.

Josh stood up. "Listen, Tori, I think you better leave."

Ari walked up to Victoria and got right in her face. "You know what? I've just about had it with all you fucking bitches. You just keep talking, but you don't ever say shit. You can't find a man of your own, so you try to take others. Women like you are nothing but pathetic, lowlife, douche twat, desperate, slut, bobblehead whores who have no respect for themselves or anyone else for that matter!" Ari balled her hands into fists.

Victoria stood there and just stared at Ari. "You know what I say to that, honey? Go fuck yourself." She smiled.

Ari glared at Victoria. "Don't call me honey."

Before I could even make a move to stop her, Ari reached back and then knocked the shit out of Victoria.

"Ari!" Ellie and Jeff both called out.

Jeff was next to Ari so fast that I didn't even see him go by me. He grabbed Ari's arm and tried to pull her away. She had hit Victoria so hard that Victoria stumbled backward and fell. Ari pulled her arm out of Jeff's grip.

She walked up to Victoria and stood over her. "The only person who calls me honey is my dad. I have one piece of advice for you. Stay the fuck away from all of us." Ari took a beer off the table and poured it onto Victoria.

Victoria jumped up, screaming.

Jeff grabbed Ari and reached for her purse. He looked back at me. "I'm taking her home."

Everything was happening so fast that I didn't even notice when Ellie had grabbed her purse to head out with them.

I ran and took her by the arm. "Ellie! Where the fuck are you going?"

"I'm going to have Jeff drop me off at Garrett and Emma's house," she said.

"Ellie, come on, that was so fucking long ago, way before you. This has nothing to do with you and me."

"Really, Gunner? If it was so long ago and meant so little to you, why didn't you tell me about it the minute she started coming on to you yesterday?"

*Fuck!* I didn't think Ellie had noticed how Victoria kept flirting with me yesterday. "Ellie, sweetheart, please don't do this. Please don't bring up something from my past that is meaningless. You're my life, Ellie. You and Alex. You know this!"

"Ellie, are you coming with us or not?" Ari asked.

Ellie looked at me and gave me a weak smile. *Thank God she's seeing how silly she's being.*

"I'm gonna stay. Put ice on your hand, sweets," Ellie said to Ari.

"I'll call you tomorrow," Ari said with a smile before she started to leave with Jeff.

"I love you, Ells. You know how much I love you," I said.

She smiled and nodded. "Oh shit! I have Jeff's truck keys."

When Ellie turned to go after them, she ran right into Jessie, Drake's daughter. Aaron, Jenny, and Dewey were following right behind Jessie.

"Oh my god, I'm so sorry!" Ellie said.

Jessie started laughing. "No worries, Ellie. How are you?"

Ellie glanced at me and then back at Jessie. "I'm good. Thank you for asking."

When Ellie looked back at me, I instantly remembered how jealous Ellie had gotten when she saw me talking to Jessie in the barn.

"Hey, Gunner! Shit, you remember all the good times we had here?" Dewey said with a smile.

"Yeah, good times." I smiled at him.

"Fuck…you and Jess had your first kiss here, didn't y'all?"

*Ah shit. Dewey and his big mouth.*

Jessie started laughing. "Yep! That's right. One of a few kisses!" She winked at me and then looked at Ellie. "We were in high school. It was so very long ago."

Ellie slowly turned and glared at me.

*Oh, son of a bitch. Why is this happening?*

"Like a sister…right, Gunner?" Ellie turned and walked off.

"Ellie!"

I followed her out of the dance hall as Jeff was about to walk back in. Then, he saw Ellie coming out. "Oh, good. You got my keys, Ells?"

"Will you drop me off at Emma and Garrett's place, please?" She handed him the keys and walked to the truck.

"Ellie! Stop!" I jogged over and grabbed her arm. "Why are you acting like this? All this shit happened years ago, Ellie. Stop being so damn jealous over nothing."

"What else have you not told me, Gunner? Any other girls gonna walk in tonight and say how they kissed you or fucked you?"

I took a deep breath and closed my eyes. *This is so stupid.* "Ellie, this was so long ago. It was before you and me, and really, the way you're behaving is stupid and childish. We're married with a baby for fuck's sake."

The moment I saw the tears forming in her eyes, I felt sick to my stomach. "Wait, sweetheart. I didn't mean to just say that—"

"Just stop. I'm leaving. I'll see you in the morning." She turned and jumped into the back of the truck.

I looked over at Jeff as he shrugged his shoulders.

"Is she pissed about Victoria? I thought she got over it."

I ran my hands through my hair as I headed over to him. "Fucking Dewey mentioned how Jessie and I had our first kiss here. The first time Ellie saw me talking to Jessie, she got jealous, and I told her Jessie was like a sister to me when I was growing up."

"Uh-huh. A sister you kiss?"

I let out a breath and shook my head. "It was high school, Jeff. I'd say that's far enough back that she shouldn't worry!"

"Dude, I would think it has more to do with the fact that you told her you were only friends, and now, she just found out that you kissed her." Jeff raised his eyebrow at me. "Y'all date?"

I looked back at the dance hall. *Fuck, this is not happening.* I turned back toward the truck. Jeff had given Ari the keys, and she had started his truck, so there was no way Ellie could hear us talking.

"For a bit, right before I started UT, but we weren't meant to be anything other than friends," I said.

"You sleep with her?"

I looked at him, and the moment our eyes met, I didn't have to give him my answer. He shook his head and walked toward the driver's side of the truck. I stood there and watched them drive off with a sick feeling in my stomach.

"I take it you never told Ellie we were more than friends?" Jessie said from behind me.

"No, no, I didn't, Jessie. The first time she saw us together, she got insanely jealous. I didn't think it would matter. It was so long ago."

Jessie let out a laugh. "Yeah, it was a long time ago. You were never worried she might ask about the first time you had sex?"

I turned and looked at her. "No. Why the fuck would she ever ask me that?" I walked past her to head back into the dance hall. *I need a damn drink.*

When I saw Scott at the bar, I walked over to him and slapped him on the back. Jessie came in right behind me, and I noticed when Scott did a double take at her.

"Holy shit, is that little Jessie Rhodes?"

"Yep."

"Damn. She grew up…and she looks like a girl. I mean, she looks like a woman…a very hot woman." Scott took a drink of his beer.

I glanced back toward Jessie. She was talking to Josh and Heather, and I assumed Heather was getting her caught up on everything.

Scott and I talked at the bar for a while longer. I lost count on how many beers I'd downed. Scott kept looking over toward where Jessie and Heather were talking.

"You should go say hi and catch up with each other. Didn't you like her for a bit in high school? Before Chelsea? Jessie always had the hots for you." I downed my beer.

Scott turned to me. "What? How do you know that?"

I looked at him and smiled as I stumbled back. *Why is the fucking room spinning?* "When I fucked her, she called out your name."

Scott shook his head. "Nice, Gunner. You're fucking trashed, dude." He grabbed my arm and walked us over toward our table.

"Looks like Gunner got himself drunk. I'm gonna take him home. Any volunteers on who can drive his truck back?" Scott asked.

I tried to stand perfectly still. *Shit, I haven't been this wasted in a long-ass time.*

Jessie jumped up so fast that it caused me to take a step back. I ended up tripping over a chair, and I started to fall backward, but Scott and Josh jumped up and caught me.

"Jesus H. Christ, Gun. How much have you had to drink?" Josh asked.

"Well, he just downed at least six beers in the last thirty minutes while we were talking at the bar. Not sure how many he had before I got here," Scott said.

"I'll drive his truck!" Jess announced. "I mean, I think he should drive with you, and I'll follow y'all in his truck."

I looked at Scott and raised my eyebrows. I was just about to say, *I told you so,* when he grabbed me, and we headed out the door.

*Shit, I wish the room would stop spinning.*

I was pacing back and forth in the living room, trying to remain calm. For the last thirty minutes, I'd been trying to call Gunner. When the bartender from the dance hall answered Gunner's phone, I was stunned. I was guessing that Gunner must have dropped it or left it on the bar.

*Where is he?*

I grabbed my cell and called Heather.

"Hey," I said.

"Hey, sweets. Is Gunner home yet?"

"Um…no. When did he leave?"

"Well, he was really wasted, so Scott was giving him a ride home, and Jessie was following them in Gunner's truck."

*Oh, just great. I can't believe he got drunk.* "Well, I guess that's my fault he got drunk. I acted like an insecure, childish brat," I said.

"No, sweets. He really shouldn't have lied to you about Jessie," Heather said.

"Where are you?" I asked.

"Oh, um…Josh and I are, um…well, we're heading home…or I mean, back to my house."

I let out a laugh. It was going to be their home before the accident happened. Josh had almost his whole apartment packed up and ready to move in with Heather. My heart started aching for them both.

"Okay, sweets. Well, drive safely and call me tomorrow." I hung up and started pacing again.

I'd decided to have Jeff just drop me off at home. I had hoped Gunner would have just come home right after I left, so I hadn't bothered to pick up Alex. I'd thought we could make up. *Gah!* I'd wanted him so bad all night, and then that stupid Victoria had gone off and ruined everything.

Just then, I heard two vehicles pulling up. I didn't have any of the lights on, so I walked up to the window and peeked out. Scott was helping Gunner out of the truck, and then it looked like Gunner was pushing Scott away. Jessie walked up and grabbed Gunner by the arm. Then, Scott and

Jessie started to bring Gunner up toward the front door. I was just about to open the door for them when I heard Gunner talking to Jessie.

"I'm really sorry I's your first, Jessme."

*Her first? Her first kiss? Her first love? Her first crush?*

"Drew, you're really drunk, and you need to sleep this off before you talk to Ellie. Do you think she's asleep?"

"Shheee's probably at my Graaaammm's house," he said with a slur.

"Oh, okay. Well, you can make it inside the house and to bed on your own, right?"

"Don't worry, Jessme. I won't try anything on yous. I wuv my wife very much."

I rolled my eyes.

Jessie laughed. "Drew, I know you better than that, and I know how much you love Ellie. Just do me a favor. Always be honest with her, Drew. Honesty is so important in a relationship."

When I heard a bang on the door, I jumped back.

"Jesus, Gunner, be careful," Scott said.

Gunner started laughing. "Don't worry, Jessme. If shheee ever asks who I fucked and wost my virgin…virginity to behind the barn at sixteen, I'll be sures to be honest and tell her it was yous."

I threw my hand up to my mouth. *Oh. My. God. No!*

"Nice, Gunner. Really nice, you asshole. You make a lousy drunk," Scott said.

"Fuck off, Drew," Jessie said.

I stepped back away from the door. My hands were shaking. *He slept with Jessie? She was his first? That motherfucker!*

I reached out, grabbed the door, and opened it as fast as I could. I stepped back when I saw Gunner come flying into the house. When he landed, he hit his head on the tile floor.

*Oh shit!*

"Motherfucker! What in the hell just happened?" Gunner sat up and grabbed his head.

When I looked over at Jessie, I saw she was looking at me. I noticed a tear rolling down her face as she held her hand up to her mouth.

She slowly pulled it away. "Oh god, Ellie…"

Scott helped Gunner stand up, and then he asked where our bedroom was. I told him and then turned back toward Jessie.

"Was he your first?" I asked.

She nodded, and I sucked in a breath of air. *Fuck.*

"Ellie, it wasn't anything like that. I mean, we weren't meant to be together. We were friends…almost like brothers and sisters even."

"Uh-huh…brothers and sisters who sleep together?"

"Drew and I started talking about it when we were behind the barn one day. He mentioned he'd never had sex, and I couldn't believe it. I mean, all the girls around here loved it whenever he came to town, and they were always throwing themselves at him. I was only fifteen at the time, and well…one thing led to another, and we—"

I shook my head. "I really don't want the details of the first time my husband ever had sex." I needed air, so I walked out onto the porch.

"Of course. I'm sorry. It's just that…well, Ellie, it didn't mean anything to either one of us. We were curious, that's all. I'd heard my brothers go on and on about it, and well…I wanted to know. I begged Drew. I told him if my first time was going to be with anyone, I wanted it to be with one of my best friends."

I spun around and looked at her. "Funny because most girls want it to be with someone they love!" I shouted at her.

"I know, Ellie, I know. I wasn't a normal girl. I was such a tomboy, and I didn't want to be a virgin when I started school, so…I guess you could say we both used each other." She looked away. "Believe me, I think back to that afternoon, and I wish I could take it back. I wish I would have saved myself for when I met the man of my dreams. But I can't take it back, and I'll never experience that magical moment…ever. I cried afterward, and I told Drew how stupid I was for talking him into doing that with me. I felt so guilty, and I kept saying how I'd never get my special moment. He apologized to me for five years after that. Every time he saw me…he would say how sorry he was that I never got my special moment."

*Oh my god. No wonder he wanted to make our first time together so special.* "That must have hurt you for him to say he fucked you behind the barn." I walked closer to her and took her into my arms.

She started crying. "He didn't mean that, Ellie. He doesn't have a mean bone in his body. But you should know everything." She pulled back and looked at me as she took a deep breath. "When he came here the summer before he went to college, we started dating. It was for a very short amount of time, and I think he only did it out of guilt. I don't think either one of us wanted to date each other. It was awkward. Maybe we were just trying to make each other feel better. I was actually totally in love with one of his friends," she said with a laugh.

*Do I really want to hear this?*

"We only lasted for a month and a half."

"What happened?"

She looked away and then back at me with a weak smile. "Um…I called out someone else's name while we were having…um…"

*They dated…and slept together more than once. I think I'm gonna puke.*

"He told me y'all were just friends," I said, tears sliding down my face.

"Ellie, why would he tell you? Why would he want to hurt you or make you doubt him?"

I let out a gruff laugh. "Well, I can tell you I certainly doubt him now!" I turned away.

"Please don't, Ellie. He loves you so much. Please don't let something that happened so long ago get in the way of something so beautiful."

She was right, and I knew it, but it didn't mean I had to like it.

We sat down on the porch swing and talked for a few minutes longer. I slowly started to feel like an insecure fool again.

"Can I ask you something, Jessie? And you don't have to answer if you don't want to."

"Of course you can!"

I peeked up at her and smiled. "Whose name did you call out?"

Even in the dark, I could see the blush on her face.

She looked back at the door and then at me. "Uh…Scott's."

I let out a gasp. "Oh my god! No!" I grabbed her hand.

She smiled and nodded. "Oh my god, Ellie, I've never told anyone that! I've never told anyone at all about how I feel for Scott. Only Drew knew."

"Wait. What? How you feel? Oh, Jessie…are you still in love with him?"

She gave me a weak smile as she nodded.

"Why haven't you told him or gone after him?"

"He's been dating the same girl since high school. It's the reason I left Mason. I couldn't stand seeing them together. It drove me crazy. Then, I heard they were getting married, so I just knew I would never come home. I'm almost done with vet school though, and I wanted nothing more than to work around here, but—"

I jumped up. "Jessie! He's not getting married!"

Jessie stood up and grabbed my hands. "What? How do you know?"

I let out a laugh. "Okay, Scott loves to torment the hell out of Jefferson. Jefferson thinks Scott has the hots for Ari, but he doesn't at all. Jefferson told me tonight that Scott's fiancée left him! She told him she didn't love him."

Jessie dropped my hands and put her hands up to her mouth. Then, she started pacing.

"Jessie, what's wrong? I thought that would make you happy?"

She stopped and looked at me. "Oh, Ellie, it makes me very happy…and scared as shit, too. Scott's only ever looked at me as Dewey and Aaron's tomboy sister."

I looked her up and down. She was breathtaking. She was about my height and weight, but she had blonde hair and the lightest of green eyes. And at the moment…she was totally freaked out.

*Well, shit. I sure don't need to worry about her having feelings for Gunner.* "Um…well, I can tell you that you're certainly not a tomboy anymore, sweets."

"I would have to agree," Scott said from behind me.

I closed my eyes and wondered how long he had been standing there. Jessie spun around, and her mouth just dropped open.

"Who said you were a tomboy?" Scott asked.

"What?" Jessie and I said at the same time.

Scott laughed. "Ellie, you said she wasn't a tomboy anymore. Who said you were, Jessie?"

"I…um…well, nobody said it. I was just…um…I just…"

*Oh. My. God. This poor girl can't even talk!* "Jessie just mentioned to me how she used to be a tomboy when she was younger, and I just said she certainly wasn't anymore!" I laughed. "Hey, by the way, is Jessme your nickname?"

Jessie laughed. "No, Drew's just a really bad drunk. He never could talk right whenever he got drunk!"

Scott threw his head back and laughed. "Damn straight." Then, he looked at me. "That boy loves you so much. He was actually crying when I threw his ass on the bed. He was begging me to go and get you. Kept saying how he hurt you again. I hope everything is okay between y'all."

I smiled at Scott. I was starting to warm up to this guy…even though he lived for tormenting Jefferson. "Yeah, everything's fine. I just had some old…issues…pop up, but I've got it now." I winked at Jessie.

Scott took in a deep breath and slapped his hands together, causing Jessie and me to jump. "Oh shit! Sorry, ladies." He looked at Jessie.

With the way he was looking at her, I could tell he had a thing for her. "You need a ride, don't you, Tiny?"

*Tiny?*

Jessie frowned at that nickname. "Yeah, I'm staying with Aaron and Jenny, so if you wouldn't mind dropping me off there, that would be great." She walked up and hugged me. "Go love on that drunk bastard," she whispered in my ear.

I let out a giggle as I pulled back and smiled at her.

As I watched them walk toward Scott's truck, I noticed Scott inching closer and closer to Jessie. He jogged ahead of her, opened the door for her, and then he held out his hand to help her up into the truck.

*These Southern boys…damn, they sure know how to melt a girl's heart.*

I stood in the doorway of our bedroom, just watching Gunner sleep. He was passed out cold. Scott had somehow managed to take off Gunner's boots, pants, and his shirt. *Thank God he was wearing underwear.* As he started mumbling in his sleep, I smiled, thinking back to the first time I'd spent the night with him…when he was drunk.

I somehow managed to take off his underwear. I started stripping off my clothes, and then I climbed on top of him. He was lying on his back, so I straddled him. I leaned down and put my lips up against his ear. "Damn you, Drew Mathews. It's been six weeks, baby," I whispered.

I moved a little, and I could feel his dick slowly getting harder. I smiled as I rubbed against him. I threw my head back and moved my body over his. *Oh god, I want him so badly.*

Then, I felt his hands on my hips. I looked down, and he was looking up at me.

"Baby, I'm drunker than all get outs," he said as he pouted.

I let out a laugh and lowered myself to kiss him. "I know you are, baby…but I want you so bad."

I moved against him, feeling him grow harder.

"I thought yous hated me. God, please don't ever hate me. My life would be nothing withouts yous and Awex."

*Oh my god. I love him. I love him. I love him.* "I've waited over six weeks to have sex with you, Gunner. We're having sex whether you can move or not. Just don't throw up on me!" I moved up and then slowly sat back down on him.

*Oh god.* It hurt, but it felt like heaven at the same time. *Jesus…he's filling every ounce of me.*

"Holy hell, Ells…Jesus, you're so warm. Yous feel so good. Move, baby…please move."

I started moving up and down, in circles, all over him until I found that perfect spot. *Oh god, yes…there it is.* "Oh, Gunner…it feels so good. I don't want to come yet." I slowed down.

"Ells, I'ms not going to last much longer, baby," Gunner panted.

I started to move faster. "Oh god…oh yes, Gunner! That feels so good."

Before I knew it, I was calling out his name. He sat up and wrapped his arms around me as he moaned in pleasure.

We just sat there and held each other for a few minutes until my breathing got under control.

"Fuckin' A, baby. Drunk or not, that was amazing!" I said with a giggle. "Gunner?" I tried to pull back from him, but he had his head on my chest, and all his weight was leaning up against me.

*Oh. My. God. He's fucking asleep?* I reached behind me and pulled his arms off of me. I watched as he fell back and hit the pillow.

"Feels so damn good, baby."

I just stared at him. "We're done," I said.

"Hmm…Ellie…yous feel so good, baby."

I slowly got up and off of him. I kneeled down next to him. "Gunner! We. Are. Done. As in…we're finished having sex." I watched him roll over as he tried to reach for me.

"Oh yeah, baby…smex with yous amazing. God, I love you, Ells."

I shook my head while my drunker-than-drunk husband was lying there, sleeping. My heart filled with so much love for him. I knew with every ounce of my being that he only loved Alex and me.

*I'll have to apologize tomorrow…but he still has to make up for this in the morning.*

# Chapter Twenty-Three
## Josh

*Jesus H. Christ.* My hands were sweating, and I had to keep wiping them on my pants. I glanced over at Heather when I was stopped at a stoplight. She was looking out the window.

*Is she just as nervous as I am? I mean, it's not like we haven't had sex before. Fuck. I don't remember having sex with her.*

"So which way should I go?"

"At the next light, you'll want to turn right." She looked at me and smiled. "Sorry, I guess I kind of forgot that in your mind, you've never been to our…I mean, my house before." Her smile faded a bit.

"So, I was getting ready to move in?" I asked.

"Yeah…I mean, you pretty much made the decision. You were packing up your place. After your accident, your mom and I went to your apartment to get you some clothes. That was when I saw all those packed boxes. I think you were going to surprise me with moving in sooner," she said with a wink.

As I turned right, we started driving through a neighborhood. It had mostly bungalow-type houses, and they were cute as fucking hell. When I came up to a stop sign, Heather pointed to the house on my left. It was across the street on the corner. The lights were on, so I was able to get a good look at it.

*Red tin roof. Looks like a white clapboard house.*

"Just go straight down the driveway, and the detached garage is behind the house."

I pulled in and headed back to the garage. I saw a two-car garage, and the doors looked like barn doors. I put the truck in park and shut it off.

"You ready for the tour…again?" Heather asked with a laugh.

I turned and grabbed her hand. "Wait, you walk from here to your house…alone…in the dark?"

"Um, yeah. I guess if I get home after dark, I do. Why?"

"It's dangerous!"

"What?"

"Heather, I'm not so sure I like the idea of you walking so far in the dark. Anyone could just pull up and grab you. Where the fuck was I when you bought this house?"

She sat there, stunned, as she stared at me. "Well, uh…we weren't really together when I bought the house," she said.

I turned back and looked at it. There was a huge deck in the backyard. *Damn, we could have some fun parties on that thing.* I looked over to my left, and there was a smaller deck with an outdoor table and grill. *Ah hell yeah. This place fucking rocks. The lot is big, and if we put up a fence, I could get a dog.*

I looked back at Heather. "Two decks?"

She smiled and nodded.

"Did we ever have any parties here?"

She started laughing. "Yep! We had a party here last fall, celebrating Ellie's, Ari's, and my birthday. It was a blast. You kept hounding me to put up a fence, so you could get a dog!" She laughed some more.

My heart stopped. I reached over and pulled her to me. I took her mouth with mine. *Oh god, she tastes just like honey. So damn sweet. I want her so much. I need her so much.* I slowly pulled way and smiled.

"Wow! What was that for?" She smiled and looked into my eyes.

"Can I still move in?"

The look she gave me sent a chill up and down my spine. The lust in her eyes was beyond anything I had ever seen before.

"Yes," she whispered. "Josh?"

"Yeah, princess?"

"Will you please take me inside and make love to me?"

My heart slammed in my chest. *Motherfucker.* I never moved so fast in my life. I was out of my truck and on the passenger side so quickly that I thought I even surprised her. After opening her door, I helped her down, took her in my arms, and kissed her again. The low soft moan that came from her lips ran through my whole body.

She pulled away, grabbed my hand, and started walking us toward the deck with the table and grill. After she got out her keys, she was trying to unlock the door, but her hands were shaking, so she could hardly get the key in.

*Holy hell. She's just as nervous as I am. How about that?*

When I put my hand over hers, she stopped moving. I turned her around and backed her up against the door while I took the keys out of her hand. I put the key in, and just as I was about to unlock it, I leaned down and started kissing her. She threw her arms around my neck and kissed me back with so much passion that I thought I would explode.

I pushed open the door and slowly walked her backward into the house. I kicked the door shut with my foot, and we kept walking until we hit the kitchen island. I picked her up and set her on the island. All the while, we never once broke our kiss.

*Heaven...I'm in heaven.* I pulled my lips away and rested my forehead against hers. "I've waited so long for you."

"I've always been yours. I'll always be yours."

"For infinity?"

She let out a giggle. "Yes...for infinity."

It was pitch dark in the kitchen.

"The lights?" She pointed behind me, next to the door.

Once I turned them on, I saw the size of the kitchen.

"Holy hell, this kitchen is huge, and that island—"

Just then, an image of us on the island flashed into my head.

"Have we..." I started to ask, pointing at the island.

She smiled and nodded as her cheeks flushed.

*Fuck me, that is such a turn-on.* "How long ago?" I asked.

"What?"

"How long ago was it when we made love on this?" I winked at her. I just wanted to see her blush again.

"Oh...um..." She closed her eyes and smiled.

*She must be picturing it.*

"Heather?"

She snapped open her eyes, and there it went. Her cheeks flushed, and my dick got rock-hard.

"Late November maybe." She looked down and away.

I placed my finger on her chin and pulled her face back toward me. I could see her chest quickly moving up and down.

"Breathe, princess."

"Oh god, Josh. I've missed you so much, and I have no idea why I'm so nervous and scared, but this...this..."

"Feels like our first time?"

"Yes!"

"Well, for me, it kind of is!" I said with a wink.

She started laughing. "Yeah, I guess it is. I kind of have the advantage. I know what you like me to do!"

*I need to be inside her...right now.* "Condoms?"

Her smile faded for a second, and she looked like she wanted to say something, but she stopped herself. Then, the smile spread across her face, even bigger than before.

"No, babe, we don't need one."

My heart started pounding stronger. *She must be on the pill? Sex with no condom! Shit, this just keeps getting better.* I pulled her closer to me. "Wrap your legs around me, princess."

"Your ribs, Josh," she whispered.

"They're fine."

"Do you want a tour of the house?" she asked with a smile.

I threw my head back and laughed. "No…the only thing I want is for you to tell me where the bedroom is." I looked into her eyes.

She smiled, and my heart fell to my stomach. *Shit…I don't want to fuck this up.*

I slowly let her slide down my body, making sure she felt how much I wanted her. She raised her eyebrows and let out a giggle.

*My god, she's breathtaking.*

Heather grabbed my hands and led me through the kitchen, dining room, and out to the living room. I looked around, trying to see if anything, anything at all, would spark a memory.

*Nothing.*

"The master bedroom is upstairs." She turned to me with the sweetest smile I'd ever seen.

My heart was beating harder and faster with each step I took. Once we got upstairs, I looked around. "Jesus H. Christ. The whole upstairs is the master?"

"Yep! The couple who had it before me remodeled the whole house. Wait until you see the master bath. There are two bedrooms downstairs, too. One is a guest room right now, and the other is an office, but I'm going to change it to a baaa…um…well, someday it will be something different." She stopped talking and turned away.

*She was going to say baby's room. I wonder if we talked about having a baby soon. Holy shit.* I tried so hard to not freak out. "So…can I see this master bathroom?"

She smiled that beautiful smile and nodded.

The moment we walked in, I noticed the cabinets. I closed my eyes as I pictured taking a blindfold off of Heather.

"Did I make these cabinets?" I asked.

She spun around and looked at me. "Yes! Oh my god! Do you remember making them, Josh?"

I had to laugh at how excited she got every time I seemed to remember something. "I remember taking a blindfold off of you…and we were standing in this bathroom." I looked around. *Fuck, I do good work!*

She put her hands on my chest and started pushing me out the door. "I have to go pee," she said with a wink.

"Again? My god, girl. It's all that water you were drinking tonight!" I pulled her to me and kissed her before she closed the door.

I headed toward the bed and took a good look around. She had her iPod sitting on her iHome, so I reached down and hit play. Tim McGraw's "One of Those Nights" started playing. I'd heard this song this morning, and it had made me think of Heather. I smiled to myself, thinking how perfect this song was.

I walked over to the dresser and saw a picture of us fishing somewhere. Heather was holding a giant-ass bass, and she had the biggest smile on her face. I took off my boots and then pulled my T-shirt out of my pants. I opened a drawer, and it was filled with my clothes. I smiled as I took out my favorite T-shirt from high school.

*Why can't I remember? I just want to remember what it was like to be with her.*

"I love that T-shirt," Heather said from behind me.

I turned around and sucked in a breath of air. My eyes traveled up and down her body. With a wicked smile on her face, she was leaning up against the doorjamb, wearing only a pink lace bra and matching panties.

*Holy shit…I can't even think straight.* "Heather…I, um…I can't even fucking think straight while looking at you in just your, um…your…um…" I just kept staring at her. *She's perfect. There isn't a single thing I would change about her.*

She let out a laugh as she started to walk toward me. By the time she reached me, George Strait's "Give It All We Got Tonight" started playing. She placed her hands on my chest and looked up at me. She slowly moved her hand down. She took the T-shirt I was holding out of my hand, and she tossed it to the floor.

"I, um…that was my favorite shirt in high school," I whispered as I placed my hands on her hips. *Oh god…her skin is so soft. I'm not gonna last five minutes.*

She licked her lips. "I know." She slowly started to lift my T-shirt up.

I reached down and helped her get it off. The way she was looking at my body was like she'd never seen it before. I couldn't be any more turned-on if I wanted to be.

"Dance with me?" she asked.

I pulled her closer to me as she placed her head against my chest. *She fits so perfectly in my arms.*

"I'm so scared, Josh," she whispered.

*What? Why in the world is she scared?*

She pulled away and looked into my eyes. The tears rolling down her face about gutted me.

"Oh, baby…please don't be scared. I promise…it's going to be perfect."

I wiped away her tears as she gave me a weak smile. For a brief moment, it almost seemed like she wasn't scared of making love with me. She seemed to be scared of something else, something she was holding back from me.

I walked her toward the bed as she started to unbutton my jeans. I leaned down and took her lips with mine. The sweet, soft moan she let out rolled through my body with such a warm feeling. I reached behind her and used my hand to unclasp her bra. I slowly slipped it off her, and then I just stared at her beautiful skin.

*So fucking beautiful. I love this girl. I feel it one hundred percent in my heart. I love her more than anything.*

I looked into her beautiful blue eyes and smiled as she smiled back at me. I kissed her so softly. When I pulled away, I noticed her biting her lower lip. I reached up with my thumb and pulled it out of her teeth as I shook my head.

"I want to do that." I noticed her whole body tremble. "Lie down, princess," I whispered against her lips.

# Chapter Twenty-Four
## Heather

The moment he told me to lie down, my heart dropped into my stomach. *Oh god…I want him so badly. How is he making me feel like this is our first time all over again?* I started to move back onto the bed as I watched him take off his pants. My heart was slamming in my chest. I was lying down just as "Storm" by Lifehouse started to play. I closed my eyes and fought back the tears. *Breathe…oh god. Breathe.*

I opened my eyes and saw Josh standing there, looking at me. *Oh. My. God. He has tears in his eyes.*

"I want to lose myself in you…and I pray to God I also find myself in you, princess."

He slowly moved onto the bed and over me. He captured my mouth with his and kissed me like I'd never been kissed before. I wasn't even aware that he was taking off my panties until I felt his hands lift me up. My body shivered under his touch.

"I love you, Josh. I love you so much. Please…please," was all I could manage to get out.

Josh leaned his forehead on mine. He took in a deep breath and then slowly let it out. "I'll love you until the day I take my last breath." He took his hand and placed it on the side of my face before moving it down my neck, to my chest, and then lower to my stomach. He stopped right on my stomach and smiled.

I sucked in a breath of air. *Does he know? Impossible…he couldn't know.*

"Maybe someday, we can fill this whole house with kids," he said with a smile.

I felt a tear rolling down my face. He moved his hand lower, and the moment I felt him touch my clit, I bucked up my hips. Then, I felt his fingers inside me, and I almost came. *God, I need him in me so bad.*

"Heather…fuck, you're so wet, princess." He started to move his hand in a way that drove me to the edge in no time.

"Yes," was all I could get off my lips.

"Tell me what you want, Heather."

*Oh. My. God. I can't stop it.* "Oh god, Josh. I want you…I need you so badly. I need you."

"I love you, baby." He took my nipple into his mouth.

It hit me so hard and fast that I couldn't help but yell out in pleasure. "Oh, Josh! Oh…oh god…please don't stop."

Before I even had a chance to come down from the incredible orgasm I'd just had, I felt him slowly entering my body.

*Oh my…he feels so good.*

"Good god…Heather, you feel like heaven." Josh started to move so slowly. "You feel so damn good."

I pushed my hips toward him. *I need him to go faster, harder.* "Josh…go faster! Please move."

He let out a laugh as he pulled back and looked at me. "Okay, princess, but this is, like, my first time with you. I just want to savor every second."

I pulled his face to mine and kissed him like I'd never kissed him. He smiled against my lips.

"I love you," he said.

I smiled. "I love you more."

"I love you more times infinity," he said with a wink.

He made such sweet, slow love to me that I almost wanted to cry. I pushed my hips up and grabbed him by the ass. *I need more.* I forced him over and got on top. The moment I sank all the way down onto him, I threw my head back and moaned. *Holy hell, this feels so damn good. I've missed him so much.* I started to give him a taste of his own medicine as I slowly, oh-so slowly moved up and down and then around.

When Josh let out a moan, I smiled, knowing I was making him feel so good.

He grabbed on to my hips and tried to get me to move faster, but I stopped moving altogether. His eyes flew open, and he smiled that damn smile of his. The dimple on the side of his cheek melted my heart in an instant.

"Baby, I really need you to move."

I moved slightly and smiled.

"I'm gonna flip your ass over and take you from behind unless you move," he said with a smile.

I raised my eyebrows. From just him mentioning it, I almost felt like I could come again.

He sat up and took me in his arms as I started to move.

*Oh. My. God. This feels so good.* "Oh god, I'm going to come again, Josh."

I threw my head back as we both cried out in pleasure.

The next thing I knew, I was lying across his chest, listening to him trying to catch his breath. I smiled to myself as I thought about how wonderful it was to be with him again.

*He's mine again. He will always be mine.*

When I rolled off of him, he took me in his arms, and I felt myself going to sleep, falling into a dream.

*On my way to the bonfire, Ari reached out and grabbed my arm.*

*"Maybe you and I should take a walk, Heather."*

*"Why? It's getting cold, and I just want to sit by the fire."*

*Ari looked back over at the fire. When I followed her eyes, I saw Josh and Victoria hugging. My stomach turned, and I wanted to throw up.*

*Then, it happened. He dropped to one knee and held out a ring box. Victoria's hand flew up to her mouth as she let out a small scream.*

*My eyes moved from her to Josh. When he glanced over at me, I wanted to scream,* No!

*But I couldn't move.*

"Heather? Heather! Baby, please wake up!"

"No! No, you can't marry her! You love me! No!" I sat up with sweat pouring off of me. *Oh my god! I had the dream again.* It was the same stupid dream I'd been having for the last few weeks. *Shit!* I placed my hand on my chest. *I can't breathe.*

"Baby, take a deep breath." Josh wrapped his arms around me.

*Oh, thank you, God. He's with me.*

"Jesus, Heather, you scared the shit out of me. What in the hell were you dreaming about?" Josh asked as he ran his hand through my hair.

I shook my head. "Nothing. Just a nightmare that I'm hoping I never have again." I looked up and smiled at him.

"Shit, I hope not."

I felt his hand move up and down my side. I started to get that familiar ache between my legs. I would have to ask Ari if this was just a part of being pregnant or if it was just because I'd missed Josh so much. Either way, I wanted him again. I glanced up at the clock and saw it was six in the morning. When I looked back at him, he smiled and tapped my nose with his finger.

"Want to go take a shower?" I asked, scrunching up my nose.

He laughed. "Again?"

I nodded and smiled. "It's such a big shower, and I don't want to be in there all alone."

"Shit, Heather. I never knew my equipment could perform so much. I'm really happy about it and all, but baby, this'll be the fourth time. I don't want you to be sore."

I pushed him onto his back and crawled on top of him. I rubbed against him until I felt him growing hard. I bent over and kissed one nipple and then the other before I jumped off of him.

"Okay. Well, you know where I'll be if you change your mind," I said over my shoulder as I winked at him and made my way into the shower.

After we made love in the shower, we got dressed, and then I finally gave Josh a tour of the house. I made us breakfast, and we ate it on the back deck. We talked about Josh wanting a dog, and I answered a million questions he had about us.

It was a perfect morning. It almost felt like things were back to normal. Josh went back upstairs to get ready to leave since he was heading to his apartment today to grab a few things and finish packing to move in with me.

I smiled, thinking about when he'd asked if he could still move in. *I really need to tell him about the baby. I'm so scared he's going to think I'm trying to trap him.*

"Hey, you look like you're a million miles away."

I stood up and walked over to him. *I just need to tell him.* "Um…Josh, I kind of want to talk to you about something."

"Sure, princess. Anything you want to talk about, I'm all ears," he said with a smile.

Just as I was about to start, my cell phone rang. I glanced down and saw it was Amanda. *Shit!* She was on her way to see Brad, and I was sure she was upset.

I looked back up at Josh and frowned. "Amanda is going to see Brad today, so I better get it." I let out a sigh.

Josh grabbed his truck keys and then gave me a quick kiss on the lips.

"Hey, Amanda. Hold on real quick," I answered. I looked Josh in the eyes. "I love you. Please be careful driving." I kissed him again.

"I'll be back soon. I don't think it will take me long. Are you staying here?"

"I have to run a few errands, but I won't be gone long. I'll be waiting for you," I said with a wink.

The smile that spread across his face caused my knees to go weak.

He slowly backed away and turned to leave. "Be naked!" He walked down the steps and out to his truck.

I giggled as I watched him walk away. *Damn, that boy has a nice ass.*

"Hey, Amanda. I'm so sorry. Josh was just leaving to head back into Austin." I sat down.

"Did you tell him about the baby?"

"Uh…no, not yet."

"Oh Jesus, Heather. You can't keep putting it off. Look at the situation I'm in now because I didn't tell Brad the moment I found out I was pregnant."

My heart broke for Amanda. "What time are you going to see him?"

"I don't think I can do it. I've pretty much gone through half this pregnancy without him here. What if he can't give up the drugs? And, of course, there's also the fact that he made out with that bitch."

"Oh, Amanda, please go. I know you're angry, but you'll always second-guess yourself if you don't go. I know he hurt you, but I also know he is hurting so, so much. Ellie said Brad cries every time he talks to Gunner, and Brad always says how much he hates himself for what he has done to you."

Amanda was silent for a good two minutes. I heard her softly crying.

"I just love him so much…and I hate him so much, too, Heather. I gave up all my dreams for him. I went to work for his fucking mother even though I hate her, and I did it for him. I've changed myself, so I could fit into their stupid high-society life…all because I loved him so much. In return, he just pushed me away when he should have been pulling me in closer, so I could help him. How do I move past this?"

I took a deep breath in and let it out. Everything she'd said was so true. She'd had dreams of moving and living near the ocean, so she could work as a marine biologist. She'd talked about it since we were freshmen in high school. She'd given it all up to work as the office manager for Brad's mom.

"I don't know, sweets. All I know is…if you love him and he loves you, then you'll find a way to make it through this. I think Brad was just as unhappy as you were, but he was too afraid to stand up to his parents. That was where the drug use came into play. I think he just wanted to find an easy way out…a way to forget."

"Yeah…well, I wish I had a way to forget the last six months of my life," she said.

"I know, sweets. I know you do."

"Heather?"

"Yeah?"

"You need to tell Josh about the baby. I know you're hoping he'll get his memory back, but if you keep waiting…you're going to be four months pregnant like I was. Then, you'll have to figure out a way to tell him and also explain why you waited so long to tell him."

"I know. I almost told him right before you called."

Amanda took a deep breath in and let it out. "I just pulled up to the rehab center. I wish y'all were here. Oh god! What if his parents are here?"

I let out a laugh. "Amanda, you said you were just meeting with the counselor and Brad. Baby, take a deep breath and decide right now. Are you going to forgive him and stand by his side to help him through this drug problem? Or are you going to hold on to your anger, raise your child as a single mother, and walk away from the love of your life?"

"Okay…well, right now, I'm going with option two—anger and single mother. That pretty much sums up how I'm feeling toward him. When I see him, I might change my mind, but I seriously think I'm just gonna want to junk punch him."

"Good luck, sweets. I love you," I said.

"Thank you, babe. I'll call you after I leave. Plus, I want to know what last night was like."

I laughed. "Bye, sweets. Talk to you later." I set my phone down on the table, and then I closed my eyes as I thought about the last few days.

The image of our baby on the monitor as the nurse had congratulated me popped into my head.

My eyes flew open. "Oh god. Why didn't I just tell him the moment I found out?" I said out loud.

I picked up my phone and looked at the time. I jumped up and ran into the house, heading upstairs to change out of my pajamas. I wasn't going to waste another moment. I would just go to Josh's apartment and tell him.

I grabbed his T-shirt off the floor and slipped it over my head before I pulled on a pair of jean shorts. I smiled as I thought about telling him. The way he'd put his hand on my stomach last night as he mentioned kids warmed my heart.

*Oh shit. He said "someday," meaning…not right now. What if he freaks out about it? He was just getting used to the idea of us, and now, I'm going to throw a baby into it.*

I shook my head and cleared my thoughts. *Amanda's right. I need to do this.*

I ran downstairs and skidded to a stop. *Fuck! My car is at Josh's parents' house.*

Neither of us had given a second thought about leaving my car behind when we headed to the dance hall yesterday. I glanced over and saw my dad's car keys hanging up next to the back door. Although I had kept my dad's Lexus, I would only drive it every now and then. Smiling, I walked up and grabbed the keys.

"Okay, Daddy, let's go tell Josh he's gonna be a father."

I sat there, bouncing my knee up and down, as I ran my hands along the thighs of my jeans.

"Brad, just take a deep breath. She's going to come," Bryan said as he smiled.

"My parents are not going to be here, right? My fucking mother is the cause of all this."

Bryan let out a laugh. "Brad, you're a grown man. You made the choice to take drugs."

I looked down at the ground. I knew he was right, but at this moment, I hated my mother. She had constantly pushed Amanda and me, and she was the reason Amanda and I had fought in the first place.

"I know what you're thinking, Brad. Yes, your mother played a big role in all of this, but you have a decision to make right now. Do you continue to let your mother control your world? Or will you do what you wanted to do when you first met Amanda?"

Just then, I heard her voice, and I jumped up. The door opened, and Amanda walked in. For a brief moment, it almost looked like she was going to run into my arms. As I glanced down at her stomach, my heart started pounding. She was a lot bigger. I looked back up into her eyes, and I smiled. The look she gave me was blank, like she had nothing left to give. Her eyes were bloodshot, so I knew she must have been crying. This couldn't be good for her or the baby.

Bryan got up, walked over to Amanda, and shook her hand. "Amanda. It's a pleasure," he said as he gestured for her to take a seat.

"Bryan, the pleasure is mine."

The moment she spoke, her voice ran through my whole body. She looked over at me and gave me a weak smile before sitting down across from me. Bryan had only put three chairs in the room, and he'd purposely placed Amanda's chair across from me.

"You look breathtaking. You're getting bigger," I said as I smiled.

She placed her hands on her stomach and nodded. "Yeah, she's been moving around a lot more lately."

My heart dropped into my stomach, and I felt like I was going to throw up. *She found out the sex of the baby without me.* I tried to talk, but nothing would come out. I cleared my throat. "You, um…you found out the sex of the baby?" I felt tears building in my eyes.

Her eyes snapped up and met mine. "No! I would never…I mean…" She took a deep breath and looked away from me. "I was waiting to see if you could there when I have the next sonogram. Well, I mean, I was going to ask you today if you wanted to be there."

I smiled, and my eyes captured hers. "Yes. More than anything, I want to be there."

She nodded and attempted to smile. "Okay. Well, it'll be just a few more weeks, and then we'll know."

Bryan cleared his throat and then began our session. He talked about how well my treatment was going, how he thought I might be able to finish up the program a few weeks early, and how I should handle the situation with my mother. I looked at Amanda as Bryan started talking about my mom. Amanda began moving around in her seat.

"Brad, would you like to tell Amanda what we talked about?"

"Um…well, Bryan and I talked about how I needed to tell you everything. I haven't told you that Michele has been blackmailing me the last few months."

Amanda's body looked like it was shaking. "Why?"

"Money. She just wants money from me."

She took a deep breath and looked into my eyes. "What is she blackmailing you with?"

"A video."

"Oh. My. God. You didn't…you didn't sleep with her, did you?"

"What? God no, Amanda. I already told you that I just kissed her, but she…she, um...she had a camera. She recorded me taking the drugs, and then…me, um—"

"You kissing her? You touching a woman who wasn't your wife while you were higher than a kite?" Amanda shouted at me as she stood up.

"Amanda, why don't you sit and calm down? It's not good for you or the baby to get so upset," Bryan said.

Amanda just turned and looked at Bryan. "Fine." She sat back down and put her hands on her stomach as she frowned.

"What's wrong? I jumped up and went over to her.

She stood up and moved away from me. "Don't touch me!"

"What?" I almost fell to my knees.

"Just don't touch me, Brad. I can't stand the thought of you touching me right now."

I looked over at Bryan and then back at Amanda. "Amanda, please don't say that, baby."

"Don't call me *baby*."

My heart started pounding in my chest. "Amanda...god, please don't do this."

"Why don't we all just sit back down? Amanda, Brad wanted to say some more things to you."

Amanda took a seat as she gave Bryan a dirty look.

I almost wanted to laugh. *My feisty girl.*

She looked over at me and raised her eyebrow, signaling for me to get on with it.

I cleared my throat, looking first at Bryan and then back at Amanda. "Well, first off, I know that asking for your forgiveness is a lot, but—"

"You think?"

I took a deep breath. "I'm ready to get down on my knees and beg you to please forgive me. My life is nothing without you. I love you so much, and it absolutely kills me that I've hurt you. I promise you...if you can find it in your heart to forgive me...I promise, baby, I'll do everything in my power to make it up to you every single day for the rest of our lives. I'll be the best husband and father I can be. I would lay down my life for you."

Her eyes filled with tears as she shook her head. "I gave up my dreams for you. I became something I wasn't just to make you happy, so you could keep your goddamn parents happy. Do you know what it's like to walk into your college classroom pregnant and have everyone stare at you? Do you know what it's like to tell your parents that you're leaving your husband because he's taking drugs? That he flipped out on you one night and told you to give up the baby? Oh, and then to say...by the way, Mom and Dad, the night I got pregnant, my husband forced his high-ass self on me!"

I was doing everything I could to keep from crying.

Bryan cleared his throat. "Amanda, you have to know that he was not the Brad you met and fell in love with."

"At this very moment, I have to say no...I can't forgive you. I'm not sure I'll ever be able to forgive you for the way you treated me during all those months or for making me go through half this pregnancy by myself because I thought you were no longer in love with me."

I fell down to my knees and looked up at her. "Please, God, no. Amanda, please don't give up on me. I'm begging you, please. Baby, I love you more than anything or anyone."

I saw a tear fall from her eye.

"How does that make you feel, Brad? Do you feel like shit? Do you need a hit to forget all this pain?"

"Amanda!" Bryan said.

"I want you to hurt like how I've hurt. I want you to feel the pain I felt when you forced your drunk, high-ass self on me and then left me alone for days."

I could hardly see her through the tears in my eyes. *She hates me.*

"Amanda, please calm down," Bryan said.

Amanda looked over at Bryan and then at me. "I'm sorry, Brad. I don't think I can do this right now." She started to make her way to the door.

I jumped up. "Amanda, please! I'm begging you to just give me a second chance."

She turned back to me, and tears were falling like rain down her face. Just as she was about to open the door, I heard one of the nurses telling someone not to come into our room.

Amanda glanced over at Bryan and then me. "I'm sorry. I just can't do this right now, Brad. I won't give up on you, but I just can't do this right now."

When she opened the door, my mother and father were standing in front of her.

"What's going on here?" my mother said, looking around.

"Excuse me. I was just leaving."

My mother grabbed Amanda by the arm and forced her to stop. "Oh no, you're not. We're all going to sit down and talk about this. That is my grandchild you're carrying, and you will not walk away from your marriage and abandon your husband like this!"

"Mom—"

"How dare you! How dare you even show your face here! If it weren't for you and your mind-controlling, bitch-ass ways, none of this would have happened," Amanda said.

My mother sucked in a breath of air and looked back at my father.

"How dare you talk to me that way! I've done nothing but set up everything, so you and my son could live a comfortable life with no worries."

Amanda let out a laugh as she tried to yank her arm out of my mother's grip. "I don't want your money. I'm moving as soon as I graduate from school. You will never tell me what to do ever again."

"Don't blame this on me. You were the one who couldn't keep your husband happy. God knows how you treated him to drive him to drugs."

"That's enough! Let go of my wife right now, Mother."

Amanda and my mother both snapped their heads toward me.

"What?" my mother said.

"Let go of my wife's arm now. As a matter of fact, I need you to please leave. You weren't invited to this meeting." I started shaking but not from the desire for anything. I didn't need alcohol or drugs. All I wanted was my wife. I longed for her touch and only her touch.

"Brad, I think maybe you're just upset and not thinking clearly."

"No, Mom, I haven't been this clearheaded in a long, long time. I stand behind Amanda one hundred percent on whatever decision she makes."

I glanced over toward Amanda. She was just staring at me…stunned.

"Dad, I didn't want to do this now, but I see I have no choice. I'm going to quit my job with the company."

"What?" Amanda and my mother said at the same time.

My father nodded as if he knew it was coming.

"I'm sorry, Dad, but working for you and taking over your company is just not my dream." I looked at Amanda and smiled. "Not our dream."

"What in the hell are you talking about?" my mother said. She turned and looked at Amanda. "You will get back in there, and we will talk about all this nonsense!"

Amanda shook her head. "No. You can't tell me what to do any longer. As soon as I finish school, I'm moving."

My mother put her hand to her chest. "You can't move away. We'll never be able to see our grandchild if you move."

"Exactly," Amanda said with a smile.

"Bradley, talk some sense into your wife. Tell her you made a mistake."

"I already asked Amanda to forgive me. I'll do whatever she asks of me."

My mother started laughing. "What are you trying to say, Brad?"

"I'm saying that I'll stand behind Amanda and whatever decision she makes, Mom. If that means she's moving to pursue her dream, then I'm moving with her—either as her husband or to be near her and the baby."

"What if she divorces you? Are you just going to pine after her and follow her like some lost little puppy?"

"Carol, that's enough. I think we need to leave and let Brad and Amanda work out their problems on their own," my father said as he tried to take my mother's arm.

My mother turned and looked at me. "If you do this…if you leave your father's company and follow this lowlife piece of trash around the country, I promise you, son, you will regret it. You will not see a dime from us!"

"Carol!" my father said as he tried to get her to stop talking.

"No, it's okay, Dad. Go ahead, Mom. Make the same threat you've been making to me for the last three years. I don't care anymore. Some things are more important than money." I looked over at Amanda, who was now standing there with her mouth hanging open. "You didn't like Amanda the moment you laid eyes on her. You've made our lives a living hell because of it. Well, no more. I'm done. Please leave now, and the next time you want to visit, I suggest calling ahead."

I turned and went to sit back down. I raised my eyebrows at Bryan as he smiled and gave me a thumbs-up.

*Holy fucking shit! I just stood up to my mother! Finally, after all these years, I spoke my true feelings.*

I could hear my mother bitching the whole way out.

I sat down in the chair and put my head in my hands. "Oh god. I just lost everything—my wife…my parents…my job. Motherfucker. Everything is gone."

## Chapter Twenty-Six

### Amanda

I watched Brad as he sat down in the chair. When I heard him say he just lost everything, I couldn't catch my breath. I turned and walked out of the building and to my car as fast as I could.

*Oh. My. God. Now, he decides to stand up to the witch. Damn it!*

I almost started jogging. I needed to get away. I got into my car and started it up. Christina Aguilera's "Stronger Than Ever" started playing, and I put my head on the steering wheel.

*I really have to stop listening to this song!*

Just then, I heard someone knock on my window. *Motherfucker. If it's Carol, I'm going to punch her fucking lights out.*

I slowly looked up and saw Bryan standing there. I opened the car door and got out.

"Oh my god, I'm so sorry I went off on him like that!" I immediately broke down into tears. "I just wanted him to hurt as much as I've hurt. Oh god…I don't want to walk away from him, but I'm so angry with him." I fell into his arms, sobbing. "I just don't know what to do. I love him so much, but I hate him so much, too."

"I know, Amanda, and what you did was exactly what I told Brad would most likely occur."

I pulled away and looked at him. "What?"

"Brad knows how much he hurt you. He might have mentally prepared himself for what just happened, but he was not prepared for it emotionally. He needed to see and hear how he has hurt you. He needed to see how his decision to do cocaine cost him everything. In order for him to never want to touch it again…he needs to see the destruction he has caused."

"You knew I would react that way?" I asked.

He nodded with a weak smile. "Unfortunately, it's all part of the job."

I leaned back against my car. Just then, I felt the baby move. I closed my eyes and put my hand on my stomach. *He's never even felt the baby move. I wouldn't let him touch me. Oh, God, please help me.*

"Amanda. Before Brad's parents showed up, he was going to read this letter he wrote to you. He wanted to read it himself. Things got a little crazy though when his psycho mother showed up."

I let out a laugh. "Bryan, I'm pretty sure you're not supposed to call her that."

He shrugged his shoulders and smiled. "Probably not, but in the years I've been doing this...Jesus, I've never seen such a controlling parent. Anyway, read the letter, Amanda. He also put a CD in there for you."

He leaned down and gave me a small hug. "Good-bye, Amanda. I hope to see you again soon."

"Good-bye, Bryan. Thank you for bringing this out to me," I said as I tried to give him a smile.

I took a deep breath and got back into my car. I opened the envelope, and I pulled out the CD and put it into my CD player.

Vince Gill's "I Still Believe in You" began playing, and I instantly started crying. *Oh, Brad...oh my god, I love you so much.* I slowly opened the letter and tried to read it through my tears.

> *My dearest Amanda,*
>
> *No matter how many times I say I'm sorry, I know it will never change the fact that I hurt you. I can never take back the moment I started to use cocaine. When I'm lying in bed at night, I think about how I hurt you and how I left you for days to wonder why I acted the way I did, and all I want to do is just scream.*
>
> *Bryan once asked me, "If you could go back in time and change one day, would you pick the day you started to use drugs?" I didn't even think twice about it. I knew what day I would go back to. It would be the day you told my mother you wanted a small wedding outside by the water, and she laughed and said that was nonsense. I saw the hurt in your eyes. That was the moment I gave her control over our lives. The more I pushed you away, the emptier I felt inside. I thought drugs could help me, but I know now that you are the only thing in this world I need to get through anything.*
>
> *All I can say is that I love you, Amanda. I've loved you ever since the first moment I laid my eyes on you. I will do everything in my power to make it up to you. I promise you...I'll do whatever you need me to do to make you*

*happy again. I just want you and our baby. I want that life
we dreamed of the night I asked you to marry me.*

*I love you, Amanda. I'll love you until the day I die.*

*—Brad*

I leaned my head back onto my seat and cried hysterically while I
listened to the words of the song he'd picked out. When I felt the baby
moving, my eyes snapped open.

*I won't give up on him. I won't give up on us. He needs me now more
than ever, and I need him.*

I reached for my keys, turned off my car, and got out. After I made my
way back into the rehab center, I saw Bryan talking to someone.

"Excuse me, Bryan?"

He looked at me and smiled.

"Can I please talk to my husband?"

"He's taking a walk on the property. He's probably down by the pond.
It's a secluded and serene area, and it's one of his favorite places to sit."

"Will you show me?"

Bryan walked me outside and down a path. We talked about how
Brad's treatment was going.

"Amanda, I really think with the proper support system, Brad can
make a full recovery."

I smiled, knowing that all we needed was each other and our friends to
help us get through this.

Bryan came to a stop and pointed. When I looked over, Brad was
sitting on a bench, staring out at the water.

"Thank you, Bryan," I said as I began heading toward the love of my
life.

*We are worth fighting for. We can do this together—him, me, and the
baby.* I tried so hard not to start running.

I stopped right behind him and fought like hell to hold back the tears.
"Brad."

He turned around, and the moment he saw me, he jumped up.

I couldn't think of what to say to let him know I wouldn't abandon
him. Then, it hit me.

*He just needs to hear six simple words.* "I love you and forgive you." I
broke down and started crying.

He shook his head, and I saw the tears falling from his eyes. When he
reached out, I slammed myself into him and hugged him. He pulled away
and grabbed my face with his hands. Taking my lips with his, he kissed me
as if it were our first kiss, and I let out a moan.

As our lips parted, I said, "I've missed you so much."

"I love you, Amanda. I love you so, so much, and I'm so sorry…" He trailed off as he began crying.

I took his hand and placed it on my stomach, and the moment he touched me, the baby gave a big kick.

Brad cried harder as he fell to his knees. He put his face right up to my stomach. "I'm so sorry. Oh god, I'm so sorry."

I ran my hands through his hair as he calmed himself down and started talking to our baby. My heart was beating so fast, and I couldn't believe how much she was moving around. She knew it, too…

*Your daddy is finally back, baby girl.*

# Chapter Twenty-Seven
## Josh

I walked into my apartment and looked around. Almost everything was packed up and ready to be moved. I glanced to the counter and saw a picture of Heather and me. I went over, picked it up, and smiled. In the photo, Heather was sitting on my lap, and we were both laughing. It looked like we were out in the country—maybe at Gunner's or Jeff's place.

I sucked in a deep breath, tucked the picture under my arm, and sent Heather a text message, letting her know I was at the apartment. I wanted to hurry, so I could get back to her.

When I heard a knock on the door, I let out a small laugh, thinking it was Heather. *She must be feeling the same way I am.* I hadn't wanted to leave her this morning.

I started to open the door as I laughed. "You couldn't stay away either, could…uh…Victoria?"

Victoria was standing in front of me. I eyed her up and down. She looked terrible.

"Is everything okay?" I noticed the black eye she had from Ari knocking the shit out of her.

She was holding a giant bottle of water.

"You thirsty?" I asked.

She glanced down at the water and smiled. "Something like that. Do you mind if I come in? I've been waiting for you to get here." She pushed past me and walked into the apartment.

*What the hell does she mean she's been waiting for me?* "Um…listen, Victoria, I don't think it's such a great idea for you to be here. I mean, with everything that has happened, it's probably best if you just leave."

She spun around. "What's wrong, Josh? Scared by a little temptation?"

I rolled my eyes as I walked by her. "No. I'm just saying…I don't think we really have anything left to talk about, do you?"

She opened the water bottle and lifted it to take a drink. As I turned around to set the picture down on the counter, I heard Tori yell.

"Son of a bitch, look at this!"

I spun around and her light blue shirt was drenched in water. "What the fuck happened?"

"I'm such a klutz. I went to get a drink, and it all poured out on me. Shit! I have to meet my mother in thirty minutes for lunch. Can I borrow a T-shirt and put this in the dryer?"

"Yeah, sure, but I'm not really sure where all my shirts are."

She smiled and tilted her head. "Thanks! I really appreciate it. Damn, I can't believe that happened. Be right back."

I started to move some of the boxes. Then, I pulled out my phone and called my dad.

"Hey, Josh! You at your place or still with Heather?"

"Nah, Heather is running some errands in Fredericksburg, and I'm at my apartment."

"How is she running errands when her car is here?"

*What?* "Oh shit! Neither of us thought about that this morning. Ah hell, let me call her real quick. I'll call you back, Dad."

"Okay, talk to you later."

*Son of a bitch. I left her stranded.*

I was just about to call Heather when there was another knock on my door. I walked over and opened it to see Heather standing there.

"Hey!" she said with a smile.

"Hey, I was just about to call you! My dad said your car is at their house. I thought I left you hanging."

She started to walk in, but she stopped as she looked past me. "Oh my god…no…"

I turned around to see Victoria. She was wearing nothing but my white button-down shirt with half the buttons undone.

"Oh, hey there, Heather." Victoria was looking at Heather with an evil smile on her face.

When I looked back, Heather had tears in her eyes.

*Motherfucker.* "No, wait! Heather, wait…before you go jumping to conclusions, this is not what it looks like!"

I spun back around to Victoria. "Tori, what the fuck are you doing?"

When I turned back to Heather, she was gone. *Oh Jesus. This is not happening.*

I looked back at Victoria. "Put your fucking clothes back on, and get the hell out of my apartment now!"

I took off after Heather. She was just about to get into a car.

"Heather! Please wait!" *Wait…whose car is that?*

She started the car and locked the doors.

"Heather, please wait! You have to let me talk to you. You have this all wrong! Heather, I was just calling you!"

I was banging on the window as she put the car in reverse and started backing up. As she began driving off, I ran after the car, yelling for her to stop. After she pulled out into traffic, I turned and ran back to my apartment. *I am going to kill Victoria.*

When I walked into my apartment, Victoria was sitting on a bar stool, still dressed in only my white shirt.

"Get the fuck out! Now!"

I ran into the laundry room and took her shirt out of the dryer. *Where the hell are her pants?* I went into my bedroom, and when I saw them on the bed, it all became clear to me. She must have heard Heather at the front door. *She did this on purpose. Fucking bitch!*

I came back into the living room, and she was still sitting at the bar.

I threw her clothes at her. "Leave."

"Josh, wait! Don't you remember what it was like? We were so good together, baby. Let me give you something to relax a bit, and then I'll take care of you like I used to."

I just looked at her. Just the sight of her turned my stomach. "Get the fuck out of my apartment, or I'll call the police and have them remove you."

"Josh, we're meant to be together. You don't love Heather. She's a fucking elementary school teacher. You want someone who's fun. You want me, Josh. You need me."

I shook my head to clear my thoughts. An image of another girl standing in front of me, saying the same damn thing, popped into my head. *Fuck!*

*"You need me, Josh. You don't love Heather. You need me."*

Just then, the night of the accident came back to me. Lynda had shown up at my mother's Christmas party. She had begged me to come back to her. She'd kept repeating how I needed her and how I couldn't possibly love Heather. I'd turned and left the party to head out to Mason to ask Heather to marry me.

*Heather is the only one I need. She's the only one I want.*

Then, it all came flooding back—every memory, every tear, every laughter, every fight, and every time Heather and I had ever made love.

"I remember everything."

Victoria stood up, looking confused. "What?"

I walked over, picked up her clothes, and grabbed her by the arm.

"Let go of me, Josh!"

"If you just caused me to lose the only girl I've ever loved, I'll make sure Ari gives you a matching black eye."

I opened the door and pushed her out before I slammed the door in her face. I locked the door and pulled my cell out of my back pocket. I called Jeff and Ari's home number.

"Hello?"

"Ari!"

"Hey! What's up, asswipe?"

"I need your help," I said.

"What's wrong? Is Heather okay?"

"I remember you saying that Heather has a special spot that was just her and her dad's. You said she would go there whenever she was upset. I need to know where that is, Ari."

"What did you do to her? I'll fucking kill you if you hurt her. Wait…how do you remember me telling you that?"

I shook my head, not wanting to waste any more time. "I remember everything, Ari. Victoria said something that triggered a memory from the night of my accident, and then it all came back to me."

"Oh my god, Josh! That's great! But why is Heather upset? Victoria…what did the douche twat do?"

I quickly told Ari everything that had happened. "Then, Victoria started talking shit about how we belonged together and how I needed her. That sparked the memory of Lynda."

"Oh holy hell. Have you tried calling Heather?"

"No! I called you 'cause I figured that spot might be where she's going. She doesn't know I remember everything, so she won't think of me asking you. Please, Ari…please tell me where she could have gone."

"Um…okay, you know the gazebo down at Zilker Park? The one that looks out to the river?"

"Yep, I know it."

"That's probably where she went."

*Yes!* "I knew I could count on you, Ari."

"What happened with the bitch?"

I ran and grabbed my wallet and truck keys. "I threw her ass out, dressed in nothing but my white shirt."

"Ah shit. I always did like you, Josh."

I laughed as I ran out to my truck. "Ari, can you do me another favor?"

"Will it make my girl happy?"

"I'm praying to God it will." I took a deep breath and told her my plan.

I pulled up and parked right in front of the gazebo. I looked around the parking lot and saw Heather's dad's Lexus. I rolled down all the windows in my truck, hit play on my stereo, and turned up the volume before I jumped out of the truck and made my way over to the gazebo. I saw her standing there, staring out over the water.

When Ed Sheeran's "Kiss Me" started playing, she spun around. She just stared at me as she started to slowly shake her head.

"Nothing happened between us. I swear to God. She stopped by and spilled water on her shirt. She asked me if she could dry it 'cause she was meeting her mom. She must have heard you at the door, so she put on that shirt with nothing else. I swear, I didn't ask her to come over. She said she'd been waiting for me all morning. I promise you, princess, I would never hurt you. I love you and only you. I want to spend the rest of my life with you, Heather. I need you more than the air I breathe."

Tears were rolling down her face as she walked up to me. "Why are you playing this song?"

I smiled as I wiped away her tears. "Because it's your favorite song, princess…and it reminds me of one of the most amazing moments of my life…making love to you in the rain."

She began crying even harder. "Do you remember?" she asked in between sobs.

I placed my hands on the sides of her face and leaned down to kiss her tear-soaked lips. "I could never forget a love as strong as ours."

She looked so confused. "How much do you remember?"

I kissed her again and poured every ounce of my love into the kiss. I slowly pulled away and rested my forehead on hers. "Everything."

She reached her arms around my neck, and I lifted her up as she cried. She wrapped her legs around me and held on to me so tightly I could hardly breathe. It was as if she were afraid I would leave her again.

*Never. I will never leave this girl.*

"Oh my god, Josh! I've missed you so much. I've needed you so badly!"

I walked over to the bench, and she slowly started to slide her body down against mine. I sat down and pulled her onto my lap. She buried her face into my chest and cried.

"Shh, baby. I'm here. I'll always be here for you."

"I was so scared, Josh. You have no idea how scared I was."

*Why the hell was she scared? Scared I would never remember her? Scared I wouldn't want to be with her?*

"Shh…breathe, princess…just breathe."

She pulled away and looked at me. I wiped away her tears and pushed her blonde hair behind her ears.

"I was coming to your apartment to tell you something. I, um…I was so afraid to tell you. I wanted to wait until you got your memory back, but no one was sure when that would happen. I was going to tell you this morning, but then Amanda called. So, I rushed after you—"

"Heather, baby, slow down. You're talking too fast. You can tell me anything." My heart was pounding. *Now, I'm scared. Is something wrong with her? Is she sick?*

"Well…um…"

She gave me the most beautiful smile. I smiled back just because she looked so damn happy.

"I'm pregnant."

*Oh. My. God. We're having a baby?*

I grabbed the back of her neck, pulled her to my lips, and I kissed the shit out of her. I wasn't sure how long we sat there, just kissing each other and whispering how much we loved each other, before I heard someone clear his throat. I pulled away from her lips and turned to see a police officer.

"Um, sir, is that your Ford truck?"

I let out a sigh. "As much as I want to say no, yes…yes that is my Ford truck."

Heather started laughing. I stood, picked her up, and carried her back to my truck.

"I can walk, you know!"

I smiled and put her into the truck through the window.

I turned back to the officer. "Sorry."

He just winked at me with a grin.

I ran around, opened the door, and got into the truck. I looked over at the love of my life. "Can I take you somewhere?"

She giggled and nodded.

I winked at her. "We're going for a ride in the country, baby."

I glanced over at Josh and smiled. He was humming along to the radio, and he looked so damn happy. The moment I heard "Kiss Me," my whole world had stopped. Ari had called to tell me that Josh was looking for me. She'd told me everything that Josh had said about what happened with Victoria. *That bitch left out the fact that Josh had his memory back!*

I thought we were heading back to my house, but it looked like we were heading to Mason. "Josh, you really want to go visit our friends? I thought maybe we could…you know, go back to the house," I said as I peeked over at him.

Josh looked over and smiled at me. *Oh god, that smile of his just melts my heart.* My heart started pounding, and I just wanted to be with him.

"I have a surprise for you."

I finally figured out that we were heading to Jeff and Ari's place. Josh had stopped at a gas station, and I could see him talking on the phone, wearing the goofiest grin on his face.

When he got back into his truck, I asked, "Who were you talking to?"

"Jeff. He's helping me out with a little something."

When he grabbed my hand, the butterflies took off, and I giggled.

"What's so funny?"

"Nothing. It's just…well, when you reach for my hand like that, I still get butterflies in my stomach."

Josh glanced over and then quickly looked straight ahead again. The dimple on the side of his face was such a turn-on. I'd never seen him so happy. He asked a few questions about the baby, and I told him I'd just gone to the doctor for my first appointment last Friday. Then, we talked about changing the office into a baby room. He was so excited, and I was completely shocked at how he was not freaking out in the least bit. I was still freaked out, but he seemed…he seemed so happy.

I looked out the window, and then I closed my eyes as I pictured Josh as a dad, holding our child in his arms. My heart swelled as I felt tears building in my eyes.

"We're here!"

I watched as Josh punched in Jeff and Ari's gate code. The farther we drove, the weirder Josh acted. He seemed nervous as shit. *Is he nervous about telling Jeff and Ari about the baby? He has to know I already told them.*

Josh took a left turn, and we started heading toward the barn.

"Are they down at the barn?"

"Um…Jeff is."

Josh parked the truck, and I saw Jeff coming out of the barn with Rose and Tulip, their newest horse, saddled up. When I looked back at Josh, he was rubbing his hands on his pants.

Josh jumped out of the truck and looked back in at me. "Hold on a second, princess."

He ran over to Jeff. Jeff glanced over at me sitting in the truck and smiled as I waved at him. Then, I saw Ari walking out of the barn with Luke.

*What the hell is going on? Who's going for a ride?*

Josh went over to Ari, and she nodded and started laughing. He leaned down, hugged her, and kissed her on the cheek. Then, he ran back to the truck and opened my door. He held out his hand for me and helped me out. I noticed when he reached back into his truck and grabbed something out of the glove box before closing the door.

Then, Josh jogged up and took Tulip's reins from Jeff.

Jeff walked over and handed me Rose's reins. When I gave Ari a confused look, she just winked at me.

"Um…you want me to take Rose for a ride? We just got here!"

I watched as Josh hopped up onto Tulip, and then he looked at me with that panty-melting smile.

*He's up to something.* I shook my head and climbed up onto Rose.

"Y'all have fun!" Ari called out.

Josh rode up next to me and reached out for my hand. I turned to Jeff and Ari. They were just standing there with shit-eating grins on their faces.

*Yep, something's up, and I'm the only one left in the dark.* I smiled at Ari, shaking my head. I glanced back to Josh before we started to head off in the direction of the river.

"Are we going somewhere special?"

"Yes, ma'am, we are."

"You gonna tell me what's going on?"

Josh started laughing as he dropped my hand. He kicked Tulip and took off into a gallop. I shook my head and gave Rose a small kick to get her going.

After a short ride, I knew fairly quickly where we were heading—to our spot along the river where we had first made love. I smiled at the memory. Then, I thought about the night I was pretty sure we'd conceived the baby. I put my hand on my stomach.

When we started to round the corner, I looked ahead. I sucked in a breath of air when I saw a blanket lying on the ground with buckets of roses surrounding it. *Oh. My. God. I've never seen so many roses in different colors.* As we got closer, I glanced around at everything. There was a small table with two glasses next to a bucket with a bottle inside. Near the table was a picnic basket.

Tears began building in my eyes as we came to a stop. I jumped when I felt Josh put his hands on me. I looked at him and smiled as he was waiting to help me down. I swung my leg around, and as he grabbed me by the hips, he gave me a smile that drove me insane with lust.

He took my hand and walked me over to the blanket. Josh pulled the bottle out of the bucket of ice, and I laughed when I noticed it was grape juice.

Josh smiled. "Only the best for my two favorite girls."

My heart dropped in my stomach. "Girls?"

"Yep!"

I laughed and shook my head. "What makes you think it's a girl?"

"I just know it's a girl. It's really weird, but last night…which, by the way, was incredible…" He winked. "When I placed my hand on your stomach, I didn't know at the time you were pregnant, but for some reason, I just knew when the time came, it would be a girl."

I grinned and placed my hand on my stomach. "I think it's a boy."

"Nope. I've noticed that you've been sick. It all clicked on the drive up here. Considering how you keep throwing up…it's a girl."

I laughed and gave him a little shove. "I'm telling you…it's a boy."

He reached for me and pulled me up against him. "Maybe it's both!" he said with a wink.

My heart started pounding. "Oh dear god…don't say that, Josh!"

He shook his head and laughed. "Shit! Better not say that…I'll jinx us."

From the flowers to the picnic, everything was just perfect. *How did he do all of this? When did he do all of this?*

When he placed his hand on my stomach, it just dropped. He looked into my eyes and gave me that panty-melting smile of his.

I giggled. "When did you do all of this?"

He laughed as he glanced around. "When I kicked Victoria out of my apartment, I called Ari. Once she told me where you might be, I asked her if she would do me a favor and call Jenny. I'd already talked to Jenny about this, so she knew what I wanted. I'm not as romantic as that bastard Gunner, but…" He started laughing.

I reached up and kissed him. When he let out a small moan, an ache grew between my legs. Then, I pulled back and gave him a confused look.

*Wait. What does he mean he talked to Jenny about this? About what?*

He smiled as he stood up. He walked over to where his iPod was connected to a speaker. He reached down and pushed play. Brad Paisley's "She's Everything" started to play, and I instantly felt tears building in my eyes.

"Dance with me, princess?"

I nodded as he helped me up and took me into his arms. We slowly started to dance, and he began singing the lyrics to me. I laughed when he changed the words from brown hair to blonde hair.

I couldn't believe that just a few hours ago, he couldn't even remember this spot, and now, we were dancing here, surrounded by beautiful flowers. I closed my eyes, and I just listened to him singing to me. I felt so happy that I could hardly breathe.

*Breathe, princess.*

I tried so hard to stop myself from sobbing. I could feel Josh's breath on the side of my face as he sang to me.

*Oh, Daddy…I think you would have loved him. I'd be lost without him in my life. Thank you for bringing him back to me.*

The song came to an end, but we were still dancing. All I could hear was the sound of the river, and I thought back to the first time we'd made love. It was in this very spot. I smiled when I remembered how scared I had felt. I wasn't sure how long we were in each other's arms, dancing to the sound of the river, before Josh slowly pulled away.

As he stared at me, his eyes were filled with so much love that I had to suck in a breath of air. I'd never seen him look at me like that before.

"Heather…even when I couldn't remember our love, I felt it in my heart. I knew that you were my only reason. I knew you were my every breath. I could never live this life without you. I wouldn't want to live it without you. I want to wake up every morning to your beautiful face, and I want to fall asleep every night with you wrapped up in my arms. I want to watch your stomach grow with each child we have."

Tears were rolling down my face, and I started crying harder the moment he mentioned having children together. My knees felt like they were about to give out on me.

"I want to make a porch swing and hang it up on the front porch of our house. I want us to sit in it every single night as we talk about how blessed we are to have each other's love. I want to be with you every single moment of the day…and when I'm not with you…you will fill my every thought."

I watched as he reached into his pocket. As he pulled out a ring box and slowly got down on one knee, my hand flew up to my mouth, and I started to cry even harder.

"Heather, if your daddy was still here, I would have asked him for your hand in marriage. I would have told him that I'd spend the rest of my life taking care of you and our children. I went to a church one day, and I sat down and had a talk with him. I'm pretty sure your dad somehow put the fear of God in me 'cause when I walked out of there, I went and asked Mark, Jeff, and Gunner for your hand in marriage, and each looked at me like I was nuts."

I couldn't help it, but I started to laugh. He flashed me that breathtaking smile of his. Dropping down onto my knees, I placed my hands on the sides of his face, and then I kissed him. I kissed him with so much passion that I was sure we would both melt on the spot. I leaned my forehead against his, like we always do, and I smiled.

"Um...baby, I wasn't done yet," he said.

"Oh...oh, I'm so sorry, Josh. I was just so moved that I had to kiss you!"

I went to stand up, but he grabbed me and kept me on my knees.

"Heather Lynn Lambert, would you do me the honor of becoming my wife and making me breakfast every morning for the rest of our lives?"

I let out a giggle. When he opened the box, I sucked in a breath of air as I saw the most beautiful diamond inside. *Holy hell. Oh. My. God.* My eyes snapped up to his face and then back down to the ring. When I looked back at him, he had a single tear rolling down his face.

I reached up and wiped it away. "Yes. Yes, I will make you breakfast every day for the rest of our lives."

I'd never seen him smile so big. He pulled the ring out of the box and gently took my hand in his. Shaking my head, I looked down at the beautiful princess-cut diamond framed by sparkling round diamonds. It was stunning. The white gold band was covered in a ribbon of diamonds. As he placed it onto my finger, I noticed his hands were shaking.

*Is he nervous?* "Josh...this is the most beautiful thing I've ever seen. It's...it's just breathtaking," I said, staring into his green eyes.

With a smile, he placed his hands on each side of my face and pulled me in for a kiss. Right before my lips touched his, he said, "You have just made me the happiest man on earth, and now, I'm going to make mad, passionate love to you."

I smiled back and giggled. "Okay!"

As he slowly started to sit back, he brought me with him until I was lying on top of him. He rolled us over and just stared into my eyes. He got up on his knees and started to unbutton my pants. My heart was pounding while every memory of us making love flooded my mind—the first time we'd ever made love in this very same spot, in the back of his Dodge truck after we'd left his friend's wedding in Abilene, on the kitchen island in my house, incredible wall sex in the shower, inside the tent when we had gone camping at Guadalupe River State Park during a terrible thunderstorm…and the day in the rain when we'd conceived the child growing in my stomach. I would never forget that day…or this day…ever.

He slipped down my pants. Smiling, he placed his finger along the edge of my panties and slowly moved it along my stomach. I sucked in a breath of air. His touch was driving me insane. I needed more. I closed my eyes as my whole body began trembling.

"Josh…" I couldn't even get anything else out of my mouth.

"I'm so sorry I forgot you," he said.

My eyes flew open, and I looked straight into his. A tear was rolling down his face, and my heart broke into a million pieces. I started to sit up, but he stopped me. He leaned down and kissed me. In all the times we'd been together, I'd never felt such passion from him. Josh was always so sweet and slow in his lovemaking, but this…this felt like pure passion and lust.

"Jesus, Heather…I want you so badly."

I grabbed his hair and pulled his lips back to mine. We kissed like we hadn't seen each other in months. We barely stopped kissing to take off our shirts. He pulled my bra and panties off so fast that I didn't even realize I was naked until I was watching him take off his jeans. He moved over me and tugged on my lower lip with his teeth. The moan he let out moved through my whole body, and I swore I was on the verge of coming.

"Oh. God. Josh, please…I want you so much. I just want to feel you inside me."

"Not yet, baby," Josh whispered against my skin.

The next thing I knew, his mouth was on my nipple, sucking and pulling, as I felt his hand sliding down the side of my body. The moment he touched my clit, he moaned, and I felt like I was about to come. I started to call out his name when he pulled his hand away.

"Oh my god, Josh! Why did you stop?"

Then, I felt his lips kissing the side of my left hip. As he slowly made his over to the other side, he barely touched around my clit with his thumb.

*I'm going to die if he doesn't make love to me soon.* My hands were running through his hair, and I let out a moan as he started to kiss down the inside of my leg. *Jesus H. Christ. Is he going to—*

Before I even had a moment to think of what he was about to do, his mouth was on my clit. I screamed out his name as I grabbed on to his hair and arched my back. Then, I totally left this earth. I'd never in my life experienced such an intense and long orgasm. It felt like it would never stop. I almost needed it to stop, so I could breathe. Just as I was coming back down, he moved his mouth lower, placed his fingers on my clit, and let out a long deep moan.

*Holy hell...not again.* "Josh! Oh my god...Josh...I can't...oh god, Josh!" All I could do was repeat his name.

By the time he was moving back up my body, I was panting and gasping for breath. He kissed my stomach and made his way up to my chest where he took my nipple in his mouth again. I must have been holding my breath because after he softly placed kisses on my neck, he leaned up to my ear.

"Breathe, princess," he whispered.

"I've never—"

He let out a laugh. "I know, baby."

"I want you inside me, Josh. Now!"

Before I could even say another word, he entered my body with a fast and hard thrust.

*I can't believe it...* "Motherfucker! Not again!" I yelled as Josh was moving in and out of me hard and fast.

We both called out each other's names, and then Josh told me how much he loved me while we both came together. I'd never experienced such passionate lovemaking in my life. It was...amazing.

Josh started to kiss around my face, and when he moved to my lips, I turned away quickly.

"Are you kidding me? I don't think so!"

Josh smiled. "What? You don't want to taste yourself?"

"Um...I think I'll pass!"

He started to laugh, but then he looked at me as his smile faded just a little. "Fuck, Heather...that was the hottest fucking thing ever."

I wanted so badly to ask if that was the first time he'd ever given a girl oral sex, but I knew better. As much as I wanted to believe it was, I knew it wasn't. Lynda had made sure of that.

"Was that..." I stopped myself. *Why did I even start to ask?*

"Yes," Josh said with a smile.

I shook my head, confused. "Yes? Yes, what?"

"Yes, that was the first time I've ever done that," he said as he blushed.

"That can't be true!" *Why in the world would he lie to me?*

"What?" he asked.

"Well...I mean, Victoria said she used to have oral sex with you all the time, and Lynda said you used to—"

Josh pulled back and sat up. "Lynda said what? And when the fuck did she talk to you about us?"

*Oh shit.* "Josh, you know…none of that matters now. It's you and me forever, so whatever you did before me isn't important."

"It's important to me, Heather. I just told you I've never given a girl oral sex, and you're basically calling me a liar."

"No, I'm not!"

"Then, tell me what Lynda said."

*Oh god! How did this perfect moment turn into a disaster? Oh yeah, when you opened your big mouth, Heather!* I smiled and leaned over toward him. "Josh, I don't want to ruin this moment by talking about Lynda or anyone else."

As he turned away from me, he grabbed part of the blanket, covered himself up, and looked out at the river.

*Fuck me.* I took a deep breath. "Lynda used to send me text messages or sometimes emails. She would describe how y'all would have sex in the car, bathtub, at a park one time…" I started to shake my head. *I really don't want to think about this.* "She told me your favorite thing to do was…was…"

Josh snapped his head back to look at me. The expression on his face was pure horror, like someone had just told him the worst news of his life.

"Um…she said it was you giving her oral sex. She said you first did it at Jeff and Ari's wedding." I felt tears stinging my eyes.

Josh's jaw dropped. "When?"

I felt a tear slide down my face. "I just fucking told you when!" I got up and started to reach for my clothes to get dressed.

He grabbed my hand and pulled me back down. "When did she tell you all this? When was she sending you these texts?"

"Ever since we've been together," I said in between sobs.

"Oh. My. God. Heather, why didn't you ever tell me?"

He moved me onto this lap, and he began stroking my hair as I cried harder. All those months of holding it in and not telling him, all the built-up anger and jealousy…it was finally being released.

"As God as my witness, Heather, none of what she said is true. None of it. I never did anything like that with her."

"You didn't give her oral sex at Jeff and Ari's wedding?"

"You're the first girl I've ever done that to! I never had sex with her in a bathtub or in a park. None of what you just told me is the truth. Heather, she was just lying to you, princess. Oh fuck! I'd like to go break her fucking neck for hurting you all those months."

I buried my face into his neck. For some odd reason, I was so relieved. I knew Josh had been with lots of girls in the past, but to hear details from one was just pure hell.

"If she ever calls or texts you again, please tell me, Heather. I want us to be one hundred percent honest with each other. Promise me?"

I pulled back and looked into his eyes. *I love him so much.* "I love you…more than I love anything in this world."

He placed his hand on my stomach and smiled. "Not for long!"

I let out a laugh.

He kissed me so softly and sweetly on the forehead. "I have one more thing to ask you."

My heart started beating faster. *Victoria.*

"What did Victoria say to you?" he asked.

I closed my eyes. "The first day when you woke up, I was in the restroom with Amanda, and Victoria came and told me how much you loved getting a blow job from her."

He placed his finger under my chin and pulled me toward him. When I thought about where those lips had been, I wanted so badly to pull away from his kiss…but I couldn't.

What started out as an innocent kiss quickly turned passionate.

Once again, we were completely lost in each other.

# Chapter Twenty-Nine
## Josh

I held Heather in my arms while she slept. My mind was racing with a million different things. So much had just happened in the last five hours. I'd gotten my memory back, I'd found out I was going to be a father, and I'd gotten engaged. I'd also found out my two ex-girlfriends were nothing but bitches. If I ever saw them again, I would give them a piece of my mind. *I could just unleash Ari on their asses.*

I slowly ran my finger up and down Heather's side. Her skin felt so amazing. I wanted nothing more than to wake her up and make love to her again.

I smiled as I thought about everything she had done to keep Tori's claws from getting into me. She'd taken a leave of absence from a job she loved, and she'd moved in with my parents just to be near me. That last one alone meant she would be getting the wedding of her dreams.

"What are you thinking about?"

I smiled as the sound of her voice moved through my whole body. *Damn, the things this girl does to me.* "How I want to give you the wedding of your dreams."

She moved and put her hands on my chest. Resting her chin on top of her hands, she smiled at me.

My heart dropped to my stomach. "If you only knew what your smile does to me...or when those beautiful blue eyes of yours look into mine."

"Oh yeah? What do they do?" Her smile grew.

"They make me weak in the knees. I feel like I've just hit a dip on an old country road while going seventy miles an hour, and it just takes my stomach away."

Her eyes instantly filled with passion. She got up and crawled on top of me. When she slowly started to grind against me, I let out a laugh.

"I don't think he can. After last night, this morning, and just a bit ago...you've exhausted him." I sat up and took her into my arms.

She laughed and hit my back. "You know what I want to do?" She nibbled on my ear.

"What? I'll do anything you want."

"I want to go tell your mom and dad that we're getting married."

I pulled back and smiled at her. "Yeah?"

She nodded and smiled. "Yeah! How do we break the news to them about being grandparents?"

I started laughing. "Hey! You never told me when the doctor said your due date was."

The blush that covered her cheeks caused my dick to jump. *Why does that turn me on so much?*

"Well, I kind of said that I thought I knew when we'd conceived the baby, so…" She giggled as she blushed even more.

"How do you know?" I asked, shocked.

"Oh shit! I didn't tell you."

While she told me about how all the medicine she had been taking when she was so sick had caused the birth control pills to not work properly, I started daydreaming about her holding a baby girl in her arms.

"So, that's the due date they gave me," she said.

"Wait. What? I didn't hear the date."

She let out a laugh. "Did you hear anything I just said?"

I smiled, and I kissed her again. "Yes, ma'am, I did, but I got carried away, dreaming about you holding our little girl."

"We're due on September seventh."

I smiled as I felt my dick getting harder. I gently took her off my lap, laid her down, and rolled on top of her. "He's ready."

She grinned from ear to ear as she wrapped her legs around me, and we made love again.

By the time we packed everything up, I sent Jenny a text, telling her she'd knocked yet another one out of the ballpark. I was ready to get to my parents' house. I was excited to tell them that Heather and I would be getting married, but I couldn't wait to see my mother's face when we told her about the baby.

"Jen said to just leave it all, and she and Aaron would come and pick it up. You ready to head back?"

Heather smiled and nodded as she got up on Rose. The whole way back, we talked about the wedding. Heather admitted that she was worried about what her school administration would think about being pregnant and not married. We decided that she would take the rest of the year off and go back next fall…if she wanted to. I had a feeling the moment she saw that baby, there would be no way in hell she would want to leave our little girl.

"How soon do you want to get married?" I asked.

She smiled and bit down on her lower lip.

I let out a moan as I watched her nibble on it. "Princess?"

She turned to me. "Yeah?"

"Stop biting your lip."

She let out a small laugh and looked straight ahead. "Right away. Since Ari and I are both due in September and Amanda's getting bigger by the day, I want to get married right away. The sooner, the better! What about you?"

"I'd marry you today if you said you wanted to."

We talked about our ideas for a wedding. We'd never really talked about marriage before, but I wasn't surprised to see we wanted the same thing—something small near the ocean with just family and close friends.

When we made our way up toward the barn, Ari was leaning up against the door with a smile.

"Jesus, Mary, and Joseph, I thought y'all got lost." She winked at me and then glanced over at Heather.

"Nope, not lost at all," I said with a wink of my own.

"Pregnancy makes you feel like the damn fucking Energizer Bunny, huh, Heather?"

I glanced over to my girl to see that she was blushing. I laughed, and I had to adjust myself as I got off the damn horse.

Jeff came walking up and slapped me on the back. "Congratulations, dude...on getting your memory back and landing the girl of your dreams."

I smiled as we headed into the barn. "Where's Luke?"

Jeff turned to me and laughed. He opened a stall door a little and gestured for me to look in. Luke was sound asleep in his car seat.

My heart melted at the sight of him. "Right where he belongs—in a damn horse stall like his daddy."

Jeff laughed. "Dude, he said 'dada' the other night. I about came out of my skin. It was one of the best moments of my life."

I watched Jeff as he stared at his son sleeping. *Shit. The four of us have come so far.* Then, it hit me. *We are all going to have kids.* "Holy shit."

Jeff looked at me, confused.

"Jeff, by next fall, we're all going to have kids!"

He threw his head back and laughed. "I know, right? Hey, have you seen Brad?"

"Not yet. He was supposed to be meeting with his counselor and Amanda today, right?"

"Yeah, he was. Has Heather heard from Amanda?"

I shook my head. "Not that I know of."

I could hear Heather and Ari laughing outside. The sound of Heather's laugh did things to my body that drove me insane.

Jeff put his hand on my shoulder. "Moves right through your body, doesn't it?"

I looked at him, confused. "What?"

"The sound of her voice or laughter. Sometimes, I find myself catching my breath when Ari walks into a room, talking or laughing. I still can't believe she's mine."

I turned and watched the girls walking into the barn. Ari was holding Heather's hand, and Heather had the most beautiful color on her cheeks.

I whispered, "She's glowing."

Jeff let out a small laugh. "Yeah, she is, dude. They both look breathtaking." Then, he smiled and gave me a wink. "If Heather's anything like Ari is when she's pregnant, you are gonna be fucking exhausted all the time, dude!"

We both started laughing as Ari walked up and peeked in on Luke. When Luke made a noise, everyone got quiet.

Ari turned and glared at Jeff. "If you wake him up, you're playing with him until bedtime."

After picking up Heather's dad's car from the park, I pulled up to my parents' house and watched as Heather parked. I jumped out of the truck and jogged over to her. My mom and dad still didn't know I had my memory back. I opened her door, and the second she got out, I pushed her against the car and started to kiss her. She pulled back some and started laughing.

"I want you, princess," I whispered. I kissed her neck and blew in her ear before I kissed her earlobe.

"Oh god, Josh...don't do that to me. You know how much I love that."

I smiled and started to laugh. "Let's just tell them another time. Come on, let's sneak away before they—"

"Josh?"

*Oh holy shit.* I snapped my head up and saw Lynda standing on the steps next to my mother...my very angry mother.

"Joshua Michael Hayes, where in the hell have you been? Your father and I have been worried sick! The last we knew you were at your apartment, and then you just disappeared."

Heather started to giggle.

I looked back at her and winked. "Do I take care of my mom first or the bitch?"

Heather brought her hand up to her mouth, trying to stop herself from laughing. Then, her face turned pale. "Oh my god! Oh shit!"

"What? What's wrong?"

"I think I'm gonna get sick!"

Suddenly, she pushed me out of the way, ran over to the grass, and started throwing up.

*Well, damn…that hit her fast.*

My mother was down and by Heather's side in two seconds flat.

"Heather, honey…oh, baby girl, are you sick again?" My mother turned to me and smiled.

*Why the fuck is she smiling? My future wife is throwing her guts up, my ex is standing ten feet away, and my mother is happy?*

I glanced toward the door and saw my dad standing behind Lynda.

I walked over to Heather. "Baby, are you alright?"

"Please, Josh…just see what she wants."

My mother gave us both a confused look.

As I faced Lynda, I let out a sigh, deciding to just get it over with. "Lynda, what do you want?"

Lynda looked at my mother and then back at me. "I, um…I just wanted to talk to you and see how you were doing."

I walked over to Lynda's car and opened the driver's side door. "You and I no longer have anything to say to each other. I need you to please leave…now."

Lynda looked stunned. She slowly started to make her way to her car. She stopped right before she got in. "I don't understand."

"Let me explain it to you. I'm with Heather. I'll be with Heather until the day I die. I love her and only her. I will only ever love her. Don't ever text, email, or call her or me again. Do I make myself clear?"

"But I—"

I leaned closer to her. "I know all about the lies you were feeding her. I'd die to protect her from being hurt. I never want to talk to you again. Ever."

She turned and got into the car but not before looking over at Heather, who was now just standing there, watching us.

I shut her door and watched her drive off. When I turned back around, my mother was standing there with tears in her eyes. *She must know I have my memory back.*

"Mom—"

She held up her hand and shook her head. "Give me a second here to bask in this wonderful feeling."

I smiled at Heather. *Yep, she knows.*

"I have waited for so long…for you to tell that bitch to take a hike! Oh. My. God! You don't know how happy I am right now!"

My dad started laughing as my mom walked up to him. He held up his hand, and they gave each other a high five.

*What the fuck?*

I looked over at Heather, and she just shrugged her shoulders. I headed over to Heather, grabbed her hand, and walked her up to my parents, who were still laughing and celebrating.

"Jesus H. Christ, y'all. Did you really not like her that much?"

My mother turned around and let out a gasp. "Wait a minute. How did you know that was Lynda?"

I smiled.

My mother screamed as she grabbed me and pulled me into a hug. "Oh my god! Do you remember?" She pushed me away from her and looked me right in the eyes.

"Yeah, Mom…I remember everything."

My dad took both my mother and me into his arms. He looked at Heather and smiled. "Baby girl, get your ass in this hug!"

Heather started laughing as she walked up. I pulled her in closer to me, and we just stood there, enjoying our group hug for a few moments.

"Hold everything! How did it come back? Heather, why do you have your dad's car? What the hell is going on?" my mother rattled off.

Heather started to giggle. She looked at me and then over to my mother. "It's kind of a long story, Elizabeth, but after Josh left our house this morning, I needed to tell him something…in person. We both forgot that I'd left my car here yesterday, so I took my dad's car."

"And while I was at my apartment, Victoria knocked on my door."

My mother looked confused. "How did she know you were there?"

"I'm guessing she heard me last night when I was talking about heading into Austin to my place," I said with a shrug of my shoulders.

After we explained everything, my mother smiled.

"How did you know where Heather would be?"

I shook my head as I looked at the love of my life. I noticed how she'd been hiding her left hand in her pants pocket or behind her back. "Ari told me."

Heather shook her head and let out a laugh.

"Okay, so where the hell have y'all been the last few hours, Josh? I've been trying to call both of your cell phones. Your father and I have been a nervous wreck."

I grinned as I held out my hand toward Heather. I glanced over toward my parents. "I'm so sorry y'all were worried. I took Heather back to Mason."

"Mason?" both my parents asked at the same time.

"Yep. There was a certain spot I needed to take her to…so I could ask her to be my wife." I lifted up her hand and kissed the back of it, making sure my parents could see the ring.

My mother started jumping up and down, and my father winked at me. The next thing I knew, my mom had Heather wrapped in her arms, and they were both crying. When I looked at my dad, he just shrugged his shoulders and smiled.

"Just go with it, son. They're happy tears. They can turn that shit off and on like magic."

My mother pushed Heather away and giggled. "And?"

Heather started shaking her head. "Um…and?"

My mother put her hands on her hips and looked between Heather and me. She raised her eyebrows at both of us.

"And…we wanted to go out to eat and celebrate tonight," I said.

She slowly grinned, and then she winked at my dad. "Okay…dinner it is."

My mom hooked her arm around Heather's, and we made our way into the house.

*Damn! I can't wait to see her face when she finds out we're pregnant!*

We walked into Hut's Hamburgers while Josh and his dad talked about the business. During the whole drive over, Elizabeth had talked my ear off about the wedding. She hadn't asked yet when we wanted to get married. *Thank God!* I knew if I were to tell her as soon as possible, she would figure out I was pregnant.

She smiled at me. "I love the idea of a wedding on the beach."

We all slid into a booth, and I sat across from Elizabeth.

"I do, too. I can picture it all in my head!" My stomach did flip-flops just from thinking about marrying Josh.

Josh reached down, grabbed my hand, and placed it on the table. When I glanced down at my beautiful ring, tears began building in my eyes. So much had happened in the last twenty-four hours. I looked over and just stared at Josh as he talked to his father.

*I love this man with every breath I take. I'm going to be his wife…and have his baby. Please don't let this all be a dream.*

*Breathe, princess.*

Josh turned to me. Leaning down, he whispered against my ear, "Breathe, princess."

I smiled as I placed my right hand on my stomach. I could feel that my parents were with me. They were always with me, and I swore that my father would talk to me through Josh.

Josh kissed me gently on the lips. "I love you."

"I love you more times infinity!" I said with a giggle.

"I love you just a little more than that." He laughed as he turned to his parents. "Heather and I are getting tattoos."

I choked on my water.

Elizabeth reached across the table and grabbed my hand. "Honey, are you okay?"

I looked at Josh. "What?" *I can't get a tattoo while I'm pregnant!*

When I looked back at Elizabeth, she seemed like she was upset. "When? What are y'all getting?" she asked as she tried to smile.

*Oh shit! Is she upset that I want to get one? Josh already has tattoos, so why would she be upset if I want one?*

I grinned and shrugged before I glanced back at Josh.

"Well...we're each going to get an infinity symbol on our right wrists. Isn't that right, baby?"

I nodded. "Yep."

Elizabeth just stared at me.

"Because our love is so strong, faithful, and never-ending. Right, babe?"

*Why does he keep bringing me into this?* I nodded again. "Ah...that's right."

"I see. Well, I love that idea," Elizabeth finally said. "When will you be getting this done, Heather?"

*Ah shit. Oh no!* I tried to kick Josh with my foot.

Greg yelled out, "Ouch! What the hell? Which one of y'all just kicked me?"

Josh started laughing.

"Josh!" I said with pleading eyes.

"Not until after September seventh, Mom! Sorry, Dad. Heather kicked you."

My jaw dropped open. *How is he so calm when he's about to tell them about the baby?*

Greg looked at me. "Heather, why?" he asked with a laugh.

"I'm so sorry, Greg. I was trying to kick Josh. I guess my aim was off a bit."

I looked over at Elizabeth, and she seemed confused.

"Joshua Hayes. Why do you have to wait until after September seventh? I'm at a total loss right now."

Josh turned to me and smiled. I peeked up at his parents, so I could see their faces when they heard the big news.

"Well, the reason we have to wait until after September seventh is because...that's when the baby is due."

It took a few seconds for it to sink in for Greg, but Elizabeth immediately screamed out and then threw her hand up to her mouth.

"I knew it!" Elizabeth called out.

"What?" Josh and I both said at the same time.

"What do you mean?" I asked.

"Oh, Heather...that first day you started throwing up, I knew. The moment I laid eyes on you, I knew. Your skin was glowing, and you just had a look about you."

I sat there, staring at her. *How do these women know this shit? Is it like some gift God gives you after you have a child of your own?*

Josh started laughing. "Mom, you knew Heather was pregnant? For how long?"

Elizabeth smiled and shook her head. She reached across the table and put her hand on mine. With the way she was looking at me, I couldn't help but smile back at her.

"The day Heather decided to move in with us. I didn't know for sure, but I had a feeling." She winked at me.

"I'm so happy for both of you!" Greg said. He called the waitress over and asked for our check.

"Greg, we haven't even ordered our food yet!" Elizabeth said.

"Shit, my son just told me I'm going to be a grandfather. I want steak and wine, damn it!"

By the time we made it back to Josh's parents' house, Greg and Josh were toasted. Elizabeth and I made our way into the kitchen as the guys went into the game room to shoot pool.

Elizabeth leaned up against the counter and smiled at me. She had been doing that all night, and it was starting to freak me the hell out.

"Let's talk wedding. How soon?"

"Soon…as in, like, the next month."

When Elizabeth began jumping up and down, I had to start laughing. I felt my phone vibrate in my back pocket, so I reached for it and saw a text from Amanda.

*Amanda: I know it's late, but can I call you?*

I sent her a text back, telling her to call me. I told Elizabeth about what was going on with Amanda and Brad and that everyone was worried about them both, especially since Amanda had gone to Brad earlier today and no one had heard from her.

My phone started ringing, and Elizabeth went to check on our drunk boys. I laughed before I answered the phone while stepping outside.

"Amanda? Are you okay? We've been worried!"

Amanda laughed. "Oh Jesus H. Christ, Heather! I've never been better!"

*What?* "Did you go and see Brad?"

"Yes, and I ran into his parents there."

"Oh shit, Amanda! That couldn't have turned out well."

She laughed. "Actually, it was probably the best thing to happen. Brad pretty much told them to shove it, and we, um…we worked everything out.

I mean, it's going to be a rough road ahead and all, but I think we're going to be okay!"

I could hear the happiness in her voice, and my heart swelled with love for them.

"Oh, Amanda! This makes me so happy. And the baby…he's happy about the baby?"

She let out a sigh, and I could almost feel her smiling through the phone.

"Yes! I spent the whole day with him!" She started laughing. "I don't think I was supposed to, but I did. I went to his sessions with him, we ate lunch and dinner together, and…well, let's just say they all pretended not to notice when I went back to his room with him!"

"Amanda! You didn't! Oh please, tell me y'all didn't!" I started to giggle.

"Fuck yes, we did! Do you know how fucking horny I've been all day? I haven't felt his touch in months. Oh, Heather, it was amazing. I don't know if it was because of the amount of time we've been apart, the fact that I'm pregnant, or if it was the thrill of being sneaky."

When Josh came outside, I sucked in a breath of air at the sight of him. He was giving me that big ole panty-melting smile of his as he stumbled over to me. I was guessing he'd had more to drink while shooting pool. I smiled as he attempted to sit down next to me. When he fell out of the chair, I let out a laugh.

He yelled, "Oh shit!"

"What the hell was that?" Amanda asked.

"Josh is drunk."

"Have you told him?"

"Oh. My. God. Amanda, I have so much to tell you, but yes! Yes, I did tell him."

"And?"

"Well, let's just say I'm now engaged and planning my wedding with Elizabeth. We told them tonight about the baby, and…oh yeah! Josh has his memory back!"

He got up and started to move on top of me. I tried to push him away, but he just smiled at me.

"I want to make love to you…but shhh, be quiet…my parents can't hear!"

Amanda started laughing. "Sounds like you have some sneaking of your own to do. I'll let you go! I'm heading out to your place in the morning to pack up my stuff. I have so much to tell you, and it sounds like you have so much to tell me! I'm so, so happy for you, sweets! I knew that boy would remember your ass soon enough!"

I laughed. "I love you, Amanda! See you tomorrow." I hit End and leaned back in the chair. It wasn't lost on me that we were in the same lounge chair we had made love in.

Josh got on top of me and attempted to sit up.

"You're drunk," I said with a smile.

"Baby, I'm happy!"

I laughed as I glanced toward the kitchen window. I saw Elizabeth blowing me a kiss before she mouthed, *Good night.* I waved, and Josh tried to turn to see what I was waving at. When he started to lose his balance, I grabbed him by the shirt. He smiled as he leaned down. As he started to kiss me, I wanted nothing more than to make love with him at this very moment.

"Josh…we can't do this here, not with your parents being home."

He pulled back with a pout. "Let's go to my place then," he said.

"How about I help you up to your room, so you can sleep off your…happiness?"

By the time I got him upstairs and into his room, he had attempted to take off my shirt twice. He'd succeeded in unbuttoning my pants and somehow unhooking my bra.

After he fell onto the bed, he looked up at me with those beautiful green eyes of his. When he smiled at me, my stomach started doing crazy things. I reached behind me and closed his bedroom door.

"Ah hell…that's what I'm talkin' 'bout!"

I smiled as I pulled my shirt over my head and took off my bra. I stood there as his eyes moved up and down my body. I unzipped my pants and slowly started to slide them down.

"Son of a bitch. You're so fucking beautiful." Josh sat up, supporting himself on his elbows.

The lust in his eyes drove me insane. I could feel how wet I was, proving how much I wanted him. *Am I really going to do this with his parents at home?*

Then, he laid back and motioned for me to get on top of him. He gave me that crooked-ass smile of his with that damn dimple.

*Oh god…that dimple gets me every time. Yep, I'm going to make love to the father of my unborn child.* I made my way to his bed. I started to unbutton and unzip his pants. He lifted his hips, so I could pull them off. I smiled when I saw that he had gone commando. I was turned on even more, knowing he hadn't been wearing underwear the whole evening.

I snapped my eyes back up to him. "How drunk are you?"

He lifted his head and laughed. "Why? How drunk do you need me to be?"

"Are you going to remember this in the morning?"

His smile faded. "Of course I am, princess. I'm not that drunk!"

I looked down. *Okay, I can do this.* Leaning over, I kissed his stomach, and he let out a small moan. *At least he knows enough to be quiet!* I took him in my hand and started moving it up and down over him. He was so hard, and I knew he wanted me just as much as I wanted him.

I slowly inched down, and then I licked the tip of his dick.

"Jesus, Heather! If you do that, baby, I'm going to come. Honestly, baby, I want to remember this!"

I let out a small laugh before I took him into my mouth. I started to move my head up and down. When it hit me, I gagged just a little. *Okay...it's okay! I can do this. One more time.* I tried again, and this time, I started to go faster.

Josh moaned, grabbed my hair, and pushed me farther down.

*Nope! This shit ain't happening! I pulled away and started gagging so bad that I knew I was going to throw up.*

Josh started laughing.

*That bastard!*

"You think that's funny, Joshua Hayes?" I said in between my gagging fit.

"No, ma'am!" he said as he continued to laugh.

I jumped up, ran into his bathroom, and hit the floor in front of the toilet. It was nothing but dry heaves.

*Okay, so maybe giving my first blow job while pregnant wasn't the best idea I'd ever had.* I sat back and leaned against the wall. *Thank goodness, I didn't throw up.*

After a few minutes, I finally felt better enough to stand up and go back into his room. When I walked out of his bathroom, he was sound asleep. I started to laugh as I made my way over to his bed and crawled in next to him.

He wrapped me up in his arms. "I love you, princess. I love you so much."

"I love you, too, Josh. More than you'll ever know."

I drifted off to sleep and into a wonderful dream of Josh and me with a little girl in blonde curls, wearing a yellow sundress, running up ahead of us.

*Chapter Thirty-One*

*Josh*

I walked back and forth in the barn, trying to settle my heart rate down. Gunner came up behind me and slapped me on the back.

"Dude, don't worry. It's the most magical moment of your life!"

"Shit, Gunner…what if they find something wrong? Ah hell. Maybe we shouldn't do this before the wedding. We should wait."

Gunner just stared at me, and then he busted out laughing. "Damn. I thought I was a nervous wreck. Dude, calm down. It's going to be all good. You're gonna see your baby today, and then we're all heading to the coast for your wedding tomorrow. It's going to be perfect."

I knew Gunner was right. *It's all going to be okay. I'm just nervous about the wedding. The baby is fine. Heather is fine. Everything is going to be fine.*

I looked up and saw Jeff walking into the barn. Gunner and I must have read Jeff's T-shirt at the same time because we both started laughing.

"Where in the hell did you get that shirt?" Gunner laughed, pointing at him.

Jeff slapped his hand away and looked down at his shirt.

"I know your wife doesn't know you have that shirt on," Gunner said with a smile.

"Y'all like it?" Jeff said with a grin. "Shit! Ari wears what she wants to wear, so I wear what I want to wear."

Gunner just shook his head. "Uh-huh."

I laughed and re-read his shirt.

*Endangered Species*

*The Long-Haired Beaver*

Jeff walked up to me, and we slapped hands before he brought me in for a hug and slapped my back. "You ready to see your baby, dude?"

With that, the anxiety hit me all over again.

Jeff must have noticed because he started laughing. "Josh, it's gonna be fine. You're going to be in awe at the sight of your baby."

I shook my head to clear my thoughts. "Okay…well, what did y'all want me to drive all the way to Mason for anyway?"

"So, we know Brad's been out of rehab for about a month or so, and he's doing really well," Gunner said with a smile.

"Yeah, we had lunch with him and Amanda two weeks ago," I said.

"Did they mention that they are moving after the baby is born?" Jeff asked.

*What the fuck? Moving?* "Moving? Where? They didn't say a word to Heather and me about moving."

"I guess Brad's dad actually did something nice for him. He got Brad a job with another advertising agency here in Austin, and they are willing to let him work at their branch in Florida," Jeff said.

*Florida…holy shit.*

*That's right.* Amanda's degree was in marine biology. Brad was moving, so Amanda could follow her dreams.

I smiled as I looked between Gunner and Jeff. "Damn. That's fucking awesome, but at the same time…Florida? It's so far away."

Jeff just stared at me. "Jesus H. Christ. When did you grow a vagina, dude? Are you going to cry?"

"Fuck off, Jeff! Asshole!"

"Assmole, Jeff!"

Jeff closed his eyes and shook his head. I turned around to see Matt running into the barn as Ari stood there with her hands on her waist.

*Why is it she shows up with Matt when I'm the only one swearing?*

When Matt ran up to me, I bent down ready to take him in my arms.

"Josh! I've missed you, Josh, so much! I'm going to hug you now."

I laughed as Matt gave me a big ole hug, and I returned one just as big. "Hey, little buddy! I've missed you, too. Have you been a good boy?"

He nodded and turned to look at Ari, who flashed him a smile. "Josh, Ari said that you're going to see your baby today. Can I see her, too?"

I laughed before I gave him a quick kiss on the head. "I wish you could, buddy, but not today. You see, I'm taking Heather to the doctor, and we are going to use a special machine that will be able to see the baby. The baby is only about ten weeks old in Heather's belly, so I think it's gonna look like a peanut."

Matt laughed. "You're such an assmole, Josh!"

I smiled as I stood back up and looked at Ari, who was holding her stomach.

"So?" I smiled.

Ari was just about to start talking when she noticed Jeff's T-shirt. "Oh. My. God. What in the hell are you wearing?"

Gunner had taken Matt and walked him over to see Rose's new colt. He turned around and yelled over his shoulder, "I told ya!"

Jeff gave Gunner the finger before smiling at Ari. "What's wrong with my shirt, baby?"

Ari glared at him. "Well, since you seem to like long-haired beavers, I can arrange for that."

I started laughing.

Jeff's smile dropped. "Um…no. No, that's really okay, baby. I'm not a fan of the long-haired beaver at all! I'm more partial to the hairless beaver."

The next thing I knew, Jeff was taking off the T-shirt and tucking part of it into the back of his jeans.

Gunner died laughing, which caused Matt to laugh.

Matt finally stopped laughing as he looked up at Gunner. "Why are we laughing? Should I take off my shirt, too?"

Ari walked up to Matt and reached for his hand. "No, buddy, don't take off your shirt. Let's go in and see Mommy. You can try on your new outfit for Josh and Heather's wedding." As she walked by Jeff, she reached behind him and grabbed the shirt out of his pocket. "I needed a new cleaning rag."

I had tears coming out of my eyes as I watched Ari walk out of the barn with Jeff's T-shirt.

When I was finally able to stop laughing, I managed to get out, "I'm the one with a vagina, dude?"

Jeff looked at Gunner and then me and shook his head. "Fuck off, both of you! Let's talk about doing something for Brad and Amanda, like we were supposed to. Assholes."

As we waited for the doctor, Heather reached over and took my hand in hers. "So, you never did tell me what y'all are going to do for Brad and Amanda?"

I knew she was just trying to keep my mind busy. *How is she so damn calm?* "I was going to tell you about it. Jeff and Gunner already talked to Ari and Ells, and they're totally on board with the idea."

She smiled at me, and my heart melted.

"Okay. You're going to have to tell me the idea, babe, for me to be on board, too."

"What? Oh yeah, right. Okay, so when I told you that they're moving to Florida, you already knew. I love how I'm the last to find out, but that's beside the point."

She started to giggle as she rolled her eyes.

I let out a sigh. "They wanted to pull together some money to give to them before they left. To help them get settled and all. With Brad's parents totally cutting him off, they're not going to have much of anything after they sell the house. His mother is insisting that they pay back everything his parents paid for in regard to the wedding."

"Wait a minute! That bitch was the one who wanted the big fancy wedding, and now, she wants them to pay her back for it?"

I nodded. "Yep. She always has been a bitch."

I was just about to keep talking when Dr. Johnson walked in. Heather was so happy that the same doctor who had delivered Alex was also going to deliver our child.

When he held out his hand, I stood up and shook it.

"Josh, Heather, how are y'all doing?"

"Good!" we both said together.

Heather quickly glanced over at me and winked.

"So, how are Alex, Gunner, and Ellie doing?"

Heather let out a laugh. "Alex is doing great! I can't believe she's two months old already."

Dr. Johnson sat down and looked over at me. "Josh, you doing okay, buddy? You look a little white."

"I'm good. I'm fine. I'm just ready to see my baby girl and make sure she's okay."

He smiled. "Baby girl, huh? Well, we might be able to hear the heartbeat if we're lucky."

Heather snapped her head over toward him. "But I'm only ten weeks! Can the sonogram machine pick that up this early?"

He started laughing. "We actually just got this new sonogram machine in. It's capable of picking up the heartbeat as early as eight weeks, so let's keep our fingers crossed. So, Josh, you think it's a girl? Heather, how about you? Any guesses?"

Heather smiled and nodded. "Well, everyone keeps telling me it's a girl because of the morning sickness I've had. By the way, that's not limited to just morning, so why they call it that, I don't know. I just have a strong feeling it's a boy."

The nurse walked in, and Dr. Johnson stood up. "Well, let's get the show on the road and see us a baby."

After they put some jelly shit on her stomach, he started moving the contraption all around. I couldn't see anything, but then a small lima bean thing appeared. That was when we heard it—the baby's heartbeat. Heather looked up at me as a tear rolled down her cheek.

I leaned down and kissed her on the lips. "I love you." I looked back up at the monitor. "Does she look okay?"

Dr. Johnson laughed. "Yes."

Then, he made a funny face, and it almost sounded like the heartbeat was echoing. He started moving that little contraption all over the place as he pushed down more on her stomach.

Heather must have noticed it also because she frowned at me. She turned back to the screen. "Is everything okay?" she asked.

I looked up at the nurse, who was smiling.

Just then, there were two distinct heartbeats.

"Are you picking up my heartbeat also?" Heather asked.

"Or mine 'cause it's pounding loud enough in my chest!" I said.

Dr. Johnson and the nurse started laughing.

As I looked back at the screen, I saw it. Another little lima bean showed up.

"Oh. My. God. Is that another…" Heather's voice trailed off.

"Wait. What? Why are there two lima beans?" I glanced down at Heather.

She was smiling so big as she looked at the monitor, and then she started crying.

*What in the hell is going on?*

Dr. Johnson turned and smiled at me. "Josh, I think you should sit down."

"Why? Is something wrong with her?"

The nurse came and stood next to me.

*Oh god! Something's wrong. Why is Heather smiling? She's crying and smiling? Who does that?*

"Josh, it looks like y'all might both be right."

"Both be right about what?" I asked.

I felt my legs about to give out, and the nurse grabbed on to my arm.

"The two lima beans are two babies. Y'all are having twins."

*Twins? Holy hell. We're having twins!* I stared down at Heather with tears in my eyes. She was looking up at me with most beautiful smile I'd ever seen on her face. *Twins.*

## Chapter Thirty-Two
## Gunner

When I heard Ellie scream, I ran into the kitchen, trying to get ahead of that bastard dog of hers. Of course, he cut me off and got to her first.

*If he didn't watch over Alex like he did, I swear I'd…I'd…ah hell. I love that damn dog.*

"What's wrong?" I asked.

Ellie turned around and gave me the biggest smile I'd ever seen. I smiled back at her just because I couldn't help myself.

"That's so wonderful, sweets! Don't worry. He'll snap out of it soon enough. Just splash some cold water on his face," Ellie said with a laugh.

Reaching down, I started to rub Gus on the head as I listened to Ellie's side of the conversation.

"Okay. Heather, honey, it's all going to be beautiful, so please don't worry! Okay…see you in a bit." She hung up the phone and walked over to me.

As she kissed the shit out of me, I placed my hands on her hips and pulled her closer to me.

She slowly leaned away but not before she let out a small moan.

"Damn, Ells…what was that for?"

She smiled and scrunched up her nose. "Do I have to have a reason to kiss my husband?"

"No, but I sure as hell want to know what I did, so I can do it more often."

She laughed and gave me another quick kiss. "That was Heather on the phone."

"I gathered. I take it from your smile that everything turned out good?"

She started to giggle. "Yep! Except Josh nearly passed out."

"Pussy."

"You're one to talk!"

"I tripped!"

"Uh-huh. Well, anyway, Heather had a bit of news to share."

Her smile grew, and this time, she began hopping up and down. I couldn't help but laugh at how giddy she was acting.

"Are you going to tell me? Or do I have to kiss it out of you?"

"Oh! I kind of like that idea…but I can't wait another second. They're having twins!"

*Wait. What?* "Ellie…did you just say they're having twins?"

She shook her head and started to clap her hands together.

"Oh my god, Gunner! We're going to have five kids all around the same age. Five! I can't wait to tell Grace and Emma. I would give anything to see Elizabeth's face when they tell her they're having twins."

"Shit, I'd have given anything to see Josh's face when he found out they're having twins!"

She threw her head back and laughed. "Heather told me the nurse had to hold up Josh, so he wouldn't fall over, and the whole way home, he just kept repeating the word *twins*."

"How is Heather taking it?"

Ellie walked over to the refrigerator, took out a few bottles, and started packing them into the diaper bag. "She's over-the-moon happy."

The way she was moving around and humming was turning me on. I looked at the clock to see how much longer Alex would be napping for. I slowly made my way over to Ellie and put my hands on her hips. As I pulled her closer to me, she leaned her head back, resting it on my chest. I started inching my hand up her shirt to her chest. When I slipped my fingers into her bra, she let out the sweetest sounds ever.

I moved my lips to her ear. "I want you, Ells."

She lifted her head and looked over toward the clock. As she turned around, she gave me that smile I would lay down my life for. When she started to lift up her shirt over her head, I took off my shirt and unbuttoned my pants. She pushed my hands out of the way, and then she started to slide my pants down my legs.

The moment I felt her lips on me, I let out a gasp. "No, Ells…I want to be inside you…now," I said as I pulled her back up. After I slipped off her panties, I placed my hand on her and slowly slid two fingers inside her. *Oh Jesus H. Christ, she's so wet.*

"Gunner, please…I want you now."

I picked her up and walked her over to the other side of the kitchen. Leaning her up against the wall, I kissed each nipple as I listened to the sweet little noises she was making. Then, I adjusted her some before I entered her warm body.

She threw her head back against the wall and moaned.

"Ells…you feel so damn good, baby."

"Oh god, yes…Drew."

I began moving faster and harder as she held on. She started to say how close she was, and just as I was about to come, the doorbell rang.

I instantly stopped moving.

"No! No, no, no, no! Fuck! Gunner, no, please don't stop."

"Ells, someone's at the door."

She grabbed my hair and pulled my lips to hers as she tried to move herself against me. "Move, Gunner. Fuck! I was so damn close!" she said against my mouth.

Then, I heard the one thing I would never want to hear while my dick was inside my wife.

Gramps came walking into the house as he called out for us, "Drew? Ellie?"

Ellie's eyes widened as she whispered, "You didn't lock the door?"

"Fuck! I forgot!" I whispered back.

"Oh my god, Gunner! Put me down!"

I damn near dropped Ellie to the floor. We both hit the ground and started crawling over to the other side of the kitchen. I heard Gramps's footsteps getting closer, and by the time, we made it to where our clothes were on the other side of the island, he called out our names again.

"Drew? Ellie? You around?"

We stopped and didn't move an inch. I put my finger up to my mouth for Ellie to be quiet. Gramps turned, headed back down the hall, and started to go upstairs. I'd never in my life seen Ellie get dressed so fucking fast. After we both began giggling, we couldn't stop.

Gramps must have heard us because he called out again, "Drew? Ellie? Where are y'all?"

I jumped up and quickly opened the back door as Ellie looked around while she continued to laugh. She grabbed a basket and ran over to me just before Gramps got into the kitchen. I shut the door, acting like we had just walked in.

"Hey! There you two are. Where in the hell were you? And is Alex napping?"

With Ellie still in a giggling fit, I nodded. I knew if I were to open my mouth, I would start laughing.

"Drew, what in the hell is Ellie laughing about? Girl's got damn tears running down her face."

Ellie held up her hand for Gramps to stop talking. I just shrugged my shoulders as I did everything I could not to look him in the eye.

"Your dad said y'all were going out boot-stompin' in Luckenbach again tonight."

Then, it happened. I went to talk, and instead, I lost it, which caused Ellie to laugh even more.

Gramps just stood there, looking between Ellie and me. He looked confused as hell as to why we were both laughing.

When we heard Alex crying through the baby monitor, Gramps's face lit up. "I'll go get her since you two can't get seem to stop laughing about whatever in the hell it is you're laughing about."

Once I heard him walk up the steps, I grabbed Ellie and pushed her against the wall. "I'm going to finish what I started later tonight."

She instantly stopped laughing as she grabbed behind my neck and pulled me to her mouth. I wasn't even sure how long we were standing there, kissing, before I heard Gramps clear his throat.

I slowly pulled away from her lips. "I love you so much."

"I love you more."

When Alex let out a little cry, Ellie smiled and headed toward Gramps.

"I've already changed her, so she is fresh and ready to go!" Gramps smiled at Ellie.

The look on Ellie's face was pure love.

*God, just from watching her move around the kitchen, my heart swells up with so much love for her.*

"Do you want to feed her?" Ellie asked.

Gramps laughed and started toward the living room to go sit down. "Hell yes, I want to feed my girl."

I leaned up against the doorjamb, watching my grandfather feeding my daughter in his arms. When Ellie came up and stood in front of me, I wrapped my arms around her.

Leaning down, I whispered in her ear, "Another one?"

She turned her head and smiled at me. "I thought you'd never ask!"

Just then, the doorbell rang.

"Today is the day for company, I guess," I said.

Gramps smiled and went back to humming to Alex.

I headed over to answer the door, and when I opened it, I almost fell over as I recognized the person standing there.

*Oh holy motherfucking shit.*

Ellie's mom was smiling at me, holding a basket filled with…gifts.

I took a few steps back, turned to Ellie, and tried to smile. "Wait in the living room, okay, sweetheart?"

Her smile faded. "Why? Who is it, Gunner?"

"Ellie, please just stay inside."

I walked outside and shut the front door behind me. "What in the hell are you doing here? And how did you get on our property?"

Her smile faded for a quick second before she tried to smile again. "Um…your main gate was open, and the young man working on it brought me up here. I hope I didn't get him into any trouble."

I looked around her and saw Dewey's truck driving off. *Fuck! I can't be mad at him. I never told him about Ellie's mother.* "Why didn't you call first?"

She shook her head. "I've been calling Ellie's cell phone for months, but she hasn't returned my calls. I've been sober for over a year now. I just wanted to talk to Ellie. I know I could never apologize for the pain I caused her..." Her voice broke off as a tear rolled down her cheek.

I almost felt sorry for her—almost. "Mrs. Johnson, I'm sorry you made such a long trip out here, but I really think it would be best if you let Ellie decide if she wants to speak with you."

She nodded. "I spoke with Sue yesterday. She let me know that both Jeff and Ellie now have kids and..." She started crying and then quickly composed herself. "I'm so sorry. I didn't mean to cry like that. It's my own fault. I don't deserve their forgiveness. I have no right to even ask this, but...Gunner, will you please do me a favor?"

"Of course I will."

She reached into the basket and pulled out a letter. As I went to take it, I noticed her hand was shaking.

"I also bought some things for the babies. Sue told me their names were Luke and Alexandra."

I smiled and nodded before I looked down at all the gifts in the basket.

"I'm not trying to buy their love. I just...I don't know. I just wanted to do something. I've been working for a doctor's office for nine months now. I'm actually going to nursing school. I was in nursing school before the kids' father left and my world fell apart. I should be done this summer."

"That's wonderful...Mrs. Johnson. I'm sorry. I don't even know your first name."

She let out a small laugh. "My name is Sharon."

I held out my hand and shook hers.

She smiled as she handed me the basket. "Well, please let Ellie know that I'm here if she needs...um...well, I know she doesn't need me. Please have her call me if she's willing to give me a second chance. I understand that your mother is very kind to Ellie. I'm so very...um...so very happy that she, um..."

"It's okay, Sharon. I understand what you're trying to say. Is your phone number in the letter?"

"Yes. I wrote each of them a letter. I do love both Ellie and Jeff. I don't know that person who treated her daughter with such hate. My husband was my life. I gave everything up for him, and he just walked away from me, like I was nothing. When he told me that he'd only stayed because of Ellie...well, I guess I used that against her even though the poor soul had nothing to do with any of it. I see that now, but I didn't see it when I was drunk. All I looked for was a way to drink away the pain. Ellie is so much stronger than I ever was." She shook her head as if she were clearing her thoughts. "Anyway, I'm so glad she found you, and you took her away from me. It was a blessing in disguise. It took losing everything to see what I had."

I didn't know what to say, so I just stood there, staring at her.

"Well, good-bye, Gunner. Thank you for your time."

As she turned and started to walk toward her car, I noticed it had new plates on it.

A few months back, Jeff had told me that his mother had contacted him through his lawyer. She'd wanted to sell their house and buy a condo to get away from all the bad memories. Ellie had wanted so badly to ask where their mom had gone, but she'd avoided the subject, and Jeff had never given Ellie a reason for selling the house. Later, Jeff had mentioned to me that he'd let his mother keep all the equity in the house since it was really her house, but for the last nine months, she had been sending money to his lawyer to pay the equity back to Jeff.

She looked back one last time and gave me a weak smile as I heard the door open behind me. I spun around to see Ellie walking out.

"Mom?" Ellie barely got out.

Sharon didn't hear Ellie, and she was just about to get into the car.

Ellie called out, "Mom!"

Sharon stopped and snapped her head up toward the house.

"Ellie," Sharon said as she started to cry.

Ellie grabbed my hand before she started to walk us toward her mother. My heart was beating a mile a minute.

"Ellie," Sharon said as tears were rolling down her face.

*Lord, please don't let her mother hurt her again. Please.*

# Chapter Thirty-Three
## Ellie

"Mom? Why?" I asked on the verge of tears.

My mother started to move toward me as she began crying harder.

I tried like hell to hold back the tears, but seeing my mother standing in front of me, crying…I finally allowed myself to let it go.

I must have missed when Jefferson had pulled up, but I could see him now out of the corner of my eye. He was standing near his truck with Ari. I glanced over toward Ari, who was holding on to Luke. She covered her mouth with her free hand as tears rolled down her face.

My mother stopped right in front of me as she began wiping away her tears. "Ellie, I have so much to say to you, and I don't even know where to begin. I can only ask for your forgiveness. I was in the dark for so long, but I've been sober for a while now. I have a steady job, and I'm finally seeing the light. I need your forgiveness to help me stay in the light."

"Mommy…please don't ever hurt me again. I need you so much, Mom. Please don't go."

She took me in her arms as we both continued crying.

"I promise, baby…I promise to never hurt you again."

When I looked over at Jefferson, I noticed he was wiping tears away from his face. Leaning over, Ari said something to him. She took his hand and led him over toward us.

"Um…" Jefferson tried to talk, but he had to clear his throat. "Mom?"

Mom turned around and sucked in a breath of air. Jefferson pulled both of us into his arms. After a few minutes, my mom started talking.

"I talked to Sue, and she told me about the babies, and I just…I'm so sorry. I just had to try and come see you. Come see both of you. I've been sober for over a year now, and I'm…" Her voice cracked as she looked between Jefferson and me. "I'm so sorry I hurt you both. I'd give anything to take it away."

When I looked toward Ari, she was smiling and crying, and in her arms, Luke was just watching the whole show. I had to smile. He looked exactly like Jefferson, but he had one hundred percent of Ari's personality.

"As God as my witness, I promise you both that I'll never hurt or leave either one of you again. I don't deserve your forgiveness, but I swear to you, I will earn back your love with every ounce of energy I have in my body."

Jefferson took a step away and smiled at our mom. "Mom…I have someone I'd like for you to meet," Jefferson said as he reached out for Luke.

"Dada!" Luke laughed.

Mom gasped and started giggling as more tears rolled down her face. I couldn't help but smile.

I glanced at my mother. I needed her more than I ever thought I did. My heart actually felt like it was finally healing.

Jefferson grinned so big. "Mom, any special name you want him to call you?"

She shook her head as she wiped away the tears. "Whatever he wants!" she said.

"Luke, can you say hi to your Gramma?"

Luke looked right at Mom. It was as if he were looking into her soul with how he was staring at her.

"Well, hello there, my sweet baby boy! You look exactly like your father."

"I told you!" Ari said with a laugh.

Mom turned toward Ari and smiled. "Arianna, sweetheart, how are you?"

Ari let out a small chuckle. "I'm doing wonderful. Thank you, Mrs. Johnson."

"Please, sweetheart, call me Sharon."

Ari nodded. "Sharon, it is!"

"Does he really look like me, Mom?" Jefferson asked.

Sharon smiled and nodded. "Spitting image of when you were his age. He might be just a tad more handsome though." She winked.

Jefferson threw his head back and laughed, and then he held Luke out toward our mother.

She looked shocked. "Are you sure?"

Jefferson nodded. "Everyone deserves a second chance," he said as he looked at me and winked.

When my mother took Luke in her arms, I could tell she was fighting back the tears.

"I'm so happy to meet you, Luke."

I walked up and kissed Luke on the cheek. "Luke, can you say Gramma?"

As Luke stared at her, he laughed, and then everyone began laughing with him.

Then, Luke said, "Mam."

Everyone stopped.

"What did he just say?" Ari and Jefferson asked at the same time.

My mother started to giggle as she said, "Gramma."

Luke laughed again. "Mam!"

My head snapped up at Jefferson. "Is he…"

Ari laughed as she started jumping up and down. "I knew he was going to be brilliant!"

My heart started pounding. "I think he's trying to say it, Mom."

"Mam!"

I looked over at Gunner and then back at my mother.

*Is this all happening? Is my mother standing in front of me with Luke in her arms? Is she really sober…and happy?*

"Jefferson, I think Luke heard you calling her mom, so he's trying to do the same!" Ari said.

Jeff started laughing.

Gunner reached for my hand, and when I turned to him, he was looking back toward the house. I glanced over, and I saw Garrett sitting on the front porch, holding Alex. When Garrett gave me that knock-me-over smile of his, I started to laugh. He must have been watching this entire thing take place. After I nodded, he stood up and began walking toward us with my precious baby.

Jefferson, Ari, and my mom were laughing, still trying to get Luke to say *Gramma* instead of *Mam*.

When Garrett reached us, my mother looked at him and then Alex. As she started crying again, my heart broke all over.

*She wasted all those years. She missed everything—my wedding, my pregnancy, and the birth of my child.*

Jefferson reached for Luke, and I was shocked when Luke started crying.

"Mam!"

Jeff and Ari looked stunned.

"Wow, Sharon. That didn't take long for him to fall for you!" Ari said with a giggle.

Mom smiled and kissed Luke on the cheek. "I'm going to meet your cousin, my sweet little man," she said as she handed Luke to Jefferson.

Garrett smiled as my mom turned back to Alex. "Mrs. Johnson, it's a real pleasure."

"Mom, this is Garrett Mathews, Gunner's grandfather. Garrett, this is my mom, Sharon," I said.

My mother went to shake Garrett's hand, but instead, he grabbed it and kissed the back. I watched as a blush crossed my mother's cheeks.

*I wonder if my father was ever romantic with her. Did he treat her like Gunner treats me? Or how Jack treats Grace? Did he love her like Garrett loves Emma?*

"The pleasure is all mine. It's an honor to meet you," my mother said.

I took Alex from Garrett and kissed her on the forehead. As I glanced over to Gunner, I saw him smiling at me with tears in his eyes. I couldn't pull my eyes away from him. His gaze held mine, and my heart swelled with so much love for him.

*He's my rock. He's the air that I breathe. I don't think I could have done this without knowing he would be right by my side.*

I turned and faced my mom. The moment I saw her tears, I felt mine. *I'm really going to do this. I'm going to open my heart to her and trust that she won't break it.* I glanced one more time at Gunner, and he nodded and winked at me.

"Mom…" I barely got it out. I had to clear my throat. "I'd like for you to meet our daughter. Her name is Alexandra Eryn Mathews. We call her Alex for short."

My mother allowed her tears to fall like rain. She finally let out a deep breath as she looked me in the eyes. "She's the most beautiful thing I've ever seen besides you, your brother, and Luke. Ellie, she's…she's…"

"Perfect?"

My mother laughed. "Yes! She's perfect. How old is she?"

"Almost ten weeks old." I smiled.

"May I?" my mother asked as she extended her arms.

"Yes! Of course."

I placed my child into the arms of the woman who had hurt me more than I cared to even remember. At the same moment, the memories of all the times she'd loved me came flooding back into my mind.

I thought of a time when she had taken me shopping for an Easter dress.

As she was putting up my hair, she'd said, "Your eyes are the most magical things I've ever seen, Ellie."

Another time, she had taken me to the park, and we'd chased one another for hours. Whenever she would catch me, she would laugh and tickle me.

At night, she would sometimes read me a love story about a prince who saved the princess from a terrible dream, and then they lived happily ever after.

*Oh. My. God. Why didn't I remember any of this until now? Why has my mind been filled with all the bad memories?*

My mom had been talking to Alex, saying how beautiful she was, while I was lost in my memories.

"The story."

My mother looked at me, confused. "You want me to tell her a story?" She laughed.

"No, Mom. I just remembered the story you used to tell me every night. It was the one about the prince who would come and save the princess from her terrible dream. She was trapped in a nightmare and wanted so badly to escape."

My mom's smile faded just a bit.

"Mom…that was you, wasn't it?"

"Ellie, how do you even remember that? You were so little when I told you that story."

I looked at Gunner. "Gunner, will you please take Alex for a bit?"

"Um…sure, babe."

My mother handed Alex to Gunner and then glanced between Jefferson and me.

"Can the three of us go for a walk?" I asked Jefferson and my mom.

"Of course," Jefferson and my mother said at the same time.

I watched as Gunner, Garrett, and Ari walked into the house. Ari turned back with a worried look. I smiled and nodded. She mouthed, *I love you*, to me and blew a kiss.

Jefferson put his arms out for my mom and me to take.

We walked a good quarter mile in complete silence.

"Mom, did Dad treat you good while he was with you?" I asked.

My mother stopped walking. She sighed as she looked over toward a tree. "Can we sit down, kids? I have a story to tell you. It's one I should have told you years ago. Really, I should have told someone years ago."

Jeff led us over to an oak tree where we all sat in a circle on the ground.

My mother took a deep breath and slowly let it out. "I was sixteen years old when I met your father. He swept me off my feet and promised me the world. Of course, it was easy to fall for him. He had your handsome looks, Jeff, and your breathtaking, beautiful blue eyes, Ellie."

I looked over at Jefferson and smiled.

"All my girlfriends told me how lucky I was to get the most popular boy in the whole school. He played football as the star quarterback. He had big dreams of playing in college and then going pro. We dated all through high school. Our senior year, he was signed on with the University of Texas."

When my mom glanced at Jefferson, he seemed to stiffen up just a bit.

"Anyway, I was thrilled because we wouldn't have to leave Austin. My parents didn't really have the money to send me to school, so I made sure I got good grades, and I ended up earning a scholarship to UT. My parents and your father were beyond thrilled. As a graduation present to your father, his parents bought him a small house close to UT. On graduation night, he asked me to marry him. I'd never been so happy in my life. I was madly in love with him and ready to start a life with him."

I grinned and looked at Jefferson. "So, you were high school sweethearts?"

She smiled and nodded. "Yes. Your father is the only man I have ever dated or been with."

*Wow.*

"Things were wonderful for the first year. I was doing well in school, and your father was beyond happy. He was playing football and getting his degree in engineering. He was preparing to take over his father's company after he graduated UT."

Jefferson glanced over at me. He seemed to be putting two and two together...and so was I.

"Then, I got pregnant. I was so happy and so excited, but I was also shocked as shit!" My mother laughed. "Your father was playing in a game against Texas A&M in College Station, so I decided to drive there and surprise him with the big news. I was late, and the game had already started, so he had no idea I was there. After they won, I made my way down to the sidelines where everyone was celebrating, and I saw your dad talking to a girl. I had seen her before at the home games. I'd even talked to her a few times. Angie...she was the sister of another player."

She stopped talking as she stared out to where the cows were now grazing. She smiled slightly and shook her head. Then, she took another deep breath and let it out. "I was just about to call out his name when he leaned down and kissed her."

*Oh no! Oh god, my poor mother.*

"I just stood there like a fool and watched them. It wasn't just a small kiss. It was filled with passion. I wanted so badly to look away, but I couldn't. When your father pulled away from her, he looked up and saw me standing there. His smile faded, and all I could do was walk back to my car. I felt completely numb."

"Ah shit, Mom." Jefferson reached out for her hand.

She grinned, putting her hand in his and placing her other one on top of Jefferson's. "He called out after me, but I kept walking away. He finally caught up to me and grabbed my arm. He asked for me to let him explain. I couldn't even think straight. The only thing I got out was that I wanted to surprise him. I said I had news to share with him. He placed his hands on my face and started kissing me. I was so lost in the kiss and the love I had for him that I just melted. Afterward, he told me how much he loved me and only me and how he had made a mistake by kissing Angie. Oh, he went on and on. I shook my head as I blurted out that I was pregnant."

"What did he do?" I asked.

"He smiled and picked me up. He kept telling me how happy he was." My mother smiled and let out a small laugh. "I believed him."

Jefferson looked toward me. "Mom, did y'all ever talk about this girl, Angie, again?"

She shook her head. "No. He never brought her up, and I didn't either. He'd promised me it was just that one time, and it would never happen again. Your father had talked me into giving up school for a while, so I could stay home with Jeff. I wanted nothing more than to become a nurse, but he said I could go back once you started school, Jeff.

"Then, one night, I decided to have my parents babysit Jeff, so I could surprise your dad with an evening alone together. We hadn't been out in so long, and I just wanted to spend some time alone…well, you know how that is. Jeff, you were two years old at the time, and you were so full of spit and fire." She laughed. "I just needed a break."

Leaning back, she let the little bit of sun peeking through the branches hit her face. "Considering my last surprise didn't go over so well, I should have known it was a mistake to surprise him. He was interning at his dad's engineering office, so I knew where he was. After I dropped off Jeff, I called the office at lunchtime to see how his day had been going, and he told me he was going to be working about an hour later than usual that night. I thought that was perfect. I planned on dropping by the office and waiting for him, so we could go to dinner and maybe a movie. When I got there, the security officer let me in. The closer I got to the office, the more apparent it became that he wasn't alone. When I heard laughter—his and a woman's—my heart started pounding. I opened the door a little, and I saw him in his chair…with Angie sitting on his desk."

I let out a gasp.

"I had the same reaction! His tie was off, and he was massaging her bare feet. I watched his hand moving up and down her leg. I wanted to throw up. I pushed the door open more and said something about her being his reason for working late. Of course, it was déjà vu. I left, and he ran after me. I couldn't believe I was so stupid, but at the same time, he was my entire life. My heart was shattered. Again."

"What happened, Mom?" Jefferson asked.

"He asked Angie to leave, and then we fought like we had never fought before. It just so happened that she was interning there, too, and he said he'd run into her, but nothing else had happened. The more he talked, the more upset I got. When I told him I was going to leave with Jeff and stay with my parents for a few days, he blew up. He grabbed me, and one thing led to another. Before I knew it, he had me on the sofa, and—"

I put my hand over my mouth. "He didn't force you, did he?"

She had tears in her eyes. "No. I loved him so much. I would have done anything for him…anything to be with him. Later, I found out I was pregnant again. Things were never the same. He grew distant, but when you were born, Ellie, he seemed like he was happy again. It lasted for a few years. Then, one day, he came home, and Angie was with him. He told me he was leaving me for her, and the only reason he'd stayed as long as he did was because he felt guilty for 'knocking me up with another baby.' Those were his words, not mine."

*Oh Jesus. I think I'm going to be sick.*

"Jesus H. Christ, Mom. He said that to you?" Jefferson shook his head.

She smiled and nodded. "When he left, my world just fell apart. I had no job, no money, and a broken heart. A friend of mine came over one night and talked me into going out. I got drunk and had so much fun," she said with a gruff laugh. "It was the first time I didn't actually think about him. Since the alcohol seemed to help me forget, I moved from beer to hard liquor. The only problem was that the hurt turned to anger. I started to blame you, Ellie, for everything. He would show up randomly while you kids were at school. He'd tell me how sorry he was, and then before I knew it, I was sleeping with him."

She shook her head and glanced up at me. "After you left, Ellie, I realized all the time I'd wasted being angry. I almost ruined your life and that caused me to wake up and see that I needed to be rescued from the hell I was living in. So, I decided I was checking into rehab and making a new life for myself. If I got myself clean, I knew the first thing I was going to do would be to ask forgiveness from both of you."

"Oh god, Mom. What a dirty, rotten bastard," I said.

She laughed and agreed.

"When was the last time you saw him, Mom?" Jefferson asked.

"About a year ago." She smiled. "I was on a date, believe it or not!"

Jefferson and I both laughed.

"With my counselor." She held up her hands. "I know! I know!"

"How did you feel when you saw him?" I asked.

"Free—like his hold on me was finally broken." She shook her head. "I need you both to know something though. I have no doubt in my mind that at one time, your father was just as much in love with me as I was with him. And I truly believe he loved you both. But now, I have someone in my life who is my prince. He literally rescued me. Just like in my story, Ellie."

We talked for a bit longer before making our way back to the house. Garrett invited my mother over to his house to meet Emma, Jack, and Grace and to spend more time with the kids. Since we were all going out, Luke and Alex were going to stay with them tonight.

As we sat in Emma's kitchen, I watched as my mother talked with two of the most important women in my life, and a sense of calm came over me. My mom was holding Alex in her arms when she looked over at me and smiled. I got up and walked over to her.

"Grace, could you please hold Alex for a bit?" my mother asked as she turned toward Grace.

Then, she held out her arms for me, and I walked right into her embrace.

"I'm so sorry for all the pain and hurt I caused you," she whispered into my ear.

"I love you, Mom. I really do love you." I pulled away from her and smiled.

She laughed while she wiped the tears away from my face as I did the same for her.

"I love you, too, Ellie Marie Mathews. I love you so much. Thank you. Thank you so much, baby girl, for giving me a second chance. You have no idea how much I need you and your brother."

Jefferson came into the kitchen and took a good look at us before he walked up and wrapped his arms around us. "Mom…"

"Yes, Jeff?"

"I forgot to tell you. You're gonna be a grandmother again."

# Chapter Thirty-Four
## Jeff

"What are you smiling about over there?" Ari asked, reaching for my hand.

"The look on my mom's face when I told her she was going to be a grandmother again."

Ari started laughing. "Yeah, it was priceless. I'm so glad she finally made the move to come and see y'all, Jeff."

I smiled as I thought about Ellie. I knew how she had dreamed of this moment, especially when she'd found out she was pregnant. I remembered the day we'd walked along the river when she told me how much she wished our mother could help her through her pregnancy because she felt so scared. My heart had broken for her. She'd had Grace there, but it hadn't been the same thing.

"I can't wait to see Amanda! I feel like I haven't seen her in so long! I wonder if she'll have the baby before she graduates," Ari said.

"I just hope everything works out for them with the move. I hate that they are moving to Florida."

Ari grinned. "We'll have a place to visit now, I guess."

I glanced over and smiled at her before looking straight ahead.

"Okay, why in the hell is Gunner not going? It's a damn green light!" Ari said.

After sitting there through the whole green light, I jumped out of my truck and ran up to his. I was about to knock on his window when I saw that he was kissing Ells.

*What in the fuck?*

I banged on the window, and they both jumped.

Gunner rolled down his window. "What's wrong?"

"You just sat through a damn green light while you were sucking face with my baby sister, you douche."

Gunner gave me that damn smile of his. "I can't help it if I sweep your baby sister off her feet, dude," he said with a wink.

Ellie started laughing as Ari honked the horn.

"Fucker!" I jogged back to my truck and jumped in, shaking my head. "Stupid romantic ass."

Ari started laughing as Gunner punched it when the light turned green again, and we made our way to Luckenbach.

As soon as we pulled up and parked, Ari jumped out of the truck and ran over to Ellie. I knew she had been dying to talk to her. Gunner smiled and gave me another wink.

*Bastard. Thinks he's all romantic and shit. I can be just as romantic as his ass.* "Keep on smiling, dude. I've got my game on tonight," I said as I slapped his back.

Gunner started laughing. "Yeah, okay…if you think you've got what it takes to outromance me, dude, bring it."

"Oh, I will. I am! You wait and see."

I turned around to see Heather with a big-ass smile on her face as Ari and Ellie attacked her. They each grabbed her arm and started heading into the dance hall. I watched as they walked by. They were talking so damn fast that my head was spinning from just trying to figure out what they were saying.

*Baby…twins…cribs…wedding…*

Gunner turned to me, and he looked just as confused. I shrugged my shoulders and glanced back to see Josh walking up with the biggest damn smile I'd ever seen on his face.

I stuck out my hand to shake his. "Congratulations, Daddy!"

Josh laughed. "Twins! Can you fucking believe it? Twins."

Gunner started laughing as he slapped Josh on the back. "Let's buy you twin beers."

When we walked in, I saw Scott right away. "Ah hell. What's Scott doing here?"

Gunner shook his head. "Dude, he's not after Ari. He never was. He just likes fucking with you."

"How do you know that?"

Gunner looked over toward Scott and then back at me. "Look at who he's watching like a hawk. He can't keep his eyes off her."

Josh and I both noticed at the same time, and then we both asked, "Jessie?"

"Yep. He stopped by the other night, and we had a few beers. He opened up and said he hasn't been able to stop thinking about her since the night he drove her home after they dropped off my drunk ass."

"Really? Jessie, huh?" I said with a smile on my face.

"Dude, Ari is so head over heels in love with you. You ain't got nothing to worry about," Josh said with a chuckle and started toward the bar.

After about four beers, I was feeling pretty good. Ari was having fun, and Ellie was so damn happy that my heart was overflowing.

That was when I saw the bastard talking to the DJ. *What in the hell is his romantic ass up to?* "Ah hell…what's he doing, Josh?"

Josh looked over toward Gunner and shrugged his shoulders. "Don't know."

Gunner started to walk back toward us, but he was focusing only on Ellie.

"Holy hell, Ellie. That boy is looking at you with nothing but love in his eyes," Amanda said.

I glanced over at Brad and Amanda. She was sitting on his lap, and his hands were on her belly. I smiled, thinking about how far they had both come in the last few weeks.

Then, Kenny Chesney's "Because of Your Love" started to play. Gunner walked up and reached for Ellie's hand. "Dance with me?"

Ellie smiled and stood up as he kissed the back of her hand. As they were heading out to the dance floor, Gunner turned around and winked at me.

I watched while they were dancing, and Ellie buried her face into his chest. I had to hand it to him. He made my sister happy. I grinned just a bit at the thought of my best friend and sister being so in love with each other.

"He loves her so much," Ari said from behind me. She put her arms around me and kissed my cheek.

"I know he does."

"He's so sweet with the way he's always sweeping her off her feet."
*Wait. What?*

She moved around and sat down next to me, facing Amanda and Heather.

"Did Ellie tell you how he packed up everything the other day and took her and Alex to the river for a picnic?" Heather asked.

The other two sighed.

I looked over at Josh, and he just smiled and shrugged his shoulders. Then, I glanced toward Brad.

"Don't even try, dude. He's got us all beat," Brad said.

*Fuck this shit.* I stood up and walked over to the DJ. *I can be just as romantic as Gunner.*

I asked the DJ to play a certain song, and he gave me a thumbs-up. When I went back to our table, I noticed Brad and Josh laughing at me.

*Bastard friends.*

Ari tilted her head at me and smiled. Gunner and Ellie were standing there, talking to Heather, when I sat down.

Leaning down, Gunner whispered in my ear, "Hope you picked a good song."

I snapped my head around to him. He started laughing, and I was just about to curse his ass out when "Like Jesus Does" by Eric Church started.

I jumped up and pulled Ari to me. "I love you, Ari." I kissed her with as much passion as I could. When I moved away, I picked her up and carried her out to the dance floor. After I slowly let her down, I kissed her again. "This song is for you, baby."

I saw the tears building in her eyes. She grabbed the back of my neck and brought me in for another kiss. Her low moan moved through my body like water.

She pulled away from my lips and looked up at me. "I love you so much. You have no idea how much I love you."

I smiled at the love of my life as I wiped away the tear rolling down her face. "I think I have a pretty good idea. I love you, too, baby…so damn much. You will never know how much I need you. My life would be nothing without you and Luke." I placed my hand on her stomach as I looked into her beautiful green eyes. "And our baby girl."

She buried her head in my chest as she started crying. Then, she began laughing as she looked up at me.

"What if it's a boy?" she asked with a wink.

I shook my head. "Nope. I feel it in my soul. Our baby girl is sending us her sister."

She looked into my eyes and smiled. "I feel it, too."

We finished off the dance and then danced to the next song.

Afterward, we walked back toward everyone. Gunner was sitting there with that damn smile on his face. I smiled right back. *Take that for romance, you ass.*

Brad started laughing.

"What? I totally had that," I said as I gave Brad a dirty look.

Brad shook his head and whispered something into Amanda's ear. Amanda got up and moved to another chair as Brad started walking up to the DJ.

I glanced over toward Gunner.

He started laughing. "Dude, what the fuck did you start?"

I grinned and shrugged my shoulders.

Brad turned and came back with a big-ass smile on his face. He walked up to Amanda and held out his hand. She looked up at him as she put her hand in his.

He pulled her closer to him. "Will you dance with me to the next song?"

Amanda smiled and reached up to kiss him. "Of course I will."

Just then SafetySuit's "Never Stop" started playing as Brad led Amanda to the dance floor.

I looked at Gunner.

He just started shaking his head. "Fucker…that's a good song."

Gunner looked at Josh, who was taking a drink of his beer as he shook his head.

*Damn it.*

"Look at those two cutting it up out there!" Ellie walked up and sat on Gunner's lap.

Sitting down next to me, Ari watched Brad and Amanda dance. "I'm so glad they worked things out. I pray that Brad stays strong."

I couldn't pull my eyes away from Ari. She was so beautiful.

She looked back at me as she tilted her head. "They're gonna be okay, right?"

"Yeah, baby. They're gonna be okay."

Scott walked up and reached out his hand toward me. I stood up and shook it. He reached for Gunner's hand. "Hey, Gun."

"What's up Scott?" Gunner said with a wink.

"Hey, Scott. Listen, I'm really glad you're gonna make it to the wedding," Josh said, standing with a smile.

Scott grinned and looked at Heather and then back at Josh. "You know it, dude. Oh, I've been meaning to tell you that the office furniture you made me is great. I've gotten so many compliments on it. I also gave out your phone number to a few people."

Josh nodded. "I really appreciate that."

"You're very talented, Josh. I see you going really far with this." He looked at Heather and gave her a big smile. "Congratulations. I heard you're having twins."

Heather smiled and blushed.

"So, who all is heading to the beach for the wedding?" Scott asked.

"It'll mostly be just family and friends along with a few business associates that I've known since my dad ran the business."

"Is Jenny helping to plan it?" Scott asked.

When I looked over at Gunner, he smiled and winked at me. We both knew where this was going.

Heather smiled. "Yes! She's amazing. I mean, only Jen could put together a wedding in just a few short weeks."

"An out-of-town wedding to top it off!" Josh said with a laugh.

Scott smiled. "So…is Jessie going to be there?"

Heather perked up a bit as she snapped her head over toward Ellie. "Yep, Dewey also," Heather said.

Brad and Amanda came back to the table as I noticed Josh walking away.

"Hey, Scott. Damn, man, it's been a long time."

"Hey, Brad. Shit, it has been. How are you doing?"

Brad looked over at Amanda and put his hand on her stomach. "Pretty damn good!"

Scott glanced at Amanda's pregnant belly and laughed. "I'd say so."

Brad and Scott talked for a bit as I looked around for Josh. He was talking and laughing with the DJ.

*Ah, so the little bastard is going to have his hand in the romance department this evening.*

Gunner reached up and handed Scott a beer as Scott sat down.

Then, Gunner turned to me. He leaned in toward me, so only I could hear him. "Does he think he stands a chance?" Gunner looked out at Josh.

I laughed. "I guess he does. This should be interesting to watch."

Gunner and I both sat back and started to drink our beers as we watched Josh talking to the DJ.

"He's probably asking the DJ to recommend a good song," Gunner said with a chuckle.

Brad sat down as he started laughing. "Think so? This is gonna be good. Gotta give him props for trying though. I think I have both of y'all beat with my song."

Gunner and I both looked at Brad as he smiled and took a sip of his Coke.

"Ari cried," I said.

"Oh, come on, dude," Brad said.

Scott asked, "What in the hell are y'all talking about?"

Gunner looked over at the girls and saw they were deep in conversation. "We have a little romance contest going on. Trying to see which one of us can outromance the other with our song choices."

Scott's mouth dropped open. "That's fucked up, y'all. Do the girls know what you're doing?"

At the same time, Gunner, Brad, and I all said, "No."

Josh shook the DJ's hand, and as he started to walk back toward us, he had a cocky-ass smile plastered on his face.

*Poor guy. He really doesn't stand a chance.*

He walked right past us and up to Heather. He took her hand and pulled her up to him. "I have something special just for you," Josh said before he kissed the back of Heather's hand.

Gunner muttered, "Pesh," under his breath.

Ellie smacked Gunner on the back of his head. "Knock it off."

Just then, the DJ asked for everyone's attention. "Listen up, y'all. I've had a special request from one very lucky man in the house tonight. He's getting married in a couple days."

Everyone started to clap and whistle.

"Ah hell," Gunner and I said at the same time.

Brad and Scott started laughing.

"Josh, bring your beautiful future bride out onto the dance floor," the DJ said.

Josh started leading Heather out to the dance floor. As he passed us, he smiled and winked. "Watch how it's done, gentlemen."

"Little bastard!" Gunner called out, earning another slap on the head from Ellie.

We watched as Josh walked Heather out to the middle of the dance floor. Her face was bright red, and when he kissed her on the cheek, all I heard were *oohs* and *aahs*. Someone handed Josh a microphone, and then he got down on one knee.

Brad, Gunner, and I all leaned forward.

"What in the hell is he doing? He can't ask her to marry him. He's already done that!" I said.

Ari smacked me on the shoulder. "Be quiet for Christ's sake!"

"Holy hell, she's already crying, and he hasn't even started talking yet," Brad said.

"Heather, I never in my life thought I could be as happy as I am in this very moment. The idea of spending the rest of my life with you just about brings me down to both knees. I cannot wait to make you my wife. I want to make all your dreams come true. I want to be the best husband and father to our unborn babies as I possibly can."

Josh put his hand on her stomach and then kissed her belly as Heather brought her hand up to her mouth. He looked up at her and smiled.

"Is he crying?" Scott asked.

"Bastard," Gunner, Brad, and I said at the same time.

"Shh!" Ellie, Amanda, and Ari said at the same time.

"Princess, I want to be your everything." He stood up and took Heather in his arms as Keith Urban's "Your Everything" started to play.

"Oh. My. God. If that is not the most romantic thing ever!" Ellie said.

Gunner snapped his head around and looked at her.

I was still staring out at them. They were the only two dancing as everyone stood around and watched.

"Holy hell, that just swept me off my damn feet! Heather is so lucky!" Amanda said.

Brad choked on his drink.

Ari walked around and sat on my lap. Her eyes looked like they were filling with tears as she watched them dancing.

*Jesus H. Christ. Is she about to cry?*

"So incredibly romantic…wow. Heather really is lucky." She turned to me and smiled. "I think Josh won by a landslide. Don't you think, babe?"

Scott busted out laughing as I just looked at her.

All I could do was let out a small laugh before I grabbed her and brought her in for a kiss. I pulled slightly away from her lips. "He certainly did."

When she gave me that drop-dead beautiful smile of hers, my heart started racing.

"I love you, babe." She captured my lips with hers.

I kissed her and poured as much love into the kiss as I could. When she ran her hands through my hair, I wanted to just rip off her clothes and take her right here and now.

"Get a fucking room. This is a public place."

My heart stopped the moment I recognized the voice.

Ari slowly pulled away and looked at me. "You might want to make sure I don't lay eyes on that bitch, or I will kick the shit out of her. Pregnant or not."

As I looked to my left, I saw Rebecca walking off in the other direction with—*oh fuck!*—Victoria.

*How in the hell did those two hook up again? Have they even seen each other since college?*

Victoria was watching Josh and Heather dance.

As the song ended, Josh dipped Heather and kissed her. The whole place went crazy, clapping and hollering out.

When I glanced back at Ari, she was staring at me, and then we turned and looked at Heather walking back with Josh. She looked so happy, and I knew exactly what Ari was thinking because I was thinking it, too.

"How did she find out we would be here, Jeff?" Ari said with anger in her eyes.

"I don't know, baby, but we're not going to let them ruin this night."

Ari stood up as she glared at Victoria and Rebecca. "No. No, we're not."

When Heather walked up to us, I could tell she was flying high. I smiled as Ellie gave Heather a big hug, and the tears started to build up in Heather's eyes again.

"I just can't believe how perfect he is!" Heather said as she wiped away a tear.

"Who would have thunk it? My little manwhore, Josh," I said with a wink.

When Jennifer Lopez's "Dance Again" started, I looked out and saw Rebecca, Victoria, and some other bitch dancing.

*I think I'm going to puke.*

"What in the fuck are they doing here?" Amanda said.

*Shit!* I was hoping my girls wouldn't notice them, but considering the bitches were dancing like sluts right in front of us, it was hard to miss them.

I glanced over to the guys. I smiled because none of them were even looking out toward the dance floor. I also noticed when Jessie was walking up, Scott was following her every move. *Interesting.*

"Do they think they are getting the guys' attention?" Ellie asked.

"I might be six and a half months pregnant, but I can still kick some ass," Amanda said, swinging her hands all around.

I peeked over at Heather.

She grinned as she looked back at me. "Lady Marmalade."

I smiled at her and shook my head. I turned to Amanda and laughed as I glanced down at her stomach. "Can you Lady Marmalade…with that stomach of yours?"

"Fuck you, bitch. I can move better now than I ever have before. Bring it."

Ellie started jumping up and down. "Yes! I love that song!"

Then, Heather did something I never thought I would see. She went out to the dance floor and walked right between Victoria and Rebecca as she made her way to the DJ. I glanced over toward Josh, who was watching her. As she came back, she purposely cut between the dancing slut group again. Victoria never took her eyes away from Heather as she made her way back to Josh with an evil grin on her face. He took her in his arms and kissed the living shit out of her. Victoria stopped dancing and walked off the dance floor.

*Hells yeah, I'm going to buy some kick-ass outfits for the twins to show their mama how proud I am of her!*

I noticed when Heather whispered something into Josh's ear. I saw his whole face blush.

*Wow. That boy has it bad for her. There is no doubt about it. My little manwhore is no more.*

When the DJ announced "Lady Marmalade," Ellie and Amanda both let out, "Eeeppp," as they headed toward the dance floor. I walked up to Heather and hooked my arm in hers.

"Let's show these bitches how to really dance, like the sluts we're not but they are," Heather said.

Josh and Jeff tilted their heads as they just stared at her.

"Don't listen to her. She's just trying to be a badass." I looked at Heather and smiled. "Baby steps, sweets. Baby steps."

We walked onto the dance floor right when Lil' Kim began singing. Ellie started dancing, and then Amanda, Heather, and I followed suit. I turned and smiled at Jeff as he watched us dance. Using my finger, I motioned for him to come and dance with me.

Jeff got up and walked right up to me. He grabbed me, pulled me right into him, and started grinding on me. I laughed as I watched Josh, Gunner, and Brad get up and start dancing with us.

Jeff laughed as he leaned in toward my ear. "Jesus, Amanda can move that pregnant stomach, can't she?"

I looked at Amanda and smiled.

Ellie grabbed Jessie as she was walking by and dragged her out onto the dance floor. I looked around for Scott, but I wouldn't dare go get him. Jeff would have a heart attack.

Then, I saw Heather run over and pull Scott out to the dance floor. She so strategically put him right next to Jessie. When Jessie turned around and saw him there, she blushed, and he smiled.

"Do you think Scott likes Jessie?" I asked Jeff.

He looked over toward them. As he turned back to me, he smiled.

"Yeah, I thought so, too!" I said.

Brett Eldredge's "Don't Ya" started to play. I watched as Josh grabbed Heather, and they took off two-stepping. Gunner picked up Ellie and spun her around before they went back to sit at our table. Amanda and Brad took off dancing.

I looked at Jeff and winked.

"I'm reading your mind, baby!"

Jeff walked up and took Jessie's hand. "Two-step with this cowboy," he said.

Jessie started laughing.

Scott gave me a smile and shook his head. "He'll beat my ass!"

I laughed as he took me in his arms, and we started dancing.

Scott and I only danced around the floor one time before Jeff brought Jessie right up next to us. I saw Jeff's smile a mile away, and I had to giggle.

"Partner switch!" Jeff yelled as he spun Jessie right over to Scott.

"Wait! What?" Jessie said.

Scott smiled and held out his hand.

The moment he swept her away, I jumped into Jeff's arms.

"Take me home and make love to me, cowboy."

"It would be my pleasure. Let's blow this place, and take advantage of a free night."

I raised my eyebrows up and down as he took my hand and led me off the dance floor.

Ellie smiled as we walked up. "Heading out, I take it?"

"Yep, but I have to piss like a racehorse again," I said as I grabbed Ellie's arm to go with me.

Heather came up behind me. "Oh hell, so do I. I'll go, too."

"Me, too! This kid, I swear, is camped out on my bladder." Amanda kissed Brad before joining us.

While we started making a beeline to the restroom, Ellie and Amanda were taking bets on whether Heather or I would deliver first.

"That's not fair," I said over my shoulder as I walked into the restroom first. "Heather is having twins. She's gonna pop before me."

When I turned around, I came face-to-face with Rebecca. I instantly balled up my hands into fists. Then, I looked over at Victoria.

She looked down at Heather's stomach. "You sure got knocked-up fast."

I went to say something, but Heather stepped in front of me.

"Hello, Tori. Your eye healed nicely," Heather said.

Victoria looked over at me and smirked. "So, how far along are you?" Victoria asked Heather.

Heather just stared at Victoria.

"I heard you and Josh were getting married. Did he get you pregnant and feel sorry for you?"

I saw Ellie coming up from the side, but Amanda grabbed her and started laughing.

"Holy shit, Victoria. This is your dark alley, sweetheart. If you were smart, you would just keep your mouth shut and take you and your lying whore friend here and leave," Amanda said.

Rebecca let out a gasp and started to walk over to Amanda.

I stepped in front of Rebecca and pushed her back. "You take one step toward her, and I'll make sure you're limping out of here, you fucking bitch. I'm so sick of you and your bitch-ass friends doing nothing but causing drama. You lost." I looked at Victoria. "You both lost something you were never even in the running for. So, move on, ladies, and go find your own men."

Rebecca looked at me and laughed. "Come on, Tori. They're not even worth it."

Victoria started to leave, but then she stopped right in front of Heather and grinned. "I bet you've never even given him a blow job before, have you, Smeather?"

The next thing I knew, Heather reached back and then knocked the hell out of Victoria. Rebecca screamed and jumped out of the way. She looked at me like I was going to punch her. She stepped back and then took off for the restroom door.

Victoria grabbed her jaw and glared at Heather. "You bitch!"

Heather walked up to her and gave her a push, causing her to fall back into the sink. "If you ever so much as get within ten feet of me, Josh, or any of my friends...I'll make sure I break your goddamn nose next time."

I stood there, stunned. I looked back at Ellie and Amanda. Ellie's mouth was hanging open, and Amanda had a smile as big as the Texas sky. I looked back at Victoria.

"Don't worry. I have no intentions of being anywhere near you or your crazy-ass friends!" Victoria started to walk off, and she made sure to stay as far away from Heather as she could.

The moment the restroom door shut, Heather grabbed her hand. "Oh my god! Oh holy shit! I think I broke my hand!"

Ellie went running over and looked at Heather's hand. "Oh no. It's swelling. Josh is going to kill us!" she said.

"Oh. My. God! I'm getting married in two days, and I just broke my hand!"

I walked over and turned on the cold water. "It's okay, sweets. It's your right hand." When I turned around with a wet paper towel, Ellie, Heather and Amanda were all staring at me. "What? It's not like it's her left hand for Christ's sake."

When we walked out, Josh was making his way toward the restrooms. He took one look at Heather holding her hand, and he ran right up to her. "What happened?"

"Oh my god, Josh! I punched her! You would have been so proud of me. I threatened her, too!" Heather said proudly.

Josh looked like he was stunned. He glanced over at me, and I just shrugged my shoulders.

"I think she broke her hand, Josh. We need to get her to the hospital," I said.

"Wait. Who did you punch?" Josh asked as Jeff, Gunner, and Brad walked up.

"Baby, are you okay?" Brad asked Amanda.

"Oh hell, I've never been better! Ari told off Rebecca and pushed her against the wall, and then Heather pulled out her inner bitch and knocked the hell out of Victoria. It was one of the best moments of my life."

I looked over at Jeff. The smile that spread across his face made the butterflies in my stomach take off. *Shit, I want him so badly.* I smiled and winked at him.

"My feisty mama!" Jeff walked up and grabbed me.

"Only you would get turned-on by that, Jeff," Gunner said. He turned to Josh. "Do you want to leave and take Heather to the hospital in Fredericksburg?"

Josh smiled as he looked at Heather. She blushed as she started to laugh.

"My little Rocky!" Josh said. He kissed Heather, picked her up, and carried her out of the dance hall.

We all spent the rest of the night sitting at the Fredericksburg hospital while they X-rayed Heather's hand. Heather quickly came down from her high when the idea of wearing a cast on her hand during her wedding hit her full force.

When Josh and Heather walked out, her hand was wrapped in just a bandage, and we all let out a sigh of relief.

"It's just a bad sprain," Josh said with a smile.

I glanced over toward Ellie, and we both laughed. It seemed like just yesterday when that had been Ellie.

Jeff stood up and walked over to Josh. He slapped him on the back. "Well, let's get you two home and rested up. We've got a wedding in two days."

"Whose idea was it to go out tonight? I'm never going to be able to drive to South Padre Island tomorrow," Brad said with a yawn.

"Brad, are y'all sure you want to stay at the hotel tonight? You can stay with Heather and me," Josh said as he looked back at Heather and smiled.

"No, dude. We appreciate it, but I got my girl a nice room at the Inn on Barons Creek." Brad smiled at Amanda.

Josh grinned, looked around at everyone, and then took Heather in his arms. "Alright, y'all, let's get some rest, so we can head out tomorrow. I've got a very important date with the woman of my dreams in a couple days."

Once we walked into the house, I headed over to the sofa and collapsed onto it. I was so tired, so hungry, and so proud of myself for not beating the living hell out of Rebecca.

When Jeff leaned up against the wall and smiled at me, my heart dropped to my stomach, and I had to push my legs together.

*I love him so much.*

"No baby in the house, and it's the middle of the night, so no Garrett knocking on our door."

He started to walk over to me with nothing but pure passion in his eyes. He dropped to his knees and pulled me to him. After I wrapped my legs around him, he stood up and began walking us toward our bedroom. I put my arms around his neck and just held him as tight as I could. He smelled so good, and I just wanted to lick every part of his body.

He made his way over to our bed, and he slowly began to place me onto it. When I was lying down, I looked up at him and smiled. *He's so damn handsome.* I still had a hard time believing he was really all mine.

He stood up and gave me the most smoldering look I'd ever seen. "Stand up, Ari, and take off your clothes. I want to watch you."

*Oh. My. God. I think I just felt a rush of water between my legs.*

I got up and stood in front of him. He walked backward, sat down in the chair, and just stared at me.

*You can do this, Ari.* I smiled at him. I wanted to turn him on as much as he was turning me on. I leisurely started to pull my T-shirt over my head. Once I had it off, I put my hands on my stomach and moved them up and over my chest and then around to my back to unsnap my bra. I never took my eyes off of him. I gradually took off my bra and dropped it to the floor. I placed my hands on the sides of my neck and slowly moved them down. As I started to play with my nipples, I watched as Jeff licked his lips and adjusted in his seat. I smiled, knowing that I was driving him crazy.

*Time to step it up, Ari.* I gently moved my hands down and started to unbutton my pants. I slowly took them off and kicked them to the side. Then, I placed my hand into my panties as I used my other one to touch my nipple. I threw my head back and let out a long low moan.

"Motherfucker," Jeff whispered.

I smiled as I heard him moving around. I snapped my head forward and watched as he started to undress. When I began to remove my panties, he stopped undressing to stare at me. I took a few steps back and got onto the bed. Lying down, I continued to touch myself.

The next thing I knew, he was crawling on the bed.

"Not so fast." I held him up and away from me. I slid out from underneath him. "Lie on your back, Jeff."

He smiled, and I'd never seen him move so damn fast in my life.

I got off the bed, stood at the end, and smiled at him. "Feel on yourself, baby."

He lifted his head and looked at me, confused. "What?"

I glanced down at his harder-than-rock dick and licked my lips as I snapped my eyes back up at him. "You got to watch me touch myself. Now, I get to watch you."

"Ari..."

"Please, Jeff." I placed my finger inside my mouth.

"Fuck me."

"That's what I intend to do," I purred as I gave him a sexy smile.

He quickly took himself in his hand and started to move it up and down.

*Jesus, Mary, and Joseph. I had no idea how much this would turn me on!*

"Oh god, Ari...I want you so much, baby."

As I stood there, watching him play with himself, I got more turned-on by the second. It took every ounce of strength I had to not crawl on top of him. I focused on his facial expressions as I listened to him whispering my name.

When he lifted his head, he gave me a pleading look. I slowly got on the bed, crawled on top of him, and sank down onto him.

Jeff grabbed my hips. "Oh god...you feel like heaven, baby."

I didn't want to rush it, but something snapped, and I just let loose. I wanted it deeper...harder. I threw my head back as he reached around and grabbed my ass.

The next thing I knew, I was having one of the most intense orgasms of my life. I couldn't do anything but call out in pleasure.

I didn't even realize when he'd flipped us over, so he was on top. I grabbed on to the edge of the bed and arched my back to get more of him inside me.

"Harder, Jeff! Oh god! I'm going to come again!"

I couldn't believe what I was feeling. It was amazing, and it felt like it could go on forever. I called out his name as he called out mine.

Lying there, holding each other, we both caught our breaths.

"I love you so much, Arianna."

This overwhelming feeling of love just swept over my whole body. I ran my hands through his hair as I started to cry. He pulled away and wiped my tears as he smiled at me.

"I love you, too, Jeff. I love you so much. You have no idea how much."

He lowered his lips to mine, and he kissed me so slowly and sweetly. "I do, baby, because I feel the same."

When he rolled off of me, he pulled me to his side. My breathing finally started to settle as I drifted off to sleep, next to the only man I'd ever loved...the only man I will ever love.

## Chapter Thirty-Six
### Jessie

I still couldn't believe how wonderful this evening was turning out to be. Scott and I had danced together most of the night. When we weren't dancing, we were sitting and talking about horses, me moving back to Mason, and Josh and Heather's wedding. He'd even asked if I wanted to drive to South Padre Island with him.

I looked around, but I couldn't find Dewey or Aaron. *Dewey wouldn't leave without me. He's my ride.* I reached for my cell phone and hit Dew's number.

"Hey, little sister! You gettin' you some tonight?"

*What in the hell is he talking about?*

"Stop being such a dick, Dew. Where in the hell are you? This place is closing up, and I can't find you anywhere."

Dewey started laughing. "Damn that Ari. She told me you were riding home with Scott, so I left over an hour ago, Jessie. I guess Ari thought you were getting some tonight, too."

My heart dropped to my stomach. *Oh. My. God. I'm gonna kill Ari!*

I watched as Scott walked up and shrugged his shoulders. He'd gone looking for Dewey outside. I smiled and shook my head.

"Okay…well, I'll be sure to have a talk with Ari tomorrow. Thanks, Dew."

As I hung up, I felt the heat rising in my cheeks. *What if he doesn't want to give me a ride home? It's not out of his way since he passes the Mathews' place on his way home…but still. Shit, Ari!*

"What's wrong, Jessie? You look like you're going to be sick."

"Um…well, it looks like I have no ride home. Dewey left. Ari had told him I was getting a ride home with you, but I can have him come back and pick me up."

Scott's face lit up, and for one brief moment, I was happy that Ari had pulled this stunt.

When the DJ announced the last song, Scott reached for my hand. "One more dance?"

As we walked out to the dance floor, Garth Brooks's "To Make You Feel My Love" started playing. I felt like I was going to start crying. *Why do I care about him so much? I just keep hurting myself.*

He pulled me into his arms, and we slowly started to dance. I'd never danced with anyone who two-stepped so gracefully. My heart was beating so hard and fast that I was sure he could hear it. As we danced, he held me closer, and I dared to let myself believe he might be interested in me.

I fit so perfectly against him as he held me while we danced. All five foot three inches of me was wrapped in his strong arms. As the song started to come to an end, he pulled back some and looked into my eyes. I lifted my chin, and before I knew what was happening, he kissed me. I didn't mean to do it, but I let out a moan as he bit down on my bottom lip.

"Jessie…"

I couldn't even talk. My heart was pounding. I'd dreamed of this moment for so long that I just wanted to freeze it in time. I was so afraid that I was dreaming. He captured my lips with his again, and he kissed me with so much passion I wanted to cry.

He moved slightly away from my lips. "Will you come home with me, Jessie?" he whispered.

*Holy shit. Is this really happening?* I looked into his beautiful blue eyes and smiled as I barely had the strength to answer him. "Yes."

The next thing I knew, we were outside, and he had me pressed up against his truck. His hand was up the back of my shirt, and I couldn't even think straight. Everywhere he touched, my skin was on fire.

I tore my lips from his to catch my breath. "Scott, I don't do this kind of thing."

He gave me a confused look. "What kind of thing?"

"This…kissing a guy in a parking lot and saying I'll go home with him. I just wanted you to know that this isn't me."

The smile that spread across his face made me weak in the knees. I felt myself slowly sliding down his truck before he grabbed me and lifted me up. He carried me to the other side, opened the passenger door, and set me in the seat.

"I don't do this kind of thing either, angel. I've never been with anyone besides Chelsea."

My heart slammed in my chest. *What did he just say?* I could barely get it out. "What?"

He smiled, leaned in, and kissed me again before he shut the door.

*I can't breathe. He's only slept with one person—his high school sweetheart...his ex-fiancée...the only other girl who knew how much I lusted after him. Well, Heather, Ari, and Ellie also know, but they don't count. Do I tell him I've only been with Gunner? Oh shit. Oh god, I feel sick.*

He jumped into his truck and looked at me with a big ole smile. I couldn't help but smile back at him.

*Jesus H. Christ. I'm really going home with Scott Reynolds...to his house...alone...with Scott Reynolds. Oh holy hell.*

The drive to Mason was filled with laughter. I wasn't sure if we were both just nervous as hell or what. The ache between my legs needed relief so damn bad that I was ready to touch myself just to get it over with. It's been so damn long since I'd even been with anyone, so I was incredibly scared.

"I have to pee!" I shouted.

Scott looked at me like I was crazy. "What? Right now, Jessie? You can't wait a few more miles?"

I shook my head. It'd hit me like a ton of bricks. *I have to pee now! What the fuck?* He needed to pull over, or I was going to piss in my pants.

As soon as Scott pulled the truck over, I jumped out and dropped my pants right on the side of the road. The moment I started to pee, I moaned in relief.

"Shit, Jessie...don't make noises like that!"

I had to giggle. Then, I moaned again. This time, it was a little louder and lasted a bit longer. I smiled as I hopped up and was about to get my pants back on.

Then, he grabbed me and pushed me up against his truck. He kissed me and placed his hand on my bare stomach. I had the strangest feeling in my stomach. I'd never experienced this before—this intense feeling of need for someone.

He slowly slipped his hand into my panties. I felt the flood of wetness the moment he brushed against my clit.

"Oh god," I said against his lips.

"Jesus...you're so wet, angel. I need to get you home, Jessie."

"Yes...touch me, Scott."

He moved his other hand up my shirt and under my bra. The second he pinched my nipple, I felt it building.

*Jesus H. Christ. Could I have an orgasm this easily?*

Then, he slipped his fingers inside me, and that was it. I grabbed his hair and threw my head back against his truck as I cried out in pure pleasure.

As I finally came back to earth, I looked into his eyes as his lips brushed against mine.

"Oh god, Jessie...I want you so badly."

At this point, I was ready to drop to the ground and tell him to have his way with me. My chest was moving up and down so hard and fast.

"Let's go." He reached down and pulled up my pants.

I couldn't even think straight. *That was...that was...amazing.*

As we drove up his long-ass driveway, I could hear my heart beating. I'd dreamed of being with him since the first time he kissed me back in high school. Every damn time he'd called me Tiny, my heart would skip a beat. My brothers had known I liked him in high school, and they'd teased me about it.

Scott pulled up and jumped out. I looked over toward his garage. A dark BMW was parked there. *Huh, I couldn't picture Scott driving a Beemer.*

He opened the passenger door and reached in for me before I could attempt to get out of the car myself. After carrying me up the stairs leading to the front door, he slowly slid me down his body, and I could feel how much he wanted me. He put his key into the lock and pushed me back against the door as he started to kiss me. He opened the door, and he began walking me backward into the house, never breaking our kiss.

Then, I heard someone clear her throat.

Scott pulled away from me and looked to his left. "Chelsea?"

*Chelsea?* I turned to see his ex-fiancée sitting on the sofa.

Scott instantly stepped back and away from me, leaving me stunned for a second.

*Are they back together? Did he just get caught cheating? No...he told me tonight she'd left him for one of his best friends.*

Scott quickly looked at me. He must have realized what he had done because he took a step back toward me and grabbed my hand. "What in the hell are you doing in my house? How did you get in here?"

Chelsea held up a key as she looked at me like I was something she needed to get rid of and fast. Her expression should have dropped me to the ground. Then, it seemed like she was trying to make herself cry.

She stood up and turned back to Scott. "I really needed to talk to you. You weren't home, so I figured you wouldn't mind if I waited. I didn't know you were bringing a…friend home with you." She glanced back over toward me.

"Um…Jessie, you remember Chelsea?"

I nodded and tried my best to smile at her.

She looked me up and down and then turned back at Scott. "I'm really upset, Scott. I need to talk to you…in private," she said with a quick look in my direction.

Scott glanced at me and then back to her.

It should have been a no-brainer. *Tell her ass to leave and come back tomorrow.*

"Um…uh…Jessie, would you mind if I talked with Chelsea for just a bit?"

"Yes…Jessie, maybe you could go outside for a bit? Take a little walk in the moonlight. Better yet, Scott, maybe Jessie should go home."

"Um…" was all Scott said.

*Wait. What? Does he really want me to go outside and take a walk at one thirty in the morning?*

"Listen, Chelsea, it's late. Why don't you crash in the guest bedroom? Then, we can talk before I leave town tomorrow."

"What?" Chelsea and I both said at the same time.

She snapped her head over at me, shaking her head. "Why? So, you can fuck your little friend here? You want me to just sit in another room while you screw someone else?"

"No! I just meant that instead of you leaving so late, we could just talk in the morning. Jessie can sleep in another bedroom."

*Oh. My. God. It's happening all over again. How stupid could I be? What in the world ever made me think I could take the place of Chelsea Mason?*

As I glanced over at Scott, I did everything I could to keep back the tears. "I have a better idea. Why don't you just take me home? Then, y'all can have your privacy to do whatever."

Chelsea smiled at me. "That's a great idea."

Scott snapped his head from me to Chelsea. "Chelsea, will you just shut up?"

She looked stunned as she sat back down on the sofa.

I turned and pushed past Scott, making my way to his truck.

"Jessie, please wait. Jess! Stop, please."

I spun around. "I just want to go home!" I shouted. I took a deep breath and slowly let it out. "Either you take me home now, or I can have Dewey come pick me up. Hell, at this point, I'll walk home."

Aaron and Jenny lived right down the road, right before the Mathews' place, so I decided to head that way as I started to walk down his driveway.

"Stop! Please just let me take you back inside." He grabbed my arm and spun me around. "Please, Chels, let me take you back inside."

*I'm going to be sick. He just called me Chels. Don't cry. Do not cry.*

As a tear rolled down my face, he looked at me like someone had just kicked him in the stomach.

"My name is not Chels."

He closed his eyes and dropped his head. "Fuck, Jessie...I didn't mean—"

"Please...please just take me home," I whispered.

He nodded as he let me walk past him toward his truck. I opened the door and slammed it shut before he could even try to help me in. He walked around the front of his truck and looked back at his front door. When I turned back toward the door, I saw Chelsea standing there.

*Fucking bitch. I hate her.*

He got in his truck, started it up, and headed down the driveway. "Jessie—"

"Please just turn on the radio. I really don't want to talk to you."

He let out a sigh as he reached for the stereo. Right when he turned it on, Hot Chelle Rae's "Why Don't You Love Me" started to play. Looking out the window, I let out a gruff laugh and just let the tears fall.

*How could I let this happen? Again.*

I didn't even care that he knew I was crying. I didn't care about anything anymore.

"Jessie, please—"

I shook my head and prayed for God to please just let me get home fast. I closed my eyes as I listened to the words of the song. *What a perfect fucking song. I'm so tired of being hurt.*

He pulled up to Aaron and Jenny's house, and I jumped out before he could even put it in park.

He got out, ran over to me, and grabbed me. "Jessica, please let me talk to you."

I looked up at him and laughed. "Do you remember the first time you kissed me?"

He closed his eyes and then opened them again. "Of course I do...under the bleachers after football practice."

"Do you remember why you walked away from me?"

He just stared at me. His eyes filled with sadness.

"Well, let me refresh your memory. After you kissed me, you pulled away and looked into my eyes. At that moment, I gave you my heart and soul. Only, you threw it to the ground and stomped on it. Chelsea walked by and said, 'Hi,' to you. You took one look at her and turned back to me with a smile. Then, you laughed and said, 'Thanks for the kiss, Tiny!' before you ran after her."

Scott went to say something but then shut his mouth. I stepped away from him and started to walk up the stairs leading to the front door.

"Jessie…I was an idiot, and we were in high school. I had no idea you felt like that about me. I thought you were just Aaron and Dewey's—"

I turned and looked at him. "Little, tiny sister…yeah, I know."

"Jessie, please drive with me to the coast tomorrow. Please."

I shook my head as I felt tears building again. As one dropped, I turned away from him. "This was a mistake. It was all just a mistake. I was stupid to think you'd ever be interested in me like that."

"Fuck, Jessie. Would you please just stop and let me talk to you? Chelsea is not a part of my life anymore. I want to get to know you more, angel. I want to be with you, Jessie. Please don't do this."

"When I saw you look at her…" I sucked in a breath of air, trying to stop myself from crying. "And you didn't tell her to leave and come back tomorrow, Scott. You made your choice…and again, you picked her."

I ran up the stairs. I opened the front door and shut it before he could say anything. Leaning against the door, I listened as he started his truck and then headed down the driveway. I slowly sank to the floor as I let the tears fall freely.

*I was so stupid to think anything could ever happen between us.*
*Never again.*

# Chapter Thirty-Seven
## Scott

When I pulled into my driveway, I saw Chelsea's car still sitting there. I slammed the steering wheel. "Fuck!"

I walked into the house and looked around for her. "Chelsea?" *Where in the hell is she?*

"I'm up in your room," she called out.

My heart started to pound. *Ah shit.*

I headed to my room, wondering what in the hell she was doing there. The door was cracked open. When I pushed it open, I saw Chelsea lying naked on my bed.

*Oh fuck.*

She smiled and gestured for me to come to her. For one brief second, I wanted nothing more than to go and make love to her, but then Jessie's smiling face popped into my head and brought me back to my senses. I thought about Chelsea saying that she never loved me and she was leaving me for Mitch.

"Get dressed, Chels, and meet me downstairs." I turned and walked away.

"Scott! If you walk any farther, you will never have another chance with me. Ever."

I closed my eyes and let out sigh. "I'll see you downstairs."

I reached for my phone in my back pocket and sent Jessie a text message.

*Scott: Making Chelsea leave. Please let me pick you up in the morning. Please.*

I waited a few minutes, and when she hadn't replied, I decided to call her. I hit dial on her number, and after three rings, it went to voice mail. "Jessie, I really need to talk to you. Please call me back. Chelsea is leaving, and I…well, I just really need to talk to you."

"I don't think I've seen you resort to begging before, Scott. If it's sex you want so much, you had your chance a minute ago."

I turned and glared at her. "What the fuck are you doing here anyway?"

"I had a fight with Mitch."

*You have got to be kidding me.* "And?"

She shrugged her shoulders. "And that's it. He said some mean things, and I was upset, so I decided to come see you. Maybe leaving you was a mistake. I mean, we were so good together." She made her way over to me and went to sit in my lap.

I put my hand up to stop her. If she had come to me a few weeks ago…I probably would have been a fool and taken her back. But now, there was Jessie. Something about Jessie made me feel all weird inside. It was like nothing I'd ever experienced with Chelsea. When I'd touched Jess, it felt like fire was moving through my body. When I'd kissed her, I just wanted to crawl deep inside her. I'd never experienced anything like that before. With Chelsea, it had all been just…sex.

*Damn it! I screwed up so badly.*

"Let me walk you out." I stood up, took her by the arm, and started walking toward the front door. I opened the door and gave her a little push out. "Next time you have a fight with your boyfriend, don't come here. As a matter of fact, don't come here ever again unless you call first. I also need my key back."

She just stood there and stared at me. "Are you kidding me? You're going to pick some country bumpkin over me, Scott? Have you been drinking or something?"

"Chelsea, Jessica has more class in her pinkie finger than you do in your whole body. I've never in my life met anyone who makes me feel the way she does when I'm with her. Will you please leave now?"

"You just made the biggest mistake of your life."

"No…the biggest mistake of my life was walking away from her in the first place."

She turned and stomped off toward her car, bitching the whole way.

I looked at my phone. *Nothing.* I headed back in and made plans to get up early, so I could go to Jessie's and beg her to drive with me to the coast.

I had some serious making up to do with that girl. I just hoped I wouldn't fuck it up. Last time, I'd walked away from her because I was scared to death of the strong feelings I had for her.

*This time, I'm not going anywhere.*

# Chapter Thirty-Eight
## Josh

After I loaded up the last of our suitcases, I started to make my way back into the house. I saw Mrs. Smith walking down the street with her little monster dog who hated me.

*I'm gonna get a giant-ass dog and have him eat that thing.*

"Josh! Hello, darling. How are you feeling?"

I gave her my best smile, which always made her blush. "I'm feeling wonderful, Mrs. Smith. Thank you. I'm about to be married to the most beautiful girl in the world. What could be better?"

She laughed and looked around for Heather. "Where are you taking her for the honeymoon? She said you wouldn't tell her."

*Nosy-ass neighbors, I swear.* I smiled as I shook my head. "Oh no. I know how you women are. Y'all stick together! The minute I tell you, you'll tell Heather."

"Oh no! I won't. I promise." She winked.

Just then, Heather walked out of the house, carrying her wedding dress in a white bag. I'd felt tempted to look at it when she was in the shower, but I didn't.

"Saved by my bride-to-be," I said with a laugh.

Heather looked between Mrs. Smith and me before she started laughing. "Are we about ready to go?" Heather asked with a wink.

*God, I love this girl. How did she know I needed to be saved from the nosy neighbor?* "Yep! Just about." I turned back to Mrs. Smith. "You have a lovely day. See ya later, little puppy." I quickly moved away and started back toward the house.

Heather's mouth dropped as I left her to fend for herself with Mrs. Smith.

I walked into the house and did a quick once-over since we wouldn't be back for almost two weeks. I smiled when I thought about how surprised Heather would be when she found out we were going to Italy.

When I picked the girls' brains about where to take Heather, they all agreed on Italy. Heather had visited there a few times with her mom and dad. I was worried it would bring back memories, but Amanda had said Heather had talked about going back almost as soon as her parents had died.

Heather had a small pouch that she kept on her dresser. I'd asked her once what it was, and she'd told me it held rose petals from a flower her parents had given her. They'd planned on going to Italy for Heather's high school graduation present. They had wanted to stand on the ocean shoreline and drop the petals into the water. Her father had said it would be a way to celebrate her moving on to the next phase of her life.

I picked up the pouch and put it in my backpack. I opened up my dresser drawer and took out the ring box. I slipped it into my backpack beside the pouch. I smiled and headed downstairs. I stopped and looked into the empty bedroom that would be the nursery. I already had an idea of the cribs I wanted to make. I'd drawn them up and sent them over to my dad to get his thoughts. He loved them, and he'd asked if he could help make them.

When I felt Heather's hand on my shoulder, I turned to look at her.

"What are you thinking about? Nervous? Getting cold feet maybe?" she asked with a wink.

"Hell no. Thinking about the cribs," I said with a grin. I kissed her quickly on the lips before walking toward the kitchen.

When I heard her sigh behind me, I tried so hard not to laugh.

"Josh, come on. Why can't I see your drawings for the cribs? All these secrets! Do you know what it took for me to get Mrs. Smith to try and find out where you are taking me for our honeymoon?"

I spun around to look at her. "You didn't?"

She laughed, and the blush that filled her cheeks caused my dick to jump.

"Heather, here I was, thinking that the woman was just being a nosy neighbor, and you asked her to pump me for information?"

She laughed as she walked up to me and placed her hands on my face. She reached up as I leaned down, and she kissed me so sweetly that I just about dropped everything.

Then, she let out a moan.

*Fuck it.*

I dropped the backpack and started walking her back into the living room. Right before we got to the sofa, I reached down to unbutton her jean shorts. We never once took our eyes off of each other.

"Whatcha doing?" she asked.

"I'm getting you undressed."

"How come?"

"Because I'm going to have mad, passionate sex with you on our sofa."

The smile that spread across her face about knocked me down to my knees. *There's not a damn thing I wouldn't do for this girl.*

"You know...when I start getting bigger, Ari and Ellie said we'll have to try different positions. I was thinking we should probably practice some now. Don't you think?" She raised her eyebrows.

*Motherfucker. I think I just died and went to heaven.* "Damn, princess. I think I just came in my pants."

She threw her head back and laughed. "Want to?"

Sex with Heather was always amazing. I loved the fact that she'd tried three times to give me a blow job, and each time she'd gagged so much that she ended up with dry heaves or throwing up in the bathroom. Usually, we stuck to one of us being on top, or our favorite way was with her on her side.

*Fuck.* I was getting hard just thinking about what she had in mind. "Fuck yes, I want to. What are ya thinking?"

She slowly took off her shirt and then her bra. Then, she slipped out of her panties. She stepped over to the sofa and got on her hands and knees with her ass facing me. I'd never taken off my clothes so fast in my life.

She looked over her shoulder at me. "From behind?"

*Ah, fuck yeah. I'm not going to last a minute.*

I got behind her and touched her beautiful bare ass. When I moved my hands around her and grabbed her breasts, she threw her head back and moaned. I used my knee to spread her legs apart more. I gently entered her and started to move. As she let out a gasp, I stopped moving.

"Are you okay, baby?"

She pushed her ass into me. "Oh my god...it feels like it's so deep inside. Move, Josh!"

I started to slowly move in and out. *Fuck, this feels so damn good.*

"Touch me, Josh! Please touch me."

The moment I touched her clit, she started calling out my name. Next thing I knew, I was pulling her toward me. When I sat back, she started moving up and down. I cupped her breasts and started playing with them. She rested her head back on my shoulder as she started to cry out again.

"Oh god! Oh god, Josh!"

I didn't last another minute. I leaned down and gently bit on her shoulder as I started to come.

*Fuck me. Why does every time with her feel like the first time?*

Heather collapsed onto the sofa, and I followed. She rolled onto her side, so she was facing me.

"Oh. My. God! Why have we never done it that way before?" Heather smiled at me.

I smiled back before I kissed her. As many girls as I'd been with, I'd never tried that position before. Really, I'd never had them on top ever.

"I'm so glad you found me," I said.

Tears began building in her eyes. "You found me and saved me."

"I love you so much, Heather. I'll love you forever…for infinity."

She kissed me softly on the lips and then rested her forehead against mine. "I love you, Josh. I'd be lost without you. I'll love you for infinity…plus a little more."

I smiled and kissed her nose. "We better get going, babe. We have a long drive, and with your pee breaks, it will take us twelve hours to get there!"

She jumped up and started getting dressed. Lying there, I just watched her. I'd waited for so long to find her, and now, she was almost officially mine. When I glanced down at her stomach, I felt mine take a dip. I'd never thought I could ever be this happy.

I looked over at my iPod sitting on the iHome. I got up and pulled on my pants before walking over to find the song I wanted. When "Bless the Broken Road" by Rascal Flatts started to play, Heather turned around and looked at me. I gave her my crooked smile, the one that I knew melted her heart, and I held out my hand. She walked up to me and then placed her hand in mine. Pulling her in as close to me as I could, I sang the lyrics to her as I ran my hand through her beautiful blonde hair. When I heard her sniffling, I knew she was crying.

As the song ended, I leaned back and wiped away her tears. "I've never in my life…ever…felt this way with anyone. You're the air that I breathe, the light in my darkness, the hope of my future."

She started crying harder as she shook her head. "Josh…" Her voice cracked as she looked up at me with those beautiful blue eyes. "When my parents died…I never thought I would ever feel love again. I didn't want to feel it because I was so afraid of getting hurt. But when you snuck into my heart…I…I didn't want to do anything else but love you. I'd rather love you than never have you in my life. I love you with every ounce of my being. I can't wait to be your wife and the mother of your children. Most of all, I can't wait to sit on our front porch when we're eighty years old, bitching about the young couple next door who play their music too loud."

I started laughing as I pulled her to me. After I kissed her, I asked, "You ready to be Mrs. Joshua Hayes?"

A tear rolled down her face as she nodded. "More than anything."

As we pulled up to the Peninsula Island Resort and Spa, my heart started pounding. Of course, Jenny was standing outside, waiting for us.

"Holy hell. What time did they get here?" Josh started laughing.

I smiled, but I felt sick to my stomach. *I'm getting married tomorrow. Tomorrow.* When I glanced over to Josh, he was smiling as he put the truck in park. As he hopped out, I saw Jenny walking up to the truck. She knocked on my window and gave me the sweetest smile as she winked at me.

I slowly opened the door, and she held out her hand for me. When I got out, she leaned up next to my ear.

"It's okay to be nervous, but everything is going to be beautiful," she whispered.

I smiled as I took her into my arms and hugged her. "Only you could plan a wedding in a few short weeks, book everyone's rooms, and make me feel better with just a simple sentence!"

"I love my job! What can I say?"

Aaron walked up. "What did Josh take? He's high as a kite!"

I looked over at Josh. He was talking away to the bellhop, who was helping him take out the luggage from the back of the truck.

I had to laugh. "He talks a lot when he gets nervous. I think he's feeling the same way as me."

Aaron started shaking his head as he walked toward Josh. They shook hands, and then Aaron leaned in and said something to Josh. Josh snapped his head up and glanced over at me. When I smiled, he gave me that damn panty-melting smile back.

*Yep. I can't wait to be his wife.* He winked at me, and I started giggling. *If we can both make it through this night, we have it made.*

"I have you both booked in the honeymoon suite, but Josh won't be staying in there tonight."

I spun around and stared at Jenny in shock. "Why?"

Jenny laughed. "Tradition, sweetheart. Y'all can go one night without seeing each other. I promise!"

"Has anyone told Josh this? I'm pretty sure he won't be happy with this arrangement." I was secretly thanking the heavens that Josh and I'd had sex right before we left.

Jenny smiled as she glanced over at Josh. "Yep, Aaron is telling him right now. He'll be staying in our two-bedroom condo with us tonight."

I turned and peeked at Josh. His smile faded as he shook his head. Aaron slapped him on the back as they began walking into the hotel. I smiled at Josh and shrugged. *If I know Josh, he's already thinking of a way to get to me tonight...and that is fine by me!*

I looked up and saw Gunner's truck pulling up with Jeff and Ari right behind him. I jumped up and down as Ellie, Ari, and Jessie all jumped out and ran over to Jenny and me.

"Holy hell! We have to get you caught up on so much!" Ari said.

Gunner walked by and rolled his eyes. "Holy shit. For the last two hundred miles, all I heard were three girls doing nothing but bitch and put curses on poor Scott Reynolds."

When Ellie turned around and glared at Gunner, he must have realized what he'd said wrong.

"Did I say poor? I meant, that dirty, rotten bastard, Scott Reynolds."

Jeff started laughing as he walked up. "Speak of the devil."

I turned to see Scott pulling up. Jessie and Ellie grabbed my arms, and we started to head into the hotel.

Ari called over her shoulder, "We're going for a walk on the beach, boys! Behave!"

After Jessie filled me in on everything that had happened with Scott, my heart was breaking.

"Then, to top it off, we ran into Chelsbitch this morning at the gas station," Ellie said with an eye roll.

"Did you just call her Chelsbitch?" I asked with a laugh.

"Yep! Anyway, that bitch walks up to Jessie and says, 'Thank you so much for leaving last night. Scott and I were able to catch up...if you know what I mean.' Ugh! I wanted to punch her in the throat!"

When I looked at Jessie, she was attempting to smile, trying to show she wasn't bothered by it all, but I knew exactly how she felt. *Been there, done that.*

"Jessie, I thought he called you and said she left?"

She shrugged her shoulders. "He did. He must have tried calling until four in the morning."

I took a deep breath. "From my experience with the ex-bitches, they lie out of their asses. I find it hard to believe he would call you until four in the morning if he was having sex with Chelsea."

Jessie's eyes lit up just a bit.

Ari nodded in agreement. "You know, Heather is right. If he was calling and texting you, I highly doubt that she was there."

I looked back to the hotel and saw Josh walking down toward us. The smile on his face took my breath away.

"It's amazing how they can keep doing that, isn't it?" Ellie said.

I glanced over at her. "Do what?"

"Take our breaths away with just a smile."

I looked back at Josh as he was making his way over to us.

"Yes," Ari, Jessie, and I all said at the same time. Then, we started laughing.

I hooked my arm around Jessie's as we headed over to Josh. "Give him a chance, Jessie. If I learned anything from what happened between Josh and me, it was that if you want something bad enough, you fight for it. Don't let some jealous ex-girlfriend get in the way. Just take it slow."

She looked at me and grinned as Ellie walked up and took her other arm.

"Ells, I've been meaning to ask you. Did you ever talk to Gunner about…well, about what happened with me and him?" Jessie asked.

Ellie smiled. "Yes. The next day, we took Big Roy and Rose out for a ride, and we had a long chat. Everything is fine, and Gunner promised to never hold back the truth about anything ever again. It actually taught me a lesson. It helped me to bury some of those old insecurities a little deeper. Plus, we ended up making love by the river. It was magical!"

I smiled as I thought about the wonderful time Josh and I had spent together on the riverbank where he'd asked me to marry him.

"Wow…what a lucky guy I am. Look at these four drop-dead beautiful girls all walking my way," Josh said with a smile. He took me in his arms and kissed me like he was saying hello after not seeing me for months.

When he pulled away from my lips, I smiled. "Wow."

"I missed you," he said.

"You better get it in now. Jenny will have her locked away tonight with heavy security watching," Ari said.

Ellie started laughing.

Jessie giggled. "I actually heard her ask Aaron if they should hire someone to watch Heather's door because she didn't trust Josh!"

Josh smiled and shook his head. "Damn. That girl knows me too well." He winked and kissed me again.

The rehearsal on the beach had been flawless, and everything had gone smoothly. Everyone was now on the island, and we were making our way to the hotel restaurant for the rehearsal dinner.

After kissing and hugging, laughing and talking, we were finally sitting down to eat. Jeff, Gunner, Ellie, and Ari all gave speeches. I had never cried and laughed so much in my life. The night went on, and I told Josh it was probably one of the best nights of my life.

Then, Jenny came to me and said Josh wanted me to meet him outside.

When I found him, he was looking out at the black ocean. He was wearing a gray pullover with white linen pants, and I had been lusting after him all night.

I walked up to him and wrapped my arms around his waist. "Are you nervous?"

He laughed. "Yep! You?" He turned around and looked into my eyes.

I caught my breath as I just lost myself in those eyes. I barely whispered, "Yes."

He took my hand, and we strolled along the beach for what seemed like forever. We talked about everything from us both being scared to death…to why we were scared…to the babies and how I'd decided to stay home with them…to Josh's business and how it had just taken off…and then my parents.

"More than anything, I wish they were here, princess."

He held me, and I leaned my head back on his chest and stared out at the ocean.

"I feel them with me. That might sound weird, but I do." I let out a small laugh and shook my head. "Sometimes, I swear that my dad talks through you!"

Josh asked, "Why's that?"

"Just from little things you say to me. You say something to me right at the exact moment I need to hear it. Sometimes when I'm scared, I can hear my dad whisper, reminding me to breathe, and then you say it within in a few seconds."

He held me closer. "We better get back."

"Are you going to behave tonight?"

Josh threw his head back and laughed. "I almost paid Aaron two hundred bucks to set up a blanket down here, so I could make love to you on the beach, but I wanted to save that for our honeymoon."

*Oh my god! Where is he taking me? To a beach? He must be taking me to a beach somewhere. Act cool, Heather. He just slipped up. He might give you more!* "Sounds like heaven!"

"That is, if there is a beach around where we're going," he said.

My smile faded, and my mouth dropped open. *He did not just do that! Bastard!*

## Chapter Forty

### Josh

I sat and watched as the sun moved above the horizon. When I felt a hand on my shoulder, I looked up to see my father standing there. I smiled as I motioned for him to sit down. We sat there for a good ten minutes, just watching the sun rising on one of the most important days of my life.

"Did you write your vows?" he asked.

"Nope."

He laughed. "Holy shit, you're more like me than I thought."

I glanced over at him as he looked out at the ocean. "Dad, can I ask you something?"

He looked at me and smiled. "Always, son."

"Do you ever look back on your life and regret things you did?"

He let out a gruff laugh and shook his head. "Not so much anymore, but when I was younger, I did. Sometimes in life, when we're looking for something, we don't know the right way to go about looking for it. We want it so desperately that we search for it in all the wrong places, for all the wrong reasons, and with all the wrong people."

I sighed, looking back out at the ocean. "I've never in my life felt the way I do when I'm with her, Dad. All those other girls…they meant nothing. I never felt anything but emptiness afterward. When I look at Heather though, when I look into her eyes, I pray to God that I'm not dreaming. I'm so afraid this is a dream, and I'm going to wake up, still searching for that one person who moves my heart and soul. She's the air that I need to breathe."

My dad put his hand on my back and winked at me. "It's not a dream, son. It's very real, and you're both very much in love with one another. In a way, I think you rescued each other."

I nodded as I thought about what he'd just said. "Is it wrong I just want to say to her what's in my heart? That I'm not planning it out beforehand?"

"Hell no, it's not wrong. It's your wedding. You do what you feel in your heart is the right thing to do. I think you could tell a joke, and Heather wouldn't care. That girl is over-the-moon in love with you."

"I'm over-the-moon in love with her, too." I started laughing. "Especially with how she keeps trying to trick me into telling her where I'm taking her for the honeymoon!"

My dad laughed and slapped me on the back. "I'm proud of you, Josh."

I snapped my head over to my father. "Dad…"

He looked at me with tears in his eyes. "I am. I know I've never said this before, but when you were in high school and you told me you wanted to follow in my footsteps…my heart filled with joy. I actually had to walk outside because I didn't want to cry in front of you."

"Dad…I never knew that it made you so happy."

"What makes me happy, Josh, is that you followed your dreams. You go for what you want, and you absolutely excel at it. Your mother and I are so proud of the man you've become. You help people, and you don't even think twice about it. You give your love with your whole heart, like the way you love Matthew. When I see you with him, my heart swells up. And the way you love Heather…you take care of her and put her needs before yours. Even when you lost your memory, you still put her first. Yes, son, you've made your mother and me so very proud. I'm so damn blessed to call myself your father."

I felt a tear rolling down my face. "I love you, Dad."

"I love you, too, Josh."

When my dad slapped the shit out of his legs, I jumped. "Fuck, Dad! You just scared the shit out of me! We were having a moment."

He stood up and reached down for my hand. "Moment is over, son. Let's go. You're getting married in a few hours, and I have to go and give your mother a wake-up call." He wiggled his eyebrows up and down.

"Oh, for the love of God…I didn't need to hear that, Dad. Shit, I think I'm going to hurl."

"Josh?" Gunner said.

I turned around, looked at my three best friends, and smiled. "Jesus H. Christ. If I were a woman, I'd be wet right now from the sight of the three of you!"

They all laughed.

Brad walked up and shook my hand. "You look pretty damn good yourself."

"It's getting close to that time. Did you want to walk down to the beach and check everything out?" Gunner asked.

"No."

Jeff started laughing. "Why the hell not?"

"I want to be surprised!" I said.

The three of them just stared at me.

"Pussy," Brad said.

"Shut the hell up, you bastard!"

Gunner winked as he said, "You know when I said I was going to push you in the water? Dude, I was only kidding."

I smiled as I sat down. "I really do want to be surprised. I think Heather does, too. She told Jenny she wanted it simple with only a white arch sitting on the beach. I trust Jenny. I've seen her plan three kick-ass weddings so far, so I'm pretty sure she's got this."

"Okay. How about a beer from the bar then?" Jeff asked.

"Fuck yes!" I jumped up.

Just then, Matt came running in with his dad, Mark, right behind him.

"Josh!" Matt yelled.

I bent down and held out my arms for him.

Like always, he stopped, just short of me. "I'm going to hug you, Josh," he said.

"Go for it, buddy!"

He slammed into me, and I hugged him back.

He pulled away and smiled. "Guess what?"

"What?"

"Jeff and Ari found a place that has horses! They are going to take me for a ride on the beach!" He started to jump up and down, and he looked at Jeff, who was smiling at him.

"Oh yeah?" I said.

He turned back to me. "Yeah, and guess what else?"

"I give up!"

"Josh...you assmole...you didn't even try to guess."

I smiled, glancing up at Mark. Sue and Mark had pretty much given up on trying to stop Matt from saying *assmole*.

"Um...your mommy and daddy are going with you?"

"Nope! Better! Luke is going with us."

"That's pretty cool, buddy. How lucky are you that you get to be with him on his first ride on the beach?"

"I know!"

"Come on, Matt. Let's leave the big boys to get ready now. One hour, guys...don't forget." Mark looked right at Jeff. "Don't get him drunk. One beer, and that's all." He took Matt's hand, turned, and left.

Jeff gave me a shocked look. "What the hell? That man has no faith in me whatsoever."

Gunner, Brad, and I all lost it and started laughing.

Gunner slapped Jeff on the back. "Come on, let's all go grab a beer."

As Gunner and Jeff began walking out, Brad grabbed my arm. "Josh, can I talk to you for a minute?"

As Gunner shut the door, Brad turned and smiled at me.

"What's up, dude?" I sat down.

Brad took a seat across from me. He smiled and let out a laugh. "Dude, out of all of us, I honestly never pictured you getting married. I'm so damn happy for you, Josh."

"Thanks, man. I appreciate that…I think."

He looked down at the ground and then back up at me.

*Oh fuck. What if he's doing drugs again? Or he wants to do drugs again? Dude, don't do this on my wedding day.*

"We're going to find out the sex of the baby when we get back."

I slowly let out the breath I'd been holding. "That's awesome, dude!"

He nodded. "Yeah, I know. But, um…I'm scared, Josh."

"Of what?"

"What if something's wrong with the baby because I was taking drugs when I got Amanda pregnant? She hasn't said anything, but I know if it's crossed my mind, it's crossed hers. I'm so scared."

"Dude, it's going to be okay. Everything has been good in the pregnancy so far, right?"

He nodded.

"Brad, you made a mistake. Stop beating yourself up every chance you get because you slipped up and made a bad choice. I honestly believe in my heart that you're going to have a beautiful, healthy baby. Dude, don't worry."

He stood up and let out a sigh. "You're right!"

I got up and looked at him. "Can I ask you something? Friend to friend."

"Of course, Josh."

"Have you wanted to…"

He grinned and shook his head. "Not one damn bit. I've never felt so much peace and happiness in my life. I actually love my job right now. It doesn't hurt that it's one of my dad's biggest competitors! I'm looking forward to becoming a father. Amanda was so excited about starting a new career, but she's decided she's more interested in becoming a mom more than anything."

I grinned. "Does that mean y'all aren't moving to Florida?"

"Nobody knows this yet, but I talked to my boss and asked what the chances of me staying in Austin would be. I got hired on for their Florida office, but he said they are so happy with my work that they were actually going to offer me a raise to stay in Austin. This couldn't have happened at a better time. Amanda and I talked about it, and we are still selling the house to pay my parents back what they want. Then, we're going to look at some land outside of Dripping Springs. It's close enough for me to get to work and for Amanda to go visit the girls when she wants."

"Ah hell, Brad. You don't know how happy this makes me." I walked up and gave him a quick hug.

"Let's keep it between us for right now. I think Amanda wants to tell the girls herself, and I'm going to tell Gunner and Jeff later today."

"Will do, Brad. Gunner and Jeff will be just as happy." I slapped him on the back before we left the room and made our way down to the bar.

As we walked by the windows, I looked down at the beach. I could see the white arch in front of the chairs covered in the light blue fabric Heather had picked out. I quickly turned away as my heart started pounding.

*In one hour…she's going to be mine.*

# Chapter Forty-One
## Heather

I stood there and looked at my beautiful wedding dress hanging up on the door. I closed my eyes and thought about the day I'd found it.

"I don't want to try on another dress. I'll just wear jeans!" I said to Ari and Ellie.

Amanda held out another dress. "Oh hell…this is the one, Heather!" she said with a gasp. "Ouch! Motherfucker!"

We all turned and looked at her.

"Big kick!"

I sighed and shook my head. "That was what Ellie said about the last one, and Ari said the same thing about the one before that."

Amanda handed the dress to Rachael, the sweet, patient girl who had helped me try on at least twenty-five gowns so far.

*Okay, so maybe it was only ten, but it was enough to make me hate the color white now.*

"Oh! This is a beautiful one." Rachael hooked my arm and dragged me back into the dressing room.

As she helped me get dressed, I begged her to make it all stop. "Please…Rachael…don't let them make me try on another dress! I'm starving, and I have twins to feed. I just want to go eat!"

She smiled as she did up the back of the dress. "Do you want another banana, honey?" she asked as her eyes filled with sympathy.

"No. Thank you though."

When she stepped back, she put her hands to her mouth.

*Huh…she hasn't done that yet.*

"Heather, slowly turn around and look."

I rolled my eyes at her exaggeration about the dress. She was good at it, but this one topped all the others.

When I looked in the mirror, I sucked in a breath of air. "Oh. My. God. I look like a—"

"A princess," she said.

I felt tears building up in my eyes. I knew why I was being such a brat. I wanted my mother here. I had Ari, Ellie, and Amanda, but it wasn't the same.

"This one is called the Gemma, and it's made by—"

I spun around to face her. "What?"

"What?" she said.

"What's the name of this dress?"

She gave me a confused look. "The Gemma?"

I started to walk past her, heading straight to the girls. As soon as I came out, all three of them gasped.

"Oh my god! Oh my god! That is beautiful. I knew it would look beautiful on you!" Amanda said as she rubbed her stomach.

Ellie clapped, jumping up and down. "Holy hell! That's perfect, Heather."

Ari was smiling from ear to ear.

"Ari…" I couldn't talk.

"Oh, baby girl…that is the dress. See, you're even crying! They say when you put it on and cry, that's the dress. Did she cry when she first saw it, Rachael?"

Rachael laughed. "Yes, but she really freaked out when I told her the name of the dress."

Ellie laughed. "What's the name?"

"The Gemma."

I started crying harder. Before I knew it, I was sandwiched between my three best friends.

Amanda looked me in the eyes.

"Did you know?" I asked her.

She shook her head and smiled. "No."

"Okay, y'all…I'm so confused here," Rachael said.

Everyone pulled back and turned to face her.

"My parents died in a car accident a few years ago. My mother's name was Gemma."

Rachael got tears in her eyes and shook her head. "Motherfucker."

Ari laughed. "Hell, I knew I liked you for a reason."

After Rachael got her composure, she began telling us about the dress. "This is a strapless A-line taffeta gown with an exquisite hand-draped sweetheart bodice. The band is garnished with Swarovski crystals with matching floral embroidery and beading throughout the full skirt, corset back bodice, and chapel-length train. It is designed by Sophie Tolli, an Australian designer."

Ari looked at her and frowned. "Why can't y'all just say it's a beautiful dress with crystals wrapping under her breasts—which, by the way, your big-ass tits fill out very well—and it has a gorgeous train? That I get. All that other talk is like wah, wah, wah."

*Poor Rachael. Girl never stood a chance.*

"You're lost in thought, baby girl." Elizabeth placed her hand on my shoulder.

I smiled. "I was thinking about the day I found this dress."

"You mean when I found it!" Amanda called out.

Jenny walked up with a huge grin on her face. "It's time to put it on now, Heather."

I turned to Elizabeth. "Would you help me?"

She smiled with tears in her eyes. "It would be an honor."

I took off my robe and looked at myself in the mirror. I placed my hands on my stomach, and I could just barely see a little bump. I glanced at the pale blue strapless bra with the matching panties that Ari had bought and then the matching garter belt that Ellie had given me. The beautiful blue antique hairpin that Amanda had let me borrow looked beautiful in my hair. She said she had worn it on her wedding day, and before her, her mother, grandmother, and great grandmother had worn it on theirs. It held up half of my hair while the other half fell down in soft curls falling around my shoulders.

I reached up to touch it.

"Don't touch your hair!" Jenny yelled out.

"Do you think Josh will like all of this?" I asked without even thinking that I was asking his mother. "Oh my god! I didn't mean to ask you that, Elizabeth." I felt my face flush from embarrassment.

She laughed, looking at my reflection in the mirror. "Sweetheart...I think he's going to pass out when he takes off your wedding dress."

I peeked up at her and smiled.

After the dress was on and everyone had smoothed it out, I slipped on a pair of white flip-flops adorned with crystals. They were Ari's idea since there would be no way I could walk on the beach in heels. Next came my mother's wedding veil. She had given it to me when I turned eighteen. I smiled as Ari placed it on my head.

"Oh, Heather! It looks beautiful on you," Ari said.

I tried so hard not to cry.

I glanced over at my three best friends and smiled. They were each dressed in a beautiful light steel blue strapless bodice with a taffeta knee-length skirt.

Jenny walked up and handed each of them a bouquet of bright blue hydrangeas. I smiled because hydrangeas were my mother's favorite flowers. The stems were wrapped in a beautiful bright blue satin fabric with white lace and silver accents. Then, she turned and handed me my bouquet.

I sucked in a breath of air. "Oh, Jenny! It's beautiful." I fought to hold back the tears.

The bouquet was filled with light blue hydrangeas and white roses. The stems were wrapped in a white silk fabric and pinned with mother-of-pearl pins.

"Jenny, did you make these?" I asked.

She nodded.

"Thank you so much. All I had to do was leave the flowers up to you, and I knew you wouldn't let me down. How did you know about the hydrangeas?"

"I asked Ellie." Jenny smiled over toward Ellie.

I walked over to Ellie and hugged her. "Thank you, sweets," I whispered.

"I love you, Heather," Ellie whispered back.

I pulled back and stared at the three of them for a few seconds. "Y'all ready to do this?"

Ari laughed. "The question is…are you?"

"Never been more ready in my entire life."

Jenny turned to me. "You have your vows written down?"

"Um…I decided to just wing it."

"What?" all four of them said at the same time.

Elizabeth started laughing.

"Oh. My. God. Heather! It was your idea to say your own vows. Poor Josh probably spent days on his, and you're going to just *wing it*?" Amanda said.

I laughed as I shook my head and started toward the door. I stopped and turned to them. "I'll bet each of y'all that he doesn't have his vows written down. He's going to do the same thing as me."

"Shit, I'll take you up on that. A hundred bucks says that boy pulls out a piece of paper or stumbles on his words 'cause he forgot them," Ari said with a laugh.

"I'm in," Ellie said.

"Oh hell yes! I'm in, and I'll double that shit!" Amanda said.

Jenny laughed. "Come on, ladies. Let's get a move on, shall we?"

Amanda walked out first, then Ari followed, and Ellie was last.

Ellie turned and kissed me on the cheek. "They're with you, sweets," she whispered in my ear.

I smiled and nodded. "I know. I feel them with me."

I watched as Ellie started to walk around the corner. I took a deep breath, looked up, and saw Josh's dad standing there.

"Greg, what are you doing here?"

He smiled as he came up to me. "Heather, you're breathtaking. Josh is going to…well, to be blunt and honest, he's going to shit his pants when he sees you."

I couldn't help but laugh. "I hope he has a reaction but not quite like that."

"Josh didn't want you walking down the aisle alone, so he asked me if I would do the honors."

I felt tears building in my eyes. *Thank God I have on waterproof makeup.* "I would love that," I barely got out in a whisper.

"You ready, baby girl?"

I nodded as I took his arm. We rounded the corner, and I didn't look up until we were out on the light blue runner. The moment I lifted my head, the only person I saw was Josh. I sucked in a breath of air as I looked at him.

"Oh. My. God. He looks amazing," I whispered.

Greg laughed. "He does look pretty sharp, doesn't he?"

I turned to Greg and smiled. "Just like his father."

"Now, you're just suckin' up to find out where he's taking you!"

I laughed as I put my eyes back on the love of my life. My heart started beating faster, and the butterflies were going crazy in my stomach. *He looks so handsome…and hot as hell!*

He was dressed in a white button-down shirt with a light blue tie and white linen pants. When I looked down at his feet, I busted out laughing.

"He has on flips-flops, Greg!"

"He said if you got to wear comfortable shoes, so did he."

The chairs were all covered in a light blue fabric with white bows. At the end of the aisle, there was a small makeshift tent made from white lace fabric with a table under it. The table had four beautiful vases with light blue candles in them.

When we walked up, Greg placed my hand in Josh's hand, and Josh just stared at me. I saw the tears in his eyes, and I did everything I could to hold mine back.

Gunner leaned forward and bumped Josh. "Josh…"

Everyone started laughing.

Josh looked me up and down and then stared into my eyes as he shook his head. "You're so beautiful. You leave me speechless, princess."

Greg said, "Damn, I taught that boy good."

I turned to Greg as Elizabeth smacked him on the arm.

I smiled and looked back at Josh. I never stopped gazing into his eyes. I barely even heard the preacher talking.

"Josh, Heather, are you ready to say your vows?"

Gunner had to snap us out of our endless staring contest.

"Josh, say your vows," Gunner said.

"Heather, first, I just need to say…wow…baby, you look beautiful."

I smiled. "So do you!"

Then, he squeezed my hands and gave me that smile that drove me mad. "I didn't write down any vows because I wanted to speak straight from my heart."

*Yes! I just won four hundred bucks!*

"The first time I ever saw you, something happened inside of me. The only thing that was important to me was to get to know you more. I wanted to see you smile that beautiful smile of yours, hear that amazing laugh, and see those beautiful blue eyes light up. The first time you touched me, I wasn't really sure what happened. I'd never felt the things I felt when I was around you. I just knew I wanted to feel that way for the rest of my life."

I felt a tear rolling down my cheek as I watched one roll down his face. *He's really going to be mine—forever.*

"I want to wake up every morning and see your beautiful face looking back at mine. I want to go to sleep every night to the taste of your sweet lips on mine. I want to watch you with our kids and see what an amazing mom you'll be. I want to sit on our front porch every night and tell you how much I love you."

I started to cry harder. *I'm never going to be able to say my vows now.*

"Princess, you're the air I breathe. I'd be completely lost without you. I love you so much." His voice cracked, and he smiled. "I'll love you until the day I take my last breath, and I'll be forever faithful to you."

When he finished, I glanced up at Gunner. He looked like a proud father who had just given birth.

I looked into Josh's eyes. I was about to start talking when…I went blank.

*Nothing. Oh my god. I wonder if I can just say ditto? I can't breathe. Oh shit! This was my idea.*

Josh gave me the sweetest, most beautiful smile ever.

*Breathe, princess.*

I took a deep breath and slowly let it out. "Josh, as I stand before you, my heart is filled with so much love that it scares me sometimes. I love you so much, and I need you so much more. The first time I saw you, I instantly felt something deep down inside. I fought it for so long until I realized that without you in my life…I had no life. When I close my eyes each night, I thank God for you. You rescued me and showed me that it was okay to live again, to want to be happy again. I've never been so happy in my entire life. I can't wait to spend every minute of my life with you. I can't wait to put up that fence and get you your dog."

Josh started laughing as he shook his head.

"I can't wait to watch your business grow as I stand by your side and support you one hundred percent. I want to hear the first sounds of our children with you. Thank you for never giving up on me. Thank you for loving me and for giving me hope again. I love you so much, Josh. I'll always love you…for infinity."

I watched as a tear rolled down his face. I reached up and wiped it away as he grabbed my hand and kissed the back of it.

*Never in my life would I ever again feel as happy as I do right now.*

Josh and I decided to have all our pictures taken on the beach. We did pictures with our family, friends, and the wedding party. Then, the photographer told us to have fun. That was all Josh had to hear. He picked me and carried me into the surf.

"Oh my god, Josh! My dress!" I screamed.

He laughed. I looked back at Ari, Ellie, and Amanda as they were all just laughing, too.

He started to kiss me as he slowly lowered me into the water. I completely forgot about everything but the love of my life, who was kissing me so passionately that I almost started crying. When he started to drop to his knees, I did also. I could feel the surf crashing up on us.

He cupped his hands on my face and slightly pulled away as he rested his forehead on mine. "My god, I love you."

I smiled as a wave crashed into me, pushing me against him. We both started laughing.

"Josh, you're soaking wet!" I said with a giggle.

He pushed pieces of hair away from my eyes and laughed. "So are you, princess."

I wasn't sure how long we were sitting in the surf, just kissing and talking.

The photographer cleared her throat. "Josh and Heather, I think I got some wonderful shots. Shall we move to the reception now?"

I looked up at her and then over to our friends. Ellie was crying, and Ari and Amanda were smiling from ear to ear.

I glanced back at Josh and smiled. "What am I going to wear to the reception?"

He gave me that drop-dead gorgeous smile of his. "I bought you a dress for the reception. I also had Ari buy you double of what you're wearing under your dress." He wiggled his eyebrows up and down.

I shook my head and giggled as I looked over at Ari. She was dancing with Jeff. I could hear the music from the reception, and I could see some of the tables outside on the patio and the beach.

"Did you plan this?"

"Yep. I thought they would make some badass wedding pictures."

I slammed my body into his and hugged him. "Oh my god. I love you, Joshua Michael Hayes."

As Josh and I walked into the reception room, I let out a gasp. We had both agreed we wanted to see it for the first time together.

"Oh, wow. It's beautiful!" I said.

"Wow!" Josh let out a laugh.

The tables were covered with white lace and a beautiful light blue fabric runner. Each table had clear vases filled with sand, shells, and white candles in the center along with the most gorgeous arrangements of flowers I'd ever seen. White lights were everywhere. There was a table off in the corner covered with tiny white chair picture frames. Some had a picture of Josh and me, and the others had our wedding date.

I looked over at the wedding cakes. There was a white three-tier cake with white and light blue seashells cover it. I smiled at how Jenny had included every single thing I'd requested. I noticed the cupcake display, and I grinned as I saw the light blue cupcakes with the letters J and H surrounded by a heart on top of each one. Josh hadn't wanted a groom's cake, so we went with the cupcakes. I loved them. They were perfect.

When I turned to look at Josh, he had the biggest smile on his face.

"Damn, that girl is worth every dime we paid her!" he said with a laugh.

"Yes. Yes, she is. Do you like everything?"

He looked at me and laughed. "Princess, I would have been happy with anything. As long as I was the one putting this ring on your finger, I would have worn a box if you told me to."

I smiled as I reached up and kissed him. "Thank you for this beautiful dress."

He wiggled his eyebrows up and down and winked at me. "The best part will be taking you out of it."

"Alright, y'all. Get your horny asses in there, and greet your guests," Gunner said. He walked up and kissed me on the cheek.

Josh grabbed my hand, and we made our way into the room.

I took a deep breath and let it out. Everything was going too smoothly. I had a feeling in my gut that something was going to happen. I just didn't know what or who it would be.

## Chapter Forty-Two
### Josh

I watched as Heather moved from person to person. She was smiling, laughing, and just being Heather. I'd never met anyone who could be so damn polite with such Southern charm.

*Fuck, I love her more than life itself...and she's all mine.*

"Dude, you better stop eyeing your wife like you want to devour her. These old folks might start talking," Jeff said as he handed me a beer.

I looked around. The wedding reception was perfect. The room led to an outdoor covered patio right on the beach. I watched as Matt played with Luke and a few of Heather's cousins' kids. My mother was talking to Sue and Grace while Emma was talking to Sharon.

"Dude, thanks for inviting my mom at the last minute," Jeff said.

I smiled at him. "Christ, Jeff, you know I'd do anything for you and Ellie. I'm just glad to see she's clean and back in your world." I glanced over, and Sharon was holding a sleeping Alex while she was laughing at something Emma had said.

I looked back over toward Heather. "I can't believe she's mine." She was breathtaking in her dress. *I just want to see what's under it.*

"There goes that look again. Dude...how fucking horny are you? I thought I was bad," Jeff said.

I threw my head back and laughed. "Ah shit, Jeff. I've never been so happy in my life. I thank God every day that I got a second chance with her. I feel closer to her now than I did before the accident, and I didn't think that was even possible."

"Man, I totally get what you mean. After Ari lost the baby, we grew so far apart, but once we got things worked out, it was like we were closer than ever. Even now, I feel like I fall in love with her more every day."

I glanced over at Brad and Amanda dancing. She looked so happy and relaxed.

"Did Brad talk to you and Gunner?" I asked.

"About staying?"

"Yeah."

Jeff smiled and nodded. "I was so fucking happy that I almost kissed his ass."

I let out a laugh.

Gunner walked up and sat on the other side of me. "Heather just offered me four hundred dollars to tell her where you're taking her on your honeymoon."

I snapped my head over to Gunner. "What? Are you kidding me?" I laughed. "That girl loves surprises, but she can't ever be patient enough for them." I shook my head as I watched Heather, Ellie, and Ari all make their way over to us.

"Jesus H. Christ. How in the hell did we get so lucky with them?" Gunner asked.

Jeff and I just shook our heads.

"Hell if I know, but I'm sure glad we did." I said. I smiled as Heather came and sat down on my lap.

"I love you," she whispered against my ear. "It's almost time for our dance."

I looked into her eyes. "You want to know what song I picked, don't you?"

She sighed and nodded. "Yes!"

"Oh, stop being such a brat, Heather. You told Josh he could pick the song. He won't let you down. If he does, I'll junk punch him," Ari said.

I turned toward her. "Thanks for the vote of confidence, Ari."

She shrugged and winked at me. "Anytime, sweets!"

I saw my father walking to the middle of the dance floor with a microphone.

"Can I have everyone's attention, please?" He looked over toward Heather and me and smiled just a bit. "I've been told that the first dance as husband and wife is coming up, but another dance needs to be done first."

I felt Heather stiffen in my arms.

My dad made his way to us and looked down at Heather. "Heather, from the moment you stepped foot inside our world, I have loved you like a daughter. So much so that I've wanted to kick my own son in the ass when I thought he had hurt you in some way or another."

Everyone let out a laugh, and I hugged Heather tighter.

He took a deep breath and slowly let it out. "I could never, ever replace your father, and I would never want to. I feel it so deep inside of me that he would want you to have your father-daughter dance at your wedding."

When Heather's body jerked just a little, I knew she was trying to hold back from crying.

My dad reached out his hand for Heather's. "It would be my honor..."

She slowly stood up and reached for his hand as he handed me the microphone. When they started heading out toward the dance floor, she looked back at me. I felt like someone had just kicked me in the stomach. The look of pain on her face about killed me.

My dad said something to Heather, and she snapped her head up to him. Then, Faith Hill's "There You'll Be" started to play. I watched as Heather buried her head into my father's chest and grabbed on to his shirt. I heard as Ellie and Ari started crying.

"This song was played at Heather's parents funeral," Amanda said to Brad.

*Jesus...all I want to do is take away her pain. My sweet, beautiful girl.*

*I promise you...I'll never let anyone or anything hurt her—ever. I'll always love and protect your daughter. I promise.*

I watched as my dad talked to Heather. She nodded once but kept her head buried in his chest. My heart started beating faster, and I felt my chest moving up and down. I couldn't hold it in anymore. I just let the tears fall.

Gunner put his hand on my shoulder.

"I'd do anything to bring her parents back for her. I wish I could take away her pain. I'd take it in a heartbeat and not think twice about it."

"I know you would, Josh, and she knows that, too. All she needs is for you to just love her."

I looked at Gunner and then back out to the dance floor. Just then, our eyes met. The tears falling down her face made me sick to my stomach.

"Fuck."

Gunner squeezed my shoulder. "Smile at her, Josh."

I did exactly what Gunner had said. She slowly smiled back as the song ended.

"Go to her, dude."

I stood up and started to walk out onto the dance floor. As soon as I got to her, she turned and slammed into my body. My dad put his hand on my back, and then he turned and walked away.

"I love you, princess. I love you so damn much, and I wish I could take away every ounce of pain."

When her eyes met mine, I wiped away her tears.

"Would it make you feel better if I told you where we're going for our honeymoon?"

She smiled the biggest smile ever. "Yes! Plus, it'll save me four hundred dollars," she said with a giggle.

The DJ announced, "Ladies and gentlemen, I think it's time for Mr. and Mrs. Hayes' first dance as a married couple. Heather, Josh wanted to say a few words to you before the song."

I saw her eyes building with tears again.

"No more sad tears, baby. It's only happy tears from now on, okay?" She nodded and smiled.

"I didn't think I would ever find love, but you proved me wrong, Heather. You said I rescued you, but you rescued me when you walked into my life."

I placed my hands on her face, leaned down, and kissed her so softly on the lips. I slowly pulled away as Lila McCann's "When You Walked into My Life" started to play. I put my forehead against hers and sang along with the lyrics as we started to dance.

When my princess started crying, I captured her lips with mine. She wrapped her arms around me and held on to me so tightly. My chest felt like it was going to explode at any moment with all the love I felt for this girl.

*I'll always love her. I'll always protect her. I promise you.*

She pulled away from my lips and smiled as she let out a little giggle. "I kinda think you got Gunner beat in the whole romance department."

"Fuck yeah, I do!"

We both laughed as I glanced over at Gunner. I looked back at her and put my hand on the side of her face. "I love you. I'll always love and protect you, princess."

"Forever?"

I pulled her closer to me. "Forever plus infinity."

# Chapter Forty-Three
## Gunner

"Well, I'll be goddamned. I think that boy just outromanced you, Gun," Jeff said.

I looked over at Jeff and Brad as they were both laughing. I shook my head. "I taught his ass everything he knows, damn it!"

Jeff threw his head back and laughed. "Little fucker. Wait until she finds out she's going to Italy."

Brad slapped me on the back. "I'm gonna ask my girl to dance with me. Excuse me, y'all." He walked up and swept Amanda away from Sharon and Alex.

I smiled, watching as Sharon carried a sleeping Alex around. I looked for Ellie.

"Where are the girls?" I asked.

"They went to the ladies' room with Jessie. What in the hell happened between Jessie and Scott?"

I shrugged my shoulders. "Fuck, I don't know. Something about Jessie going back to Scott's house, and Chelsea, his ex, was there, waiting inside."

"Hell, I could see why that would make a girl mad."

Scott walked up and sat down with a sigh.

"Speak of the devil," I said.

Scott looked at me, confused, and then looked out at Josh and Heather cutting up on the dance floor. "I want that. I want what y'all have."

I was shocked by what he'd said. *Ah fuck. How much has he had to drink?*

I glanced over at Jeff as he gave me a concerned look.

"Scott, how much have you had to drink?" I asked.

Scott gave me a confused look. "One beer, you asshole!"

Jeff started laughing.

I glanced up to see the girls dancing on the dance floor. Jessie was smiling while she was talking to Ari about something.

"Don't let her push you away, Scott."

He shook his head. "I'm trying, Gun. I've asked her, like, five times to talk to me, to dance with me, to kick me…anything. She won't even let me explain."

"Dude, from what I could make out by all the talking on the way here, you didn't kick the ex out. You don't bring a girl home and then ask her to step aside for the ex."

Scott sighed as he pushed his hands through his hair. "I know that. At the time, I didn't think I was doing anything wrong. Fuck, I was just surprised that Chelsea was in my house. Then, when I was talking to Jessie, I accidentally called her Chels."

"Oh…ah hell, dude. You done fucked-up!" Jeff said.

"Tell me about it. As soon as I got back home from dropping off Jessie, I had Chelsea leave."

"Wait, we ran into Chelsea on the way here, and I overheard Ells and Jessie saying how Chelsea had said she'd spent the night with you."

Scott's face fell. "What the fuck? No, she didn't! I made her leave. I mean, her ass was naked in my bed when I got home, but I walked away and told her to leave. I have to talk to Jessie." He jumped up.

Jeff got up and grabbed his arm. "Dude, don't mention the fact that she was naked in your bed. Since nothing happened, Jessie doesn't need to know that."

Scott grabbed Jeff on the shoulder and smiled. "Thanks, Jeff, and dude…I really have just been fucking with you about Ari. I know how much y'all love each other. I'd never get in the way of that."

Jeff nodded. "I know. I trust Ari. Besides, I'd kick your ass and put you in the hospital if you ever touched her."

Scott nodded. "Ah…right." He turned and started walking toward Jessie.

"You know Jessie, Gunner. What's your take?"

I looked at Jeff and then back out toward Jessie and Scott. "Shit, I know they both really liked each other in high school, but Scott was freaked out by how much he liked her. Once Chelsea Mason gave him some attention, he used that as an excuse, and he went after her. It was always about sex with Chelsea though. I just hope they don't pull a Jeff-and-Ari."

Jeff shot me a dirty look. "Fuck off, you fucker!"

I watched as Scott went right by Jessie and up to the DJ. Scott talked to the DJ for a good minute before turning back and walking up to Jess.

Hunter Hayes's "All You Ever" started to play. Scott took Jessie's hand and pulled her closer to him as they started dancing. Ellie turned to me and smiled.

I stood up and headed over to her. "Dance with me, sweetheart?"

"Always."

I took her into my arms as I started to dance with her. I held her close to me and whispered in her ear, "I love you, sweetheart."

She held on to me tighter as I moved her around on the dance floor. I glanced over at Scott and Jessie dancing. My heart broke when I saw Jessie quickly wipe away a tear.

"Gunner?" Ellie asked.

"Yeah, baby?"

"When can we go back to our room?"

I laughed as I kissed her on top of her head. "We could try and sneak away now. Your mom hasn't let go of Alex since we got to the reception. I don't think she'd even notice if we were gone!"

Ellie looked around me at her mother. She gave me the most beautiful smile as she looked up into my eyes. The passion filling her eyes had my dick jumping. I grabbed her hand and started leading her off of the dance floor. I took one look at Jeff, and he just smiled and shook his head.

"Holy hell, Gunner. You're going to pull my arm out of its socket if you don't slow down."

"I want to take you out of that dress right now. If we don't hurry, we might be having sex in the elevator."

Ellie started giggling. "That sounds like fun!"

I turned to her as the elevator doors opened. I grabbed her and started to kiss her as I walked her into the elevator. When the doors shut, I pushed her against the wall, and I quickly hit the button for our floor.

"I want you so badly, Ells."

"I want you, too, Drew."

By the time the elevator doors opened, I was ready to take her right there. I scooped her up into my arms, and I walked to our room. She laughed when I had a hard time getting the room key out to open the door.

Once we got in the room, I slowly put her down while I kissed her with as much passion as I could.

"Drew…"

"I love you, Ellie."

I reached around her back and started to take the top of her dress off. She lifted up her arms, and I slowly pulled it up over her head and then tossed it to the floor.

She laughed and hit me. "I have to put that back on, you know!"

I slid the zipper on her skirt down and then let it fall to the ground. I held her hands while she stepped out of it. I let my eyes move up and down her body. She had on a white lace bra with matching panties, and she looked breathtaking. I put my hands on her shoulders and turned her around. I started to take off her bra, and then I dropped it to the floor. I kissed her back and made my way down until I was on my knees. I slipped my thumbs into her panties, and I slowly started to take them off as I kissed her everywhere on her body. She let out a low moan as she lifted her feet, and I tossed her panties on top of her bra.

"Turn around, Ellie."

She did as I'd said, and then she started to take off her shoes.

"Keep your shoes on, sweetheart."

She sucked in a breath of air as I kissed right below her belly button.

"Lean against the wall, Ellie."

She barely whispered, "Okay."

I picked up her right leg and put it over my shoulder as I started to kiss the inside of her thigh.

"Oh god," she said as she grabbed my hair.

I just wanted to make her feel good. I wanted us to get lost in each other.

The moment my lips touched her, she started making small moans that were driving me crazy. It didn't take long before she was calling out my name. I picked her up and carried her to the bed. I got undressed and then slowly crawled on top of her. I took my time entering deep into her body. I wanted so badly for her to get pregnant. I placed my hands on her cheeks as I planted soft kisses all over her face. Once I was buried deep in her, I started to move.

She grabbed my ass and bit down on my bottom lip. "Faster, Gunner."

It didn't take long before we were both coming and whispering how much we loved each other. I stayed on top of her for a few minutes, catching my breath, as she gently moved her fingertips up and down my back.

Then, someone knocked on the door. She tried desperately to keep from laughing. I shook my head for her to be quiet.

"Gunner? Ellie?"

"Oh. My. God! It's like he has some sort of radar!" Ellie whispered.

I covered her mouth, so Gramps wouldn't hear her.

We waited for another five minutes before I jumped up and began getting dressed. Ellie ran by me and started the shower.

I followed her, reached in the bathtub, and turned it off. "What are you doing?"

"I don't want to smell like sex, Gunner!"

I started laughing. I grabbed a washcloth and ran it under hot water. "Spread your legs, sweetheart," I said as I gently cleaned her up. I looked up at her, and she had her eyes closed while she bit on her lower lip.

*Fuck! I want her again.*

When I stopped and turned on the shower, she looked at me, confused. I stood up, grabbed her hand, and brought her into the shower with me. Picking her up, I pushed her against the shower wall and started to make love to her again.

"We need to sneak away more often."

"Oh, that can be arranged, sweetheart."

After we came back into the reception area, Jeff and Ari looked at us. Ari's mouth dropped open. We walked up, and I grabbed Jeff's beer from his hand.

"You horny bastard. You had to sneak away with my sister during our best friend's wedding reception?"

I just looked at him.

"Jesus, Mary, and Joseph. Did you do it in the shower? Your hair is soaking wet in the back, Ells. Have I taught you nothing? Shower cap, bitch!"

Ellie started laughing as her cheeks flushed.

"Ah hell, come on. I don't need to hear this shit!" Jeff got up and made his way to the bar.

Ari winked at me before she followed Jeff.

Sharon walked up and smiled.

"Where's Alex?" I asked.

"Grace finally sweet-talked me into giving her up. Where did you two disappear to? Garrett went off looking for you," she said with a wink.

Ellie's flush deepened as her mother grabbed her arm and started walking off with her. When Ellie looked back over her shoulder and smiled at me, my heart dropped to my stomach. *I'd laid down my life to always see that smile on her face.*

I saw Scott sitting in a chair, drinking a beer. I went over and slapped him on the back. "So, how did the dance go?"

He shrugged his shoulders. "When we finished dancing, I asked her if we might be able to talk, and she just turned and walked away from me."

"Dude, did you go after her?"

He shook his head. "No."

"Did you ever think she might have wanted you to follow her?"

Scott just looked at me. "Why in the fuck wouldn't she just tell me to follow her? Am I supposed to read her damn mind?"

I nodded. "Yep."

Scott threw his head back and sighed. "Holy hell, I can't do this."

"If you care about her and want to have a relationship with her, you'll do it."

Scott turned and looked at me. Then, he stood up and smiled. "Well, Heather told me she saw Jessie walking down to the beach."

I gestured to the boardwalk. "You know what to do." I watched as Scott took off toward the beach to look for Jessie. *I hope that stubborn girl gives him a chance to explain everything.*

When I glanced over to the entrance of the ballroom, my heart dropped in my stomach. *What in the fuck is she doing here?*

I stood next to Elizabeth as she went on and on about the babies. All of a sudden, I felt someone staring at me. When I looked up, I saw Victoria standing at the entrance of the ballroom.

*What in the hell is she doing here? God, give me the strength not to pound the fuck out of her.*

I glanced around the room for Josh. I saw him talking to some friends from college. My head snapped back to Victoria.

I turned back to Elizabeth. "Excuse me, Elizabeth. I need to take care of something."

When I started heading over to Victoria, Gunner jumped up and came to my side.

He took me by the arm and leaned down into my ear. "Heather, why don't you let me take care of her?"

As we kept walking toward her, I turned to Gunner. "I'm tired of these crazy-ass, good-for-nothing, stupid bitches. I'm going to finish this."

Gunner let go of my arm, but he kept walking along with me. When I was standing in front of Victoria, the smile that spread across her face made me sick to my stomach. I grabbed her arm and pulled her right back out the door and down the hallway, taking her away from the ballroom.

"Let go of me right now," Victoria said.

I stopped and pushed her against the wall. "Listen here, you crazy-ass nutcase. I don't know how you found out where we were getting married, and I don't really care. You showing up here is the last straw. He doesn't love you. He doesn't want you. We. Are. Married." I pushed my wedding ring into her face. "We are having twins in September. We are in love, Victoria. He is my life, and I am his. You are nothing more than some slut who used to give him head in her car as a means to keep him around. Do you really think he wants to be with you? I feel sorry for you. Do you know why?"

She just stared at me as her smile faded. She glanced over toward Gunner and then back at me.

"I feel sorry for you because you're chasing after someone who wants nothing to do with you. It's pathetic. Try to have a little bit more self-respect, Victoria. If you do, you just might find someone is out there for you. Someone will love you for you, not just because you give good blow jobs."

Victoria opened her mouth to say something but then closed it.

"Now, I'm going to ask you politely to leave my wedding reception and never, ever contact either Josh or me again. The next time I see your face show up somewhere you aren't invited, I'm going to make sure you're the patient and not the nurse. That goes for all my friends, too. You even so much as look in Ellie's direction, and you'll regret it for the rest of your life. Do I make myself clear on all of this...Tori?"

She just stared at me. My hands were shaking, and I tried desperately to hide the fact that I was trembling from head to toe. I was surprised my voice hadn't cracked, but with Gunner standing next to me, I'd found the strength I needed to just tell this girl off.

"I just...I only wanted to say I was sorry to Josh."

"He doesn't want nor does he need your apology."

Victoria stood up a little taller and tilted her head.

"Shall I walk you out, or have you removed?"

She looked over at Gunner and made a face before she turned back to me. "Fine. I'm leaving. You can have him. He sucked in bed anyway."

Something inside me snapped, and I slapped her across the face as hard as I could. My damn hand was stinging and still hurt from the last time I'd hit this girl. "Go fuck yourself, you bitch," I said.

Victoria put her hand up to her face as tears were filling her eyes.

"I suggest you leave now before I do what I really want to do to you."

Victoria moved and started to make her way out of the hotel. I put my left hand on the wall to hold myself up as I tried to catch my breath.

Gunner squeezed my shoulders as he leaned down toward my ear. "Holy hell, girl. You just made me so damn proud, Heather!"

"Jesus H. Christ!" Ari said.

I turned and saw Ari leaning up against the wall. She was smiling from ear to ear, and I couldn't help but smile back at her.

"I knew you had that shit deep down inside you!"

Gunner and I both started laughing. He reached for my hand and smiled as he kissed the back of it. He brought Ari and me in for a hug.

I slowly pulled away and looked at Gunner and Ari. "How in the hell did she know where and when the wedding was?"

"Evil witches like her use their wicked powers to find shit out," Ari said with a smile.

"This shit stays between the three of us. Nobody else needs to know we had a visitor today," Gunner said.

Ari and I both said at the same time, "Agreed."

It was finally time for Josh and me to leave the reception. The best part of the evening was when Ellie's mom had caught the bouquet.

Josh and I were standing in the elevator as he looked over at me and winked. "Are you happy, Mrs. Hayes?"

My heart dropped when he called me that. I smiled and wanted nothing more than to be in his arms. "Yes, very happy!"

The elevator stopped, and the doors opened. An older couple walked in and smiled at us. "Oh! Congratulations!" the woman said.

"Thank you!" Josh and I both said at the same time.

"So, where are you going on your honeymoon?"

Josh tilted his head at me and shook it.

I started laughing as I held up my hands. "I swear, I didn't!"

The older couple looked at us with confused expressions.

When he slowly let that panty-melting smile of his cross his face, my heart melted.

"It's a surprise. I haven't told her yet," he said, never taking his eyes away from mine.

"How romantic. You're a very lucky young lady," she said as she smiled at her husband.

"Yes. Yes, I am."

The doors opened, and the older gentleman called over his shoulders, "Get in lots of baby-making practice!"

Josh and I both laughed as the doors shut. Before I could even say anything, he pressed the stop button on the elevator and then pushed me back against the wall.

"I love you so damn much." He captured my lips with his.

I wasn't sure how long we stood there, kissing, before the phone in the elevator started ringing. Josh pulled away from my lips and pushed the stop button back in and started the elevator again.

When the doors opened up on our floor, he reached down, picked me up, and carried me to our suite. He was kissing me as he tried to put the card into the reader. He finally got it open and took me inside.

"I'm so damn glad no one else is on this floor," he said with a wink.

"Why?"

He gave me that crooked smile of his and winked again. "'Cause, baby...you're going to be calling out my name all night!"

After he slowly put me down, I turned and let out a gasp. The room was filled with lit candles and bouquets of roses. A bottle of grape juice on ice and chocolate-covered strawberries were sitting on the small table. The bed was covered in rose petals, and it smelled like heaven.

Josh took me by the hand and led me into the bathroom. Beautiful white and light blue candles surrounded the oversized Jacuzzi tub.

"Oh my gosh…everything is so beautiful. Did Jenny do all of this?"

Josh smiled and shook his head. "Nope. I came up here while you were talking to my mom, Emma, Grace, and Sue."

"I tried to get that over-romantic, bastard best friend of mine to help me, but Garrett couldn't find him anywhere."

I smiled because I knew exactly where Gunner had been. Ellie had filled us in on their little sneak-away. "Ellie and Gunner had a little, um…alone time earlier," I said with a smile.

Josh let out a small laugh and pulled me to him. "Have I told you how beautiful you look?"

"I think maybe once or twice."

His eyes turned from love to passion in a matter of seconds. "I love you, princess."

My heart started beating faster in my chest. "Make love to me, Josh."

He laughed and shook his head. "Your wish is my command." He took my hand and led me out of the bathroom.

He reached over to his iPod sitting in the iHome, and Brad Paisley's "New Favorite Memory" started to play. I smiled as he placed his hands on my face. He brought his lips right up to mine and barely touched them together.

"I can't wait to make new memories with you, baby."

I closed my eyes as I felt my stomach twisting and turning. *Oh. My. God.* I opened my eyes and gazed into his beautiful green eyes. "You have no idea how special you've made me feel today. I just…I feel…"

As I felt a tear roll down my face, he wiped it away.

"How do I make you feel?"

"Like a princess. Like you love me more than life itself. I'll never forget this day and how you made me feel, Josh."

He leaned in and kissed me so softly that I let out a whimper. Then, our kiss turned more passionate. I needed him so badly. I started to unbutton his shirt, but our lips never lost contact with each other. After I pushed it off his shoulders, I placed my hands on his massive chest that was still covered by a white tank top. I slowly pulled away from his lips and lifted it up and over his head. When I pulled back to look at him, I noticed the tattoo on the left side of his chest. I just stared at it. It was my name in cursive, and under my name was a heart with the number two on it.

I shook my head and looked up at him. "When did you…"

He gave me that smile that just about dropped me to my knees. Snow Patrol's "Chasing Cars" started to play.

Josh laughed and shook his head. "What perfect timing for a song!"

I looked at him, confused.

"I made arrangements to have the tattoo done last night. Jeff, Gunner, and Brad were with me."

I smiled. "The number two? You and me?"

"Nope."

"The babies?"

He laughed. "No, but that would have been a good idea!"

I hit him on his stomach as I looked back at the tattoo. "What does it stand for?"

"When I gave you my heart. Who else gets to say he's fallen in love with the same girl twice?"

I shook my head and felt my heart beating faster. "What about the song?"

"I used to listen to this song over and over again—just dreaming about being with you, marrying you, having kids with you, growing old with you."

I slammed my body into his and kissed him. I needed him right this moment. I kissed him and poured as much love into the kiss as I could. "Please…please make love to me. I just want to be lost in your love all night."

"Turn around."

The sound of his voice made my whole body tremble. I slowly turned around. The moment I felt him unbuttoning my dress, my heart started beating faster.

He started laughing when he finally got to the last button. "Jesus, that was a lot of buttons!"

I tried to turn around, but he stopped me. Placing his hands on my shoulders, he leaned down and started to kiss my back. Then, he pushed the dress off my shoulders. The whole thing pooled at my feet. I went to step out of the dress.

"Wait. Fuck. If you look this amazing from the back, I can't imagine what you'll look like when you turn around."

I looked over my shoulder and smiled at him. He moved his hands up my neck and began taking the pins out of my hair. The moment my hair fell, I felt a sense of relief. When he ran his hands through my hair, I let out a soft moan.

"Oh god. That feels so good to have it down."

He kissed my neck as he placed his hands on my stomach. My whole body trembled.

"I love how your body reacts to my touch," he whispered in my ear.

"Josh…"

"Step out of your dress, princess, and let me look at you."

*Jesus. H. Christ. Why am I so nervous?*

He took my hand as I stepped out of the dress, and I slowly turned to face him. He sucked in a breath of air and just looked me up and down. I almost felt like I wanted to cover myself up, but the look in his eyes just turned me on even more.

When his eyes finally met mine, he smiled. "So fucking beautiful. I can't believe you're mine."

I couldn't even talk. I just wanted him to take me into his arms, so I could lose myself in his love.

"Heather…" He bent down and started to take the clips off of my thigh-high stockings.

I picked up my foot and set it on his leg as he gently rolled the stocking down. When he kissed the inside of my thigh, I let out a moan.

"Faster, Josh."

He let out a laugh. "Oh no, princess. I'm going to enjoy every second of this."

He repeated the same slow process when he took off the other stocking. Then, he removed the garter belt. He got on his knees and slid his finger along the top of my blue lace panties.

"Oh god…" I put my hands in his hair and tried to steady myself as he removed my panties.

*Kiss me…oh please, kiss me down there.* I was just short of begging him to touch me with his lips, his fingers, anything. I just needed to feel his touch.

"Your body is so beautiful, baby. I could stare at you all day."

"Josh…" When I felt his lips on my clit, my whole body jerked. "Oh god, yes!"

He pulled away, and I grabbed his hair.

*No!*

He kissed my stomach and then whispered to the babies before he slowly started to stand up.

My heart was pounding so hard. "Josh…I'm so turned-on right now. I just need you. Please."

He stood up and looked down into my eyes. "I need you, too, baby, but I want to savor every moment of this."

He reached behind me and had my bra undone so fast that I didn't even realize he had taken it off until he tossed it to the floor. Bending over, he took a nipple into his mouth as he started sucking and pulling.

"I think…I'm…going to…"

He let out a laugh. "What, baby? Are you going to come, baby?"

"No, you ass! I'm going to explode with desire if you don't touch me soon."

He started to walk me to the bed. When my legs hit the edge, he looked at me. "Lie down, and spread your legs open."

*I can't breathe. Holy hell. I can't breathe. I've never in my entire life been as turned-on as I am this very moment.* I sat down on the bed and moved up to the pillow. I lay down and slowly opened my legs to him. My chest was moving up and down, so hard and fast, and I just knew he could hear my heart beating.

He slowly crawled onto the bed. He kissed from my foot up to the upper thigh and then over to my other upper thigh and back down to the opposite foot. I grabbed on to the comforter and pulled on it as I arched my body up. *Why is he teasing me like this?* I closed my eyes as he started to move his way back up my leg, one soft, painfully slow kiss at a time. Then, I felt his lips right above my clit.

"Josh, please! I can't stand it any longer."

He slowly pushed his fingers inside me. "Motherfucker, Heather…you're so wet."

"I want you, Josh. I want you so badly."

"Heather…" he whispered against my skin.

The moment I felt his tongue move along my clit, I knew it would only be a matter of seconds.

*Oh, sweet heaven, this feels so damn good.* "Yes…"

I moved my hands through his hair as he kissed and sucked. I arched myself into him. I felt it building. "Oh god, Josh, don't stop!"

He kissed and sucked my clit as he moved his fingers faster.

*Jesus…I'm in a blissful heaven.*

I didn't even notice when Josh began crawling on top of me. I was just barely coming down from the first orgasm when he buried himself so deep inside me.

I grabbed on to him and called out in pleasure. "Oh my god! Oh god, Josh."

I felt his warm breath against my neck as he whispered in my ear, "I love you so much, Heather."

*Oh. My. God. Is it possible to have an orgasm on top of another one?*

Then, he said so softly and sweetly, "Oh god, Heather…I'm going to come, baby."

My world exploded with those words. He reached down and captured my lips with his as he kissed me before calling out my name. It was one of the most intense orgasms I'd ever had.

*Nothing in this entire world will ever be as wonderful as this very moment. Nothing.*

Josh leaned up on his elbows, catching his breath, as he looked me in the eyes. "I can't wait to make love to you under the stars of Italy."

*Wait. What?* "Italy?"

He smiled and kissed my nose. "Yeah, princess. Italy."

*My pouch!*

"I brought it, Heather. It's in my backpack."

I looked at him, confused, and then I realized he knew what I was thinking. "You brought my flower petals?"

"I did."

My heart swelled with more love.

"Just when I think a moment with you couldn't be any more special, you go off and do something else to top the one before."

"Are you happy, Heather?"

I smiled. "I've never been so happy in my life."

Josh rolled off of me, and I snuggled up next to him.

"Give me just a little bit," he whispered.

I listened to his breathing as it got more and more relaxed. I was pretty sure we were both going to fall asleep together.

As I looked out the window to the dark ocean outside, I thought about my mother and father. *Were they as happy as Josh and I are?* I so badly wanted to call Ellie, Ari, and Amanda to ask them if they had felt the most overwhelming sense of love on their wedding nights. My heart felt like it couldn't hold any more love.

Then, he started to mumble. I put my chin on the back of my hand and watched him sleep.

"Don't drop the babies, Jeff!" Josh called out in his sleep.

When I giggled and kissed his chest, he opened his eyes and looked down at me.

"My love will always be faithful and true to you," I said.

He moved his arm around me and smiled. "I love you, Heather."

"I love you, too, Josh."

He closed his eyes and drifted back off to sleep.

*Italy? Wow.* I closed my eyes and dreamed of Josh making love to me on a beach…under the stars of Italy.

# Chapter Forty-Five

## Jessie

"Dewey, I'm really not in the mood to go to a bar tonight. I just got back from the coast, and I'm tired."

"Come on, Jessie. You've been pouting ever since you got back. Let's just go boot-stomping."

I rolled my eyes as my brother looked at me with pleading eyes. "Fine."

We pulled up to the Wild Coyote Bar.

Dewey jumped out as he yelled, "Let's dance, baby sister!"

I laughed as he grabbed my hand and pulled me out of his truck. When we walked in, I noticed him.

"Fuck!" I said.

Dewey followed my eyes. "Alright, we're gonna have fun tonight!" He threw his head back and laughed.

Miranda Lambert's "Mama's Broken Heart" started playing as Dew pulled me out to the dance floor. I looked over my shoulder, and Scott was downing a beer as some bleach-blonde was trying to talk to him.

As Dewey and I two-stepped, he yelled out a whoop and a holler. I wanted to hide, but I knew it was too late. When I glanced over toward the bar, Scott was watching us on the dance floor.

*Shit. Shit. Shit. Maybe staying in Mason is a mistake.*

Dewey was singing along with Miranda, and I couldn't help but start laughing.

"You're crazy, do you know that?" I yelled.

"Hell yes, I know that!"

By the time we danced to three songs in a row, I was dying of thirst. "Dew, I need a beer."

Just then, Misty Rose walked by and smiled at Dewey. He turned back at me and gave me those sad puppy eyes.

I rolled my eyes and shook my head. "You're really going to leave me alone, Dew?"

He kissed my cheek. "I knew you'd understand. Open a tab. It's on me, baby girl."

I sighed as I walked away. I headed toward the side of the bar opposite of where Scott was sitting. I peeked over at him as I was walking up. He was watching me as the same blonde was still standing there, talking to him. My heart started beating like crazy. I knew that he had told me the truth about making Chelsea leave that night. There was no way he could have screwed her and sent me those messages all night. *Damn it. Why am I so scared to let him in?* I knew I wanted him more than anything. I glanced up at him again. Now, he was laughing at something the blonde had said to him.

*Yeah, I want him, but the moment I let him in, something better will come along, just like before. He'll leave me high and dry again, feeling used and abandoned.*

When I looked around, I had to smile. *Jesus, is this our high school reunion?*

"Hey, if it isn't little Jessica Rhodes. How in the hell have you been, girl?"

I laughed as I reached out and shook Jimmy's hand. "Hey, Jimmy. I've been good. How about you?"

"Well, I'm still kicking, still running this bar, and still married to the Mrs., so I'd say I'm doing pretty damn good."

I giggled as I took a quick look down the bar. Now, she was leaning toward him and talking into his ear. *Slut.*

"You want me to move, so you can throw 'em?"

I looked at Jimmy, confused. "Excuse me?"

"Those daggers coming out of your eyes. You look like you're about to pounce on someone."

I started to laugh. "No, not at all. Hey, Dewey asked if you would open a tab for him?"

"Sure can. What are you drinking?"

"A Bud Light please."

Jimmy winked and turned around.

When I glanced up, Scott was gone. *Shit! Did he leave?* I turned toward the dance floor, and then I saw him dancing with the bleach-blonde. *Asshole.*

"Well, if it ain't Jessie Rhodes. You back for good now, sweetheart?"

When I turned around, Michael McDowell was standing there with a shit-eating grin on his face.

*Oh Lord. This boy chased me all through high school.* "Hey, Mike. How's it going? Been a long time."

"I heard you're a vet now, fixin' to work at the local vet clinic here. Is that right?"

"Here's your beer, honey," Jimmy said.

I turned around, and he handed it to me. I glanced back out to the dance floor. Scott was laughing and twirling the bitch around. I practically slammed the beer in one drink.

I looked at Jimmy and raised my eyebrows. "I'm gonna need another one."

Mike smiled. "I'll take one also, Jimmy."

I glanced back at Mike. "I busted my ass to try and finish up school a couple years early, but I still have a few classes I'm taking."

When Easton Corbin's "A Little More Country Than That" started playing, Mike grabbed my hand. "Dance with me, Jessie."

With one look on the dance floor, I saw that Scott was still dancing.

I turned and smiled at Mike. "Sure. Why not?"

We walked out, and as soon as we hit the dance floor, Mike spun me around, and we took off two-stepping.

I let out a laugh as he twirled me around again. "Shit, Mike. I forgot how well you know your way around the dance floor!"

He looked down at me and smiled. I was having so much fun dancing with him. For a few brief minutes, I forgot all about Scott and the bleach-blonde.

By the time we got back to the bar, I was laughing so hard that my side was hurting. Mike and I talked for a few minutes, and then I saw a girl walking up. She reached up and kissed him on the cheek. I smiled as I noticed the way he was staring at her.

*I want that. I want to feel loved and cherished.*

Mike leaned down and whispered something into her ear that caused her to blush. I turned away and asked Jimmy for another beer.

When I turned back, she was looking at me.

She held out her hand. "Hey, I'm Mary Lou, Mike's wife."

I shook her hand. "It's a pleasure to meet you. Thank you for letting him spin me around on the floor."

She giggled and hit his arm. "He loves to dance."

"It shows."

After a few minutes, they said their good-byes, and I was left sitting there, alone. When I looked down the bar, I noticed Scott wasn't there. I glanced out onto the dance floor, but I didn't see him there either. *He must have left.* I frantically searched for the blonde. *What if he left with her?*

*Shit!* I closed my eyes and fought to keep the tears from building. *No. I won't do this again. I can't do this again.*

When Blake Shelton's "Do You Remember" started to play, I decided that I needed to find Dewey and leave. *I can't do this.* I got up, and when I turned around, Scott was standing there.

He gave me a weak smile as he held out his hand toward me. "Dance with me?"

My heart started to pound, and I felt sick. As much as my head was telling me to say no, my heart answered for me instead. "Okay."

He walked me out onto the dance floor, and he pulled me in close to him. He didn't say a word as we started to dance. I kept thinking back to him on the beach, begging me to believe him about Chelsea. I did believe him. But then, she had called, and it hit me. She was still a huge part of his life.

*Is he looking for someone to make him forget? Or is he looking for someone to love?*

As the end of the song was playing, he drew me in closer and put his mouth up to my ear. I felt the heat of his breath, and I had to close my eyes.

"Please forgive me, Jessie…please, angel. I haven't been able to stop thinking about you. It kills me that you're hurting because of me."

I leaned away from him and stared up into his blue eyes. The look in his eyes was filled with…

*Impossible. He couldn't possibly think of me that way. I'm just Tiny, Dewey and Aaron's baby sister.*

He placed his hands on the sides of my face as he leaned down to kiss me. My heart was beating so fast and hard that I was sure the whole place could hear it. Once his lips touched mine, I let out a small moan as I reached up and ran my fingers through his hair.

I wasn't sure how long we had been kissing, but the next song was already playing, and everyone was dancing around us.

He pulled away just a bit. "Please come home with me."

I smiled as I nodded. "Are you sure it's safe? No ex-girlfriends?" I giggled.

He threw his head back and laughed. "I promise. The only other living thing in that house is my cat."

As I was looking around for Dewey, he danced right on by me.

"Dew!" I yelled.

He stopped and looked right at me.

"I'm going to be, um…I'm going to, uh…"

Dewey stared at me like I was nuts. I noticed then that he was dancing with the same bleach-blonde who had been talking to Scott earlier. Scott must have noticed, too, because he started laughing.

"Dew, I'll make sure Jessie gets home...tomorrow." He winked, and then he grabbed my hand and started walking me out of the bar.

Dewey shouted at Scott, "Fucker! That's my sister you're talking about, you dick!"

I turned around and smiled at Dewey. I was blowing him a kiss while Scott was practically pulling my arm out of the socket. It wasn't lost on me that the blonde was giving me a dirty look. As soon we got outside, Scott grabbed me and began kissing me. I'd never felt so alive in my life. He reached down and picked me up as I wrapped my legs around him. He started to make his way to his truck.

That was when I heard her laugh.

"For the love of god, Scott. At least wait until you take her to a cheap motel."

Scott pulled away from my lips and smiled. "Funny, I thought I heard someone talking."

He put me down near the passenger side of his truck. His smile was breathtaking. It was slightly crooked with a dimple on each side, and it totally made me weak in the knees.

"You did hear—"

He kissed my lips before I could finish. When I felt his hand go up my shirt, I did everything I could to keep from letting out a whimper. He moved his lips to kiss along my jawline, and then he bit down on my earlobe.

He whispered in my ear, "I'm not sure I can get you home fast enough."

I looked over his shoulder, and Chelsea was standing there with two other girls, just staring at us. I smiled as I decided to give the bitch a taste of her own medicine.

Picking up my leg, I wrapped it around him as I threw my head back against his truck. Then, I just simply yelled, "Yes!"

Scott let out a moan and pulled me into him as he opened the door to his truck. "Jesus H. Christ, Jessie. I want you, angel." He picked me up and set me down on the seat.

I looked into his eyes and smiled. "I want you, too, Scott...more than you know."

He smiled as he stepped back and shut the door. He didn't even look in Chelsea's direction. I watched her while she stared at Scott as he ran around the front of his truck and jumped inside. When she quickly glanced at me, I looked away. I smiled at Scott as he looked at me with a smile that just about caused my panties to combust.

*Oh god. Is this really going to happen? Can I open my heart to him again? Will he take care of it? Or will he break it again?*

The whole way to my house, Jessie was quiet. *Does she regret this? Fuck, I hope not.*

I'd just about died when I heard Chelsea laughing, and then I'd wanted to tell her to go fuck herself when she made that smart-ass comment. I smiled when I thought about how Jessie had put on a bit of a show for Chelsea.

As I pulled into my driveway, my heart started to beat faster, and I made sure I didn't see a BMW anywhere. *Shit, Scott! Now, you're just being paranoid.* Then again, I wouldn't put it past Chelsea to find a way to get here before us.

After I parked the truck, I turned to Jess. "Hold on, angel." I jumped out so fast and ran around to the passenger side. When I opened her door, I couldn't help but smile. *Jesus, she has the most beautiful smile ever.*

I held out my hand, and she took it. After she jumped out of the truck, she looked back toward it as I shut the door. I started to walk backward as I was leading her to the front door.

She began laughing, and she stopped walking.

"What's wrong? Are you having second thoughts?" I asked with panic in my voice.

She shook her head and looked back at my truck. "Scott…you left your truck running."

Then, I heard the diesel engine. *Oh for the love of all things good. How fucking stupid.* "Oh shit! Hold on."

I ran back to the driver's side and took a deep breath. *Okay, Scott…Jesus H. Christ, calm the hell down. It's okay. It's all going to be okay.*

She was breathtakingly beautiful. Her shoulder-length blonde hair was shining in the moonlight, and I could swear those piercing green eyes were on fire. She was probably around five foot three inches, and she couldn't have weighed more than a hundred and ten pounds. She was perfect.

Then, she giggled, and it moved through my body like a jolt of lightning. *I've wanted this girl for so damn long.* I walked up to her and slammed my lips onto hers. She wrapped her arms around my neck, and I reached down and picked her up. After I carried her up the stairs, I slowly let her down as I pushed her against the front door.

"I'm going to make love to you all night, Jessie," I softly said.

"Scott…" she whispered back as she looked me in the eyes.

I thought she seemed scared. I knew she'd been with Gunner, but I didn't know how many other men she had slept with. *What if I sucked? Oh shit. What if she compares me to them?*

Her eyes were screaming passion, yet her body was shaking from head to toe.

*Is she just as nervous as I am?*

I unlocked the door and led her in. As I turned to face her, I was just about to ask her if she wanted something to drink, but then she walked up to me and grabbed my neck. She brought me down for the most passionate kiss I'd ever experienced. I picked her up again and started carrying her up to my bedroom.

I pulled away from her lips and smiled. "Do you want something to drink, honey?"

She gave me the sweetest smile back as she shook her head. "I only want you."

My heart slammed in my chest as I walked into my bedroom and slowly put her down. I placed my hands on her face and then gently kissed her on her forehead, down to her nose, and then to her lips. The moan that escaped her mouth just about had me ripping off her clothes and making love to her against the wall.

I slowly moved my hands down her shirt, lightly touching her breasts. She threw her head back and let out a whimper. I lifted her T-shirt up and over her head and then tossed it onto the chair. I took a second to look at her. I had imagined this moment since I was seventeen years old. *Jessica Rhodes is standing in front of me, dressed in a black lace push-up bra.* My hands started shaking as I reached behind her back and unclasped her bra in one movement. She raised her eyebrows at me and smiled. I let out a laugh as I took my hands and pushed the bra off her shoulders.

*Motherfucker. She had to be about a thirty-six…C-cup. I'd never seen such beautiful breasts. Chelsea was a thirty-two A, and she never liked for me to touch her breasts. Ever.*

"If you're trying to figure out my size…it's a thirty-six C." She smiled.

"Damn, I have a new talent now!" I said with a wink.

I reached up and cupped her breasts. *God, they fit perfectly in my hands.* I glanced up at her, and she had her eyes closed. Leaning down, I put a nipple in my mouth. When she brought her hands up to my hair, I felt like I was about to lose it. *Shit! I better at least last five minutes, or I'm going to be really embarrassed.* I moved my mouth over to her other breast as she began pulling my hair.

"Scott..." she whispered.

I got down on my knees and started to unbutton her jeans. Her whole body was covered in goose bumps, and I smiled, knowing it was my touch that was causing her reaction. I slowly slid down her jeans and held her as she stepped out of them and kicked them off to the side. When I looked at her matching black lace panties, I could swear my dick got harder and started jumping. I leaned in and kissed her through her panties right about her pelvic bone.

"Oh my god!" She grabbed my hair again.

I smiled. *I wonder if...*

I started to take off her panties. She lifted one foot and then the other. I stood up and took a good look at her. I pushed her back against the wall and dropped to my knees again.

"Scott...I've..."

I started to kiss her upper thigh, and the sound she was making was driving me insane. My dick was hurting so bad that I almost wanted to take myself in my hand and finish the job. I moved up her leg and around her clit.

"I've...never...oh god..."

*She's never had oral sex before?* When I looked up at her, her head was leaning back against the wall, and she had her fucking finger in mouth. *Oh hell, I'm never gonna make it.*

"Jessie...have you ever had oral sex before?" I asked.

She snapped her head down to look at me. Still biting on her damn index finger, she shook her head.

I smiled so damn big. I was going to pleasure her in this way. I loved that I got to be her first for this. As she smiled back at me, I saw the blush spreading across her cheeks.

When I turned back and blew on her clit, she let out another moan and threw her head back. Then, I oh-so lightly took my tongue and ran it along her clit. Her hips jerked, and she cried out. I wanted to go slow, but all I really wanted to do was be inside her. I gently started to kiss and lick her clit as I put two fingers inside her.

*Holy hell. She's soaking wet and so damn tight. Fuck, I want to be inside her, deep inside her.*

I slipped another finger inside and moved my tongue faster. As she started to grab my hair, I felt her tighten around my fingers.

She called out my name over and over again. "Scott! Oh…god…oh god, yes, Scott! Oh my god, I've never…felt…oh god!"

Her hips were moving so fast, and my dick was about to explode. I reached down and undid my pants. I stood up and dropped them while I watched her come down from her orgasm. I picked her up and pushed her against the wall as I lowered her onto me.

"Oh fuck…Jessie…you feel so good."

"Scott. Oh god…that was…that was amazing."

I smiled as I leaned down and kissed her neck. I wasn't sure how she would feel about me kissing her after what I'd just done. She tasted amazing, and I already found myself wanting more of her.

When I pushed myself deeper into her, she let out a whimper.

"So tight, Jess."

I moved in and out of her slowly. From how tight she was I could tell she hadn't had sex in while. It didn't take her long to start moving right along with me.

"Harder, Scott! Please...faster and harder."

*Oh god…this just keeps getting better.* I walked her over to the bed and gently laid her down. I crawled over her and slid my dick back inside her. I couldn't help but let out a moan. I'd never felt anything so wonderful.

Then, it hit me. *I don't have a condom on. Fuck!*

When I stopped moving, she grabbed on to my back.

"Scott…move! Please move."

I pulled back and looked at her. "Jessie…I forgot to put on a condom."

"Oh my god. Is that why it feels so amazing?"

I had to laugh at her response. "Um…"

She stared into my eyes and smiled. "I've never had sex before without a condom. I'm on the pill though, so…I'm totally okay with this."

I smiled as I bent down and kissed her. I placed my hands under her body and grabbed her ass as I started to move again. Before I knew it, she was calling out my name again. I held off for as long as I could before I had to let it go.

"Oh god, Jessie…I'm going to come, baby."

"Yes! Oh god, yes!"

It felt like heaven coming inside her. It was like every wish and dream I'd ever had about her just came true. I could hardly breathe.

"Scott…" she barely said.

I lay there for a few seconds before I was able to talk again. "Jessie, that was the most amazing thing I've ever experienced."

She wrapped her arms around me and held me tight. After a few minutes, she moved her legs, and I rolled off of her to lie on my side. She looked at me with the sweetest smile ever. I pushed her hair back from her eyes and smiled back at her.

"That was the most magical moment of my life," she said.

I took her hand in mine and laced our fingers together. "I've wanted to do that with you for so long," I said.

Her smile faded.

*Oh shit. What did I say?*

"Me, too." As tears started to build in her eyes, she quickly turned and got up.

"Where are you going?"

She glanced back at me. "I have to pee like a racehorse!" She wiped away the tears as she walked into my bathroom.

I sat up. *What in the hell just happened? Were those happy tears? Scared tears? Regret tears? Fuck me. If I pushed her into this too soon, I'll never forgive myself.*

I got up and grabbed a pair of boxers off my chair. I walked to the bathroom and knocked on the door. It was still open, so I peeked in. She was sitting on the edge of my tub, wrapped up in a towel, and she looked so damn cute. My heart started beating faster.

"Please tell me I didn't rush this, Jessie. I'll never forgive myself."

She glanced up at me, and that was when I saw a tear fall.

*Oh. My. God.* My whole world just stopped with that one tear. I went over to her and fell to the ground. "What's wrong? Did I hurt you? Do you regret what we did? I have to tell you, Jessica, that was one of the most wonderful moments of my life."

She smiled as she shook her head. "Oh god, no. I don't regret that at all! It was just as amazing for me. It was…it was—"

"It was, what?"

"Everything I ever dreamed it would be."

*She's thought about being with me?* My heart started to beat so loudly that I swore it was echoing in the bathroom. "Then, honey, why are you crying?"

When she glanced back down, I used my finger to lift her chin, so she would look at me again.

"I've just never felt this way before, and I'm…scared."

My heart dropped in my stomach. All I wanted to do was take her in my arms and love her again. "Jessie…" I whispered. I leaned up and kissed her lips softly. I pulled back and wiped her tears away with my thumbs. "I feel the same way."

She snapped her head up at me as her eyes grew bigger. "You're scared? Why?"

I let out a small laugh as I shook my head. "Jessie, I've never in my life experienced these feelings that I have for you. Just the sight of you takes my breath away. The touch of your hand on my body makes my skin feel like it's on fire. The sound of your laugh covers my body like a warm blanket. Your smile…my god…your smile can bring me to my knees in a second."

I watched as a tear rolled down her face. *I'd do anything for her.*

"No one has ever said anything like that to me before."

My smile faded for a quick second before I smiled at her again. I cupped my hands on her face and brought her in for a kiss. I kissed her so softly and tenderly. I wanted to make her feel how much I cared about her. I stood up with her, never stopping the kiss. I slowly pulled away, and then I reached into the shower and turned it on. She looked over and blushed.

*Why do I get the feeling she's much more inexperienced than I thought?*

I pushed the towel off of her, and I stared at her beautiful body. I could tell I was making her nervous.

"You're perfect, Jessica. Beyond beautiful."

She closed her eyes as I leaned down and kissed her neck gently. I quickly took off my boxers and helped her into the shower.

"Have you ever made love in the shower before, Jessie?"

She shook her head and looked down.

I bent down and looked into her eyes. "Just Gunner?"

She bit on her lower lip and nodded.

"I've only been with Chelsea," I said.

She gave me a weak smile.

I slowly started to kiss her. I was not going to fuck this up again. As much as I wanted to pick her up and start making love to her, I was bound and determined to make her feel special.

To make her feel…cherished.

## Chapter Forty-Seven
### Josh

"So, are you nervous, princess?" I asked.

When I looked over at her, she had her hand resting on her stomach. She was so much bigger than Ari, but she looked so damn cute.

She let out a giggle. "I'm more worried I'm going to lose my bet with Gunner. He swears it's two boys."

"I'm sticking with a boy and a girl."

She reached for my hand and kissed it. "Me, too!"

As Dr. Johnson moved the scanner on Heather's stomach, I felt tears building in my eyes. I could see both babies. I couldn't believe how well we could see them with their new scanner. I glanced at Heather as she just cried and cried.

"They're so beautiful. Oh my god, Josh…our babies!" she said between a laugh and a cry.

"So…do you want to know the sex?" Dr. Johnson asked.

He normally didn't do ultrasounds himself, but when he saw us walking into the hospital, he'd said he wanted to tag along with us.

At the same time, Heather and I both said, "Yes."

Dr. Johnson moved the scanner around and made a few clicks. As he began typing, I read the words appearing on the screen.

*Baby number one: I'm a boy.*

I jumped up and pumped my fist. "Yes!"

Heather started laughing as she grabbed my hand tighter.

Then, he started typing again.

*Baby number two: I'm a girl.*

"I knew it! Oh, I so knew it!" Heather said as she let out a squeal. "I cannot wait to tell Gunner that he owes me two hundred bucks!"

Heather and I were sitting in The Auslander Restaurant when her cell phone went off. She picked it up and let out a gasp.

"What? What's wrong?" I jumped up.

"Amanda! She's on her way to the hospital. She's in labor!" Heather tried to stand up.

I walked over and helped her up as I threw a few twenties on the table. "What about everyone else?"

"I'm on it!" Heather quickly sent out a text to Ellie and Ari.

Both had already heard from Brad, and they were on their way to Austin.

When we walked into the waiting room, we saw Jeff, Gunner, Ellie, and Ari all sitting there. Ellie jumped up and ran over to Heather.

"Well?" Ellie asked as she grabbed Heather's hands.

I noticed Heather glance over to a grinning Gunner.

"One little boy...and one little girl." She winked.

Gunner started laughing as he got up and walked toward me. He stuck out his hand. "Ah hell...congratulations, dude. That's perfect."

He reached over and took Heather in his arms. He just laughed as she bragged about winning the bet.

Jeff was next. Then, I looked at Ari standing there with a smile as big as the Texas sky.

My heart started beating faster as I glanced over toward Jeff, and he winked.

"A girl?" I asked.

She nodded, and Heather let out a small yelp. They both hugged each other as Ellie walked up and joined in on the love fest.

We sat down and talked about the ranch, Jeff's breeding business, and how well my business was doing. Finally, Brad walked out with the biggest smile plastered on his face and tears just rolling down his cheeks.

We all jumped up.

"How's Amanda?" Ellie, Ari, and Heather all asked at the same time.

Brad laughed. "She's absolutely wonderful."

"And you?" I asked as I reached out for his hand.

"It's a girl!" He blurted out. "I have a baby girl." And then, he lost it and began crying.

*Motherfucker is gonna cause me to cry.* I had to look away before I started crying.

I glanced at Jeff as he wiped his eyes quickly. I just looked at him and mouthed, *Pussy*, to him. He shot me the finger and walked up to Brad to congratulate him.

Gunner was slapping Brad on the back as he was congratulating him. When I looked back over toward Heather, she had the sweetest smile on her face. I felt tears building as I turned back to Brad. He was so damn happy.

I just stood there and glanced around at our little group. We'd all come a long way in the last few years. Each of us was married with kids and happy as hell, and it was about fucking time.

Out of the corner of my eye, I saw Victoria walking by. I quickly glanced at Heather, but she hadn't seen her. When I looked back at Victoria, she smiled at me and started my way. Then, she saw Heather, and she stopped. She turned and walked away.

*Okay...that was weird...but nice!*

As I glanced over at Heather, she was watching Victoria walk away. She started to turn back toward Brad, but then she caught my eye and gave me a wink. I had no idea what that was all about, but the fire in Heather's eyes turned me the hell on. I smiled back at her and shook my head.

"Y'all want to meet Maegan Ann?" Brad asked.

"Oh, I love that name, Brad!" Heather hugged him.

"My god, Heather...you're getting bigger." Brad laughed.

"Yep! We found out today that it's a boy and a girl." She looked back at Gunner.

I shook my head and followed everyone to Amanda's room.

After we all piled in, Amanda made everyone wash their hands—twice—and then we had to also use sanitizer. Finally, we all took turns holding Maegan. She was beautiful, and my heart swelled up so much at the sight of her. I couldn't wait to hold my own little girl and boy.

I watched as Heather was holding and singing to Maegan. *I need to get her home.*

I leaned over to Gunner. "Does it make me an ass if I want to stop and get a room tonight for Heather and me?"

Gunner looked at me and smiled. "Fuck no, dude. When we dropped Alex off at Sharon's, I'd already asked her if she could keep Alex all night. Got me and my girl a room at The Driskill."

I just shook my head. "Fucker. Of course you did."

Gunner started laughing as he shrugged his shoulders.

I excused myself and walked back to the waiting room where I pulled up the number for Hotel Ella. I reserved a room for Heather and me, and I was just hanging up when Gunner slapped the shit out of my back.

"Well?"

"Hotel Ella." I smiled.

"Nicely done," Gunner said with a wink.

"So, what brings you two handsome men to the maternity scene?" Victoria said from behind me.

I closed my eyes as I let out a breath. *Why won't this girl just go away?* Gunner glanced at her and gave her a dirty look.

"What? I don't even get a hello from the two men who know me oh-so well."

I turned around and just glared at her. "Really, Tori? What part of *fuck off* don't you get?"

She threw her head back and laughed. "You really mean to tell me that you two..." She looked us both up and down. "Are happy being married? Just being with one girl all the time? Somehow, I don't see it."

"Well, look harder. Honestly, Victoria, begging doesn't become anyone, not even a dog," I said.

Victoria's smile faded, and she tilted her head as she gave me a go-to-hell look. "You weren't that great in bed anyway. Neither of you were." She turned and walked away.

I shook my head as I turned back to Gunner.

He was watching her walk away. "Fuck."

"What? I think she might leave us alone now," I said.

Gunner shook his head and turned to me. "Yeah...but I wanted to know which one of us was better."

My mouth dropped, and I just stared at him. "What?"

"You or me. Which one of us was better? I mean, I'm sure she would say I was."

*What a bastard!* "Dude, please. I think you've got that backward. I'm pretty fucking sure she would say I was better...way better."

Gunner just smiled. "Okay, I'll let you have it."

"Oh no! There's no letting me have it, you bastard. We both know I'm way more experienced, and—"

"More experienced in what?" Heather asked as she walked up from behind Gunner.

"Um..." I looked at Gunner for help.

"Uh..." Gunner said as his head snapped over toward Ellie.

Ellie came up to Gunner and let out a sigh. "I'm exhausted. Can we go pick up Alex and head home?"

When Gunner glanced back over at me, I could see his body relax instantly.

"Sweetheart, I'm taking you to The Driskill for the evening. Your mom is going to watch Alex for us."

Ellie's face lit up as she jumped up and down. "Oh god, Gunner! I love you so much!" She slammed into his body and kissed him.

As he pulled back, he pushed a piece of her hair behind her ear.

I had to laugh because he did that all the damn time.

When I looked over at Heather, she was watching the whole thing with a smile on her face.

I walked up to her and whispered in her ear, "Baby, I made reservations at Hotel Ella for the night."

She smiled and pulled me off to the side. "I love you more than anything, but I'm not feeling very well. Can we just go home?"

My heart started beating faster. "What's wrong, princess? Do I need to call the doctor?"

She let out a small laugh. "No. I just want to be in my own bed. Is that okay? I mean, I love you so much for doing that. I just really want to go home."

I smiled as I pulled her to me. I leaned over to give her belly a kiss. "Whatever makes you happy...makes me happy."

We went back to Amanda's room and said good-bye to everyone before we walked out with Jeff and Ari.

I helped Heather into the truck and then ran around and jumped in. By the time we got out of Austin, my princess was sleeping peacefully. When I looked over at her hands resting on her stomach, I felt tears building in my eyes.

In a little less than four months, we would be parents to two babies.

*Holy hell. I sure hope I don't drop one!*

# Chapter Forty-Eight
## Heather

I sat on the porch, drinking my ice water. *I swear if it gets any hotter, I'm going to melt. This has to be the hottest July ever in Texas.*

Amanda and Brad had left a few hours ago with Maegan. She was already two months old. Josh had made a crib for her It was breathtaking, and I was so proud of him.

I had laughed at him though when he was holding Maegan.

Josh had kept asking Brad, "Have you ever almost dropped her?"

Shaking his head, Brad had just laughed each time.

*Why is he so afraid of dropping one of the babies?*

I watched as he came running up the street from his evening run.

*Oh. My. God. He looks sexy as hell, dripping in sweat, with his white T-shirt plastered to his body. Oh Lord...I want him so badly. Too bad I can hardly move.*

That was when I saw Mindy walking up to her little fence, waving for Josh to stop.

*Bitch! I just want to slap the hell out of her for her stupid excuses to get him to talk to her all the time.*

I watched as he ran his hand through his hair while he laughed at something she'd said. When she motioned for him to follow her into the house, I instantly sat up.

"You make one move to go inside that house, and you will regret it!"

I looked around when I realized I had just said that out loud.

Then, he started to walk up to her front porch.

*What in the hell is he doing?*

Just then, one of the babies kicked me so hard that I had to suck in a breath of air.

"Oh, not now, sweet babies. Mommy has to watch your stupid-ass Daddy flirt with the pretty skinny neighbor."

I watched as he lifted up a huge plant and moved it from her front porch down to her walkway. Mindy placed her hand on Josh's arm and laughed as she said something to him. Josh shook his head and waved good-bye as he turned and started to head over to our house. I stood up and put my hands on my hips.

Mindy kept her eyes on Josh as he walked away. She finally looked up and saw me standing there, and she smiled and waved. I really wanted to give her the finger, but I picked up my hand and forced myself to wave and smile back.

Then, she called out, "Thanks again, Josh! Next time, stay for some tea!"

Oh no, she didn't. *She. Did. Not. That twatface bitch of a whore! It doesn't take a gynecologist to pick out a cun—*

"Hey, babe! You look pissed. Is everything okay?"

I just looked at him. "You enjoy your run?"

He smiled up at me and nodded. "Yeah, but it's hot as hell. I should have taken Mindy up on that tea."

"Uh-huh. Well, it's not too late." I turned and walked into the house, slamming the door behind me. *Prick.* I stomped into the kitchen, opened up the refrigerator, and pulled out a beer. I was just about to open it when I realized what in the hell I was doing. *Oh god. I need these babies out. I can't make it another month. I'm going to explode.* I looked over at the watermelon and smiled. I started to take out a knife as Josh came into the kitchen.

"What in the hell is wrong with you?"

I turned around and looked at him. "Me? What's wrong with me? Oh hell, Josh, I don't know. I'm tired, I'm hot, I'm being beaten to death from the inside out by two very strong babies, you're flirting with the cute skinny neighbor almost every night after your run, we haven't had sex in almost a week, and even if we did, you'd probably be wishing it was with someone who didn't have a huge stomach in the way, and...and...I just want some damn watermelon and a fucking beer!"

Josh was just looking down at the knife in my hand. I had pointed it at him as I shouted. When my hands started to shake, I dropped the knife. Josh reached down and picked it up. He walked over to the sink and cleaned it off before he started to cut up the watermelon. I just stood there and watched him as he cut up the whole watermelon, put it in a giant bowl, and then cleaned up the mess. He turned around and set the bowl in front of me before dropping the knife in the sink.

He looked at me and let out a long breath. "I don't know what to tell you about the beer, Heather. As far as sex, I happen to love making love to you while feeling our children moving in your stomach. It's probably one of the most amazing things ever. I'm sorry I've been working late every night, but I wanted to finish up your surprise. While you were visiting with

Amanda, Brad helped me with it. I didn't realize it was causing you to think that I didn't want to be with you."

When he ran his hands through his hair, all I wanted to do was walk up and kiss him. *Oh god...what's wrong with me? Why am I being such a bitch?*

"I'm going to go take a shower and go to bed. I'm tired." He turned and headed out of the kitchen.

I just stood there and watched him walk away. I closed my eyes and felt tears building. I wasn't even sure how long I stood there.

*Shit! I hate being so moody and then taking it out on him.* I looked down at the watermelon, picked up the bowl, and put it in the refrigerator. I started to make my way to the babies' room. I opened the door, and as I looked in, my heart dropped to my stomach. I put my hand up to my mouth and instantly started crying. *The cribs.*

Two almost identical wood cribs were sitting in the room. They were breathtaking. Josh had used tree posts for the four corners and wood slates for the rails. The front right posts had a branch that extended up and over the crib. Josh had made six wooden stars that were hanging from the branch. One crib had six blue stars, and the other crib had six pink stars.

I walked in and ran my hand along the beautiful smooth wood. They were amazing, nothing like I could have imagined they would be. I'd never seen anything like them before in my life. I smiled, knowing that he had designed and made these cribs by hand just for our little buggers.

*Oh my god. I was such a bitch to him, and he had been working so hard all week to finish these. He didn't even get to see my face when I saw them. I started to cry harder.*

When I felt his arms wrap around my body, I instantly relaxed.

"Breathe, princess," he whispered in my ear.

I turned around and fell into his arms. "I'm so sorry! Oh, Josh. I'm so sorry. I love them. They're so beautiful!"

He held me tightly as he laughed. "I'm glad you love them. Dad helped me build them. He's been in town this week, helping me finish them up."

I pulled back and looked at him. "What? Your dad was in town this week? Why didn't he stop by?"

Josh smiled as he wiped the tears from my cheeks. "Dad cut the trees down for me. They all came from my parents' property. He helped me strip and stain them, and we worked on putting them together. He also brought them to the house earlier this week. I had them in the garage, and for the last two days, I was just praying you didn't have a reason to go out there."

I reached up and kissed him as I let a moan escape my mouth. I slowly pulled away from his lips, leaving only enough space just so I could talk. "Josh...I want you so much."

He grabbed me by the back of the neck and pulled me to him. He kissed me with so much passion that I thought I would explode.

"I'm going to make love to you princess." As he led me upstairs, my heart was pounding. Every time with him was like the first time. He always made me feel so special.

As he slowly undressed me, he knelt down and started talking to the babies. They began going crazy, moving all around, and we both laughed.

"Alright, y'all. I'm going to make love to your mommy, so settle down now." Josh stood back up. "Lie down sideways on the bed, Heather."

*Good Lord.* Something in his voice just sent me over the top. I wanted to come so badly that I could hardly stand it. I slowly made my way onto the bed, lying down sideways, while he got behind me. The moment he lifted my leg and started to touch me, I knew it wouldn't be long.

"Josh...yes...please don't stop." My voice sounded like I was begging.

He started to kiss my back, and for some reason, that was my undoing. I practically screamed out his name. Before I even came down, he moved inside me, and another orgasm began building. It felt like pure heaven, and I didn't want it to stop.

"Deeper, Josh..."

"The babies, Heather."

"You heard the doctor, Josh. We can't hurt them by having sex. Please..."

Josh pushed in, just a little deeper, and for the third time, I was calling out in pleasure. "Oh god! Josh it feels so good." This time, he was calling out my name along with me.

As we lay there, trying to catch our breath, I felt one of the babies moving.

"Someone really likes it when we have sex," I said with a giggle.

"Jesus H. Christ, I hope it's not the girl!"

We both started laughing as I rolled over to face him.

"I'm sorry I got jealous of Mindy. I don't like her, and she's always flirting and getting you to do things for her. I hate it."

Josh's smile faded. "I'll run back home a different way, princess. I won't even pass her house ever again. But please tell me next time, okay? Don't let it bother you until you blow. I want us to be one hundred percent honest with each other."

I nodded. "Okay...well...I feel huge and unattractive. My back and my feet hurt. I look like a whale, and I still have a month to go. Ari looks cute as a button, and...and..."

When I started crying, Josh smiled and tilted up my chin until I looked at him.

"I'm so sorry your back and feet hurt, baby. I'm going to run you a warm bath and then give you a good rubdown. You are the most attractive, beautiful, take-my-breath-away woman I've ever laid eyes on. I think you're more beautiful now than you've ever been. Your cheeks have the most beautiful glow to them. One look at you, and all I want is to be inside you and stay there forever. I'm the luckiest son of a bitch on the face of this earth because I get to go to sleep next to you every night and wake up with you every morning."

I smiled and reached over to kiss him. "Thank you," I said with a giggle.

"For what? Telling you the truth? Heather, I wish I could stand on the highest mountaintop and just scream out how much I love you. I'll always love you."

We talked for a little bit more before we both finally drifted off to sleep. I dreamed of nothing but Josh loving me all night.

I woke up to the smell of bacon. *Oh man, I've been craving bacon for two days! Josh must have run to the store to pick some up. I'm so going to try the whole blow-job thing again once these babies are born!*

When I stretched, I could feel every muscle aching. *Oh man, can I make it another month?* I slowly rolled onto my side and stood up when something red caught my eye. When I looked down at the bed, I saw blood on the sheets.

*No...oh god, no.* "Josh!" I yelled out.

I heard him coming up the steps.

"Hey, I was trying to let you sleep in. I made you breakfast." He walked up to me, smiling.

I looked down at the bed. I glanced back at him, and the moment he saw the blood, his whole face turned white.

"It's okay, princess. Let's get you dressed, okay? I'll call Dr. Johnson's office and get you in right away," he said as he turned and walked to get the phone.

*What in the hell? How is he so calm?* "Josh...do you not see the blood? It's not okay. It's blood."

Josh walked back over to me with a pair of shorts, a shirt, and my flip-flops. He smiled at me. "I know it's blood, honey. Can you get dressed while I call the doctor? Do you have a pad you can put on?"

*I just sat there, staring at him. A pad?* "Um...a pad?"

"Yeah...so when we get there, they can see how much bleeding you're experiencing. Baby...I need you to get dressed."

*Who is this person standing in front of me? And how in the hell did he think of that?*

Josh pulled out his phone while I got dressed. I walked to the bathroom and put on a pad.

*Please, God, please don't take my babies from me. Please. Daddy...help them...Daddy, please.*

When Dr. Johnson finished doing his exam, he looked up at Josh and me. My heart was beating so hard and so fast, and I knew I was squeezing Josh's hand.

"You said you had sex last night, right?"

Josh and I both nodded our heads.

Josh said, "Yes."

*Oh shit. I told him it was okay to be rough. Shit! Shit! Shit!*

"Oh Jesus H. Christ, I was too hard...oh hell." Josh stood up and started pacing.

Dr. Johnson laughed. "Josh, please sit down. It's perfectly fine to have sex right up until the babies are born. Everything is fine. There are no problems at all. The babies are doing good, Heather is doing good, all is well."

"Why was there blood?" I asked, taking Josh's hand as he sat back down.

"Well, when you're pregnant, blood flow increases to your cervix, so spotting after sex is normal. Now, from what you've described, there wasn't a lot of blood on the sheet, and hardly any was on the pad. I really think it was just from intercourse, so you have nothing to worry about."

I looked over at Josh and smiled.

He let out a breath of air. "Thank God. If I did anything to put them at risk, I'd never forgive myself."

After leaving the doctor's office, we went to lunch and then headed home. I took a nice warm bath, and then Josh massaged all over my body. I was in pure heaven. I assured Josh that it was okay to have sex, and we played in the shower some before making love.

"Heather, are you sure you feel like heading out to Mason?"

I smiled as I looked at my sweet, overprotective husband. "Yes! It's Jeff's and Gunner's birthday barbecue. It'll be fun. I need to get out and move around a bit. I promise, if I get tired, I'll let you know."

As we went out to Josh's truck, Mindy was walking by with her little white dog. Josh didn't even so much as look in her direction. He grabbed my hand, brought it up to his lips, and smiled at me. He walked me to the passenger side, opened the door, and winked at me.

As I felt that familiar buildup, I slowly licked my lips and then bit down on the lower one.

He smiled and shook his head. "Should I call and tell them we're gonna be late?"

"Yep!"

# Chapter Forty-Nine
## Josh

I rolled over and felt something wet and cold. I reached down and touched the sheets. *Wet. Heather's been eating watermelon again.*

Two nights before, Heather had woken me up, saying she had a dream about needing to go pee. In her dream, she finally made it to a bathroom and started peeing. The only problem was she'd started peeing in her sleep, too. She had eaten almost a whole watermelon earlier in the day.

I smiled as I got out of bed. *Damn, that girl sure does love watermelon while she's pregnant.* I was beginning to worry the babies would come out green and pink. I walked into the bathroom, and I was just about to lift up the toilet seat.

"Josh?" Heather called out for me.

"I know, babe. You peed the bed again." I laughed. "Damn, I didn't think I'd ever have to say that."

"Uh, Josh...I didn't pee."

I stopped and looked down at my dick. "Well, I sure as hell didn't piss the bed, Heather."

"No, Josh...my water broke."

*Wait. What?* I stepped out of the bathroom and stared at her.

She was standing up, holding on to her stomach, with her cell phone in her hand. "We need to call Dr. Johnson, Josh. I just had a contraction."

"Wait. What?" I just stood there and stared at her. *She's not due for another two weeks.*

"Baby. Will you hand me my clothes, so I can get dressed?"

*What is she saying? I need to sit down.*

She walked by me, grabbed her clothes, and started to get dressed. Then, I saw her grab her stomach.

I jumped up and ran over to her. "Heather!"

"It's okay. We probably just need to start making our way to the hospital." She smiled at me.

"Oh. My. God. It's time?"

She nodded.

"I'm not ready. They're early, Heather! They can't come early."

She laughed and walked over to me. She sat down on my lap, and I put my hand on her stomach.

"Josh, I don't think it's really up to you, babe. I'm pretty sure these two are saying they want out...now. To be honest, I'm perfectly fine with that."

I felt her stomach getting tighter.

"Shit...here comes another one, I think."

"Breathe, princess." I started to rub her back.

After the contraction was over, Heather stood up and smiled at me. "Is my suitcase in the truck?"

*Oh fuck! I forgot to do that.* I ran over to the dresser and grabbed a pair of underwear, shorts, and a T-shirt. I got her stuff out of the closet and then stuffed everything into a suitcase. I started down the steps, but then I stopped. I took out my phone and then continued down the stairs.

"Who are you calling?" Heather called out.

"My parents!" I shouted.

I ran through the living room, kitchen, and out the back door. When I got to my truck, I realized I'd forgotten my damn keys. I set the suitcase down and ran back inside as I found my mom's cell phone number.

"Josh, is everything okay? It's two in the morning."

"Holy fuck, Mom!"

"Josh! Do not swear at me like that. What in the hell is wrong with you?"

I shook my head to clear my thoughts. "Mom! Focus here. Heather's water broke. I'm freaking the fuck out, but I don't want her to know I'm freaking the fuck out."

My mother laughed.

*Oh my god! My mother is laughing at me!* "Mom, really? You're going to laugh at me now. Do you ever want to hold the babies?"

My mother stopped laughing. "You wouldn't! Oh, Josh, calm down, sweetheart. It's going to be okay. How far apart are the contractions?"

I stopped dead in my tracks. "Ah hell, Mom. I didn't look at the clock. That was my job. I fucked up my first official Dad job. Fuckin' A!"

"Josh, what are you doing right now?"

"I, um...I was putting the suitcase in the truck, but I can't find my truck keys." I looked up and saw Heather standing there, holding my truck keys.

"Oh, Heather has them! Thanks, babe!"

I ran back out the door and to my truck. I opened the back driver's side door and threw the suitcase in. I jumped in and checked the car seat again. *Shit, I hope this thing is in right.*

"Okay, sweetheart, that's good. But what are you doing right now?"

"Mom, I'm checking the car seat now!"

"Okay…my guess would be to just let that go for now since you already had that checked out four times in the last two weeks, honey. You might want to focus on Heather. I'm just saying."

I heard my mother tell my father to call Heather's cell.

"Josh, stop and take a deep breath. Will you do that for me?"

I jumped out of the truck and took a deep breath. I closed my eyes, picturing Heather and the first time we had made love next to the river. I remembered everything—how her body had reacted to my touch, every sound she'd made and look she'd given me, every time she'd whispered my name. My breathing slowed, and my hands stopped shaking.

"Better?"

"Yeah. Better. It's just that I love her so much, Mom. I don't want anything to happen to her or the little ones."

"I know, baby boy. I know. Your dad is talking to Heather now. She said her contractions are about twenty minutes apart. Honey, go back into the house and help your wife to the truck. We're on our way, okay?"

I nodded. "Okay. But, Mom…"

"Yes, Josh?"

"Hurry. Please hurry. Heather needs you, Mom, and I…I need y'all, too."

"We will. Don't worry. Women do this every day. You're married to the strongest woman I know. She's got this."

"Thanks, Mom! See ya soon." I tried to walk calmly back into the house.

The moment I saw Heather standing there, taking deep breaths, I almost lost it again.

"Come on, baby. Let's get in the truck and head over to the hospital, okay?"

"Oh, wait! Can you grab some watermelon?"

I just looked at her. "Really?"

"Hey…I remember both Ari and Ellie complaining how hungry they were. I don't want to be hungry, Josh." Tears began building in her eyes.

*No! Oh no! No, no, no! Don't cry!* "Okay, princess. Look, I'm getting it right now!" I walked over, got the watermelon out, and handed it to her.

She took the watermelon, and then she started to walk toward the back door.

*Holy hell. Who is this person?*

She turned and smiled, so I smiled back at her. I decided the best thing for me to do was to do whatever she told me.

## Chapter Fifty
### Heather

I listened as Dr. Johnson talked to Josh about what to expect during the C-section.

When I looked up, I saw Ari and Ellie walking in. I glanced over at the time. It was five in the morning.

"Hey, sweets!" Ari smiled at me.

I looked down at her huge belly and smiled. *She's next.*

"How are you feeling, hon?" Ellie asked.

"Better…now that I've had the epidural!" I said with a laugh.

After chatting for a few minutes, Dr. Johnson walked in. "Heather, it's time."

Ellie let out a little, "Eeeppp."

Ari smiled, but it faded as she put her hands on her stomach. "Oh, Jesus, Mary, and Joseph."

Dr. Johnson looked over toward Ari and raised his eyebrow. "Ari?"

She glanced up at him and nodded.

"Oh my god, Ari," I said with a smile.

Ellie looked between the three of us, and then she let out a small laugh. "This just keeps getting better and better."

Dr. Johnson laughed and turned back to Ari. "You better let your husband know and then check in."

"Ah hell, here we go again." Ari turned and walked out of my room.

I glanced over and winked at Josh. "Ready?"

He laughed. "Ready."

The moment I looked at Josh holding our son, I knew my life would never be the same. I glanced down at our daughter and smiled.

"So, have y'all decided on the names yet?" Elizabeth asked as she stood next to Josh.

Greg was sitting on the bed with the sweetest smile on his face.

I looked over at Josh, and we both grinned.

"Well, Josh picked a name, and I picked a name."

Elizabeth smiled. "Go on."

"This precious little girl's name is Isabella Gemma Hayes. Isabella is short for Elizabeth, and Gemma is after my mother." I smiled at Elizabeth as she began crying.

"And this future all-star football player's name is William Gregory Hayes. William for Heather's dad, and Gregory for you, Dad."

Greg stood up, leaned down, and kissed my forehead. "I've never been so honored in my entire life, baby girl."

I felt tears rolling down my face. I peeked over, and Josh was crying also. There was a knock on the door, and then Gunner and Ellie poked their heads in. Alex was wide-awake, and she smiled the moment she saw Josh.

"I still say that girl knows a good-looking man when she sees one," I said.

Josh laughed and showed Alex the baby. "Alex, meet William Gregory. You can call him Will."

Alex started laughing and buried her head into Gunner's chest.

Ellie rubbed Alex's back and turned to me. "Oh my god, they are so tiny! Her name?"

"Isabella Gemma. Libby for short."

"Beautiful names."

"Ellie, how is Ari doing?"

Ellie smiled and shook her head. "She's doing good, but Jefferson is freaking out."

Gunner and Josh both started laughing.

I snapped my head over at Josh and just looked at him. "Really? You're one to talk!"

Josh instantly stopped laughing and looked at his dad. "Oh, um…uh." Josh turned back to look at me. "Princess, have I told you how beautiful you look?"

"Nice," Gunner said, laughing.

As I looked around, my heart started to feel tight, and I felt like I couldn't breathe.

*My parents should be here. They should be holding my two beautiful children right now. My mom should be making plans to come and stay at my house for the first week, so she could teach me everything she knows about babies and diapers and no sleep.*

*Oh god! How am I going to do this alone? Take care of two babies? I'm going to drop one. Or what if I forget to feed one? Holy hell.*

I looked at Josh. He must have seen the panic on my face.

Ellie must have noticed it, too. "I've washed my hands twice. May I hold Libby?" she asked with a wink.

I handed her the baby as Josh handed Will to his mother. He walked over and sat on my bed. Leaning down, he kissed me so softly and sweetly that I let out a small moan.

He moved his lips to my ears. "Don't make noises like that. I've been told no sex for six weeks," he whispered.

I giggled, and he kissed my nose. When I looked over at Elizabeth holding Will, my heart got heavy again.

"Breathe, princess. They're with you, with us. I don't think it was an accident that we both came up with your parents' names for our children. I really believe they are with us, guiding us along. I wish more than anything they could be here for you...if only to kiss you on the forehead and tell you, 'Good job, you did great,' just like they knew you would. I'm so proud of you, Heather. You've made me the happiest man on earth...again! I can't wait to start this next chapter of our lives. I love you."

Tears were building in my eyes as I looked at the most important person in my world—my husband. "I'd be lost without you."

"I'd be even more lost."

"I love you so much, Josh."

He smiled and kissed my lips gently before he rested his forehead on mine. "I love you more, princess."

I let out a giggle. "I love you more times infinity."

# Chapter Fifty-One
## Jeff

I stood there next to Ari as she pushed again.

After nearly two hours, Dr. Johnson finally looked up and smiled. "One more good push, Ari, and I think we'll have it."

"One more good push! That's what you said on the last push, you bastard!"

Dr. Johnson laughed. "Come on, one more push."

The next thing I knew, I could hear the sounds of our baby girl crying.

I bent over and kissed Ari on the lips as she cried. "You did it, baby." I wiped the tears from her face.

When they placed our sweet baby girl on Ari's chest, Ari just stared at her. She looked up at me and smiled. "I think the name we picked is perfect."

I glanced down at our beautiful angel and smiled. "I agree. Grace Hope Johnson is perfect." I leaned over and kissed my sweet baby girl as she gave us a big yawn.

A few minutes later, there was a knock on the door, and Ellie and Gunner walked in with Alex. Then, Brad and Amanda followed with Maegan.

Ellie gave me a huge smile as she walked in, and then she glanced over to Grace. "Oh my god. Oh, Jefferson, Ari…she's breathtaking!"

When Alex let out a laugh, Gunner laughed. "I think she's excited about her cousin already!" Gunner reached out and shook my hand as he winked at me. "She's beautiful, dude."

I looked back at her and smiled. "Yeah, she is."

Brad walked up, leaned down, and kissed Ari on the forehead. "Job well done, Ari. She's beautiful."

Amanda smiled while she was rocking Maegan back and forth.

I glanced around and laughed. "Oh, holy hell. Do you know what it's going to be like when these three start dating?"

Gunner and Brad glared at me.

Brad shook his head. "She ain't gonna be dating…ever."

Amanda laughed. Ellie looked at Gunner and winked.

Ari sucked in a breath of air. "Heather!"

"Two beautiful, healthy babies—Isabella Gemma and William Gregory," Amanda said.

"Wow. Four girls and two boys. Five more, and we'll have a football team," Gunner said with a chuckle.

Brad glanced over at Amanda and winked. "I'm working on it."

I noticed Ellie was looking down at the ground. She glanced up and caught my eye. When I tilted my head, she gave me a look.

*Oh my god. My baby sister is pregnant.*

I raised my eyebrows, and she quickly looked over toward Gunner, who was now holding Maegan while Amanda held Alex. Ellie shook her head.

*Gunner doesn't know yet.*

I winked at her and then turned back to Ari, who was humming as she fed Grace.

I glanced around the room at everyone. I couldn't wait to see Josh and Heather's babies, and I really couldn't wait to see all the kids running around and playing on the ranch. My heart swelled up with so much love and pride as I looked at each person in this room. There wasn't a damn thing I wouldn't do for any of them.

Leaning over, I kissed Ari and then Grace.

Ari glanced up at me with tears in her eyes. "By the grace of God, he gave us hope. In that belief, we were blessed with our baby girl."

"Grace Hope," Ari and I said together.

"I thought the birth of Luke could never be topped, but life just keeps getting better and better. I owe that to you, Ari. I love you more than life itself."

As Ari handed me Grace, she smiled. "I love you, Jeff. Thank you for making all my dreams come true."

I walked around the room with my baby girl. I dreamed about taking her fishing, going hunting, and teaching her how to shoot a gun. I couldn't wait…but I could wait. I wanted to enjoy every single moment with her. "I have big dreams for you, sweetheart. Big dreams."

Gunner walked up and smiled as he glanced down at Grace. Then, he looked around and back at me. "Dude, does Ari have a plan for introducing Scarlet to the baby?"

*Oh Jesus H. Christ.* I wanted Ari to forget all about that. "Keep your voice down, Gun. I don't want to remind Ari. I'm paying Dewey to take Scarlet on a little ride once we get home with Grace."

"A ride?" Gunner asked.

I looked back over toward Ari. She was now holding Maegan and talking to Amanda, Ellie, and Brad.

"Yeah…I arranged for Scarlet to go to a doggy boot camp for a week. They're going to train her to do all kinds of shit she should already know how to do. Sit, heel, walk, roll over—whatever the fuck they do at those places. I bought myself at least a week."

Gunner shook his head. "Motherfucker. Why didn't I think of that?"

I shrugged my shoulders and smiled. "I'm smarter?"

Gunner just looked at me. "Hardly."

"Jeff?" Ari called out.

I turned and smiled at her. "Yeah, babe?"

"Before I forget to tell you, I told Dewey to cancel that whole doggy boot camp thing. Scarlet needs to be home to meet Grace," Ari said with a shit-eating grin on her face.

*How in the hell does she know these things?*

Gunner busted out laughing as he gently slapped me on the back.

"Damn…I love your wife." He walked over to Ellie and kissed her.

I stared over at Ari. She gave me a wink before she raised her eyebrow at me.

I shook my head as I looked down at Grace. "Remember this, baby girl. Nothing gets by your mama."

I peeked up and just watched as Ari laughed and talked to our friends.

*Yep, I love her more than life itself.*

# Chapter Fifty-Two
## Ari

As we pulled up to the house, I saw my mother and father standing on the porch with Luke. He started jumping up and down while clapping his hands.

Jeff parked the truck and let out a sigh as Scarlet came running up to the truck. "If that damn dog makes a move, I'm gonna kick the shit out of her."

I snapped my head to him. "You will do no such thing, you ass!"

Jeff shook his head and got out of the truck. When I looked back toward the house, I noticed Luke was wearing a T-shirt that said, *I'm a Big Brother*. I smiled as Jeff opened the door for me before getting the back door to get Grace.

"Oh!" was all my mother said as she walked up to the truck.

My father picked up Luke, and they were coming toward Jeff and Grace. I stood there as everyone tried to get a peek of the baby.

Luke kept saying, "I want Macy...I want Macy!"

"Jeff, may I?" my mother asked as she held out her hands.

I looked down at Scarlet, who was just sitting there, like the good girl she was. I knew my mother would shove the baby right in the dog's face, and Jeff would freak the hell out.

"Of course, Sue."

After Jeff handed Grace over to my mother, she walked up to the front porch and sat down with Grace. Sure enough, Scarlet came up, and my mom had her sniffing the hell out of the baby. It took everything out of me to not start laughing.

After Jeff got the baby bag out of the car, he turned around. "Oh no. Oh shit...no, no, no!" he said. "Um...Sue? I don't really want dog slobber on the baby...you know, germs and all. Maybe Scarlet can sniff Grace's butt or something...but not her face!"

My mother looked at Jeff and smiled as she stood up. She started to walk into the house but not before she turned around. "Like the great Katharine Hepburn said, 'If you obey all the rules, you miss all the fun.'" She winked, and then she went inside.

Jeff looked at me with his jaw hanging open. "What in the hell did that have to do with dog slobber on my child?" He walked past me and up the porch steps.

My father walked up to me and gave me a hug. "Oh, ma belle fille!"

"Bonjour, Papa!"

"Quel beau nom Grâce est."

I smiled as I nodded. "Yes, Grace is a very beautiful name, Papa."

As we headed into the house, my father looked at Jeff.

"Jeff, avez-vous obtenu malade?"

I let out a laugh as Jeff spun around to my dad. "No! I didn't get sick!"

My dad laughed and slapped Jeff on the back. "Way to keep going with the French, son. I'm impressed as hell."

Jeff smiled and wiggled his eyebrows up and down.

I bent down, scooped up Luke, and gave him a big kiss. "Hey, my big man! I missed you so much. What do you think about your baby sister?"

Luke smiled and pointed to Grace. "Macy!"

"Grace. Can you say Grace?"

"Shit!"

*Wait. What?*

I looked up at Jeff. "Did he just say…*shit*?"

Matt rounded the corner with his iPad as he yelled out, "Oh shit! I lost again."

Luke laughed. "Shit."

I almost fell over. My mother spun around and looked at me with that expression only a mother could give.

"What? Why do you automatically look at me?"

"Wow. I'm impressed at how clearly he says it," Jeff said.

My father walked up and hit his head from behind. "Assmole." My father winked at Matt.

*Oh my god. What in the hell is happening? My child just said, "Shit," and…and…*

"Did you just call Jeff an assmole, Dad?"

Matt looked up from his iPad. "Jeff is an assmole. Everyone knows that."

Jeff just shrugged his shoulders and took Luke out of my arms. "Hey, big boy. That's a bad word. We don't say shit."

"Shit! Shit! Shit!"

"Ah shit, Ari. He keeps saying it."

I just stood there and looked at him. *I swear if I didn't love him so damn much…*

"Nice, Jeff…swear at him while you tell him not to swear," my father said as he walked up and took Grace from my mother.

"I didn't swear at him…I…um…Ari?"

"Don't Ari me. You dug the hole, baby." I walked by and gave him a wink.

I fell onto the bed and let out a sigh. *Jesus H. Christ, I don't remember being this tired after Luke. I can't move.*

Jeff and Josh had been helping Gunner tag cattle all day. I reached over and picked up the phone to call Heather.

"Hello?"

"Jesus, Mary, and Joseph. You sound like how I feel."

"Oh my god. I'm so tired. I'd give anything to get, like, a good solid three hours of sleep." Heather yawned.

"You haven't slept for a solid three hours yet? Oh my god, Heather."

"How old are the babies?"

"Um…I sat up and looked around. Five days old now?"

Heather started laughing. "I thought it was six."

"Is Elizabeth still there, helping?"

Heather yawned again, which caused me to yawn. "Yes! Thank God, too. I don't know what I would have done if she weren't here. Josh got out of the house today for the first time since we brought the babies home. He's helping Jeff and Gunner."

"Yeah, Jeff told me. Have you heard from Ells?"

"Not today. Have you?"

"Nope. She's up to something though. She looked…different to me."

Heather sucked in a breath of air. "Amanda and I thought so, too! Like she might be—"

"Pregs?"

"Yes!"

"I wanted so badly to ask her, but if she hasn't told Gunner yet, I figured she wouldn't tell us until he knew."

"Ari?"

I yawned. "Yeah?"

"Thank you."

"For what?"

"For calling me. You have no idea how wonderful it is to hear your voice. I love you, sweets."

I felt tears building up in my eyes. "Ah hell, Heather. You're going to make me cry, you bitch!"

She let out a laugh. "I'm serious. Thank you so much for calling!"

"Same here, sweets. I love you, too. I can't believe we all have kids now…and hell, we're not even twenty-one yet!"

"Speaking of, I want to throw one hell of a party for our twenty-first birthdays. I've already got Greg and Elizabeth reserved for that weekend."

I started laughing as I lay back down. "Oh, hell yes. I can't wait to get legally wasted!"

I could hear one of the babies crying in the background.

"My free time is over! Elizabeth is napping, so I better grab him…or her…or both!"

"Alright. I love you, Heather."

"Love you, too."

I hung up the phone and closed my eyes. *Oh god…it's so quiet.* I started to drift off to sleep when I felt someone get on the bed. *Either Luke learned how to climb out of his crib, or I'm about to be kissed by a stranger.*

When I felt his hot breath next to my ear, I smiled and let out a giggle.

"I can't wait six weeks to be inside you."

I opened my eyes and looked directly into Jeff's. They were filled with so much passion.

"Me either, but we have to."

Jeff pulled away and winked at me. "But we can do other things." He raised his eyebrows.

He slowly pulled off my shorts, and then he started to kiss the bottom of my leg, making his way up. When he kissed right above my panty line, I let out a soft low moan. He moved up to my stomach.

He looked up and smiled at me. "Sit up, Ari, and let me take off your shirt, baby."

I did what he'd said. I lay back down on my side as he began to take off his pants and shirt.

"Jeff…there ain't no easy way to say this, honey, but…you stink."

He laughed as he used his fingers to gently run along my panty line. I closed my eyes and bit down on my lower lip. I grabbed on to him and started to move my hand up and down…feeling him getting harder by the second.

"Ari…" he whispered in my ear.

He slid his hand down into my panties and gently touched my clit. I bucked my hips into his hand and let out a moan. I moved my hand faster on his dick, his breathing got heavier. The moans coming from his mouth were turning me on even more. All he had to do was move a little faster on my clit, and I would be sure to come.

"Oh god, Ari…faster, baby."

I went faster and squeezed him tighter, and the moment he started to say my name, I came. Jeff captured my cries with a kiss as he rolled on top of me. Just to feel his body on mine was pure heaven.

He pulled away and smiled. "Four weeks?"

I laughed as I nodded. "Four weeks."

Jeff leaned down and kissed me gently on the lips. He whispered, "I love you, Ari. So damn much."

When I heard Grace starting to whimper, I let out a small laugh.

"My sweet baby girl...giving her mommy and daddy their time together," Jeff said with a wink.

He jumped up and headed into the bathroom. As he turned on the shower, he called out, "Close your eyes, babe. I'll be two seconds, and then I'll grab her and take care of her while you get some sleep."

"Oh, thank you, Jeff!" I closed my eyes and drifted off to sleep, dreaming of quilts, oak trees, and making love to Jeff. *Pure heaven.*

*Chapter Fifty-Three*

*Ellie*

I sat in my car and took a deep breath. I had dropped Alex off with Grace and Jack, and I'd made sure again that it was okay if they kept her for the night. I hated leaving her all night, but I wanted to spend some time with Gunner.

I wasn't expecting him to be back home so soon, but with Jeff and Josh both helping him tag the cattle, they must have finished up sooner than expected.

*Why in the hell am I so nervous about telling him that I'm pregnant? It's not like we weren't trying.*

I looked at myself in the small mirror. *Oh man, I look like shit.* My hair was pulled up in a ponytail, and I was wearing an old Longhorn T-shirt with cutoff blue jean shorts. It was not how I wanted to greet him.

After I opened the car door, I slowly got out and made my way into the house. It was so quiet, but I could hear our shower running. I smiled as I got an idea. I quickly made my way to the bedroom, and then I started to take off my clothes as fast as I could. When I heard him humming in the shower, I had to smile. I loved it when he would sing.

I opened the bathroom door, and I walked into the bathroom, naked. I peeked in and saw his back was facing me. I stepped inside the shower and wrapped my arms around him.

"Hmm…I was wondering where you were." He lifted up my left hand and kissed my wedding ring.

"I dropped Alex off at your parents' house…for the night."

Gunner turned around and smiled at me. "No shit?"

I laughed and nodded. "No shit!"

His eyes turned from love to lust in a matter of seconds, and the ache between my legs grew stronger. He reached up and pushed a piece of my hair behind my ear as he gazed into my eyes.

"I'm going to make love to you all night long." He gave me that damn crooked-ass smile of his.

"Drew?"

He was kissing my neck. "Yeah, sweetheart?"

"May third."

"Mmm…what about it?" He continued to kiss my neck as he moved his hands all along my body.

"It's, um…well…it's kind of an important day."

He pulled back and looked at me. "Oh yeah? Why's that?"

"'Cause it's the due date."

He looked at me, confused. "Due date for what?"

I picked up his hand and placed it on my stomach. It took about ten seconds for it to click.

He gave me the most beautiful smile. "Ells…you're pregnant?"

I nodded. He let out a yell as he picked me up and hugged the shit out of me.

"Oh god, Ellie, you've just made me the happiest man on earth!"

He pushed me up against the wall and looked into my eyes.

"I'm going to make love to you, sweetheart…slow, sweet love to you."

I bit down on my lip and wrapped my legs around him. As I felt him slowly enter my body, I put my head back against the shower wall and lost myself…body and soul…in his lovemaking.

I sat on the back porch, wrapped in a blanket, listening to the night sounds. I closed my eyes and thought back to the one moment that had changed everything. It was the first time Gunner had put his hands on me and took me to heaven and back.

I placed my hand on my stomach and silently thanked God for this baby. When I heard the back screen door open, I looked over to see Gunner walking out onto the back porch…butt-ass naked. I let out a laugh and shook my head.

"It's a damn good thing that it's three in the morning. You never know when Garrett will be walking up." I smiled at him.

He winked and sat down next to me on the swing. He wrapped himself up in the blanket with me. "What are you doing out here, Ells?"

"Thinking."

"Thinking about what?"

"How blessed we are. How happy you make me."

"You make me happy, too, Ellie. More than you'll ever know."

"I know we should probably wait to talk about this, but I'm thinking after we have this precious little gift…" I glanced over at him as he looked at me. "Well, I'm thinking two is the perfect number. What about you?"

He put his arm around me and pulled me closer to him. "Two sounds like the perfect number."

I slowly let out the breath I had been holding. *Why was I so scared to tell him that?* "Gunner? Will you do something for me?"

"Anything, sweetheart."

"Will you take me inside and make love to me again?"

The next thing I knew, he was picking me up and carrying me back inside. On our way to the bedroom, he hit his elbow on the doorjamb, whacked my head on the bedroom door, and stepped on one of Gus's toys. By the time we made it to our bed, Gunner was swearing, and I was laughing. He threw me on the bed and crawled on top of me.

"Oh, Mrs. Mathews, so you thought that was funny, huh?"

I nodded and giggled. "Yep!"

As Gunner kissed my neck and moved down to my nipples, I looked over and saw Gus standing in the doorway to our bedroom. I tried to ignore him, but I couldn't.

"Gunner…"

"I know, baby…I want to sugar stamp you all over your body."

*Wait. What?* "Sugar stamp?"

Gunner looked up at me with that smile of his. "Yeah…kiss you with my lips all over your body. Sugar stamp you."

I tried really hard not to laugh, but I couldn't help it. "Oh. My. God. I love you, Drew Mathews!"

He moved up and captured my lips with his as he slid his hand down and spread my legs open. He slowly began to touch on my clit. When his lips pulled away from mine, he made his way back down to my nipples. I looked back over to the doorway, and Gus was still sitting there…just staring at us.

"Um…Gunner."

"Hmm…Ellie."

"No…I mean…Gunner…" I tapped his shoulder.

"What? What's wrong?"

I pointed over to the doorway.

Gunner turned and looked at Gus. "What? The dog?"

"Yes. I can't do this with him watching us."

Gunner turned and looked at me with a funny expression on his face. "Uh…it's never bothered you before."

"It's like he knows…"

"He knows what?"

"Oh hell, I don't know. I just can't concentrate with him watching us."

"Okay. Do you want me to shut the door?" Gunner asked with a laugh.

I nodded. Gunner jumped up, made Gus go out in the hallway, and then shut our bedroom door. As he walked back toward me, I opened my legs more to him. He smiled as he grabbed my foot and started to kiss me all the way up my leg. The moment his lips touched my clit, I just about jumped out of the bed. I grabbed his hair and started saying his name over and over again. I didn't even realize he was on top of me and inside me until he started to move.

"Drew, I love you so much."

He moved so slowly, in and out of me, as he gently bit down on my earlobe. "I love you more," he whispered in my ear.

# Chapter Fifty-Four
## Josh

When I looked up, I saw Mindy walking on the street, heading straight toward me. *Shit! What is with this girl? And where in the hell is her husband all the time?*

"Hey, Josh. How are the babies?" she asked with a wink.

*Fuck me.* I glanced down the street. Heather would be coming home any second. "They're doing great. Thanks."

"How old are they now?"

"Thirteen weeks old." I looked back down the street, waiting to see my truck pull up at any moment.

Mindy turned and glanced down the road. When she turned back, she smiled and winked at me. "You must be feeling…overwhelmed. Heather sure looks…tired lately."

I just looked at her. "Yeah, she is pretty tired. It's not so easy with twins."

She bit down on her lip and then stuck her finger in her mouth. "I bet. She probably doesn't have much time to…fulfill certain needs."

*Motherfucker! This is not happening.* As I looked her up and down, I noticed her tits were practically falling out of a short white dress that might as well have been see-through.

"You like what you see, Josh?"

*Wait. What? Fuck. I wasn't checking her out!* I looked her right in the eyes. "Listen, Mindy, I don't know what kind of game you're playing, but I happen to be very, very happily married."

She smiled as she took a step closer to me. I took a step back.

"Oh, I'm happily married also, Josh. But that doesn't mean I don't like to…experiment…if you know what I mean."

"No. I don't know what you mean."

"Josh, come on. I've seen the way you look at me. I've noticed you running by my house again. I know you want me as much as I want you."

*Note to self: Don't ever run by her house again.* I glanced down the street again, looking for Heather. "Okay, I'm going to be blunt with you,

Mindy, because I don't really have time to jack around with this bullshit. I'm not interested in you, I've never been interested in you, and I'll never be interested in you. I only have one woman in my life, my heart, my soul, and in my bed. That woman happens to be my beautiful wife, and she will always be my wife. So, if you don't mind, I'd like to get back to what I was doing. You can take your pathetic, depressing, and rather sad attempt of coming on to me and turn around. Please…don't ever bother trying to talk to my wife or me again. The next time you do, I'll be sure to let your husband know what a piss-poor job he's doing at keeping his wife happy."

She stood there, just staring at me, with her mouth dropped open. She finally straightened up her shoulders, turned, and walked away.

I let out the breath I had been holding and shook my head. *Next time I see her husband, I think I'll remind him about that house he was interested in on Barons Creek.*

I walked back over and started messing with the fence again. I wanted to have it up and done before Heather and the kids came back. When I heard my truck coming down the street, I turned and watched Heather pull into the driveway as she smiled at me.

Tomorrow was the big birthday party for her, Ells, and Ari out at Ellie and Gunner's place. They all were twenty-one now, and they were more than ready to get legally drunk, except for Ells, who couldn't drink because she was three months pregnant.

Heather jumped out of the truck and shut the door. She gave me that smile that just about dropped me to my knees. She leaned back against the truck and raised her eyebrows. I waited for her to turn and get the kids out of the back. When she didn't, I looked at her funny.

"Um…Heather…don't you think it might be getting kind of hot to keep Libby and Will in the truck?"

She tilted her head and smiled. "They're not in the truck."

"What do you mean *they're not in the truck*?"

"Your mom and dad decided to come into town for a bit. They wanted some time with Libby and Will, so they rented a hotel room for tonight." She raised her eyebrows.

I almost wanted to jump up and down and pump my fist in the air. "We're alone? Like alone…alone? As in, I can walk through the house naked if I want to?"

She nodded. "Or maybe make love to your wife…in the kitchen, living room, bedroom, bathtub…you pick."

My heart dropped to my stomach. *I love this girl so damn much I can't even think straight.* "How about all of the above?"

She walked up to me and placed her hands on my chest as she reached up to kiss me. She pulled away and smiled. "I've always wanted to say something to you, and now seems like the perfect time to do it." Her cheeks turned a beautiful rose color.

I smiled, wondering what in the world she could say that would cause her to blush like that. My dick jumped, just thinking about what she might say. "I'm listening."

"Take me inside, Mr. Hayes, and fuck me."

My heart slammed in my chest as I looked at her. *Jesus. H. Christ. I wasn't expecting that.* "Motherfucker." I reached down and picked her up.

She slammed her lips against mine and let out the sweetest, sexiest moan I'd ever heard.

As soon as I shut the kitchen door, I put her down and started taking off her tank top. I barely moved my lips from hers, and I only did so long enough for us to pull each of our shirts over our heads. She grabbed me and started running her hands through my hair as she kissed me so passionately that I thought I might come just from the sheer intensity. I started to push her shorts down as she worked at unbuttoning my jeans. I kicked off my boots and helped her get my jeans off. I reached up and unsnapped her bra, and then I pulled her back against me.

"I want you so badly, Josh," she whispered.

"Do you like these panties?" I asked.

She looked down and then back up at me, confused.

I reached down, and in one quick movement, I ripped the lace panties off her body.

"Oh god." She leaned back and held on to the kitchen island. "I can't take it any longer, Josh. I need you inside me…now."

I reached out and scooped her up in my arms as she wrapped her arms around my neck.

"Your wish is my command, princess."

As I moved through the house and up the stairs, I smiled, knowing that this was the woman I wanted to spend the rest of my life with. She was the only woman I ever wanted to even touch. She would always be my last first kiss.

After I gently put her on the bed, she moved her body up, and then she lay down on her pillow. I looked her up and down as I licked my lips. Her body was beautiful and perfect. I would have never known that she'd just had twins a few short months ago, except for the scar from the C-section. I bent down and kissed along her scar as she let out a long, soft moan.

"My god, I love you so much, princess."

"Josh…"

I moved up, and while lying on top of her, I put my hands on each side of her face, and I just looked at her.

"I just want to lie like this for hours." I softly kissed everywhere on her face.

She let out a giggle. "We have three hours before your parents bring Libby and Will home."

"I can work with that." I kissed her lips so tenderly. "I just want to be with you...always. I look at you, and sometimes, I just want to cry because I love you so much. I'd never do anything to hurt you, princess."

She smiled, and I saw a tear slide down the side of her face.

I slowly entered her body as I kissed her. I reached under her and grabbed her ass as I moved and kissed her neck. She moved her hands up and down my back.

"I love you, Josh. Oh god, I love you so much."

"God, you feel so good," I whispered into her ear.

"Josh...yes...oh god...it feels like heaven."

I made sweet, slow, passionate love to her.

She grabbed on to my ass and pulled me deeper into her as she started to say my name. "Josh, I'm...oh god..."

I moved faster and harder as she kept along with me. My heart slammed in my chest when she moved her lips to my ear and whispered, "Josh, I love you so much."

"Oh god, Heather. I'm going to come, baby. Fuck...it feels so good."

I didn't move for a good minute as she gently ran her fingertips up and down my back. We didn't need to say a word to each other. I'd never felt so alive in my life.

*I'd do anything for her. I'd move any mountain and swim across any ocean just to be with her. I'd lay down my life for her.*

I walked out onto the back porch and handed Heather a glass of sweet tea. She had her hair pulled up in a ponytail, and she was wearing one of my old T-shirts with a pair of my sweatpants. She was swimming in a sea of clothes, and she looked sexy as hell.

"Thank you," she said.

I sat down and looked out into the yard. I started drawing a mental picture of the swing set I wanted to build for the kids.

"I've never been so happy in my life," Heather said as she turned to me.

I looked at her and smiled. "I feel the same way, princess. I just wish we had more afternoons like this," I said with a wink.

She threw her head back and laughed. "God...it's finally getting a little bit easier...or I'm just getting the hang of this whole parenting thing."

I nodded as I glanced back at her. She was breathtaking, and I really couldn't believe she was mine. The first moment I put my eyes on her, I'd known she was the one. When those blue eyes looked into mine, I'd known that was it. I would never be with anyone but her.

She smirked at me and tilted her head. "What are you thinking about?"

"The first time I ever saw you. You walked in with Ari, Ells, and Amanda, and my heart dropped in my stomach. Something about you just took my breath away. I'd waited so long for someone to have that effect on me, and there you were—the perfect picture of innocence mixed with the perfect amount of sexy." I let out a little laugh as I shook my head. "And it scared the fuck out of me."

She laughed and raised her eyebrows. "Same here. I just had to look into your eyes, and I knew I was in trouble. Gunner even walked up to me that night and told me to be careful with you."

I shook my head. "That fucker."

Heather laughed as she grabbed my hand, and when I felt that familiar jolt of electricity, I smiled.

*Still. She still has the same effect on me.*

"Love at first sight?" Heather asked.

I leaned over and barely put my lips to hers. "Yes…love at first sight, and a love that will forever and always remain faithful."

"Always," she said.

When she kissed me, I could practically feel her love pouring into my body.

I pulled away from her lips and gazed into her eyes. "How much more time do we have?"

She slowly let a smile play across her face. "Thirty minutes…maybe forty if they don't come back early."

I grabbed her tea and set it down on the table. I stood up as I took her hand in mine. "Perfect. Time to get our naughty on, Mrs. Hayes. My wife asked to be fucked, and I intend on doing exactly that." I watched the blush move up her cheeks.

We were both lying in bed, panting for air.

I rolled over and looked at her. "Mrs. Hayes, have you been well-fucked?" I asked as I watched her chest moving up and down.

She laughed as she nodded. "Yes! Yes, I have. Can I just say that was awesome? I, um…I'd like to do that kind of play more often." Her cheeks flooded with pink.

I reached over and untied her hands from the back of the bed. I slid her panties down her chest, and then I reached with my other hand and rubbed her wrists.

"I'm going to have to agree with you. That was pretty fucking awesome. I've dreamed of tying you up and having my way with you for way too long now."

"Hmm...I love you, baby." She rolled over and kissed me. When she pulled away, she hid her face in my chest. "I can't believe we just did that!" she said with a giggle.

She looked over at the clock and jumped up. "Oh my god! They're due back any minute, Josh!"

I sat there and watched her stumble out of bed. She ran over to the dresser to get clothes. I'd never in my life seen anyone move so fast. She glanced up at me and smiled.

"I think I'm going to have to talk my mom and dad into moving here."

She stopped, looked at me, and then gave me a bigger smile, like she knew something I didn't.

Then, I heard the doorbell ring.

"Shit, get dressed, or they'll know!"

I let out a laugh as I jumped up and grabbed her. I swung her around and then kissed the shit out of her. I pulled away and winked at her. "Princess, I'm pretty sure they already know what we've been up to."

When she looked down and away, I used my finger to pull her chin back toward me. "I love you, Heather. God, I love you more than anything."

"I love you, too, Josh." She smiled. "I have two surprises for you. One, you're about to get, and the other, you'll get during our next alone time."

*Ah hell...she can't do that to me.*

She got up, quickly threw on some clothes, and started to head downstairs.

"What's for next time?" I called out after her.

She laughed as I heard her running down the stairs.

I quickly pulled on my shorts and a T-shirt as I looked at the picture of us at Enchanted Rock. I smiled as I felt a complete sense of peace wash over my entire body.

"Yep. I'll always love and protect her. Forever."

*I promise you...*

# Chapter Fifty-Five
## Heather

I quickly made my way to the back door and unlocked it. When I opened it up, I smiled at Greg and Liz. They were each carrying a baby, and Elizabeth had the biggest smile on her face.

I instantly felt my face flush. *Oh god. What if they ever found out their son tied me up and made such passionate love to me?*

As Elizabeth walked by, she stopped and looked at me. Then, she gave me the biggest smile I'd ever seen.

"Oh...I've known that feeling before," she said with a wink.

"What feeling?"

"If that flush on your cheeks says anything, I'm going to safely assume my son makes you very happy...very happy indeed."

"Oh. My. God. Elizabeth! You did not just say that?"

She threw her head back and laughed. "Oh, the hell I didn't."

Josh walked into the kitchen and immediately took Will out of Greg's arms. "My big boy! Did you have fun with Grammy and Gramps?"

"He sure did. He also slept the whole time," Greg said with a smile.

Josh and I both snapped our heads over toward him.

"He slept that whole time?" Josh asked.

Elizabeth laughed and handed Libby to me. "Pretty much. Once all the paperwork was signed, the prince and princess woke up, demanding food, and then they nodded back off to sleep."

"What the hell? They never do that for us," Josh said.

I laughed as I watched Elizabeth shrug her shoulders and smile.

"Wait. What paperwork were you signing?" Josh asked.

My heart started beating so fast. I'd been dying to tell Josh, but his parents had made me promise not to say a word.

Elizabeth walked up and kissed Greg so sweetly on the lips that it caused me to look away. She pulled away and smiled at Josh. "Oh, it's nothing really. We just signed on the house we bought." She turned, reached into a cabinet, and pulled out four wine glasses as Greg grabbed a bottle of wine.

Josh looked at both of them and then at me. The expression on his face was priceless. He was confused as hell.

"Wait. What house? Where?" he asked.

Elizabeth turned around and leaned against the counter. "Oh, the darling little cottage house we bought here in town. It's about fifteen minutes from here."

I watched as the smile spread across Josh's face. I knew how close he was to his parents and how much he missed them. He hated living over an hour away from them.

"Y'all bought a house here?"

At the same time, Greg and Elizabeth both said, "Yep!"

"Holy hell! Mom, Dad...this is wonderful! Oh my god, I'm so damn happy. Wait...Mom, what about the law firm?"

"Well, since I now have two beautiful grandchildren, I'm going to need more time to be the best Grammy ever, so I decided to somewhat retire. I'm going to work from home, but I'm mostly just going to do consulting for the firm. I still own half of it, but I'm just becoming more of a silent partner in it."

If I didn't know any better, I would have sworn I just heard my husband let out an *eeeppp*. He walked up and hugged both of them and then turned to me.

"Surprise number one?" he asked.

I nodded and smiled. "I wanted to tell you so bad."

He walked up to me, leaned down, and kissed Libby on the forehead. Then, he kissed me and gave me that crooked smile of his.

I wanted him again, and he knew it.

"Oh, princess, I've got a few surprises up my own sleeve."

I smiled and whispered, "Bring it on."

Ells, Ari, Amanda, and I all sat on Ellie's back porch as we listened to the music the DJ, Jack, was playing. I felt guilty that we were all drinking, and Ellie was sipping on lemon water.

I looked out and saw the guys, including Smitty and a few other friends of ours, playing tag football. I watched as Scott ran up and jumped on Jeff before he brought him down to the ground.

"Jesus H. Christ, if one of them gets hurt and ruins my twenty-first birthday party, I'm cracking heads," Ari said.

"Hey, y'all," Jessie said as she walked up. She started giving everyone a kiss on the cheek.

"Jess! Holy shit, girl. Long time, no see," Ari said with a laugh.

Jessie sat down and let out a sigh. "Shit. I'm so damn tired that I can't even think straight. Between still taking classes and working at the vet clinic, I hardly have any downtime. Shit. They have me working so much. I'm pretty much on call twenty-four/seven. Do you know how many damn times people call for me to come watch their dogs give birth? We live in the damn country. They are supposed to be country folk. What the hell?"

Ellie, Amanda, and Ari let out a laugh.

"How about Scott? How are things going there?" I asked.

Jessie's smile faded for a quick second before she looked out at him while he was running around with the guys.

"I've never felt this way before. It's…It's…"

"Magical?" all of us said at the same time.

As we all let out a loud laugh, Gunner and Josh stopped and looked at us.

"What's so damn funny?" Gunner called out.

Ellie smiled. "Just girl talk, babe, but you're about to be—"

That was when Brad tackled the hell out of Gunner. Josh looked at me and smiled before he jumped on top of Brad.

Jessie let out a breath. "Yes. Magical. But I've seen so little of him lately. He's been busy himself. Jeff and Scott decided to go in on a horse together…a racing horse of all horses."

Jessie looked at Ari as she rolled her eyes.

"Scott had to leave for Kentucky twice this last month. I hate that we're just starting off our relationship, and we barely see each other."

Amanda smiled. "Well, when y'all do see each other, make it count, girl. Get your dirty on…like Heather here."

I snapped my head over to Amanda. "Amanda! Oh my god!" I felt my face turning hot as I looked at Ells and Ari, who were just smiling. I glanced back at Jessie, who was also smiling. "Do y'all know?" I asked as I glanced back at Ari.

She shrugged her shoulders. "What? You're like the most innocent one of the group. When you go all *Fifty Shades* on us…we have to talk about it."

My jaw dropped, and I just shook my head. "I'm never telling your ass anything ever again, Arianna Johnson. Ever!"

After they all laughed for a good two minutes, Ellie turned to Jessie. "Just make sure y'all find time for each other, Jess. I know how much Scott loves spending time with you."

Ari sat up and looked at Jessie. "Speaking of loves…has he yet?"

It was Jessie's turn to turn red. When she nodded, we all let out a squeal.

"How?" I asked before I took a drink of beer.

"Well…he was nervous as all get out. We were just getting back from a picnic that he'd planned. Oh, it was so romantic." She let out a sigh. "We were walking the horses and just talking, catching up on what was going on in our worlds, and Scott turned and asked me if I wanted to move in."

Everyone let out a gasp.

"Oh my god! Oh my god!" Ari said as she sat up straighter.

"What did you say?" Ellie asked.

"Well, at first, I was shocked. I mean, that's a huge step. I asked him if he was sure we were ready for that, and he just busted out and said, 'Jessica, I love you. All I want to do is spend every waking moment with you.' And I started crying. I told him…yes!"

"Did you tell him you loved him back?" Amanda asked.

"Yes! I told him I loved him, too, and that I couldn't imagine my life without him in it."

Ari and Ellie got up and started jumping up and down, which caused Jeff and Josh to do the same thing. Scott turned, looked straight at Jessie, and smiled. I could see the love in his eyes when he looked at her.

"Y'all don't think it's too soon? My father does. He wants me to get my own place."

"No! It's not too soon at all. You both love each other, and this way, you will get to see each other more often. Plus, that damn house needs a woman's touch for Christ's sake," Ari said before she downed another beer.

Ellie laughed. "Ari, you're on your way to getting drunk."

"Fuck yeah, I am!"

After another hour passed, I watched as Gunner, Jeff, Josh, and Scott all got plastered. Brad was the only one who wasn't drinking. The plan was for all of us to just crash at Ellie and Gunner's place, but Brad had told Amanda he felt like one of them should stay in control.

Gunner and Josh had made a dance floor, and Ari and Jeff were cutting up to Shania Twain's "If You Wanna Touch Her, Ask."

Then, "Buttons" by The Pussycat Dolls started playing. I grabbed my drunk husband and led him out to the dance floor. When we started moving together, I felt when his dick instantly got hard. As he moved his hands up and down my body, I ached to feel him inside me.

He leaned down and moved his lips up against ear. "I want you so fucking bad. Let's sneak away, baby."

I smiled at him as I took his hand. I started to lead him away, but then I saw Sharon and Grace walking up to Ellie. The expressions on their faces gave me chills.

*Something's wrong.*

I turned and smiled at Josh. "Baby, hold on to that thought for just one second. I think something's wrong."

I glanced back up to Ellie and Jessie. As I headed over to the back porch, Josh followed me. I got to Ellie right when Sharon put her hand on Ellie's shoulder.

Ellie turned to them. "Oh my god. Alex."

Grace shook her head. "No, sweetheart, Alex is fine. Jenny is playing with her in the house right now."

Confused, Ellie glanced between the two of them. "What's wrong? The look on your faces is scaring me."

Grace looked out at Gunner. "Ellie, how much has Gunner had to drink?"

Ellie snapped her head over to Gunner as tears began building in her eyes. She looked back to Grace. "A lot."

Grace was trying so hard not to cry.

Sharon grabbed Ellie's hands. "Baby girl, listen to me, okay? Something has happened."

Ellie started to cry as she looked up at Grace. "Jack?"

"Jack is fine, sweetheart. It's…it's…" Grace couldn't finish her sentence.

Sharon took a deep breath as I put my arm around Ellie. My heart was beating so fast that I could hear it.

"Ellie, Gramps had a heart attack. Jack is with him now, and they're in an ambulance on their way to Fredericksburg as we speak."

Ellie's whole body went limp, but Josh was standing there, and he grabbed her before she could fall.

Josh looked at Jessie and me. "Girls, I need you to take Ellie inside."

Ellie was crying hysterically now. Jessie, Sharon, and I all wrapped our arms around Ellie, and we led her into the house.

When I turned, I saw Josh talking to Grace. He started to walk toward Gunner with Grace following behind him.

After we got Ellie into the house, we sat her down on the sofa. When I looked out the window, Josh was talking to Gunner while Grace was standing next to him. Jeff put his hand on Gunner's shoulder right before Gunner fell to the ground.

He buried his head in his hands as he started crying out, "No," over and over again.

I put my hand up to my mouth and shook my head.

*Oh, God, please no. Don't take Garrett away from us. Please.*

## Epilogue
## Jessie

### Fours Hours Later...

I'd been trying to call Scott for three hours. I still wasn't sure if he knew about Gramps. When I finally got a text from him I let a sigh of relief.

*Scott: I'm home. Just meet me at the house.*

I was surprised that his text actually seemed coherent.

When I'd told him I was going to the hospital, he was so drunk that he could hardly talk. Scott's brother, Bryce, had been standing there with the girl he'd been hanging on all afternoon. Bryce had assured me he would get Scott home, so I'd decided to head out with Heather and Ari.

When I pulled up to Scott's house, my heart started pounding in my chest. There was a BMW in the driveway.

*Is that Chelsea's car? Oh god, please be Bryce's car. Please.*

As I glanced over toward the garage, I saw Scott's truck.

*Fuck. I hope he didn't drive home when he was drunk.*

I walked up the steps and put my hand on the doorknob. *Why do I have the sickest feeling in my stomach?* I turned the knob and stepped inside. I started to make my way upstairs. I could just barely overhear someone talking. The voice was coming from Scott's bedroom.

*No. Please don't do this to me.*

As I walked down the hallway, I heard a girl moaning out in pleasure. Reaching for the bedroom doorknob, I slowly turned it as I pushed it open. I took one look inside, and I saw a girl riding someone fast and hard.

*No...oh god, Scott, no.*

"Oh my god," I said.

Chelsea turned around and smiled as her eyes caught mine. "Oh, hey there, Jess! You weren't around, so I filled in for you."

"You fucking bitch!" I shouted before I slammed the door shut.

I heard a male voice call out after me, but I just ran as fast as I could. *I need to get out of this house right now.*

I ran out to my car. I jumped in, started it, and sped away. I began crying so hard that I could hardly see enough to drive.

After wiping away my tears, I slammed my hand on the steering wheel as I cried out, "How? How could I be so stupid? Why, God, why? Why would you do this to me again?"

*I'll never, ever again trust my heart to anyone…especially Scott Reynolds.*

Cherished
Scott and Jessie's Story
January 2014
Wanted Series, Book Four

*Thank You*

I'd like to thank God for the most amazing blessings in my life.

There are so many people to thank that I could write another book just to list them all.

Heather Davenport ~ Thank you for everything you've done for me! Your input and help with *Faithful* was beyond amazing. You'll never know how much I appreciate everything you do for me. You're an amazing person, and I'm so blessed to have become friends with you. You make me laugh, and I still say you have an accent!

Gary "Leo" Taylor ~ You continue to inspire me daily, and I'm so blessed we found each other and have become friends. Thank you for everything you do for me, for always just being you, and for sharing a bit of your world with me, so I can share it with everyone else. Smile hard!

Ari Niknejadi ~ I'm thinking a trip to Sea Side is in order very soon! Thanks for being my BFF and never givin' up on me!

Amanda Orozco ~ Thank you for being my couple picture pimp! You truly are the best! Thank you so much for all the help on *Faithful* and for answering all my questions.

Molly McAdams ~ You and me are like peas and carrots! You'll never know how much I look forward to our lunches. You keep my world steady and somewhat normal. Your stories make me laugh my ass off, and no one can tell a story like you! I truly believe my world is a better place because you are in it. Thank you for being such an amazing friend! Bitch, I want my copy of *Forgiving Lies*!

The "Misery Girls" ~ Y'all made me laugh so much when I needed it more than anything. Who would have thought that just a weekend retreat would end up giving me ten amazing new friends? I've never had more fun in two days than I did with y'all. One word, girls: DESTIN!

Kelly's Most Wanted ~ I'm so incredibly blessed to have such an amazing street team. I could never thank y'all enough for everything you do for me. I love y'all to the moon and back! I hope you know that!

*Wanted*, *Saved*, and *Faithful* boards ~ You girls make me smile daily. Your posts and pictures crack me up, and I love seeing the friendships that have developed from just a simple story that popped into my head. You might not see me post in there every day, but please know I read your posts daily. I hope that you enjoy *Faithful*!

My BDHM Girls ~ I miss y'all! I hate that I'm not on the board like I want to be, but know that y'all are always on my mind! I love y'all!

Jovana Shirley ~ You are by far one of the nicest people I have ever met in my life. I can't even believe how lucky I am to not only have become partners-in-crime with you but to also have become friends with you. I'm blessed indeed. You rock! Only the BEST editor EVER!

Stacy Borel ~ Thank God you are in Texas! Every day I sit down to write, I see the picture you sent me. I smile and count my blessings that you are my friend! Fergie misses you!

To all the wonderful blogs out there ~ Thank you so much for sharing my stories and for all the hard work you do for authors and readers alike.

Jemma Scarry, JoJo Belle, Rosa Saucedo, Trish Kuper, and Heather Davenport ~ The best beta readers known to man! Thank you, girls, for your honest feedback and for dropping everything when I said, "Hey…read this!" Y'all rock. Love you, bitches!

To all the amazing readers/friends I have met along this journey ~ I can never begin to tell y'all how blessed I am to have you in my life. I hope that you enjoy the continued story of the *Wanted* gang. It's been a blast to share these characters who I have come to love and adore. I can't wait to share a little bit more of the *Wanted* story with y'all.

To my family who has stood by and supported me in this crazy ride ~ Thank you so much. I have to thank my sister, Mary Hamilton, for her never-ending knowledge of all things cool and hip! My sister, Patty, for her support from day one. It means more to me than you will ever know.

Darrin ~ Right now, you are drugged up, sleeping behind me, and talking in your sleep about someone with an orange cone on their foot. I've never been so turned-on in my life. Thank you so much, Darrin, for your love. I'd be lost without you in my world. Your smile, your laugh, and your constant reminders of how much you love me MORE…mean everything to me. You just have to smile at me from across a room, and I feel your love. It's because of you that I can write the way I do. Thank you for inspiring me with your love every day. I love you, Darrin, so very much. You are my everything.

Lauren ~ No one on this earth makes me smile and laugh the way you do. You are my entire world. I'm totally going to sign you up for cooking classes though since you say I never have food in the house and don't cook anymore. Pesh…I have food in the house always! Mac and cheese makes a quick and easy meal!

Mom ~ I miss you every single day. I hope that you are proud of the things I've done and that I have finally followed my dreams. Love you, Mommy. See you later.

*Faithful Playlist*

"Please Remember Me" by Tim McGraw—Heather and Elizabeth talk about Josh not remembering, and Heather says she'll always love him.

"Everything" by Lifehouse—Josh and Heather are in the hospital when he tells her he is scared and wants to start off slow.

"Only You're the One" by Lifehouse—In the hospital, Heather tells Josh how she feels about him.

"Boys 'Round Here" by Blake Shelton—Jeff, Josh, Gunner, and Matt are fishing.

"Last First Kiss" by Ron Pope—Josh kisses Heather and (again) realizes he loves her.

"Hanging by A Moment" by Lifehouse—Josh tells Heather that he loves her and calls her princess.

"You and Me" by Lifehouse—Josh and Heather dance at his birthday party.

"Don't Happen Twice" by Kenny Chesney—Gunner sees Josh and Heather dancing at Luckenbach dance hall.

"Give It Up to Me" by Shakira—Heather, Ari, and Ellie dance at Luckenbach dance hall.

"Come & Get It" by Selena Gomez—Heather dances with a turned-on Josh.

"If All Goes Right" by Matt Kimbrow—Girls are all dancing at Luckenbach dance hall.

"Bobblehead" by Christina Aguilera—Ari lays into Victoria before punching her.

"Save Me from Myself" by Christina Aguilera—Ellie realizes how silly she is behaving for being jealous for no reason.

"One of Those Nights" by Tim McGraw—Josh walks around Heather's bedroom before they make love.

"Storm" by Lifehouse—Josh and Heather make love at Heather's house.

"Stronger Than Ever" by Christina Aguilera—Amanda is sitting in her car after Brad tells his parents he is leaving with Amanda.

"I Still Believe in You" by Vince Gill—Brad's dedicates this song to Amanda when she reads the letter he wrote her.

"I Need You" by LeAnn Rimes—Josh is on his way to find Heather after he gets his memory back.

"Kiss Me" by Ed Sheeran—Josh and Heather are at the gazebo when Heather finds out he has his memory back. She tells him she is pregnant.

"Everything to Me" by Brad Paisley—Josh asks Heather to marry him.

"Safe & Sound" by Taylor Swift—Ellie's mom shows up at Gunner and Ellie's house.

"Because of Your Love" by Kenny Chesney—Gunner tries to swoon Ellie during the romance contest with Jeff, Josh, and Brad.

"Like Jesus Does" by Eric Church—Jeff tries to swoon Ari during the romance contest.

"Never Stop" by SafetySuit—Brad tries to swoon Amanda during the romance contest.

"Your Everything" by Keith Urban—Josh swoons Heather during the romance contest.

"Dance Again" by Jennifer Lopez—Victoria and Rebecca are dancing.

"To Make You Feel My Love" by Garth Brooks—Scott dances with Jessie at Luckenback dance hall.

"Why Don't You Love Me" by Hot Chelle Rae—Jessie leaves Scott's house after they run into Chelsea inside Scott's house. Scott accidentally calls Jessie "Chels."

"Bless the Broken Road" by Rascal Flatts—Josh and Heather dance before they leave for their wedding at the coast.

"There You'll Be" by Faith Hill—Greg (Josh's father) dances with Heather for the father/daughter dance at the wedding.

"When You Walked into My Life" by Lila McCann—Josh and Heather's wedding song.

"All You Ever" by Hunter Hayes—Scott asks Jessie to dance at the reception.

"New Favorite Memory" by Brad Paisley—Josh and Heather on their wedding night.

"Mama's Broken Heart" by Miranda Lambert—Jessie walks into the Wild Coyote bar and sees Scott.

"A Little More Country" by Easton Corbin—Jessie dances with her high school friend at the Wild Coyote.

"Do You Remember" by Blake Shelton—Scott dances with Jessie and asks for her to forgive him.

"The One" by Skillet—Jessie and Scott make love for the first time.

"Mirrors" by Justin Timberlake—Josh and Heather tell each other they will love each other and be faithful forever. Eeeppp! This song is SO Josh and Heather's song! *swoon*

"If You Wanna Touch Her, Ask" by Shania Twain—Jeff and Ari dance at the girls' twenty-first birthday party.

"Buttons" by Pussycat Dolls—Everyone is dancing at the girls' twenty-first birthday party.